Exquisite Danger

An Iron Horse MC Novel

#2

By

Ann Mayburn

Exquisite Danger

For the first time in my life I know what it's like to be completely and truly adored by a man who loves me for exactly who I am, a high functioning autistic with more personality quirks than there are stars in the Texas Hill Country night sky.

Some people think my boyfriend, Smoke, is a total biker psycho, a natural born killer who will destroy anyone who threatens what he considers his. They wouldn't be wrong, but he's so much more than that. He's my dark salvation, my beloved fallen angel who is trying with all of his wicked heart to save me from what seems like an entire world bent on either killing me or a fate worse than death.

We're headed to the Denver, Colorado chapter of the Iron Horse MC, chasing after my narcissistic, junkie mother who decided to steal from some very bad men leaving her two daughters behind to pay the price for her betrayal. My twin sister, Sarah, old lady to the Iron Horse MC president, is looking for my mother as well, but Sarah's gone rogue and has no one to guard her back which worries me deeply. To further complicate matters, there are traitors in the Iron Horse MC who are working with my mother, not only helping her to escape but also informing my enemies of my every move.

The odds are stacked against me, but I will do whatever is necessary to protect those I love, and with Smoke at my side, I just might make it out of this mess alive.

Chapter One

Swan

The burning Texas sun set over the distant hills in spectacular bursts of amethyst, cardinal red, and tangerine, while a warm breeze moved over my skin like a caress. It was late summer nights like these idyllic evenings, when laughter and the smell of cooking food filled the air that made me regret ever leaving the raw beauty of the Texas Hill Country. I took a long pull from my cold beer and gazed across the yard to where my amazing man, Smoke, stood talking with my good friend Indigo's parents, Ron and Bettie. Indigo's Asian father looked like a hippie time had forgotten in his tie-dye shirt and long, silver-streaked hair. Her mother didn't rock the tie-dye, but she did personify the earth mother look with her rounded body and flowing dresses. Smoke seemed all the more dark and dangerous standing with them, like some kind of post-apocalypse War Barron…an apex predator.

Except, right now, he looked like an amused predator conversing with two earnest chipmunks.

Ron and Bettie were actually pretty sane for preppers. They were both highly educated and world-wise, but they'd talk your ear off about 'the man' if you gave them half a chance. I wondered if Smoke was perplexed or amused by them. I know Indigo thought they were just batshit crazy. They drove her nuts with their ever-evolving list of people they swore were trying to bring down the government. Funny thing was, the more you listened to them the more you started to believe that their weird conspiracy theories might have a ring of truth to them.

Memories of nights spent at Indigo's luxurious compound flitted through my mind, like sheets of paper caught in a windstorm, as the years peeled back. Ron and Bettie were more than a little odd, but they treated me like one of their own and were two of the few people I trusted on sight. They were close with my parents and would often come over to play cards on our big, screened-in back porch and laugh about the world going to hell. When I needed someone to talk to, they were always there. A bolt of melancholy tightened my chest as I realized how much I missed them…though right now I was far more interested in my man than my friend's parents.

Poor Smoke, he actually looked like he was really thinking about what they were saying and had a slightly bemused smile curving his lips. Considering Ron and Bettie were conspiracy theorists he was probably getting an earful about the Vagrants, an evil political entity Ron and Bettie believed was slowly taking over the world. That was why they'd decided to stop watching cable TV. They swore the Vagrants had implanted mind control devices in the cable boxes. We watched a lot of DVDs at their house.

Indigo had a touch of their paranoia, but at twenty-one, she was one of the best private investigators in the country, so maybe that wasn't a bad thing.

I had to laugh at myself as I watched my big, badass, biker boyfriend talking with them in their faded, flower child glory. I swear they were roughly half his massive size, and his commanding presence made them seem even smaller. My gaze trailed from his broad shoulders, to his thick thighs and tight ass before returning to his face.

From the top of his head of curly black hair to his sexy feet—no, seriously, the man has gorgeous feet—he was one hundred percent mine. The good and the bad. Sometimes I saw a hint of true darkness in him, the dispassionate gaze of a killer, and it scared me, yet aroused me at the same time. If Smoke was the king of the jungle, I was his queen, and I had a touch of his darkness myself. We were an odd couple, to be sure, but beneath our skin, our hearts beat to the same savage rhythm.

Even though my sex was still sore from the hard fuck he'd given me last night, I craved him to the point where I planned on throwing myself on him and tearing off his clothes the first second we were alone. When he'd taken my virginity he woke a hunger in me that bordered on ravenous. I wanted to devour him, to lock us away in my bedroom and make him give me pleasure until I passed out. I knew how good those perfect, full lips of his felt wrapped around my nipples and how his big hands could hold my body still while he bit me with little stinging nips that set my body ablaze.

He was a big, solid man all over, including his magnificent cock with the piercing beneath the base that rested against his balls. A shiver raced down my spine and settled in my belly as I imagined how that wonderful bit of metal would hit my clit just right, while he pounded into me from behind. Another wave of heat sensitized my pussy and I shifted, somehow drawing his attention to me where I stood leaning against a tree and watching the sun set.

When his dark gaze met mine, I swore the world hushed for a moment. Nothing existed except my pounding heart and his handsome face. The setting sun hit his cheekbones and his bold Aztec nose just right, turning him into the living statue of a warrior. Without even trying, he enchanted me, and my knees weakened to the point where I had to brace myself against the tree. I was spellbound by his dark gaze, completely ensnared by his raw, masculine beauty.

That was the only way I could describe my feelings for him. He wove some type of magical enchantment over me that held me in ethereal bondage, draining my will and replacing it with his. I gladly surrendered to him, and my breath caught at the flare of passion between us as he casually rubbed his lips while pretending to listen to Bettie yammer on about the world ending. His gaze moved over me, and I took a quick pull of my beer, trying to cool the fire he'd started in me.

I was wearing a pair of faded jeans and a black tank top with a pair of my beat up old boots, but he stared at me like I was nude and had been rubbed down with oil. His gaze cranked my overwhelming arousal even higher. I didn't like getting turned on with my parents around—it was weird—but at the same time, I craved the way the heat built between us until I was melting with it. If he slipped his long, rough fingers between my legs right now he'd find me slick with desire.

I had to tighten my grip on my beer bottle, suddenly certain that it would slip from my useless grip as my heart raced when he made his way across the yard to me. Yelling children darted past him while a few of my parents' friends tried to get his attention, but he avoided the kids and ignored the adults. His attention was focused totally on me, and I couldn't help my goofy smile as he came closer. Elation filled me and I took one step away from my tree, then another, eager to bask in his presence like a cat in a patch of sunlight on a cold winter day.

When Smoke's intense gaze focused on me like this, I knew I was the center of his universe. He looked at me in a way no one ever had, like I was more important than air and the most beautiful thing he'd ever seen. I would never, ever get tired of the way Smoke watched me. Putting a little swing in my hips, I stepped beneath the green leaves of the old tree until the toes of my battered cowboy boots were touching his black motorcycle boots. The scents of summer filled the air around us, the sun-baked earth mixed with the hickory smoke from the fire, and the sharp, sweet spice of barbecue.

The wind shifted a bit so that I became enveloped in his scent, and I stifled a groan. He smelled really, really good, a hint of sweat mixed with sun-warmed skin and his soap. He'd actually brought a bar of his personal soap with him and insisted on washing me with it when we shared a shower this morning. He seemed to get off on me smelling like his masculine scented soap. Not that I was complaining. Being bathed by Smoke was a decadent experience and one of the best ways in the world to greet the day.

I looked up and brushed a strand of hair from my face while we stared at each other like love-besotted fools. Tonight, I actually wore my high maintenance hair down and loose at Smoke's request. I was constantly moving it off my face, which was annoying, but totally worth every bit of irritation when Smoke ran his fingers through the long strands with a look of pure satisfaction. He cupped my cheek, leaned down and rubbed his nose along mine, then brushed a soft kiss over my lips. Even that modest touch made my skin tingle, and I sighed against his mouth, pressing my body against his even as I kept my hands at my side. If I touched him, I'd either grab his magnificent ass or run my fingers through his dark, silken curls while hauling his mouth to mine in a rather wanton display that would be totally inappropriate in front of my neighbors.

His tongue brushed my lips and I groaned softly, stealing a taste of him before he lifted his head and grinned down at me, still stroking my cheek in a hypnotizing rhythm. I knew I was the only person who ever got to see the soft, tender side of Smoke, and I relished his open affection for me. In the world of the Iron Horse MC, where he was the Master at Arms for the founding chapter, Smoke was feared, and with good reason. When we first met, I'd witnessed him losing his temper, and the pure rage he put off scared me. Even back then, he'd been oddly attuned to my every need and had immediately calmed himself when he saw that his anger scared me.

"Hey, beautiful baby," Smoke said with a rough purr in his voice. "You tryin' to get your daddy to shoot me?"

I laughed, very aware of my father glaring at Smoke from where he sat at a picnic table near the fire pit. A hint of unease moved through me. My dad could very well be considering how to end the life of my boyfriend, or as Smoke liked me to call him, my man. Even my dad's disapproval couldn't quell the need coiling inside of me, and I slipped my hand into Smoke's and gave a soft squeeze. Out of the corner of my eye, I watched as Mimi sat down on my dad's lap then threaded her fingers through his thick hair. He glared at her for a second before his lips curved into a reluctant smile, and his eyes filled with warmth. They were soulmates. I was happy for them and glad I'd been blessed with parents who showed me what true love meant.

"No, I don't want my dad to shoot you. He might hit something important. Something I really like." I bumped my hips to his, the press of his big erection against my body sending a shiver of electric desire down my spine and straight to my clit. Fuck.

Knowledge was a dangerous thing. I have this problem with people touching me, a sensory issue combined with a fear of strangers. Before Smoke, I'd never met a man who could touch me like he could. My body belonged to him from the very start, and he took very, very good care of it.

My sex tingled with arousal, and I rubbed against him again seeking the relief only he could give me, and the escape from my worries and fear that I could find only in his arms.

His deep chuckle vibrated against my breasts. "What naughty things are you thinking about? Is it about my tongue in your pussy, or my cock?"

I frowned up at him, trying to ignore the way my lady bits were now throbbing. Damn he had an erotic voice, all deep and growly. Male, primal, hot. "How do you know I'm thinking about sex?"

"Because you do these long, slow bites on your lower lip when you're getting turned on. Plus, your eyes get all hot and heavy, but brighter, a pure blue like a winter sky in the desert. Your beauty drives me insane. All I want to do is look at you, touch you, love you, because just being around you brings me joy. I could fuck you for days at a time, satisfy you until you don't know your own name, but now is not the time or place, so stop being so fuckin' sexy. You're killin' me."

My clit throbbed with each beat of my heart and I wished we could sneak off, but that would be impossible right now. I sighed and wrapped my arms around his waist, resting my cheek against his chest, peace filling me. "It'll be nice to go home when this is over. Where it can just be you and me together."

He made a happy sound and pulled me tight against him, his arms solid as tree trunks wrapping around me and holding me close. "I can't wait to get you home either."

"Um...Swan?" A woman's husky, low-pitched, familiar voice came from somewhere behind me.

Smoke tensed, but I squirmed my way out of his arms, already running before I'd even laid eyes on my best friend, Lyric, who stood not too far away. A hot blush covered her face as she looked down at her hands where they gripped her long, dowdy blue skirt so hard her knuckles were white. Memories of seeing her standing with that hesitant, scared posture flashed through me making my heart ache. My friend only looked like this after she'd been hurt, and considering her tender heart and trusting nature, that happened often. Lyric gave me a startled look when I came barreling at her, but it soon dissolved into laughter when we hugged and jumped up and down, talking over each other at the same time like a couple of pre-teen girls hyped up on Pixy Stixs.

I finally calmed down, took a deep breath and hugged her tight. She never wore any perfume, but she smelled like fresh air and the outdoors. Lyric had loved to play with makeup and perfume when she was at my house, but it was strictly forbidden at her religious compound. Something about vanity and temptation trying to make sinners out of men. Idiots.

She was about five-two with a curvy body and breasts bigger than mine. Her thick, waist-length, light brown hair was pulled back into the stupid braid her religious elders insisted all women wear. The fit of her dress made her body look lumpy, which was a shame, because beneath that sack-like piece of crap, she had a lovely hourglass shape. When we were young teenagers, she would come over and we'd play dress-up with Mimi's makeup and party dresses. I'd spend hours playing with Lyric's hair, brushing it until it shone in thick waves while we talked about our dreams of the future. Mimi had taught us both how to look beautiful, yet classy, and I know Lyric loved feeling pretty. But every time Lyric left to go home, she had to remove the makeup, wash off the perfume, and put on her shapeless clothing or risk punishment for dressing like a 'whore' and enticing god-fearing men.

The only reason Lyric's parents let her come over in the first place was because they did business with my dad. Hell, everyone in the compound dealt with my dad in one way or another. If you needed something, he could get it, and if he couldn't, he knew someone who could.

Beyond that, my dad owned the water rights for the entire collection of compounds, something more valuable than gold and not a luxury anyone wanted to lose. That meant if Lyric's compound wanted water, she got to come over for a pajama party. Thank God her parents allowed her to visit, because I don't know what I would have done without Lyric's caring presence in my life. She was one of the few people who'd been able to touch me without causing me pain, and in many ways, I thought of her as my sister.

With a faint tremble in her voice Lyric whispered, "I missed you."

Tears burned my eyes as guilt pierced me, and I hugged her hard enough that she wheezed. "I missed you too."

Smoke's voice, warm and rough, came from behind me. "You must be Lyric. Swan speaks very highly of you."

Lyric immediately clammed up, her lips pressing together as she turned her eyes to the ground and clasped her hands behind her back. It was ingrained in her, practically since birth, to be subservient to men so that she had a problem dealing with any male over the age of sixteen. I gently lifted her chin until her enormous, hazel eyes met mine. Lyric had the most beautiful eyes I'd ever seen, complex and doe-like in their innocence. From a distance, her eyes looked brown, but when you got close, they were actually a beautiful, light golden-brown with a starburst of hazel-green, and flecked with orange that surrounded the iris.

It was the trust in her eyes that made me decide to be as direct with her as I could. We didn't lie to each other, ever, and I wasn't going to start now. "Lyric, this is my man, Smoke. I know he looks scary as shit, but he's a part of my life now, and I love him. I would really like it if you could be friends. I know he's huge, but I swear he'd rather cut off his own hand than harm you.

She trembled hard, but when I gave her shoulder a reassuring squeeze, she darted her gaze up at Smoke and whispered a rapid spill of words. "It's very nice to meet you, Mr. Smoke."

"You can just call me Smoke, sweetheart." His voice was equally soothing as he said, "It's nice to meet someone that Swan cares about so much."

Lyric gave him a shy smile before returning her gaze to the ground. "I care about her, too. She's like my sister."

"Then that means we're family now, and I always take care of my family." He dazzled us both with his best smile, and Lyric sucked in a quick breath.

"Um...okay." She gave me a rather desperate, dazed look. I could sympathize with her feeling like that. "He's your boyfriend?"

"Yeah."

She gave a slightly shaky laugh and whispered, "Wow."

"It's so good to see you," I kissed her on the cheek then gave her another hug. A fragile innocence and sweetness seemed to radiate from Lyric, and as usual, the urge to take care of her rose in me. "Come on, let's get some food in you."

She paled, her sprinkling of freckles standing out on the bridge of her nose and upper cheeks. "Can we stay here? I had to agree to bring a chaperone with me to the party, and I ditched him."

I had to grit my teeth and take a deep breath as my protective instincts roared to life. "Why do you look scared when you say that?"

Clasping her hands together hard enough to make her skin blotch, she shook her head. "They have rules now, like any woman must be accompanied by a man of high standing in the church if she wishes to leave the homestead. Especially an unmarried woman."

"What?" I saw Smoke tense out of the corner of my eye and tried to think up a way to diffuse the situation, but I was having a hard enough time keeping my shit under control. "They wouldn't let you leave by yourself if you wanted to?"

"No," Lyric said in a flat voice and tensed. "Things are different with our new leader."

I blinked at her in surprise. "You're dad's not leading your church anymore?"

Lyric's lower lip trembled. "He died four months ago."

Right away, I felt like the worst friend ever, and my voice was thick with tears as I said, "Honey, I had no idea. Why didn't you have Dad and Mimi tell me? I would have come home in an instant."

"I asked them to keep it from you because I didn't want you to meet the new leader." Lyric turned her head and tried to wipe away her tears. "I don't want you around him. He's not a nice man. Your fresh mouth would get me in trouble. New rule: If we have a guest and they commit a transgression, then the person who invited them has to pay for it by doing penance. It's cut down on the number of outsiders coming to the Church, big time, and isolated the members from their extended families. A few of the more moderate families have already left, but the hardcore believers are gaining power…and new members. The pastor we have right now preaches fear and hate—that God is a vengeful deity bent upon bringing suffering to those who sin against Him. I've tried to debate it with the pastor, to help him see that God is love, not hate, but he seems like he doesn't even care what the Bible says. He's teaching the people lies, and they seem to be oblivious to just how manipulative he is."

I ran a soothing hand down her braid, trying to calm her before she became too upset to talk. "Who is he?"

"Pastor James Jebidiah Middleton," she replied with a note of disgust in her voice.

"How did he become the pastor?"

She sighed. "It's a long story."

"What about your Mom? What's she doing? Is she finally staying home or is she still on her mission kick?" Lyric's mother and father were home maybe two months out of the year, spending the rest doing missionary work around the world. I never understood how they could leave their daughter behind, but they often looked at Lyric more like an inconvenience than their child. If it wasn't for the fact that Lyric's strict but loving grandparents mostly raised her, I think Mimi and my dad would have had Lyric living with us a long time ago.

A light breeze blew a strand of Lyric's hair across her face. "My mother is dating Pastor Middleton."

I gaped at her. "What?"

"Yeah. He started courting her soon after he arrived, claiming God had sent him a vision about my mom. She spends a lot time now at the pastor's mansion. They're getting married really soon."

"What? He's marrying Evelyn? God sent him a *vision* about Evelyn, and they're getting married? That's so messed up on so many levels." I shuddered. "I thought your Mom despised sex. The thought of…urk."

17

"Yeah." Lyric's lips twisted in disgust. "Pastor Middleton is slick. He's handsome for an older guy, charismatic, and can be very, very charming, but he can also be scary. Things are different now, Swan. I'm trying to get my grandmother to leave with me, but her dementia is pretty bad. Some days she doesn't even recognize me. I don't know if moving her from her home would hurt her."

"Bring your grandma with you to my dad's house. You know we'll help you any way we can."

"I don't want to be a burden on your parents." I started to protest, but Lyric held up her hand and I noticed the calluses on her palms that hadn't been there before. "Besides, Pastor Middleton has spies all over the place, and there is no way I could get my grandma out with them watching me. She's totally bedridden now and needs constant care. I couldn't take her with me and subject her to the stress of trying to run away. I know it would kill her. I also know if I call the police, the whole thing would become a media circus, and we'd never have a chance at a normal life. That's all I want, the old fashioned American dream. A loving husband, kids, and a home that I could make my own, a place that would be a haven from the world where I could safely love my family with all my heart."

"What the fuck kind of hellhole do you live in?" Smoke's voice was thick and loaded with tension.

He was obviously angry and trying to contain it. I could understand that because I was in a similar situation, but I knew better than to get angry around Lyric. The fire in Smoke's eyes grew fiercer, and I sucked in a quick breath. He looked like a man getting ready to do something drastic. Worried about Smoke

18

getting wrapped up in a fight with the cult—okay, fine, I said it, *cult*—I reached out and grasped his hand. The instant our fingertips met, he visibly calmed himself.

"I know you think I'm stupid for staying, but my home wasn't always like this." Lyric darted a glance at Smoke that held a bit of anger mixed with shame. "When I was little and my grandparents headed the church, it was a good place, a happy place. My parents were missionaries, and they'd leave me with my grandparents for most of the year. I loved staying with them rather than with my own distant mother and father. Everyone helped each other out, and the sermons were about God's love and compassion. We were taught to forgive each other and care for each other like family. It was a wonderful place to grow up, if a bit strict. My grandmother is everything to me. She's the one who taught me about love and the grace of God. I can't abandon her."

She closed her eyes, and without a second thought, I pulled her into a hug, holding her tight as the tension and anguish poured out of her. Lyric very rarely talked about the negative parts of her life, and I wanted to do everything I could to give her the courage to speak up. Thanks to Smoke's unconditional love, I knew how healing and cathartic it could be to share the burdens from the past.

Lyric took a deep breath and rested her head on my shoulder. "Things at my church started to go wrong. First the measles then a bad case of whooping cough swept through our compound. Over a dozen children died, and it was like the joy had gone out of people's hearts. Everyone felt like each child in the congregation was their own, so every family suffered profound grief. Many lost their faith. They were...they are good people, but that anguish has smothered their souls. And now...now I'm afraid it's made them vulnerable to a man who cares more about wealth and control than about God. We have a curfew now. There are whispers about Pastor Middleton receiving messages from God about who the single women on the compound are meant to marry. Funny how all the attractive women get paired up with his most ardent followers."

My gut tightened, and I exchanged a heavy look with Smoke. "Has he tried to marry you off to anyone yet?"

"No." She made a sour face. "But his son has sure expressed his interest. That's who my chaperone is tonight, Clint."

"He's here with you?" I quickly looked around, ready to go pound some hypocritical ass for scaring my friend. With Smoke at my back I was pretty sure we'd make enough of an impression to buy Lyric some safety. "Where?"

"I ditched him with Shelly, Adam and Karen. They promised to keep him busy so I could talk with you."

Smoke growled behind me and Lyric shivered. "Honey, tell me where he is, and I'll make sure he never bothers you again."

She shook her head quickly. "No, please. I can handle him. No violence."

Protective feelings of love and worry swamped me. Lyric was a terrible fighter. In spite of my dad's attempts to train her, she was crippled by her fear of hurting someone. While I loved her compassionate

20

nature, I also knew that it made her prey, a plump little baby kitten that was a tempting target to the predators of the world.

"What about your Mom?" I was almost going to argue that some kind of maternal instinct would motivate her mother on some level, but then I thought about my own birth mother and sighed.

"She couldn't care less." Lyric took a step back and looked me in the eye. "My mother gets jealous of anyone who takes Pastor Middleton's attention away from her, including me. I avoid him and her as much as possible outside of church. I spend a lot of time in the fields and orchard working, but at least I have peace out there. Pastor Middleton's men don't like physical labor so they leave me alone. Plus, I'm staying with my grandmother and caring for her while my mother lives in the new mansion."

"New mansion? What fucking mansion?"

"You don't even want to know. They call it a meeting hall because the basement is the new gathering place for the congregation, but the top three floors of this building house Pastor Middelton and a few of his cronies, including his son."

"Lyric, honey," I gently held her face between my hands and met her confused and hurting gaze. "Please consider leaving."

"I want to, but I can't. Not while grandma is alive. I can't leave her with them, Swan. I just know they'll neglect her and won't care for her like I do. I can't bear the thought of her being mistreated."

"Fuck. Look, I know your grandmother wouldn't want you living like this."

"I can help you leave right now," Smoke replied in a thoughtful voice. "Got some people that owe me favors and we'll help you get a new identity, a new life. Could probably get your grandma out as well."

"What?" Lyric gaped at him, then shook her head and looked down at the ground. "No...no, it's too dangerous. You don't understand, she's one hundred and two years old, and her body is as fragile as a hollow egg. I can't move her, and I won't leave her. Please don't ask me again."

I could see that Smoke wanted to argue with Lyric, but she'd made up her mind, and trying to get her to change it would be like trying to tell the sun not to rise. When I placed my hand on Smoke's arm, out of the corner of my eye, I could see Lyric watching us carefully. Smoke looked over at me, and the frustration on his face was easy to read. For all that Smoke was a dangerous, deadly man, he also had a soft place in his heart for women in danger. Seemed to be a running theme in the Iron Horse MC. Smoke sighed as I rubbed his arm, then he gave me a little nod before forcing his mouth to relax out of its angry line.

"Your choice." Smoke turned back to Lyric. "Anytime, and I do mean *anytime* you want to leave or need help, have Swan's parents contact me. Once you get out, you can be and do whatever you want. We'll help you with school, getting a job, a new identity, and we'll find you a safe place to live. I'll leave my information with Mike. Swan loves you so that means you're family, and we take care of our family."

His words struck me on a profound level, and I lost a little more of my heart to him as I realized he meant it. He'd take care of Lyric, help her any way he could, because he loved me. I was sure he was also making the offer because he was a decent guy beneath all the violence, but mainly he was doing it for me. His love for me made my heart skip a beat. Lyric's soft sigh pulled my attention away from Smoke.

Tears shone in Lyric's eyes, and she nodded at my man with a look of determination tightening her soft features. "Thank you."

I wrapped her in a hard hug, and she snuggled into me. Lyric was a very physically affectionate person who had been born into a family that didn't encourage outward displays of love, leaving my friend touch-starved to the point that when she spent the night at my house when we were kids, we'd end up snuggled together in bed. She gave the best hugs—totally innocent, and full of comfort, making her the perfect person to cuddle. The soothing warmth of my love for my friend filled me, and when she pulled away with tears spilling down her cheeks, I used the back of my hand to wipe away a few of my own.

Lyric looked behind me, then tensed and ducked closer to Smoke. "Darn it, he's looking for me." I went to turn, but Lyric's hand on my wrist stopped me. "I'm sorry, I thought I had more time. Before I go I have a message for you from Sarah."

AUSTIN TX

Chapter Two

Smoke and I tensed at the mention of Sarah's name. "What?"

"I saw Sarah when she was here. She said she was going after your mom for stealing from her fiancé. Before you ask, she wouldn't give me details, but she seemed to have a plan. The only thing she could tell me was that her mom wasn't working alone, that there were people high up inside Iron Horse helping her, and that she's pretty sure your mom was going to the Denver area to go underground."

"Denver?" I said in a soft voice.

A low, deep growl came from next to me. "Sarah said someone in the Iron Horse is working with Billie? That some motherfuckers are double-crossing *my* club?"

Drawing in a quick breath, Lyric sank into herself, and I watched as she began to mentally withdraw again. A dark cloud of wrath was quickly building around Smoke, and he seemed to swell with anger. Shit, I knew he would never hurt me, but even I was more than a little intimidated. Lyric whimpered, and I threw an elbow at Smoke, but he already appeared chagrined as he watched Lyric standing as still as a statue. He closed his eyes and took a deep breath, the vein in his throat visibly throbbing. As he let it out the rage tensing his face faded. I wondered what he did with all that anger he bottled up inside of him.

When he spoke, his deep, mellow tone could have charmed a mermaid from the sea. "Sorry, sweetheart. Didn't mean to scare you."

Lyric didn't move so I went to her, wrapped my arms around her and whispered in her ear, "Is that all she told you?"

"No, she said you…" Lyric swallowed hard, then met my gaze. "…that you need to talk to Stewart. Sarah gave him something, and he found a lot of things wrong with it, like it was tampered with? Look, I know it won't be easy for you considering your history, but at least give him a chance to explain. When you forgive others, you forgive yourself—even if he did completely betray your trust and hurt you."

I swallowed hard, reached back and grabbed Smoke's hand. He instantly stilled, then drew me back into his embrace. The narcotic effect of his hold bolstered me, and the nausea eased. If Stewart hadn't cheated on me with my sister, I would've never met Smoke. I guess in a way it was worth enduring all the bullshit I had to go through to find myself here in Smoke's arms. I'd do it all again for him, but that didn't mean I ever wanted to see that cheating fuck, Stewart, again. The very thought made me relive the anger and humiliation. Volatile emotions that I was having issues dealing with. I hated to admit it, but having watched my father explode in anger all my life had given me the tendency to do the same when I was really stressed, and I didn't want my unwilling visit with Stewart to dissolve into me screaming, crying, and trying to kick Stewart's ass. Doing that was childish and stupid, emotions I couldn't afford to indulge right now. I'd rather suck it up and deal with Stewart in order to find Sarah and my mother.

Sometimes, being a responsible grown up sucked.

"What did she give him?" Smoke asked, his frame tight with tension.

Lyric shook her head, her gaze darting around. "I don't know, but I have to go. Clint's coming and I need to see a few more people before he makes me leave."

I grabbed her close and hugged her, whispering in her ear, "Come with me, right now. We'll get out of here and get you someplace safe."

"I can't," she whispered back. "Not yet. I promise when I do leave I'll find you, Swan."

I leaned back and squeezed her shoulders. "Please take care of yourself."

We both watched Lyric walk quickly away and I sighed. "I wish she'd come with me."

Smoke rubbed circles on my arm with his thumb. "It would hurt her more than help her if she was forced into leaving. She has a game plan in mind, and she'll go through with it. The last thing you want to do is take that sweet, stubborn little girl away from her grandmother. Lyric has to do it on her own. I know it goes without saying, but we will help her with anything she needs 'cause you love her and she's a good kid. She'll see her way outta that bullshit sooner or later."

"You sure?"

"Yep." His tone held absolute conviction, and I sighed. Though it might not be the most PC feminist thing to say, I loved it when he took over. It was amazing how good it felt to have someone I could trust, someone who I knew would have my back. He turned me in his arms so I could look at him. "You ready to go see your ex?"

I nodded then rubbed my face. "I'm sorry. This is beyond awkward. You...you don't have to go if you don't want."

He cupped my cheeks and tilted my face so he could look at me. "You still love him?"

"No, I thought I did, but what I felt for him was nothing like the love I feel for you."

His jaw softened and he closed his eyes. "You really love me?"

"You know I do, with everything I have."

I watched him process this information for a few heartbeats, as his breathing slowed and his touch gentled. Watching him calm down like this made me wonder if I had the same narcotic effect on him that he had on me. To test the question, I ran my hands up and down his biceps, indulging in a nice long grope of his thick muscles. He pushed his pelvis gently against mine, an involuntary reaction, and I bit back a moan at the sensation of his thick erection.

"I love you, and you love me. We got no problems." He closed his eyes and rubbed his nose against mine.

27

"And I do love you, baby girl," he whispered. "I'm never gonna let you go, ever, and no one is gonna take you from me. Don't care if I gotta fight the entire world to keep you safe. Got me?"

Melting against him I nodded, drowning in the warmth of his affection. "Yeah."

"Now let's go see that douchebag ex of yours so we can go back to your room and fuck."

Thirty minutes later, we were pulling through the gated, ten-foot high, steel beam-reinforced, concrete fence that surrounded Stewart's home, an adobe house set inside the hill. Like his father, Stewart specialized in hacking and there wasn't much he couldn't do in the cyber world. I'd watch in awe for hours as he worked his way into different systems while I lounged around his home and entertained myself. Now that I thought about it, most of my dates with Stewart resulted in me watching him work while he basically ignored me. At the time, I thought he was just a brilliant man who got wrapped up in his thoughts, but now I wondered. The memory was bittersweet as I climbed out of Smoke's truck.

The front door opened followed by loud, excited, familiar barking that made my heart race. I turned to face the front of the house just as Princess came barreling out to me. Standing as tall as my waist and weighing as much a tank, the beautiful Irish wolfhound I'd helped Stewart raise from a puppy launched herself at me. When we got her we'd talked about what a good dog she'd be for the children we would have someday. We even had names picked out.

Princess landed on me full force, but luckily, Smoke caught me and planted his feet, supporting both of us while Princess stood on her hind legs and planted her dinner-plate-size paws on my shoulders. I giggled as she licked me like I was made out of peanut butter.

"Princess." I heard Stewart's low, familiar voice, and my heart gave a painful thump as the past and present merged. "Get off of Swan."

Of course, Princess ignored him—she usually did—but when I did a double snap, she dropped down to a sit. Pleased that she remembered her training, I gave her some more love while avoiding her slobber. Smoke reached down next to me, and we scratched the dog's back, sending Princess into shivers of ecstasy.

I heard Stewart's footsteps as he approached us. When he spoke, I looked up at him and my stomach clenched like I'd been sucker punched. "Hello, Sunshine."

He was as stunning as ever, good looking in a supermodel way that I no longer found quite so hot. Now he was just…pretty. Perfect blond hair, dimples, and blue eyes with a charismatic smile. I always thought we'd have pretty babies. He looked like he belonged in a fashion magazine with his high cheekbones and natural pout, if you discounted his worn t-shirt and the grease smudges on his arms and face. No doubt he'd been working in what I used to call his 'mad scientist lab'. Standing, I nodded at him and tried to ignore the fact that the rose bushes I had planted had gone wild.

"Hello, Stewart." My voice was so ice cold I'm surprised the air didn't frost with my breath.

A flash of sadness filled his eyes, then he looked at Smoke. "And this is...?"

"Her old man," Smoke growled before I could respond.

Instead of looking surprised, Stewart merely smirked then winked at Smoke. "I bet. You certainly look like a daddy."

Baffled at what the hell Stewart meant, I cocked my head to stare at him, but Smoke sighed, shook his head, and his tension eased. He studied Stewart for a moment who shifted uneasily beneath Smoke's dark, steady gaze. Whatever he saw in Stewart's face didn't make him happy, and by the anger in his expression I worried that he might break Stewart's jaw.

Finally Smoke said, "She never figured it out, did she?"

Stewart gave shot me a remorseful look and shook his head. "No."

"You know she loved you, right?"

"Yeah. I knew." He looked at the ground, then back up at me with an ashamed expression twisting his handsome face. "I'm sorry I hurt her so much with my bullshit."

"What," I gritted out through clenched teeth, "the hell is going on?"

Princess whined at my feet. Smoke reached past me to soothe her while Stewart shook his head again. "Not out here. Come inside. I've got something to show you."

We made our way into the sprawling, comfortable home Stewart had equipped with every gadget known to mankind and then some. When he'd designed this place he'd done it with my help, implying that someday we'd live here together. Even though I was glad now that our engagement—which I was sure was going to happen back in those days—never came to fruition, it still hurt to look around the house and see all the things I'd bought.

Stewart had allowed me to decorate the place when he moved in, and everything was pretty much the same. Dark leather furniture, bright throw pillows, and lots of splashes of color here and there. I didn't know if it was because he couldn't be bothered to redecorate, or if he purposely left it like this after I dumped his ass. Either way it depressed me that I once thought I'd live here with Stewart for the rest of my life. I focused on Smoke's heat next to me instead of my negative thoughts and struggled to control my emotions. I'd have time to cry about it later, but right now I had to get my head on straight and remember we were here for Sarah.

Stewart led us through the cluttered space of his living room to the entrance of his laboratory situated deep in the side of the hill. I was kind of surprised that Stewart would let Smoke into his special space, but he didn't even blink an eye as Smoke followed me in. Princess scampered past us to her bed of pillows near one of the worktables and flopped down on them with a huff. I paused by the doorway, knowing Smoke was going to be a little surprised at the sight of an area big enough to house three fighter jets. While there were no actual jets, there were missile launchers, an honest-to-God top-of-the-line Russian tank, more electronics than there could possibly be uses for, as well as racks of experimental weapons Stewart had probably designed.

My dad and Stewart's family did a lot of business together and Stewart was an expert at rigging weapons with self-destruct devices and various levels of security so that if they ended up in the hands some idiot intent on detonating a bomb at the state capital, Stewart could destroy the device before any harm was done. See, what most people don't understand is that arms dealers tend to have a great deal of respect for their product, at least the good ones do. And they know the destruction that could happen if the weapons were stolen, so they'd engineer them with different devices to blow anyone who fucked with them to bits without harming the weapon itself.

As predicted, Smoke's eyes grew bigger, and bigger as he took in Stewart's toys. His hands twitched once or twice when he found something he was particularly interested in. I'm sure to Smoke, this place was like a huge toy store. After a few moments, a small smile curved the edges of Smoke's mouth. "Remind me to talk some business with you after the girls are safe."

Stewart nodded then took us over to a table and turned on a super bright light surrounding a big magnifying glass. I was pretty sure the battered office chair near the wall was the same busted ass one that had been here when I left. It seemed like no one was around to remind Stewart there was a world outside his lab now that I was gone. What an incredibly depressing thought—his home was his self-made prison.

Smoke cleared his throat, and I realized I'd frozen about a dozen steps behind them, caught up in my revelation.

With a sigh Stewart motioned to me. "Come here, I want to show you something."

We gathered behind Stewart and he picked up some kind circuit board from the table, his body brushing mine as he turned. "This is Sarah's phone, or what remains of it. Notice anything odd?"

Smoke studied it for a moment, then sucked in a harsh breath. "Fucking hell."

"Fucking hell what?" I tried to keep my irritation under control as I looked at the pile of circuit boards and wires spread out on the table. Smoke stood right next to me and I tried to ignore his nearness while I pretended to understand what I was seeing on the table as I leaned over to examine the bits and pieces. Right now, Smoke should have been all über alpha possessive about me standing so close to my ex-boyfriend, but instead, he was acting like Stewart wasn't a threat. In a crazy bitch way, I was disappointed by Smoke's lack of overprotective brooding even as I was glad that I didn't have to deal with an angry Smoke.

I needed therapy.

Smoke moved the lighted magnifying glass over a bit so I could see and pointed at something small and shiny on the table. "That brass bit right there? Tracker."

"And that's just the obvious one," Stewart picked up the sparkly purple phone case with a white rose on it. I knew right away the phone belonged to Sarah because it was her favorite color and flower. "Got another one in here that worked like a GPS tracker on a scrambled link."

"Motherfucker," Smoke said in a low growl.

"Indeed," Stewart said with his typical dry humor. "Even more of a clusterfuck when I was able to trace a bunch of the phone calls to the Iron Horse clubhouses in Denver and Austin that were all transmitted to a third party. And, two of the incoming calls, one from 'Beach' and one from 'Venom' had trackers on them as well. Someone has been listening in on you, and probably for a while. Bet you've had some unexplained shit happening for at least a couple months, people knowing where you'd be. Shipments getting screwed up. Whoever did this knows their shit, but it's a custom job. The guy who bugged your phones is good, but fortunately for you, I'm better."

A wave of anger poured off of Smoke and I flinched as he snarled, "What else?"

"I'd bet there are a lot more people whose phones are being traced, so you all need to get your shit checked out. Just keep in mind that someone with access to all those phones has been tampering with them. You've got a turncoat, so if I were you, I'd have everything checked out by at least two people. Now let me see your phone."

Smoke handed over his cell phone with a low growl. "I check it at least once a week."

Stewart scrolled through several screens, tapped several times, and then quickly disassembled the phone. He spent a few tense minutes looking it over while Smoke simmered in silent fury. "You're clean. So it would appear that whoever this was knew that you'd be paranoid about checking your phone, or they didn't have access to it."

We sat in silence while Stewart put Smoke's phone back together and handed it to him. Without looking at

34

me, Smoke gripped it tight enough I was worried it would shatter. "Gotta make some calls."

With an uneasy glance, Stewart gestured to the door leading out of the lab to the main house. "Use the kitchen. Only room in my home not set up to block cell reception. It's the third room on the right."

Smoke nodded with a distracted look, and I stared after him as he left me alone with Stewart. For what felt like forever, we stood there in awkward silence, stealing glances at each other, totally uncomfortable until Stewart sighed. He took a step back and ran his hand through his hair in a way that I used to find sexy. Now it just pissed me off for some reason.

His gaze met mine, and his cocky attitude melted away, revealing the real Stewart. "So, you really like that guy?"

Feeling unexpectedly guilty and wondering why, I nodded. "I do."

"You love him?"

I bit my lower lip, the feeling of guilt intensifying even as I berated myself for even caring about Stewart's feelings. "I do."

"Is he good to you?"

"In every way."

To my surprise, Stewart smiled. It was a small, tired quirk of his lips, but it shocked me. "Then I'm happy for you, Swan."

"You're not upset?"

"No, no. I want you to be happy. I…shit I had it all straight in my mind how I wanted this discussion to go, but now, I can't remember a word." He sighed and rubbed the back of his neck. "Okay, I owe you an apology, and not just for what you think. First, I really didn't do anything with Sarah. She arranged to have you walk in on us because she figured out my secret. I swear she didn't touch me anymore than it was necessary to jerk my pants down and shove her hands under my shirt. I let you believe she did more than that because I was pissed at her and wanted to get back at her."

"What?" I sagged into a chair near the table, my legs weak. "I don't understand. Why would you hurt me like that? I didn't deserve that, and I was feeling shitty enough as it was."

His face turned red. "Awww, fuck. I hate admitting what a complete asshole I was, but here it goes. Swan, I'm gay. I used you so my dad would think I'm straight and get off my back about finding a girl. Turns out my dad doesn't give a shit if I'm straight, gay, or trans as long as I'm happy. I was just an immature shit who thought the world revolved around me."

I gaped at him, no doubt looking like a fool while my personal history rewrote itself. My breath filled my lungs in a painful rush. "What? You're what?"

"Gay. I like guys."

"I know what *gay* means, you shithead." I stood up suddenly, anger filling my head. "You used me? You let me fall in love with you?"

"Oh please," Stewart rolled his eyes. "Love? Give me a break. I could barely even touch you and you didn't touch me. We were good friends, and I'm sorry that my actions ruined our friendship, but you never really loved me. We only kissed twice, Swan, and you acted like you were repulsed each time, so I never tried to take the charade any further than that."

I pointed a shaking finger at him, furious at the callous way he'd used me, how he'd manipulated me. Damn it, I really believed he'd cared about me, that he found me special, that I was loveable and not a freak. Tears thickened my voice as I yelled, "Well my aversion worked out really well for you, didn't it? You got a trophy girlfriend you didn't have to touch, the perfect disguise for a little boy too scared to let his Father know he likes dick. You *used* me."

His mouth opened and closed a couple times before he bowed his head in defeat. "I did, and I'm really sorry. Sarah was right. I do owe her for exposing me when she did. If she hadn't I'd probably still be stringing you along, and I'd hate myself for it."

"You said you loved me. You made me believe you loved me. Yeah, we didn't make out, but you were kind to me, you said all the right things. You manipulated and lied to me."

"I know. I'm not proud of playing you, but I did."

I looked to the door that Smoke went through, glad he wasn't here to witness my humiliation but wishing he was here so he could hold me, so he could take away the pain.

"At the very least, I thought you were my friend," I said in a tone that did nothing to hide how hurt I was. "Why would you do that to me?"

"Because I was a young, self-centered, fucking prick who never considered what I was doing to you. I've learned some hard lessons in the past few years. I've been in your shoes a little bit, and it sucks. I'm trying to make it up to you by helping you find your mom and Sarah. She said you need to head to Denver, that she'd find a way to contact you once you're there." He tugged at his shirt, then met my gaze. "Swan, I'm worried about her. She didn't look good."

My head was still reeling from the bomb that had been dropped on me, but the mention of Sarah looking bad snapped my attention back to the present. "What do you mean 'she didn't look good'?"

"Just that she appeared run down, tired. She threw up once while we were talking so it may have been the flu, but she looked like shit. When you find her, make sure you get her to see a doctor if she's ill. She's not my favorite person in the world, but I hope someday you'll both accept my apology. I don't want anything bad happening to either of you."

His sincere concern for my sister helped seep away some of my rage. "I'll take care of her. You have anything else to tell me?"

"No, nothing else. Just that I really am sorry for hurting you."

"Then we're done here."

"Swan…"

I ignored him and strode through the door feeling rather fragile, like my skin was made of glass and the maelstrom of emotions inside of me was threatening to shatter it. I hurt, bone-deep, and a spark of self-hatred burned inside of me that I'd blindly let him use me like that. Shit, I bought all of his smooth lies without a second thought. My trust was hard to earn, but I'd given it to him, and he'd shattered it along with my naïve heart. Stewart said he was sorry behind me again, but I pretended I didn't hear him and went to look for Smoke. It didn't take me long to find my man. He was flipping the fuck out on whoever he was talking to and his angry voice became louder.

"I want everyone, and I do mean everyone—even the old ladies—on brand new motherfucking burners. Tell them to go to random stores, buy their own phones and don't let *anyone* touch them. Do you understand me? Get those useless prospects to hunt our members down and tell them, in person, that this is an order from the Master at Arms. If Swan or Sarah gets hurt because you're too fucking slow getting the word out, you'll pray for Beach to get to you first. You do *not* want me to have to deal with you personally. I'm in the mood to get creative with a blowtorch, Vance. And remember what I said, no one touches anyone else's phone. Got me?"

My heart slammed against my ribs and I froze for a moment, his words rolling through my mind like fire. I trembled on the verge of freaking out, imagining now how Miguel must have earned his nickname and I wondered for a moment if I could live in his violent world. Then I had to choke back what probably would have been hysterical laughter, because right now, he was cleaning up the huge mess my mom had dragged me into. My world was about as dangerous as it could get. Even though Miguel may have done this kind of shit before, now he was threatening to torture people for me.

It was sweet in a rather psychotic way.

Moving slowly, I ran my hand along the wall and paused just out of Smoke's line of sight. He made a low growling sound, and I caught the edge of his body as he paced inside of Stewart's large kitchen. The whimsical teapots I'd placed near his sink were gone, but the gray granite with white tile was still the same. It made the sight of Smoke pacing through it, like a pissed off panther in a cage, all the more surreal. His agitation was contagious, and I found myself rhythmically flexing my hands in time with his long steps.

"I know you fucking need me back there, but get your dick out of your ass and handle this. That's a fucking order." Smoke abruptly stopped moving, his gaze going positively glacial as his lip curled in a snarl. "You may have outranked me in the Marines, motherfucker, but I'm your fucking boss now so don't try to pull fuckin' rank on me. You're lucky I don't tell Beach you're giving me shit about this. Mood he's in? He'd pull your toenails out as an example ... Yeah, that's what I thought."

He started moving again, and I debated stepping forward, but I didn't want to draw Smoke's attention right now. Anger poured off of him in waves, and I knew on some instinctive level that he needed his space. But I needed him, desperately, so I found myself staying right where I was, torn between fleeing and leaping on him.

"I'll handle Denver, personally," Smoke said in a low voice. "Have Beach call me ASAP... No, I don't want to tell you so you can tell him. Just find him and tell him to call me from a new burner. Get it done."

Smoke ended the call, and there was silence for a good thirty seconds before he spoke again. "You gonna

40

hide behind the wall all day, baby, or do I get to hold you?"

I slunk into the kitchen, my cheeks burning with embarrassment at being caught eavesdropping. "Sorry."

He looked tired as he held his arms open. "Come here."

Serenity filled me when he held me tight. He took a deep breath with his face buried against the top of my head. Okay, so maybe he was a psychopath, but he was my psychopath, and I loved him with everything I had. I looped my arms around his firm waist and cuddled close, loving how he enveloped me. Just one deep breath of his scent made me realize how stupid I was being to allow what happened with Stewart to mess with me, and in retrospect, how much I owed Sarah for trying to show me, in her own messed up way, what was really going on.

God, I was such a self-centered bitch.

Sarah tried to tell me the truth but I wouldn't listen, too intent on nursing my hurt feelings.

I started to cry, ashamed of my behavior, worrying about my sister, and Smoke made a shushing noise. "I'm sorry he hurt you, sweetheart. I'm so sorry that unworthy little prick used you like that. He should have manned up and lived an honest life instead'a dragging you into his mess."

Sniffing, I rubbed my cheek against his shirt. "Yeah he should have, and it sucks, but that's not why I'm crying. I'm worried about Sarah, and I need to talk with her so badly to apologize for being so stupid and wasting so much time sulking. I feel like we're never gonna find her or my mom. What if we don't find them, Smoke? Am I going to spend the rest of my life running?"

"Hey, hey," he said in that soothing voice of his that made me melt, "where's all this negativity coming from?"

I shrugged because I had no idea. I was just suddenly really bummed out as the revelations about Stewart, using me as a cover, settled into my mind making me feel worthless. I've known him since I was a kid, and I never had even the faintest clue that he was gay. Was I so stupid, so easy to fool, or was he a really good liar?

"We done here, baby girl?"

Unable to speak for some reason, I merely nodded.

"The let's get the fuck out of here before I kick that twink's ass for making you feel one moment of sorrow."

While I had no idea what a twink was, I was so ready to leave. When Smoke picked me up in his arms I didn't protest, merely clung to him and closed my eyes. At one point we must have passed Stewart because I heard him say something, but it was muffled.

Smoke replied with a warning growl, "What the fuck did you think your betrayal was gonna do to her? If you fuckin' knew her at all, you would know that when you broke her trust you hurt her deeply. Bet right now you're realizing how much damage you caused when you deceived her. Now get the fuck out of my way so I can take care of my woman."

Whatever Stewart said in reply was lost as Smoke carried me outside. I took a deep breath of the cool night air, glad to be out of Stewart's house. All too soon, we reached the truck and Smoke almost had to pry me off of him to get me in my seat. As soon as he hopped in the cab with me, I was plastered to his side, as much as I could be with the glove box in my way. My soul hurt, and the only balm to my pain was found in touching Smoke. Instead of objecting to my imitation of a clinging vine, he drove with one hand on the wheel and the other holding my hand.

Chapter Three

I had no idea how long we'd been driving. My mind was too stuffed full of a future without my sister and my own possible impending death. The thought of hundreds of strangers pawing at me, being inside of me, made me clutch Smoke desperately. I'd rather die in a hail of bullets or by my own hand before being sold into sexual slavery. Then it occurred to me that Smoke could be hurt, even killed while searching for my mother, and a desperate whimper escaped me before I could stop it. Shit, I usually had a better handle on my emotions, but even I had to admit that the situation I was in allowed me a few justifiable freak-outs. My mind had taken too many emotional blows and I was struggling to keep the tears at bay.

Smoke glanced down at me then swore softly. "Any cameras around here?"

I looked up, my eyes swollen from crying and scanned the area. "No, we're on the edge of my father's property. This is a back road that everyone on the compound uses. Just pressure sensors scattered around. No cameras or mics here."

"Good."

A plume of dust rose around us as he pulled over to the side of the road and parked the truck. With a gentleness that made me sigh with pleasure, Smoke pulled his seat all the way back and hauled me onto his lap so I straddled him. The steering wheel pressed into my back, but I didn't care. In the glow of the dash lights, I could see the antidote to my pain watching me with soft, concerned eyes.

"What do you need, baby girl?" he whispered while skimming his hands over my denim-covered ass.

My lower lip quivered at the obvious affection in his tone. Unable to stand the sympathy in his eyes, I focused my gaze out the back window to try and gather myself. Out here in nowheresville, the stars were spectacular on clear nights, and I inhaled sharply when Smoke cracked the windows. The air was clean and fresh, with the scent of the dark forest, so I took a deep breath before slowly letting it out.

Turning back to Smoke I examined his rough face, gentled with a small smile that was meant only for me. He adored me. It was in every nuance of his body that I could now, for the most part, read like a book. My trust in him was deep and I told him the truth without a hint of apprehension. "I need you. You make the pain go away and replace it with love, Miguel. I need to feel loved. I need to feel like I mean something to someone."

He let out a shuddering sigh and his lips softened as he crooned, "Sweet baby, you're not something. You're everything, *everything*, to me."

The moment his hands touched my skin, I closed my eyes, losing myself in his presence and delicious scent. Even though space was limited, he managed to touch nearly every inch of me, smoothing his hands down my body while nuzzling my throat with his lush lips. I swear this man was going to be the death of me. When he bit the side of my neck, none too gently, all I could do was arch back to offer him more. If I wasn't careful Smoke would devour me whole, but I couldn't bring myself to care. I was ensnared by him, absolutely lost in the arousal coming to life between us.

He lifted my shirt then lowered my bra, freeing my breasts for his greedy mouth. Grasping them in a hold just short of painful, Smoke began to suck gently on my left nipple while caressing the right with his thumb. As he licked at the distended tip, his hips rose into me, rocking me on him while I made little sounds of pleasure at his dedicated attention to my breasts. I loved how touching me seemed to drive him crazy, to break his careful control. His dick was hard enough to pound nails, and I ached to have him inside of me.

Greedy for a taste of him, I tugged his mouth away from my breast and leaned into him, our lips meeting as we both sighed in relief. I would never, ever tire of the way he kissed me, of how he'd seduce me into giving him everything he wanted. Grasping my ass, he rocked me against his hard shaft, the thick fabric of our jeans torturing my poor, wet pussy. I was so slick, I swore I could smell my musk with each breath. His hands skimmed my back, stopping at the hooks on my lacy, black bra. He played with the clasp, teasing me, turning the middle of my back into an erogenous zone with his rough fingertips. Jesus, every time he touched me I lost myself deeper in him and knew my soul had been inexorably changed because of Smoke.

"You have the softest skin." He whispered against my lips while his thick fingers teasingly flitted with the closure of my bra. "If I had my way, we'd always be naked around each other 24/7 so I could rub up against you anytime I wanted. When this bullshit is over, I'm takin' you somewhere private so I can spend all day and all night taking care of you, kissin' you, and fuckin' you. I want to make you mine in every way possible."

My heart lurched at the gentle strength and conviction in his voice. I swore it was beating hard enough that he should have been able to feel it against his palm cupping my breast.

"Please," I whispered and ground myself against him like the shameless hussy he turned me into. "I need you, Smoke."

"What do you need?" he asked in a rumbling tone while reaching between us to cup my sex. "Holy shit. Your pussy is hot as an oven. Bet it's soaking wet, so I can fuck you hard, to make you mine. Love knowin' that your tender little cunt aches because of me. Now tell me, what do you need?"

"You...I need your cock," I gasped when he gently squeezed my sex. Pleasure tingled through me as he applied delicious pressure to my clit. If only he would give me more...I could make him give me more. The thought made me feel kind of naughty, like seducing

my man was taboo. I drew a deep breath and said what
I knew would break his control. Smoke loved it when I
talked dirty to him and indulged his possessive side.
"Fuck me, fill me up with your come, mark me and
make me yours. I want your cock pushing so deep into
me it hurts. I want to feel you climax inside of me,
filling me up with you, making me smell like you...taste
like you."

For a moment, a hint of rough passion moved
through his gaze, strong enough to scare me and turn
me on at the same time. "Only me."

"Only you."

Smoke fisted my hair and tilted my head back while
he placed small, stinging bites all over my exposed
breasts. When he nipped at the very tips of my nipples,
I ground myself against him and stiffened, within
seconds of an orgasm. The delicious pain of his bites
seemed to travel from my breasts to my pussy where
the sensation became intense pleasure.

Some annoying sound poked at the edges of mind,
but I tried to ignore whatever it was and concentrate
instead on Smoke's fluttering licks to the sensitive tip
of my breast. When Smoke pulled his mouth from me, I
moaned in protest, but he sighed. "Fuck, you make me
forget where I am, who I am. I have to take this call,
babe. Shit has hit the fan back home, and I'm gonna
have to rip some motherfuckers new assholes. Just bear
with me for a few."

Without another word, he lifted me off his lap,
grabbed his cell phone, and left the truck. When the
door shut, I just stared out the window as Smoke began
to pace, his hands occasionally raised in the air. Even in
the dim light of a three-quarter moon, I could see he

was really, really pissed and perversely enough, his anger turned me on. My body still ached with unfulfilled desire, and even though I knew whatever he was doing was important, my self-interested libido didn't give a shit. With my wet pussy, my throbbing breasts, and the echoing sting of all those bites to my nipples, which throbbed in need, still racing through my nervous system. I wanted an orgasm.

Now.

I blew out a frustrated breath then went to tuck my breasts back into my bra. Handling them felt good.

Really good.

Curious to see if I could maybe take care of my problem on my own, I tweaked one nipple and shivered. While my touch was nowhere as satisfying as Smoke's, my body was primed for an orgasm. I gently ran my hands over my sensitive skin, eventually unzipping my jeans to slide my fingers inside. At the first brush of my swollen clit, I moaned softly. Smoke was still outside pacing and still on the phone. I watched him move about, remembering what it felt like when he pounded me into the mattress with a good, hard fuck.

His scent filled the truck, and I moaned again as I teased the entrance to my body, the tip of my finger nowhere near what I needed. I spread some of my arousal over my clit and began to rub it in slow circles with the tips of two fingers. In my mind, a naked Smoke stretched above me, his intense gaze boring into mine while he slid in deep. My breath trembled and that empty spot in my heart that Smoke filled with his overwhelming presence ached for him.

I was still lost in my own fantasy world when the door to my side of the truck was jerked open, and I was snatched out before I could tumble to the ground. Smoke ignored my shriek and grabbed a blanket from the backseat before carrying me over his shoulder to the back of the truck. He took the gate down, tossed the blanket onto the bed of the truck, then perched me on the blanket, all while speaking in Spanish to someone on the phone. Judging by his tone, it wasn't a happy conversation, but he gazed at me with lust and not anger. He wasn't pleased with whoever he was talking to, and it made his movements somewhat harsher than usual, more dominant.

I liked that.

He put his hand over the cellphone and said in a stern, no-bullshit voice, "Take your pants off and play with that sweet pussy for me. Fuck, the thought of being the first to do all these dirty things with you and knowing that I'm gonna be the only man you'll ever have inside of you, makes me want to give your greedy body every inch of cock it wants, and then some. I own that golden cunt."

I moaned loudly, and arched my hips up at him, begging him to touch me as he seduced me with his raw words. I wanted to argue that I belonged only to myself, but that wasn't true. Smoke owned a piece of me now, not just my libido, but a bit of my heart and soul. I should've been freaked out, but I also realized I owned a part of him as well.

I looked into his dark eyes and studied his face, and found a dizzying amount of desire mixed with rougher, darker emotions. I deliberately made a great production of taking my clothes off, putting everything I'd learned while working at a strip club to good use. My moves were controlled, the dip of a shoulder to draw his gaze to my neck, a slight arch to my back that pushed my butt out.

His voice faltered for a moment then picked back up as he traced his fingers over my bottom. The tremble in his fingertips as he stroked me made me want to drive him crazy. This man loved me. It was evident in his every caress, his every glance, and his every territorial move. Smoke was one hundred percent alpha male, and his need to assert his dominance over me never failed to turn me on. He put his hand between my shoulder blades and pushed me down, then propped my butt up so I had to curve my spine to accommodate his silent demands.

Remembering what he wanted from me, I spread my legs the slightest bit and slowly ran my fingertip over the wet slit of my sex. Smoke went silent behind me for a long, long moment. When he spoke again, his voice had a rough edge to it that hadn't been there before. I stared at the bed of the truck with unseeing eyes, my imagination painting vivid pictures of my man standing behind me, trying to concentrate on business while I tempted him with pleasure. The control that I had over Smoke with my body ramped my desire higher as I tried to entice him to touch me…taste me.

I teased myself and him, swirling two of my fingers through my arousal before sinking them slowly inside of me. I startled when Smoke grabbed my hips, but it was only so he could arch me further and spread my legs wider, leaving nothing of my body hidden from him. He stroked the back of my thigh with one hand, his voice becoming nothing but a rumbling sound in my ears as I reveled in his attention. My fingers felt good inside of me, but his cock would feel so much better.

"Touch me," I whispered.

Evidently I said it loud enough so that Smoke could hear me, because a second later he spanked my bottom hard enough to sting. I almost jerked my hand away from my pussy in surprise, but his hand cupped over mine. He moved my fingers inside of me, using my hand to touch my pussy the way he wanted me to. I gave myself over to him completely, my bite-bruised breasts crushed to the blanket and my ass feeling heated in the cool air,

When he was satisfied that I was playing with my sex as he'd silently instructed, he removed his hand for a moment and unzipped his pants to free his thick erection. Then he ran his thumb near the entrance to my body, coating it with my arousal. I tensed when that thumb began to spread my natural lubricant up to my anus, but he just played with me, toying with my body until I was trying to get him to sink his thumb into my bottom. A naughty pleasure tightened my sex, and I groaned as he slowly breached my rear entrance with his thumb, which felt gigantic.

I tensed, not sure if I liked this sensation. It was weird and uncomfortable and…ohhhh, God... Smoke was smacking my hand away so he could press his rock-hard shaft against my pussy. His thumb turned from a distraction to an erotic thrill as he slowly sank into me, now speaking in English. I had no idea what he was saying, too caught up in the press of his almost unbearably thick dick breaching me where I needed him the most. The feeling of coming together was bliss, and I moaned from deep in my chest. When he went to pull out, I squeezed my inner muscles and earned a rough, choking sound from Smoke, followed by a snarl directed at the person on the phone.

"Baby, bite down on that blanket," he whispered to me. "I don't want this dirty fucker Hustler listening to you. You get too loud and I'll stop fuckin' you."

I managed to gather the blanket, and hoped it was clean as I bit down on it. Personally, I didn't give a shit if Hustler heard me. I'd seen him getting a blowjob by a pretty, but world-weary woman. Hustler could kiss my ass about me making any noises. It felt good to moan my pleasure into the cloth, and I had no doubt that Smoke—he loved gagging me—was getting off on the sight. Evidently, I had a bit of an exhibitionist streak because the idea of Hustler on the phone getting turned on by our fucking made my pussy clench. Now, I'm not saying I'd touch Hustler, ever, but I wanted to do anything and everything, as long as I did it with Smoke. A decadent shiver went through me at the sheer naughtiness of what we were doing, and I began to rock back onto Smoke's devastating cock, enjoying the slow burn as he stretched me.

He stood still and let me experiment, his thumb still playing with my bottom. My eyelids slowly closed, and I became lost in the nothingness, my entire being focused on what kind of sensations I could coax from my buzzing nerves while rocking my hips back into

Smoke. Soon, I was making little, pained noises into the blanket. There was a place on the upper part of my pussy that felt really, really good when he stroked over it in a certain way. The ridge of the crest of his shaft was pressing into me just right, and I shuddered then grunted.

I barely moved a few inches with each roll of my hips, trying to move to maximize that wonderful, hard tingle I got with every short stroke. It almost felt like he was rubbing my clit from the inside. Another hard moan escaped me, muffled by the blanket, then both of Smoke's hands gripped my hips hard enough that it sent bright sparks of pleasure/pain surging through me.

"You like that, my naughty girl? When my cock strokes you right...there?"

I cried out as he shoved roughly into me, pressing hard on that spot and making my whole body shiver and shake.

"Yeah, you like that." His chuckle was that of a smug, self-satisfied male. "We'll have to see if I can make you squirt for me sometime. But right now, I need to fuck you before anyone else calls me."

With that he pulled all the way out until the bulbous head of his dick stretched the entrance to my sex, a cry of distress leaving my lips before I could stop it. He laughed again, but the sound turned into a growl as he began to fuck me, harsh thrusts that rocked the truck with his movements. One of his hands left my hip and wound into my hair, pulling back hard enough that I couldn't help but scream out my pleasure.

His other hand was still on my body, and he held me tight enough that I knew I would bruise, and that additional pain rocketed me into my orgasm. I shoved myself back at him, the wonderful tension in my body winding higher with each thrust until I broke for him, tiny whimpers escaping me as I tensed and released over and over, my pussy massaged by his thrusting cock through each delicious wave. I collapsed to the truck bed, and he followed me down, fucking me hard and deep. An involuntary aftershock moved through me, and my inner muscles, still buzzing after my release, clenched down on him. He bit my shoulder and ground me into the truck bed with his hard thrusts, then stilled. My body was still so sensitive, I could feel his throbbing pulses deep inside of me.

We remained joined together, our harsh pants blending with the songs of the insects and night creatures going about their business around us. It was a beautiful, peaceful sound. Smoke slowly pulled out, then melted next to me with a rough sigh that seemed to whisper through me. I blew my hair out of my eyes so I could see him and grinned at the slightly stunned look on his face. He blinked, then smiled back.

"Thanks, baby girl, I needed that."

I laughed, riding the blissful wave of my orgasm. "Me too."

He cupped my cheek. If I lived to be a million years old, I knew I would never find someone who fit me as well as my badass biker. "I love you. Best thing that ever happened to me."

"I love you too, Miguel."

He let out a soft growl but something else drew my attention, a faint beeping noise. I sat up immediately. "Get dressed."

"What?"

"Those beeps mean we've got company on the way. Call my Dad and see if he is expecting any visitors."

"Who do you think it is?"

"I'm not sure. This part of our property borders the commune where Lyric lives. They shouldn't have any reason for being out here at this time of night."

"You need to grab my gun?"

"No, that was a series of three beeps. Means vehicles approved to travel this road."

He didn't question me and got himself together while I scrambled to put my clothes back on. My feet were still bare when a truck pulled down the road and stopped in front of us, the bright lights blinding me. I raised my hand to block the glare, and a second later, a man's voice said, "Who are you and what are you doing on private property?"

Smoke talked on the phone next to me as I yelled, "My name is Swan Anderson. My father owns this property. Who the hell are you?"

"None of your business who we are. What are you doing parked on the side of the road?"

"They look like sinners to me, Clint," another man said in an arrogant, but vaguely familiar, drawling voice that held a slight slur. "Can't be Swan because she wouldn't disgrace her Daddy by fucking on the side of the road like some common whore."

Smoke froze, and his anger moved through the air like the shock wave of a nuclear blast.

Trying to diffuse the situation as quickly as I could I yelled, "I couldn't give a flying fuck what you think, but if you disrespect my father like that again, Clint, I'll let Mimi know your sterling opinion of her husband and her daughter."

I tried to get a good look at him, but the bright truck lights were right in my eyes, turning the men into silhouettes. I strained to see past the glare, but it was no use. The guy's voice sounded familiar, and that was confirmed when he said something about me most outsiders wouldn't know.

"Stepdaughter, no blood there." the first man said just loud enough for me to hear before he raised his voice, his tone dripping in sarcasm, "'Sides, we ain't scared. God will watch out for us. If I were you, I'd be more worried about what people are gonna think about you for being with that wetback *cholo*. You fucking the help? You gonna give your daddy brown Mexican grandbabies?"

Oh, hell the fuck *no*, he didn't just say that.

Smoke tensed up next to me, then repeated what the guy had just said in a deadly whisper before he looked at me, murder in his eyes. "Get in the truck, Swan." His voice was ice cold as he clutched the phone tight enough that I was afraid it would shatter in his grip.

I shook my head slowly. "No, Smoke, please." My words sounded broken. "No violence. I know they deserve having their racist asses handed to them on a platter, but not now, please."

He blinked twice before he swallowed hard. "No one talks to you like that."

"I'm okay, really, it's just words from a bunch of idiots." I reached out and hesitantly touched his bicep while the men in the truck talked amongst themselves.

They all slurred their words, and I was pretty sure they were wasted. Last I'd heard, alcohol was forbidden at Lyric's compound, and I wondered if the new leader had any idea his men were out late at night getting shitfaced and driving around with guns. A drunk man with a firearm was dangerous at the best of times, let alone if Smoke gave in to their taunts. "Please, Smoke, we don't need to borrow trouble right now."

The phone squawked, and Smoke slowly raised it to his ear, watching me with dead eyes as he listened to my father. Smoke grimaced and nodded then said in a loud voice, "Mr. Anderson would like to inform you that he has now given me approval to use lethal force to remove you from his land. If you so much as breathe on his daughter, he has promised that he will bring the wrath of God down on your compound and let the devil figure out what to do with your rotten souls. And he is calling Pastor Middleton."

The men in the truck cursed in a most unchristian manner before the one with the drawl said, "We'll pray for your whoring ways, Swan. Never too late to ask the Lord for forgiveness for you and your cum dump of a sister. Heard her pussy was as sweet as honey and spicy as cinnamon. Your cunt taste like candy too?"

That's it. I was going to fucking kill them.

Before I could leap from the truck bed, Smoke roared, "Get the fuck out of here, now, or I swear you'll know what the fires of Hell feel like."

One of their phones rang and was answered. A second later, the truck pulled out throwing a plume of dust and rocks.

I took a deep breath and let it out slowly while Smoke vibrated with anger next to me. He thrust his phone at me then said in a low voice, "I gotta go for a walk real quick."

Watching him stalk off, knowing that he needed time to cool down but still wishing he'd stay with me, I answered up the phone. "Hello?"

For the next ten minutes, I listened to my father rant about what he was going to do to those 'racist cult motherfuckers'. Evidently, my dad was in a property dispute with them at the moment over access to the aquifer on our land. The cult had grown by leaps and bounds since Lyric's father died. The new pastor brought in a bunch of his followers who were rumored to be white supremacists. My dad was concerned about their reservoir supporting the compound's ever growing population. My dad also said that the pastor was a right fucking asshole and dirty as the bottom of a mineshaft. Evidently, Pastor Middleton liked the finer things in life, and while his followers lived an austere existence, he partied it up in a mansion and owned a Jaguar.

The ride back to my parents' house was tense and anger-filled. I found myself curling up against the door next to me, breathing as shallow as possible in order to keep from attracting Smoke's attention. I felt like a deer frozen in fear as a hungry predator stalked past, praying he didn't notice me. My heart raced and my muscles were so tense I knew I'd be sore in the morning if I didn't relax, but I just couldn't. I hated Smoke's rage. It made me uneasy, but I kept reminding myself that he would never hurt me, never touch me in anger. Still, the feeling of having disappointed him tore at my heart, like I'd let him down somehow by pleading with him not to go off on a murderous rampage over words.

I went to reach for him, to try and soothe him, but before my hand touched his face he tilted away and spoke in a clipped tone, "Don't."

Stung, I jerked my hand back and wrapped my arms around myself, trying to ease the ache in my chest.

AUSTIN TX

Chapter Four

When we pulled up to the house, Smoke stormed out of the truck and met my father at the door. They talked for a few seconds before Smoke went into the house, leaving me alone in the truck. Miffed that my man had just stomped off without a word, I hopped out and made my way to my dad. He gave me a worried look, then pulled me into an unexpected hug. The scent of coffee and his cologne mixed with Mimi's perfume surrounded me, and I took a deep breath of the smell of home. All craziness aside, I knew my dad loved me, and I loved him just as much. "You okay, Swan?"

I hugged him back, relishing the rare occasion when my dad allowed me to show him physical affection. "Yeah, it was no big deal."

In fact, compared to being kidnapped by a biker gang, confronting some bigots was no big deal.

His arms tightened around me before he stepped back and ran a hand through his silver–flecked, dark hair. I gave him a moment and watched him try to control his anger, but he was having less success with it than Smoke. When he spoke, his voice came out strained. He constantly flexed his hands, but he managed to choke his temper back enough to speak to me. "Looks like I'm going to have to block access to our land on that road."

"Shit." I sighed, knowing that it would become harder for Lyric to come visit my family. "That bad?"

"They fucked with my daughter. *My* daughter." His nostrils flared. "I should burn that fucking place down. Unfortunately, Lyric's stubborn ass is still there along with a few other good folk. You know how obstinate that little girl is. She wants to protect her friends and family even though she hasn't realized yet that the fuckers she's squaring off against would crush her if she really went to war against them. As soon as that girl's gone I'm gonna deal with those hypocritical assholes. I promise you that."

Mimi came out onto the porch and laid a soothing hand on my dad's shoulder before giving me a gentle smile. "I'm glad you're okay, sweetie."

I glanced over at my dad, apprehension growing inside of me as I took in the signs of his growing rage breaking through his self-control. "Where's Smoke?"

"Come with me," Mimi murmured before placing her arm around my waist. "Give your dad a few minutes to calm down."

My dad was already storming off in the direction of his shooting range to work off his anger, and I let out a little sigh of relief.

"Okay."

Weariness dragged at me as soon as I was downstairs. The soothing purples and different shades of grey that decorated the room helped to slow my racing heart. Mimi steered me over to the couch, and I sat down on the soft suede. "What's up?"

To my surprise, Mimi blushed and dropped her eyes. "Well, I thought now that you're a grown woman in a real relationship I might share some wisdom with you about how to handle your boyfriend."

Hearing her call Smoke my boyfriend didn't sit right with me. He was so much more than that. He was my everything. I yearned to be in his arms. "Where is Smoke?"

"Your Dad sent him down to the gym to work off his stress." She bit her lip, then sat up straighter and met my gaze. "Smoke is a lot like your father in some ways, and far different in others, but he obviously worships you. Every time he looks at you it's like he's seeing you for the first time. He's completely entranced by you. So for a man who loves you, seeing you in danger and not being allowed to do anything about it, is probably eating at him right now. Miguel's the kind of man who eliminates anything he considers a threat to himself or those he loves, like a warrior of old. To have taken the path of diplomacy and peace goes against who he is on some basic level, and I'd bet he feels like he let you down."

There was a ring of truth to her words and I frowned. "How do you know this?"

"The wisdom of experience, my love. I could, of course, be totally wrong, but I hope that if I'm right, our conversation will help you be ready for the confrontation ahead of you." She smiled. "If you can manage to seduce him beforehand, it'll certainly sweeten his attitude. Even just a blowjob would mellow him out."

"Ack, Mimi!" I practically shouted as my cheeks heated. Mimi was as outspoken about sex as Sarah, in her own way. She viewed it as a natural part of life and doesn't understand why I freak out when she tries to give me tips. Memories of Sarah and Mimi talking about their sexual experiences with my Italian aunts and female cousins at Mimi's yearly family reunion still give me nightmares. I never, ever want to think of my Aunt Simone with her hairy upper lip having a threesome with two Greek guys again.

"Don't 'Mimi' me. Smoke will need to connect with you, to reassure himself that you're okay. Making love will help with that. It's nothing to be ashamed of. Sex is an essential part of a healthy relationship. And it soothes the savage beast."

I stood, my mouth twisted as if I'd tasted something sour as my mind unwillingly strayed to the thought of Mimi calming my dad down in such a manner. *Ewww.* Someone pass me the brain bleach. "Thanks for the advice, but I have to be going now."

Mimi smiled and wished me a good night. After making a pit stop in my room to switch out my plain black cotton underwear for something a little fancier, I made my way to the gym, a level below me, with seduction in mind. Lights turned on as I approached the motion sensors. I passed a set of empty storage rooms until I reached the double doors of the gym. As soon as I entered, the rough sounds of Smoke working out filled the air. I followed the sounds to where he was bench-pressing some obscene amount of weight. Hard metal music pounded from the speakers above, and I paused a moment inside the doorway to watch Smoke lift. The perfect definition of his arms, shoulders, and chest as they flexed with each movement sent a wave of heat to my pussy.

The way he gritted his teeth, the strain in his expression reminded me of how he looked when he came, and my new panties were already soaking wet. I allowed myself to eye fuck him a little bit more before walking over to the stereo system to switch the music from the angry metal to some of Mimi's yoga stuff. While the front part of the gym was devoted to weights and cardio machines, the back half was Mimi's yoga studio. It was closed off behind Japanese rice paper screens and I loved it. The tranquil space a totally different world than this spartan, masculine environment.

The weights rattled as Smoke racked them and sat up. Sweat trickled down the curve of his chest, and when his gaze met mine, the anger brewing inside of him was obvious. He grabbed a towel and wiped his face off. "What's up, babe?"

I walked slowly over to him, putting a swing in my hips that drew his gaze. "I have a surprise for you."

He sighed, then shook his head and held up his hand as if warding me off. "Gimme some more time down here. I'm not good to be around right now. Go keep the bed warm for me, and I'll be there in a bit."

I hesitated, clearly having been dismissed. I fought my natural inclination to obey his wishes, and managed to gather my courage. "No."

Looking at me clearly for the first time since the incident with the zealots, he frowned. "No?"

"No." I took a deep breath, then let it out slowly. "I know you're upset. I want to make you feel better."

He frowned at me. "And what do you think I'm upset about?"

"Well…" I struggled to recall what Mimi said. "I appreciate you not killing anyone—immensely—but I know it hurt your pride to walk away."

"My pride? You think that's what I'm pissed about?" He looked down and flexed his hands. "Swan, I'm trying really hard not to flip out right now, so I would really fuckin' appreciate it if you got the fuck out of here and left me the fuck alone. I can't take being around you right now. Got me?"

I felt as if someone had punched me in the chest, and I sucked in a quick breath. "Okay."

He said something more, but I'd already started to leave. Once the door closed behind me, I paused then leaned against the wall, hoping that maybe he'd come after me. All I wanted to do was make him happy, but he didn't want me. I heard the clank of the weights through the doors and pressed my hand to my stomach, hating the curl of nausea there. Smoke had rejected me and it hurt. Bad.

I slowly made my way back to my room, and once there, stripped off my clothes, leaving on my pretty panties that wouldn't be getting any action tonight. My lower lip trembled a time or two as the sting from Smoke's rebuff turned over in my heart, and I tried to keep any tears from falling. Objectively, maturely, I knew that Smoke hadn't broken up with me or anything, but I really didn't like the fact that I could turn to him for comfort but he wouldn't do the same with me. Didn't he want my love? Didn't he want to feel better? Did I even make him better?

I gave myself a mental slap as I realized I was falling back into an old habit I was trying to break: being dependent on a man. In my case, as a kid, I was dependent on my father's mood to set the tone of my own. Smoke didn't want me with him and that, on top of the earlier bullshit with Stewart, put me in an emotional place that I was ill-equipped to deal with. Maybe I could find refuge from my problems in sleep instead of in Smoke's body as I'd originally planned.

After turning out the lights, leaving only the nightlight on, I laid back in my bed and let my tears finally fall, soaking my pillow and feeling worthless and angry with myself for feeling that way.

Sometime during the night, my bed shifted as Smoke lifted the blankets and slipped in beside me. His skin was still slightly damp, and the smell of his soap surrounded me in a musky cloud of goodness. I snuggled back against him while he pulled me tightly into his arms and began to gently stroke my belly. Not a sensual caress but more…comforting.

"Babe," Smoke whispered.

"Mmm?" was my sleepy reply. My brain wasn't functioning yet, and I struggled to remain awake.

"I wasn't sending you away because I didn't want you there. I was sending you away because I don't like you seeing my temper. I know I have a bad one, and I hate how it scares you. It wasn't my pride that was hurt. It was the thought of anyone ever harming you that makes me crazy with worry. I love you so much, baby girl."

I tried to formulate a reply, but all I could do was pat his arm and mumble.

"I was a huge dick and I know I hurt your feelings, but I had to get you out of there. The anger...you have no idea what it feels like to be full of that much rage."

Now wide awake, I shoved him away from me hard enough that he rolled off the bed with a grunt.

Didn't know what anger felt like, my ass! I constantly battled my temper, tried to keep my shit under control. Maybe he needed to see a little bit of that anger. My sister has always said that at least once, early on in a relationship, a man needed to see his woman flip her shit. Some guys can handle it, some can't. I knew Smoke could handle me, but he needed to realize that he wasn't the only one in this relationship who had a volatile temper.

"You know what, asshole, you couldn't be more wrong. You think you're the only person in the world with anger management issues? Are you for goddamn real? Pull your head out of your ass, Smoke, and take a look around, because I guarantee you aren't the only person in this room who can lose their shit. And trust me, when I lose my temper it isn't pretty...or cute. I am capable of killing people, never doubt that."

Smoke pushed himself up off the ground, his stance clearly cautious now. "Easy. I didn't mean anything by it. I was trying to protect you. I needed a time-out to cool down."

"Then tell me that!" I was so pissed I went to throw something at him and grabbed one of my pillows and chucked it at him, hard. "Don't fucking send me away like some little girl. I'm not a child, Smoke. I'm a woman, and I won't put up with your disrespect."

That made him frown, and he looked at me with confusion. "I disrespected you?"

"Of course you did." My throat grew thick and I tried to hold onto my fury. "You talk all this shit about killing any man who disrespects me, and yet you continue to do it again and again. You think there is only one way to do things, your way. You totally disregard the fact that even though I have blonde hair and big breasts—and yes, I'm a woman—I'm actually smarter and more skilled than most special forces guys. That's a fact."

Rubbing his face, Smoke then nodded. "I know how strong you are, that doesn't mean I don't want to keep you safe, to protect you from anything that might hurt you, even me."

"I can handle you!" I practically shouted, then lowered my voice when he winced at my shrill tone. "I can take your darkness, I can take the danger, what I can't take is when you shut me out in some misguided macho attempt to keep me safe in some glass tower like a useless princess."

A smile tried to curve his lips but I glared at him. "I get what you're saying."

My adrenaline was still flowing so I crossed my arms over my chest, unable to argue with his statement but still feeling pissy. "Good."

He took a quick step forward and unfolded my arms then grabbed me by my waist, hauling me closer to him. "I'm sorry, baby. Let me apologize."

"I don't want your…"

My words died off as Smoke dropped to his knees then sealed his mouth over the crotch of my racy black panties. With perfect accuracy, his teeth grazed my clit, and a hard pulse of arousal made my breath catch in my throat. I couldn't stop myself from plunging my hands into his curls and tugging him closer.

He leaned back for a second and looked up at me with a wicked smirk. "Love those panties. So sexy."

My eyes closed when he swiftly leaned back between my legs and hooked the edge of my panties, pulling them over to expose my sex. He made a deep, sensual noise in the back of his throat and slowly grazed his knuckles over my labia before sliding his thumb over my clit. I sucked in a harsh breath and widened my stance, giving him better access to my body. Yeah, I was still pissed at him, but I justified letting him do this by telling myself I deserved an orgasm for putting up with his shit.

He leaned back on his haunches and stared directly at my sex with a hungry, ravenous look. "Gonna make you come with one finger."

"I want your mouth," I pleaded in a low whisper.

"Can't give you my mouth. I do that and I won't be able to keep from fuckin' you."

I spread my legs wider and tilted my pelvis to his face, my need for his tongue on me growing by the second. "Please."

I must have sounded as desperate as I felt because he chuckled. "Shhh, you're gonna like this."

With that, he slowly dragged his middle finger up and down my clit, moving the hood and watching me closely as he touched me. It felt good, a warm and mellow pleasure that seeped into my bones. His finger slid down and dipped into me for a moment, giving my sex something to clench onto, before sliding his wet finger up my slit to my aching nub. To my surprise, he flicked my clit and it stung making me flinch away.

"Come back here," he growled, and wrapped his arm around my hips, gripping my ass as he held me.

I whimpered when he returned to his play, my body moving restlessly against him while he built my arousal. My senses sharpened, and as I stared down at him, I took note of how incredibly fit he was, and how his muscles rippled and shifted with his movements. I placed my hand on his firm shoulder, rubbing the smooth surface before lightly running my fingers through his hair. He let out a soft humming noise that was pure pleasure.

"Look at that hard clit of yours. Love how you get off on me, baby girl."

Speech was beyond me at this point because he was now circling my sensitive nub with a firm touch that sent waves of pleasure through me. He'd found the perfect way to caress me and I shivered as my orgasm approached, but I felt empty. I needed him to fill me up, to fuck me, to make me scream his name while I came all over his cock.

"Shit," Smoke hissed and abruptly stopped touching me.

With a growl, he tossed me back onto my bed, jerking his pajama pants down enough to free his thick erection. He stroked himself from root to tip while his gaze devoured me. "You want this?"

I tried to formulate a reply, but I was way too interested in the bead of pre-cum poised on the tip of his cock

"Swan," he barked and squeezed his dick, adding more moisture to the tip. "You want this dick?

I licked my lips. "I want to lick your pre-cum."

He shuddered, then rubbed his thumb over the flushed crest of his dick, gathering up the liquid there and smearing it on his tip, making the deep pink skin shiny and tempting. "Sorry, baby, gotta fuck you right now before I bust a nut just kneeling here."

My breath came out in a harsh rush as he tossed me up on my bed on my back. He descended on me, spreading my legs with one hand while shoving his slick thumb past my eager lips and over my tongue. The taste of him exploded in my mouth just as he began to push his hard length into me. The combination slammed me straight into orgasm, my muscles tensing and my hips thrusting up into his. As I arched beneath him and chanted his name, he pounded hard and deep into me, painful enough that it startled a yelp out of me, but he didn't let up. In fact, he tilted my hips so I took him even deeper, each thrust a punishing blow to my body. I didn't know how long I could take it, but when he returned to rubbing and flicking my clit I took everything he gave me and wanted more.

"Harder," I whispered.

Smoke's savage growl seemed to reverberate in my soul, and I tensed around him. The sensation of him inside of me, his fingers playing with me, and his sweat-slick body rubbing against mine tipped me over the edge into a harsh orgasm. My body clenched down, making Smoke work to pull out of me and thrust back in. After three strokes that perfectly matched the pulsing release tearing through me, he came with a roar.

Panting, he collapsed next to me, his body gleaming with sweat and his damp curls sticking to his face. When we both settled enough to think, I languidly stroked his bicep with my fingernails and smiled. "Apology accepted."

He snorted, then hauled me to his side. "Good. Don't like you being pissed at me."

"Shhh," I gently placed my fingertips on his full, kiss-swollen lips. "Love you, but I'm exhausted. Can we just sleep?"

"Yeah, baby girl, we can sleep."

After turning off the lights he pulled me close, and it took me a long time to fall asleep as I worried about the future.

AUSTIN TX

Chapter Five

Smoke glanced over at me in the cab of his truck for at least the hundredth time, his lips moving like he wanted to say something, but once again, he held himself back. I wondered what it was that was bothering him, but my mind was more focused on where we were going. It turns out the Iron Horse MC had chapters all over the US, including Denver, Colorado, where my sister and mom were rumored to be. It had taken us two days to get up there, and I was beat. We'd be staying at one of the Iron Horse compounds on the outskirts of Denver in Golden, Colorado. For some reason that seemed to upset Smoke.

The tension in the truck built until I couldn't take it anymore. "Smoke, what's bothering you? If you don't let it out soon, I'm going to head-butt you."

His grip tightened on the wheel, and he kept his eyes on the road. "The Denver Iron Horse chapter is different from the Austin one. Since the Austin chapter is the founding chapter, the original Iron Horse MC, we tend to have members who are a little older, a little wiser. The Denver chapter has a lot of young guys, and they're wild."

"Wild how?"

"More into partying and they keep their clubhouse stocked with sweet butts. Don't get me wrong, my brothers make money and pull their weight, but they're more interested in getting their dicks wet with some random sweet butt than taking on old ladies."

"Sweet butts? Oh, the club sluts."

He shrugged uncomfortably. "Yeah. There are a few who even live at the clubhouse, and they outnumber the old ladies. I don't get involved in female bullshit, but in the few times I've been up there, I noticed that the brothers who respect their women keep their old ladies away from the clubhouse most of the time."

My stomach soured as I imagined a scene out of *The Best Little Whorehouse in Texas*. Instead of Dolly Parton greeting me with a song, it was a bunch of angry chicks trying to get my man, and I did not like it one bit. "Huh."

He sighed. "If any of those bitches give you any trouble, I want you to come right to me, got it?"

"What kind of trouble?"

My gaze went to my backpack and duffle where I had two different guns and a shit ton of ammo thanks to my dad, not to mention what was in our bags in the backseat. While we were up in Colorado, my dad was doing his own search at the places he knew Billie might run to. Mimi was staying at home in case Sarah showed up, but I had a feeling I'd see Mimi sooner rather than later, probably with some of my Italian cousins in tow.

Smoke's expression softened as his lips curled into a half-smile that made my heart speed up. "Not the kind that you need to be killing bitches over, but they may give you shit, and I know you have a temper. 'Sides, you could get hurt…or they could. Either way, it won't help you keep a low profile."

I gave him an incredulous look that he ignored. "What kind of shit are they going to give me exactly?"

I swear, a hint of a flush colored Smoke's tanned cheeks. "Chick shit. You know, just being bitches. You, my beautiful baby, outrank them, and there are a couple I've…known who are going to be pissed that I made you my old lady, especially when a few of them have begged to wear my patch. I fuckin' hate that drama caused by my past keeps coming up, and I would stop it if I could, but I can't. And I won't lie to you about this shit. Not even to make you feel better."

I wanted to ask him what the hell he meant by outranking them, but my burning jealousy seemed to take over my mouth and brain, and I only focused on the fact that I was going to be surrounded by women who knew what Smoke looked like when he had an orgasm. "How many of them have you fucked?"

"None of your business," he said in a gentle voice then sighed. "That's another thing that's gonna to piss you off. I've spoiled you, tried to keep you sheltered from some aspects of the MC life that you won't like. You have to face the fact that for a lot of guys in the world of the Iron Horse MC, bitches don't count."

"Excuse me?" My temper flared and I swore if I had hackles they'd be standing straight up.

"Just the way it is, babe. This is a man's world. They'll give you respect because you're my old lady, and if they disrespect you, they disrespect me, but you can't run your mouth to them like you do to me and Beach. These young guys are still all hung up on pride and reputation, and making a name for themselves. If you insulted them and were anyone but my woman, you'd pay a price. But as my woman, you're a reflection of me and under my protection. If you start some shit with one of the members, it'll get messy quick. I really don't want to have to deal with a bunch of pissed off brothers while trying to save your tight little ass."

I had an idea that by 'it'll get messy' he meant blood would be spilled, or in his case blowtorches lit, but there was no way I was going to sit back and let people insult, patronize, or otherwise mess with me. I'd been bullied as a child and there was no way I was going to allow myself to be bullied now. "So I'm just supposed to take their shit like a good little girl?"

Turning away from me, he quickly scanned the road before swerving around a slow moving car in the fast lane. The big engine of his truck purred, and I slid further into my comfortable seat, turning to face him full on. With my arms crossed, I glared at him and waited for him to answer. I couldn't wait to hear what kind of epic bullshit he was going to come up with to justify his statement.

His voice was unexpectedly grave as he said, "They may say some things that piss you off. They may treat you like a second-class citizen, but I need you to keep your temper in check. I'm not saying you have to take any shit from anyone—you absolutely do not have to put up with any bullshit—but if you can walk away from a fight, do it. I don't want you putting yourself in any situation where you could get hurt, got me? So don't start arguments. Walk away. You got a problem, you come to me, and I'll take care of it. We've got bigger things to worry about than you hurting some young hothead's pride."

"Got it," I knew I sounded surly as I examined my unpolished fingernails. Fuck him for making sense. Yes, I was being very moody and cranky, but I was tired. The constant tension of waiting for someone to attack us on the open road sent bursts of adrenaline through me whenever a car passed too close. We were both wound up, and it showed in the way we were snipping at each other. Even if the clubhouse was swarming with an infestation of sluts, I'd kick my way through them to reach a clean bed.

Please, God, let the room be clean. Not man-clean, but *really* clean. I sighed and returned my attention to Smoke who kept his gaze stiffly on the road.

"Look, in the world of the MC, a man's word and his reputation are more important than anything. I get respect because I've earned it and showed that I'll do what I need to do to keep it. If I let you run your mouth, I look weak, and there are men who would kill to be the founding house's Master at Arms. People respect me, and I plan to keep it that way 'cause that respect is gonna keep you alive. So just turn the other cheek, and I will destroy whoever pissed you off when the time is right."

Anger clenched my gut as mental images of me bowing and scraping to a bunch of faceless bikers came to mind even as my heart warmed at his crazy overprotective nature.

"This is bullshit."

"It is, but it's my world babe. Normally, I would've taken my time getting you used to it, would've sent you over to Scarlett's house back home so she could explain it to you, but ain't nothing normal about your life right now. I'm askin' you to hold your tongue, and I'll do everything I can to protect you and keep you safe. That means you may be spending some time alone while I try to find your Ma, and I need you to not bitch about it. Sooner we find your mom and sister, sooner we can go home. Just remember, no matter what happens you'll be coming home with me to our home. *Ours.*"

I turned his words over in my mind. My independent nature rebelled at the thought of playing a subservient role to Smoke outside of the bedroom even as the girly part of me squee'd at the way Smoke said *ours*.

Yeah, a hundred years ago, this meek and mild female bullshit might have been normal, but I was raised to be independent by a woman who would cut the throat of any man who disrespected her. My mind switched back to the sweet butts again, and I turned slightly in my seat so I was sitting up taller. I didn't like arguing with Smoke. I wanted to reach out and touch him, and reassure myself he still liked me. I was self-aware enough to realize that this dependence on him was a weakness of mine, so I made myself continue to address my concerns about all of this with Smoke.

With my heart in my throat I asked, "While you're away handling shit, will you be messing around with any of the sweet butts?"

He looked at me, and he was not pleased. A flash of disappointment streaked through his deep brown eyes, momentarily turned amber by the sunlight streaming through the windshield. "No, Swan, I won't be fucking around on you. You're the only woman I want. I won't lie—lots of my brothers ain't exactly loyal, but I am. You? You're my blessing, my redemption. You think I'd destroy us by sticking my dick in some slut? Never. No one has ever made me feel as good as you. What we have is special, and the last thing you ever have to worry about is me cheating on you. I've been through enough evil to recognize just how extraordinary you are and the chance that the Universe has given me with you. I'm not gonna fuck it up over used cunt."

I was still pissed, but his promise made me feel a little bit better, and I didn't like that I'd stung him with my words. "You sure going to the clubhouse is a good idea? I mean why don't we stay at a hotel or something?"

"Because the clubhouse is a fortress. It'll be a lot harder to get to you in there than in a hotel room. Look, the Denver chapter ain't a bad place, it's just not a place for old ladies. You'll be the first one to ever stay there for any extended period of time, so there's gonna be a learning curve with those guys. Yeah?"

"Yeah." I closed my eyes and leaned my head against the window.

"I might be blowing shit all out of proportion, things might go smooth as silk, but I wanted to prepare you for the worst case scenario so you aren't surprised about anything. Shit's movin' fast, even for me. I can't imagine how hard it is for you to deal with everything, so I'm trying my best to prepare you. At the very least, you'll have a lot of downtime for the next few days while I scout around. We'll get you set up with one of those e-readers, and I'll give you my credit card. You buy those BDSM erotic romances you like so much and pick a scene from one of your books. If you behave all day, I'll make that scene come true as long as it doesn't involve another man."

My lower lip trembled even as desire warmed the flesh between my legs. If he wouldn't want a threesome with another man, maybe he'd want me with another woman. It took me a moment to find my voice, to tell him one of my greatest fears, something I could never do with him. I know he liked it, and I was afraid that he'd get bored with me if I wouldn't—couldn't—indulge his kink. "Smoke, please don't ask me to bring another woman into our bed."

I startled when he abruptly pulled off the freeway, the wind of a passing semi shaking the truck slightly as he slammed it into park.

"What the fuck are you talking about?" He grasped my chin in a firm hold and made me look at him. "There will never be anyone in bed but us, Swan. I mean it. Yeah, I've done that shit in my past, but even a thousand women at once couldn't compete with one minute with you. Everything I need to be happy is right here in front of me."

A tear managed to escape as I imagined what it would be like to walk in on Smoke in the same way I walked in on Stewart. "'Kay."

"Have I done anything to break your trust in me?"

"No. I'm sorry, I…if you betrayed me, I don't know if I could survive it. I love you in a way I've never loved anyone. Sometimes it confuses me, becomes hard for me to understand and handle. I'm sorry I'm bad at this relationship stuff, but if you give me some time, I swear I'll get better. It's just…this is a lot to process, but I won't let you down."

"Baby," he purred in that husky voice that never failed to make my insides melt, "You're perfect just the way you are."

I nodded and held his hand tightly as we resumed our trip, and I stared off in the distance where the Rocky Mountains pierced the sky.

I must have fallen asleep because the next thing I was aware of was Smoke gently stroking my cheek. "Time to wake up."

Blinking slowly, I sat up in my seat, yawned and took a good stretch. It had been a long fucking drive. Even though we'd both taken turns behind the wheel, my energy was almost non-existent. As my brain began to come back online, I saw that we were in an industrial area with lots of warehouses off in the distance and vast tracts of land on three sides. The trees were thick, and I took a deep breath, catching some unfamiliar smells. "Where are we?"

"Welcome to the Iron Horse MC, Denver Chapter. This is the main clubhouse in Golden Colorado, just outside of Denver, that they use for big gatherings 'cause it's in the middle of nowhere, and no one's gonna call the cops complaining about noise. They got another clubhouse in the city, but that's above the club's garage and is mostly used for…business."

Taking another deep breath, I tried to clear my mind and focus on the situation like my father taught me. First thing for me to make sure was covered would be my freakish reaction to strangers. Just the thought of them touching me made gooseflesh rise along my arms. There was no way I could avoid mentioning it, but I hated how vulnerable my issues made me to new situations.

Trying to keep my tone quiet I murmured, "Hey, do they know not to touch me?"

"Yeah, I made sure Khan knows. I had Vance tell him."

"Khan?"

"The Denver chapter president. Good guy, and his old lady is as nice as can be. Normally, she'd be the one keeping the sweet butts in line, but she doesn't like confrontations like that. Too sweet, kinda like your friend, Lyric. Gentle souls. You'll meet her and some of the other old ladies tonight while I take care of some business."

"What kind of business?"

"The kind that's none of your business." I opened my mouth up to argue, but he held up his hand. "It's club business, and I can't talk about it, not even with you. Sometimes it's just better if you don't know."

I wanted to argue, but he was right. While I knew about my father's arms dealing, I'd never been officially told about it. It was kind of like an unspoken rule in my dad's house that when he had clients coming over, I'd just disappear. I'm sure if I dug deep enough I could find out what Smoke did for the club other than 'protection', but sometimes ignorance was bliss. Besides, I had enough things to worry about at the moment.

The thought that Smoke might have killed people, lots of people, troubled me if I dwelled on it too much, so instead, I forced myself to look around and find the escape routes. My father had drilled it into my head to always scope out any new place, and I fell back on hundreds of hours of training, scanning the area around me and forcing my racing thoughts to focus on one thing: Survival.

As we pulled up the wide gravel drive leading to the formidable three-story dark brick building I was officially tired of being cooped up in the truck. When we parked in the oversized, freshly paved, almost full lot I was feeling antsy enough to want out ASAP. It was late afternoon and the air was refreshingly cool and clear after the stifling heat of Texas. I did a quick look around, noting the differences between the Austin clubhouse and the Denver one. Unlike Austin, there wasn't any playground equipment here. Even in the fading light of the setting sun, I could see the landscaping around the clubhouse was lacking a woman's touch. The lawn was cut and the bushes trimmed, but that was about it other than two big, round, stone fire pits and a random scattering of picnic tables.

Dressed in a tight, black babydoll t-shirt with the Iron Horse MC logo on the front, I stretched out, working the kinks out of my back. A moment later Smoke had me turned and held me to his chest. Then he used his talented hands to gently press on my spine, causing delicious cracks that made the muscles of my upper back relax. I purred in pleasure and gave him a soft kiss in thanks as my senses hummed with delight.

"Swear to God you're the hottest piece of ass I've ever seen," he growled out.

The man was insatiable, and I loved it. My body warmed in response to his words, and I slowly raised my gaze to meet those dark, beloved eyes of his. I enjoyed a leisurely inspection of his magnificent body until I stared at his full lips, the need to taste him growing into an obsession. Passion flared between us and I barely managed to hold back a little moan as he squeezed my hips, reminding me of the way he'd hold them while he pounded into me. Just the memory of his skill in bed gave me a little shiver that left me squirming for his touch.

He placed a gentle, passionate kiss on my lips before he leaned back and sighed. "You ready to face what might or might not be happening in that club? It's almost dark and a bunch of my brothers are here, which means there might be some shit I'd rather you not see going on inside."

I snorted. "Thanks, but I already got to see an orgy at your clubhouse."

He flinched. "Yeah, sorry 'bout that. Fuckin' Vance should have taken you in the back entrance like I told him to."

With a shrug, I lifted my chin in the direction of two men walking across the lot toward us. The man on the left was just plain beautiful. Around Smoke's age with a solid body beneath his tight t-shirt, vest, and jeans, along with narrow, baby blue eyes and a cupid's bow mouth. He was like a sexy angel come down to earth with his bleached blond cap of curls, but the look in his eyes was scary. They were cold and calculating as he stared at me, then to Smoke, then back to me again.

The man on the right was the exact opposite of the blond's otherworldly good looks. He was a massive black man, with a tight military haircut and built like a brick wall. Tattoos, barely visible on his dark skin, covered his thick arms, and a rather gnarly scar ran up the left side of his neck to disappear behind his ear. He was far too rough to ever be called handsome in a conventional sense of the word, but there was something about him, the balance of the bold features of his face, that made him striking. He was the kind of guy you would stop and take a second look at walking down the street, especially when you noticed his beautiful, pale green eyes. Despite his stern, no bullshit look, he gave me a wink that I can only describe as flirty. I giggled, and he briefly smiled just the slightest bit before his expression hardened again.

Smoke sighed and shook his head as he stared at the approaching men. "Don't fall for any of their bullshit. They'll try to charm your panties off, but neither of 'em means it. I know these guys well. They're gonna fuck with me by trying to hit on you."

"Boys and their macho crap," I said with a barely concealed smirk.

True to Smoke's prediction, the blond angel reached us first and gave me a blatant going over from head to toe, but it wasn't sexual—more assessing than anything. There was something very commanding about his presence, and I found myself unable to hold his intense gaze. Then his brow furrowed and he tilted his head as he stared at me. "Holy fuck, ya look like yer sister. I mean I knew you were twins, but *damn*."

I smiled and gave him a small wave, hoping he wouldn't try to shake hands. "Hi, I'm Swan."

The big black man with the super short hair to the right of the blond guy made a low, humming sound deep in his throat. "Mmmm, twins. So nice to have you here, beautiful."

"Fuck off," Smoke replied and looped a very possessive arm around my waist. "Mine."

"Yours?" the blond asked with a surprised look warming his gaze. "What do you mean…yours?"

The guy with the pretty green eyes grinned, and I noticed he had a deep dimple in his cheek. It only added to his strong-featured appearance, and I could almost bet he was devastating when he turned on the charm. When he caught my considering look, he smiled even more and gave me another wink. Yep, not a man who would ever grace the cover of a magazine, but I'd bet, despite his lack of traditional good looks, he had no problem finding a woman with his abundance of natural charisma. I grinned at him and he smiled back.

Smoke didn't like that one bit. "Swan is my old lady, so keep your fuckin' hands off, and mind your fuckin' manners."

The angel made a choking sound, and I looked over at him then back to the green-eyed man who was staring at me like I was some new, exotic species of plant that had suddenly sprouted from the ground. The blond guy rubbed his mouth. "Vance never said anything about Swan being your old lady."

The scar on the black man's neck moved as he swallowed hard, his gaze darting between me and Smoke. "We got some…ahhh...entertainment inside. Something she might find objectionable if she's anything like Sarah."

Making a groaning sound, the blond guy looked to the sky. "If she's anything like Sarah, objectionable is far too mild of a word."

"Swan's worse," Smoke muttered, ignoring my glare.

Worse? What the hell did he mean by worse?

"Fuck," the blond said and gave Smoke a dark look. "Tila got together a bunch of the sweet butts to give you a welcome party. We thought you were just on guard duty with Swan."

"Tila? Sweet butts?" I asked, then gave Smoke a narrow-eyed look. "What kind of party is he talking about?"

Smoke glared at the blond. "The kind I have no fucking interest in attending."

The big man with the gorgeous eyes held his hands up, the cut muscles of his arms flexing. "Sorry, man, we didn't know." He turned his gaze on me. "Swan, nice to meet you, my name's Hulk. Please don't judge us by the trash inside. We meant no disrespect to Smoke, but there is no way we can stop a party once it's started. Brothers would get irate."

I couldn't help but smirk. "Hulk, like The Incredible Hulk? I guess I can see it with all your muscles."

A true smile with a killer dimple lit his face, turning him from average to handsome. "Thank you, but that ain't the part of me that is so big it makes women call me 'incredible'."

I was sure my face was as red as a boiled lobster. All I managed in reply was a weak, "Oh."

"Shut the fuck up"—the blond shook his head at Hulk—"or Smoke's gonna drive some railroad spikes through your eyes before lighting your dick on fire."

"What?" I choked out.

"Nothin'," the blond replied and tipped his head in my direction with a small smile. "Name's, Breaker."

"Nice to meet you, Breaker." I took a step closer to Smoke. I wasn't comfortable in this situation at all.

Imagining the reason he would be called 'Breaker' made me queasy.

Smoke instantly wrapped his arm around my waist. I glared up at him then sighed. I was thankful for his constant support. It wasn't his fault they'd set up a...party...for him. If I wanted him to be understanding with me, I had to return the favor and realize some things were out of his control. Remembering our earlier conversation about stupid macho shit, I managed to almost smile at him. It was weak, but better for his 'rep' than stomping on his foot and yelling at him for banging half of the eligible female population in the US.

His expression eased, and he gave me a pat on the butt. "Swan, go grab your backpack. Hulk will get a prospect to guard it for us."

I wanted to argue with him about basically commanding me to fetch our shit, but the serious look on his face when I glanced at him stopped me. "'Kay."

As soon as I left, the men huddled together and began speaking in low, rapid voices. Unable to listen in without being obvious, I strolled back to the truck as they moved closer to the clubhouse. When I got to the truck and reached up to open the door, my gaze caught on my wrist cuffs as the beautiful silver gleamed in the soft light. Smoke had put them on me this morning, gently kissing my pulse points before sliding each silver and turquoise cuff in place. The look of satisfaction in his eyes as he examined my adorned wrists had made my heart race. I stared at the gleaming metal for another moment before reaching into the back and grabbing my heavy pack. I'd packed a suitcase at my parents' house, and my Dad had included a few gifts for me that I hoped were overkill, including a couple grenades, an assortment of knives from Mimi, and my sniper rifle.

With a sigh, I shrugged my pack on, grabbed my duffle, locked the doors and set the alarm. After taking a deep breath, I turned back to where the men continued to talk intently as they slowly walked together, now almost directly in front of the clubhouse. I started to make my way to them, but before I got very far, the front door of the clubhouse opened. An older, stunning, blonde woman dressed in a sparkling raspberry cocktail dress and mega high heels came strolling out with a cigarette dangling from her cardinal-red lips. Her hair had been teased into a helmet of shellacked dark blonde. She wore a lot of makeup and had a worn-out, jaded air about her. Well, until she spied the men. Then her face lit up, and she pitched aside her half-smoked cigarette before launching herself at Smoke with a squeal and a bubbly, "Hey sugar. I missed you! Been too long since you been up here to visit. We're gonna have fun tonight. I've got five other girls lined up begging to get face-fucked."

Smoke stared at her in shock and loathing as she hauled herself up his body with her hands clasped around his neck, then wrapped her legs around his waist. To my utter disgust, her skirt rode up, revealing that she wasn't wearing any underwear. Smoke gave her a startled look before she planted a kiss right on his lips. A low growl escaped me, and my temper didn't just flare, it exploded in a jealous rage. I pulled her off of Smoke by her crispy, hairspray-coated hair even as Smoke shoved her away him with a repulsed snarl. Between the two of us, we had that nasty bitch on her ass on the ground in a heartbeat. I was yelling at her before she took her next breath. "Get your fucking skank hands off of him!"

"You fucking, stupid twat!" she screeched while trying to pick herself up in those ridiculous high heels. "What the fuck is wrong with you?"

None of the men went to help her, but Smoke held me back when I was about to launch myself at her when she flipped me off. More sluts came pouring out of the club, all dressed in some version of what passed for party-time-whore. They gave me curious looks, their gazes pinging between me and Smoke. A few gaped at me and I gritted my teeth when I heard Sarah's name whispered from dozens of lips in a hiss.

The blonde on the ground stood up and started to come at me, but Hulk threw his arm out and grabbed her around the waist, hauling her to his side. He spoke in a low, even voice. "Don't fuckin' do it, Tila. You two may go way back, but that's Smoke's old lady, not one of his girls."

For a brief moment pain flashed through her gaze. "What?"

Instead of answering her, Hulk turned his hardened gaze on the other women hovering around with more than a few giving me a very unfriendly looks. "Listen up, bitches. This is Swan. She's Smoke's old lady and Beach's sister-in-law. You better not give her any shit or you'll be answering to me, got it? Now get your fuckin' asses inside and take care of my brothers."

Smoke's hold on me loosened enough that I could move a little bit and I sucked in a deep breath. My temper strained against the mental leash I'd put on it, and I hated the shaky feeling that came from an extended burst of adrenaline. Breaker watched all of us in silence, his face expressionless except for a slight frown turning down the edges of his pretty lips. I met his gaze and his eyes had resumed that flat, scary look. He slowly shook his head before speaking in a near whisper, "You're gonna be trouble."

Before I could stop myself, my snark came out full force. "As long as none of those sluts leave their slime on my man, we're all good."

Hulk laughed while Smoke sighed heavily enough that his chest pressed into my backpack. "Babe…"

Not feeling the least bit contrite I glared up at him, glad Tila apparently wore kiss-proof lipstick. Just the thought of her mouth on his, of her germs festering on his lips, and my blood boiled again. "We need to disinfect your mouth where she touched you."

Smoke closed his eyes and his nostrils flared. "Chill out, babe. Nothin' to get upset about. You're my old lady, the only woman I'll ever be with again. That bitch does not matter. Understand?"

Conscious of the two men watching us with interest, and remembering Smoke's warnings about lipping off, I managed to say in what I hoped was a meek voice, "Sorry."

The deep rumble of Hulk's laughter rolled through the now empty yard. "Damn, you remind me of Sarah."

Eager for the distraction, I glanced at him. "Do you know her?"

"Met her at Sturgis a few years ago when she was beating some chick's ass, and she's been up here a time or two with Beach. Nice lady, would give you the shirt off her back if you needed it-as long as you were on her good side. Piss her off and watch out, she'll tear you a new asshole without breaking a sweat."

I vaguely remembered that Sarah had to do a publicity tour with *Playboy* when she was the centerfold for their biker bitches edition, and I wanted to ask more about Sarah, but Smoke cut me off. "Let's take this shit inside. Khan here?"

The momentary lightheartedness went out of Hulk's expression. "Yeah, he's here."

He turned without another word, and I noticed for
the first time that his Iron Horse MC vest had the words
'Master at Arms' on the back just like Smoke's did, but
it didn't have the three-bar patch that Smoke wore on
the front of his vest. The bottom rocker on Breaker's
vest had his name instead of a rank, and I wondered
what his job was within the club. The three men
surrounded me as we entered the clubhouse, and I had a
brief glimpse of walls hung with neon beer signs,
American flags, Iron Horse MC flags, and sluts with
more bikers sitting on wide, battered, leather couches
along with three pool tables and a couple dart boards.
Instead of pool balls on the green felt surfaces there was
a woman in a tiny denim skirt being rather vigorously
fucked by one man while giving another a blowjob.

I must have made a sound because Smoke shot me
an undecipherable look while Hustler moved to block
my line of sight. Why the hell did all of the Iron Horse
guys have to be so big? It was like trying to look
through a wall. All around us, the party raged and men
began to shout out to Smoke, basically treating him like
he was the shit. Smoke raised his hand in greeting and
said hi to a few of the guys, but he didn't stop to talk,
and for that, I was thankful. There were a lot of people
in this party space that took up almost the whole first
floor. A vast bar, tended by women in tiny vests with
huge tits, sat against the opposite wall. There was a big
mirror behind it, and I caught glimpses of more sexual
activity going on in the dimly lit area of the room. I
promised myself I would never sit on any of these
couches.

A woman in shorts small enough to pass for panties scurried up and said in a squeaky voice, "Can I get you something to drink, Smoke?"

He shook his head and gave her a small smile while she tried to keep up with our long strides. "I'm good."

I decided that studying Smoke was a safer bet than exposing myself to the depravity surrounding me. As much as I loathed it, I had to admit to myself that I was one of those stupid bitches who couldn't handle her jealousy. I hated every woman who looked at him with lust in their eyes, wondering if he'd fucked them and or if he'd smiled at them like he smiled at me in bed. A bitter taste filled my mouth as the unwelcome picture of him fucking Tila, making her orgasm, and her falling asleep in his arms while he held her.

For once, Smoke appeared too distracted to notice me, and I wasn't sure how to handle his lack of attention. I'd grown so used to being the center of his universe that I felt bereft at how withdrawn he appeared. Maybe he was really pissed about the incident out front, and I promised myself I would try harder to hold my temper. The chilling thought that I'd reacted like my Dad sent a shiver down my spine. I was barely aware when we took a wide set of stairs guarded by two stone-faced bikers to the second level. They were slightly older than the majority of the guys downstairs, and I got a distinct feeling that they were all business.

The two floors were so different that I did a double-take as I gazed around me. The landing with another set of stairs leading to the third floor was big enough that a black leather couch and table had been set up beside the stairs on the gleaming oak floors. The walls were off-white and there was no graffiti or posters, just a large, framed Iron Horse MC flag that had seen better days. I was sure there was some story about how it got so beat up, and I let myself be distracted by fanciful musings. I admit it, I sometimes hide inside my head when things get too stressful. Without a doubt this was a dangerous thing. My father used to flip his shit when I'd space out in the middle of his training, but I don't process stimuli in the same way most people do.

I often wondered if my unease around strangers was worse because I'd been raised in the middle of nowhere. Even so, the members of the compound all had a communal meal together at least once a month, and hundreds of people attended, not to mention my parents' friends and their kids stopping by. Someone was always celebrating something. Even at the compound, among people I'd grown up with, I would have to seek out space to do what I liked to think of as updating my software with new information. While I did this, my mind would go into kind of a wandering state that was like dreaming even though I was awake. I wouldn't see the world around me or pay it much attention, instead reliving snapshots of my day. Afterwards, I would always feel better and be able to handle people again, but during that time I was kind of useless.

I'd retreated into that dream-like state, and I guess that's why I didn't register the guys with machine guns at first. They were guarding the entrance to a hallway leading to what looked like a high-end office. We passed them, and they both nodded to Smoke with looks of extreme respect. They gave me quick, curious glances but didn't say anything. The men parted to reveal an intimidating guy who was probably in his late fifties, early sixties. He had a full head of silver hair cut into a flattop and a rocking Fu-Manchu mustache that hung past his tanned chin. Deep lines radiated from the corner of his eyes and his hands were tanned and weathered. As his dark gaze took me in, I thought I detected some Asian ancestry. He wasn't particularly handsome, but he was commanding and definitely intimidating. As I came out of my waking dream state, the filter on my mouth had yet to engage, and to my horror, I found myself speaking my thoughts out loud.

"Do they call you Khan as in *Star Trek* or as in a Mongolian king?"

AUSTIN TX

Chapter Six

Miguel 'Smoke' Santos

I held back a groan as Khan stared at Swan, obviously thrown off his stride by her question.

Welcome to my world.

That gorgeous creature kept me constantly on my toes, asking me questions or doing things that caught me by surprise. I'm good at reading people, one of the things that have kept my evil ass alive over the years. Swan was like a complex, intricately beautiful, confusing million-piece puzzle. At first, her thoughts seemed totally random, but I quickly realized that Swan saw the world differently than I ever would, and she was truly brilliant as well as easily distracted. She'd ask me things sometimes that made no sense to me at the moment, but as I thought about it later, I could almost see the leaps of logic she took. It made her endlessly fascinating to me even if I wanted to gag her at times like this one.

Khan wasn't exactly a nice guy. He didn't tolerate bullshit from anyone and was utterly ruthless about the defense of his club and family. I did a run with him once where we were picking up some shit from a dealer out in the middle of nowhere in Colorado. The bastard, all jacked up on coke, had tried to get mouthy with Khan and give us inferior product. That shit did not fly with Khan, and before I knew it, Khan had shot the two bodyguards and had the dealer's hand pinned to the table with a knife that held him in place as Khan beat the hell out of him. I've seen and done a bunch of shit, but that was a brutal beating even by my standards. Afterward, Khan went home to his sweet little PTA wife and kids with the dealer's blood still under his fingernails.

The really fucked up thing was that Khan had left the doors to the dealer's cabin open so the wildlife could get to him and his dead bodyguards.

With those thoughts in mind, I moved to shove Swan behind my back in case Khan flipped out, but Khan gave me an odd look before turning his attention back to Swan. "Which one do you think?"

My entire body tensed and I quickly glanced around the room, cataloging items I could use as weapons. Khan was fucking touchy about his pride and just because you were a woman didn't mean he'd let you get away with shit. Yeah, we were friends, but business was business, and Khan was big on maintaining his reputation as a psycho. He said once that his reputation was what kept his family safe. I understood that, but I was almost afraid of what kind of honest shit was going to come from Swan's mouth that might set him off before he realized she truly meant no harm.

Instead of answering right away, she looked around the room, giving me a glimpse of her perfect profile and smooth, tanned skin. Shit, even now, I couldn't wait to get inside of her, to make her scream my name while I fucked her, made her mine, but none of that was going to happen if I couldn't keep her safe. With that in mind, I began to calculate ways to incapacitate my brothers long enough to get my woman out of here.

Agitation filled me and it took a great deal of effort to remain still and store the energy necessary if I needed an explosion of movement and power. I started to sink into my killing zone, that headspace I'd learned to access while in the Marines and used more often than I liked with Iron Horse. I tried to keep the violence inside of me from detonating by focusing on the golden fall of Swan's hair down to the sexy nip of her slender waist, to the cradle of her hips where she would someday carry my children.

She's the future I've always wanted, and the prospect of growing old with her kept me from crossing the line from man to killer.

On some level, I knew I was overreacting, but I just wasn't rational about Swan and fury filled me at the thought of anyone harming her.

Before I could do something stupid, Swan said, "I'm going to go with *Star Trek's* Khan."

I had no idea how Khan had gotten his name. That bit of information was strictly between him, Beach, and Hustler but the corners of his lips twitched and his posture relaxed. "Why d'you think that?"

Swan moved a step back and sought me out, her hand gripping mine as soon as she found it. I know it was selfish of me, but I loved the fact that whenever she was scared she turned to me, even if she didn't realize it. Khan's gaze wandered down to our linked hands and that smile twitched on his lips again. I gave Swan's hand a reassuring squeeze while the tension eased inside of me, and my muscles relaxed as the adrenaline drained from my system. That twitch of the lips was Khan's version of a full blown smile, and for some reason, he seemed highly amused, in his own stone-cold way, at something he saw on my face before he turned back to Swan.

She licked her lips, then said in a soft voice, "Because of *The Wrath of Khan*, of course."

Khan leaned back in his chair and linked his wind-roughed hands together, then studied my woman. "Clever girl."

I knew it was a compliment, but Swan didn't seem so sure. She pressed her body against mine, and I automatically wrapped my arms around her and gave her a soothing rub on her arm. This got some raised eyebrows, but fuck'em, this was my old lady, and I'd do with her whatever I wanted. Khan especially, had no fucking leg to stand on as he smirked at me. Even though he could be a monster, that fucker worshiped his wife—and we all knew it. Want to commit a painful suicide? Call Khan's wife a cunt and you'd be dead within hours after Khan treated you to his unique brand of retribution.

"Wish I could say it was a pleasure to have you here, Swan, but it's not. You're bringin' a shitload of trouble with you." Swan started to say something, but I tightened my hold on her and she kept quiet. "Fortunately for you, I like trouble. Keeps my brothers on their toes and weeds out the weak prospects. Plus, you're Smoke's old lady and Beach's sister-in-law. That means you're family. So we're gonna do whatever we can to help you find your Ma and Sarah, but we're gonna do it quiet. Only the men in this room know why you're really here though I'm sure rumors will spread."

This caught my attention. I'd talked to Beach on and off but he was dealing with a shit storm back in Austin as they tried to weed out the traitor or possibly traitors. "What's our cover story?"

He shifted his dark gaze from Swan to me and my woman sighed in relief. "Beach is spreadin' the word around that you're looking for a couple of new Enforcers and you're up here checking out some men while we do business. The lovely Swan is with you 'cause you made her your old lady, and with all the shit going down over her Ma, you want to keep her close and away from Austin for a bit. I've told my men that keeping your old lady alive and well is part of the way to impress you so you're gonna have prospects and brothers falling all over themselves to protect your woman."

Groaning, I removed my arms from Swan and began to pace the room. Fuckin' Beach. It was a good plan that would help keep Swan safe, but now I'd have to deal with recruiting a new Enforcer without my usual attention to detail. That position was no fucking joke, my Enforcers—Hustler was a perfect example—were my right-hand men, and each of them had a particular strength and purpose. Hustler was our con man. He could talk his way out of any trouble and get even the most reluctant marks to lower their guard.

Not only did I have to worry about whoever I picked fitting into my clubhouse, I also had to worry about what they would do at my company. All of my Enforcers worked for me along with my civilian employees. This allowed them to have access to the best surveillance equipment and weapons out there without raising the suspicions of the cops. I paid really fuckin' well, and I only employed the best, so a new Enforcer who hadn't been properly vetted would throw off my whole operation and weaken me in the eyes of the employees and brothers. In my world the weak were killed and eaten.

I made too much money and worked too fuckin' hard building that company and my life to allow that shit to happen.

This was exactly what I didn't need to deal with at the moment, but I couldn't protest. It was probably the best way to keep Swan alive and gave me the freedom to work my way through Denver looking for any hint of Billie and Sarah. Swan, no matter what she wore, was too stunning not to draw attention, which was something I didn't need while trying to blend in. My concentration would also be divided between protecting my woman and doing what I had to in order to get information. The bottom-of-the-barrel people who would know if Billie was in the area were the kind of people I didn't mind torturing to get the answers I needed, but I sure as shit couldn't do that if Swan was with me.

Khan placed his elbows on his desk and studied me then cut his gaze to Hulk. "Go set Swan up in her room. Me and Smoke got some shit to discuss that ain't fit for a lady's ears."

My first instinct was to protest, but I knew Hulk and Khan would be insulted if I implied that their protection wasn't enough and I didn't trust them to take care of my old lady. Instead, I turned to Swan, and my heart ached at the fear in her eyes. While I loved that she looked to me for comfort, I didn't want her to become totally dependent on me. She was an incredibly strong woman, and I would never take her hard-won self-reliance from her to satisfy my own selfish desires.

"Go on with him, baby. I'll be there as soon as I can."

She frowned and chewed on that lush lower lip of hers. "Okay. Umm…what about the rest of our stuff?"

Hulk moved next to her and patted her on her bare upper arm below the short sleeve of her shirt. Swan recoiled instantly with a pained sound, and before I knew it, my hands were wrapped around Hulk's throat. In his shock, he actually let me pin him there. It wasn't the click of a round being chambered behind me that made me release him, but the soft sound of dismay that Swan made and her hand on my arm. The silver of the wrist cuff she wore marking her as mine gleamed in the light coming from the brass lamps scattered around the room.

"Smoke," she said in a low voice, "he didn't mean to hurt me. Please, let him go. He's been nothing but kind to me."

Anger rolled off of Hulk. "What the fuck? All I did was pat her shoulder."

"Smoke, please." The pain and embarrassment in Swan's voice made me feel like an asshole as she looked at Hulk, her cheeks scarlet. "It's okay. You didn't know."

"Smoke, let him go," Khan said in a deadly voice.

We turned to him, and when Swan saw the gun, her hand twitched in the direction of her backpack. Thank fuck she didn't go for her own weapon.

"Do not point a gun at my man." Any hint of emotion was gone from her voice, replaced by a chilling tone that I wasn't used to hearing from her. It was easy to get distracted by her stunning looks and her innocence, and forget that she'd been raised to be a merciless killer by a man I was pretty sure was half crazy. She purposely moved in front of me and Breaker snorted, which pissed me off. At some point, I was going to beat that fucker's ass.

Khan narrowed his gaze and something dark moved through his expression. "Little girl, you're playing in a man's world now. You don't get to tell me what to do."

I went to put my hand over Swan's mouth, but she easily ducked out of my grasp. Goddamn Mike and his SpecOps bullshit he'd taught her made her nearly impossible to control.

"None of that matters to me, Khan. I love Smoke, and keeping him safe is above any law or rule, man's world or not."

Her words were so cold, I was surprised she wasn't wreathed in ice and Khan blinked, clearly thrown off by this beautiful, sweet creature basically telling him that she didn't give a fuck about his threats and would be more than happy to take him on. I wanted to grab her and drag her out the door, but she was strung as tight as a trip wire and ready to snap.

I was surprised that it was Breaker who stepped in between his Prez and Swan. He looked down at her and said in a gentle tone I'd never heard him use before, "Why did you act like it hurt when Hulk touched you? That wasn't bullshit. He really caused you pain. I don't see any injury that he could have hit, so what's going on Ms. Swan?"

Her gaze met his and some of the life returned to her eyes along with an embarrassed flush. "I have an issue about being touched. If I don't trust you, the feeling of your skin on mine is like bugs crawling beneath my skin, like spiders and centipedes are squirming through my muscles. I'm okay if I'm wearing clothes, but bare skin to bare skin isn't good."

Moving to my woman's side, I guided her away from a frowning Breaker. "Baby, look at me."

She reluctantly raised her gaze to mine, and I swept her hair back from her face. We stared into each other's eyes for a moment before she let out a harsh breath. Tears turned the blue of her eyes to silver then she wrapped her arms around me. Her voice hitched as she whispered against my chest, "I'm sorry I overreacted again, Smoke, but I couldn't let him shoot you."

All I wanted to do was comfort her, but this was exactly the kind of shit I was talking about, her mouth getting her into trouble she didn't need. Knowing my words would upset her, I kept my voice low but serious. "He wasn't going to shoot me. Do you really think I

106

would just fuckin' stand there and take it? What did I say out in the truck?"

She flinched like I'd hit her and pushed away from me. "I understand."

I was pretty sure she didn't understand shit, but I needed to get her out of this room. We were both ready to argue and take out our tension and frustration on each other right now, and this wasn't the time or place. Even worse, she looked hurt beneath her anger. That killed me, but she'd just have to deal with it for a bit. There were too many undercurrents in play. As much as I wanted to fuck her to sleep, she needed her warrior right now, not her lover. It sucked, but I kept my expression stern as she stared at me. "I won't be long."

Lowering her voice further, she leaned in and whispered, "I'm sorry. Please let me stay. I won't do it again."

Conscious of Khan and Breaker watching us closely, I had to keep my expression stern as I said, "Baby, go to our room. I'll be there soon."

"Right."

Her lips tightened and I could clearly read on her expressive face that she thought this was a bunch of bullshit. I didn't disagree, but like it or not, she had no place here right now. If I kept her around, Khan wouldn't feel free to talk, and I needed all the information I could get. Shit, the last thing I wanted after a long day of driving was a fucking argument with Swan, but I didn't have time to explain shit to her.

Hulk followed her out, being careful not to touch her as he held the door open.

As soon as the door shut, leaving me alone with Breaker and Khan, the older man glared at me. "Why the fuck didn't you tell us about her phobia?"

I shook my head and returned to pacing. Anger filled me and I needed to swallow it down to stay control. "Did you talk to Vance?"

"Briefly."

"He didn't tell you about her issues?"

"Nope, we just talked about that clusterfuck of a mother of hers. Beach didn't say anything either, but then again, he's busy as fuck." Yeah, I needed to have a long talk with Vance about priorities. "Los Diablos are pissed that Swan got away. They've been giving Beach a hard time on top of Sarah being missing and finding the traitor in the club, so the man has a lot on his mind."

Khan put his gun back in his shoulder holster. I took a seat in one of the chairs across from his desk and Breaker took the other. The tension was still high in the room, and I wondered if I'd harmed my relationship with these men. If I had, I wasn't gonna apologize for it. I was known for my explosive temper, and Khan had every reason to think I would have crushed Hulk's throat. I'd calmed down somewhat over the years, but when I was younger, I'd given my temper free reign and done some extremely violent and extremely stupid shit. I could fuck a man's world up in terrible ways without a second thought and sleep just fine.

"Brother," Khan spoke with a tired note in his voice I wasn't used to. "You've got a couple rats in your clubhouse down in Austin, and if there's rats there then there are probably rats here as well. Billie came here for a reason, and it's too big of a coincidence that some bad shit's been happening around these parts. Nothing we can pin on anyone, but a whole lotta *coincidences*."

"What kind of *coincidences*?"

Breaker made a low growling noise. "Deals going bad, cops being exactly where we were, and last week, one of our prospects died in a motorcycle accident. He was on his way home from the clubhouse. It looks like while he was here, someone fucked with his bike."

"Motherfucker." I shook my head in disbelief. "Why didn't you tell us?"

For a brief moment Khan looked chagrined. "Didn't want to say anything until I was sure. I know we're a new chapter for Iron Horse, and I've been trying to make sure shit is going smooth. Beach pissed off a lot of people who thought their city should be next in line to start a new chapter for the MC when he made us official. We may be a new chapter, but we've got pride in our club, and I didn't want Beach to feel like he'd made a mistake."

If anyone thought that being in an MC was all about fucking women, fucking off, and getting drunk, along with some shady dealings they were way wrong. There were as many political pitfalls in the MC as in the US Congress, made all the more complicated by the strong egos involved and the fact that violence was a part of our lives. A man didn't rise up in the ranks of the MC world by being kind and compassionate. Don't get me wrong, we didn't patch in serial killers—too much bullshit to clean up—but the men in this building were tough, arrogant, and deadly with a total disregard for any authority that hadn't earned their respect. If it ever came out that Khan was unable to find who was fucking with him he would have been branded as weak, and someone would have tried for his position.

Didn't mean it wasn't stupid of him to hide it, but I understood.

Rather than tearing into him, as Master at Arms for the founding chapter it was my duty to keep all of my brothers safe, I pushed that bullshit to the back of my mind for another day.

"You able to find out anything about Sarah or Billie?"

"Sure did."

I sat forward, adrenaline pumping into my veins. "What?"

"We got footage on our security cameras of Sarah driving past the clubhouse a couple times, scoping it out, three days ago."

Relief filled me. "How did she look?"

"Hard to say, she was in her car, but she hasn't been back since that day."

"Beach know?"

"Yeah." He sighed and drummed his fingers against the table, his gaze distant. "We haven't heard any mention of Billie, and I've gotta wonder why Sarah is so sure she's here."

"No connections to the area?"

"Not that we can find. Billie moved around a lot, not surprising considering she's run a scam on everyone she's ever met, but we can't find any direct connection to the area. She grew up in Idaho and her parents passed away years ago. No brothers or sisters, and her family hasn't heard from her since she was kicked out of her parents' house at seventeen for stealing from her grandmother. Every man she's ever been with probably wants the bitch dead, so I'm not sure where she's finding a spot to hunker down considering she's got a U-Haul full of missiles."

I shook my head, marveling at how fucked up my life had become. "I'm gonna start looking for Billie tonight. Swan is stayin' here."

Breaker chuckled. "Oh, she's gonna love that, you goin' off on your own. Your girl was ready to gun down Khan's ass for looking at you wrong. She had something in her pack, didn't she? Saw the way she twitched before she went all Ripley on you."

"Ripley?"

"Yeah, Ellen Ripley from the *Alien* series. Now that was a badass bitch."

Ignoring Breaker, Khan studied me. "We'll do everything we can to help you, but I gotta tell ya that you're lookin' for a needle in a haystack."

"More like a dirty needle in a crack house," Breaker added with a grin.

That fucker lived to push people's buttons, so I didn't bother to respond. "I got some contacts here that might be able to give me a lead. You also need to know that you probably won't be alone in guarding Swan. I have no doubt her stepmom and dad are gonna want to help out."

With a grunt Khan frowned at me. "Her daddy is Mike Anderson, right? We've dealt with him before. He's crazy, but fair. We gonna have him in our clubhouse?"

I laughed and shook my head. "Nah. He's getting together with some buddies to go to places he knows of where Billie's hidden in the past. We'll probably get personal attention from Swan's stepmother. I think you know her. Used to go by Mimi Stefano, now known as Mrs. Mike Anderson."

"Lady Death? Shit." The color drained a bit from Khan's face, and he sat back in his chair. "Is she gonna wanna stay here?"

"No, thank fuck. I doubt we'll even notice it if she's around. She won't want Swan to know she's here, but no way that woman is leaving her little girl unprotected. I'm warning you right now, don't fuck with her."

"You think I want to have my dick sliced open and my guts yanked out? No thanks. That woman is almost as crazy as her husband. I've seen my wife go into protective mama bear mode, and the thought of Mimi Stefano feeling like her cub is threatened is the shit of nightmares. You do not want to mess with an angry mama bear."

"Especially one who can peel your skin off your hide with a good, sharp knife."

Breaker made an uncomfortable noise and I met Khan's gaze. "So what are we gonna do here to keep my old lady in one piece?

Breaker's gold wedding band flashed as he leaned against the wall next to the windows, the light of the lamp catching it. "We're gonna have a prospect and a brother guarding your old lady at all times. Not gonna say she'll be totally safe 'cause shit happens, but we're gonna do our best. Can your little girl really handle herself?"

Without hesitation I said, "Absolutely. Think about who raised her."

"Good point. In that case, keep her armed. If I've got rats in my house they might try to make a move on her while you're gone."

A sudden thought came to me that I didn't like one bit. "You using her as fuckin' bait?"

"Keep your panties on," Breaker muttered in a low voice. "We aren't gonna let anyone get near her, but we will watch and see who is giving her special attention. I understand that you don't like it, and I wouldn't put your old lady in harm's way unless we absolutely have to, but this is bigger than just her. If we don't get that shit back from Billie, we, everyone—my family and my brothers—are in danger."

I rubbed my face with a weary sigh. "I'm so fuckin' ready for this bullshit to be over. And Swan ain't gonna be happy about being stuck here without me. She already got into it with one of the sweet butts."

"Which one?"

"Tila tried to mark her territory with Smoke in front of Swan." Breaker crossed his arms with a shit-eating grin. "You know how Tila's had a thing for his ugly ass for years. She laid a big, wet kiss on Smoke, then Swan ripped her off and threw her to the ground." He turned to Smoke. "Thought your little girl might break Tila's neck, old man."

Khan's lips twisted into a barely-there amused smile while I grimaced. "Keep the sweet butts away from my woman."

"Don't worry, brother, we will." Breaker smirked. "Can't say I wouldn't be happy to see Swan kick some of these bitches' asses. The Prez's wife and my wife are sweet, kind, wonderful women who hate fighting. They understand that there will always be pussy for the brothers, and they also know that Khan and I don't sample any of that used snatch, so they have no reason to come in here and clean house. It's made some of the sweet butts, like Tila, think they run the place. You can bet that she'll try to get back at Swan, so I'd tell your old lady to carry that big ass knife I saw pressed up against the side of her bag."

I sometimes forgot how much Breaker noticed. His joking asshole persona made people see him as less of a threat, and I wondered if he'd make a good Enforcer. With this in mind, I switched the topic from Swan to the second part of the plan to keep her safe. "You serious about the Enforcer position?"

Breaker and Kahn exchanged a look, then Kahn nodded. He leaned forward and his silver mustache twitched. "I'm hoping you'll consider Hulk."

That surprised me. "Your Master at Arms? You want to get rid of him for some reason?"

With an intense look he nodded. "Yep, but not like you think. He's the best Master at Arms a man could ask for, trust him with my life, but Denver ain't no good for him anymore. Some bad shit happened with his family. His ex-wife drove wasted with their daughter in the car close to two years ago. Crashed and his daughter died instantly, but his ex lived."

"Shit, I had no idea."

"He wants it kept quiet. Doesn't want to have anything to do with his ex, but he still sees her around town."

"I'm surprised she's still alive."

"Would love to take that piece of trash out." Breaker shook his head. "Can't kill her, Hulk has forbidden it."

"He what?"

Now it was Khan's turn to shake his head. "Said he wants the bitch alive, grieving every day for the loss of their child like he is. Said, for a parent, losing a kid is hell on earth, and he wants her to suffer."

We were all silent for a moment, and I sifted through my memories of the few times I'd met Hulk's daughter. She'd been just a toddler, cute with big cheeks and a mop of curls. And to have his ex-wife be the one to have killed her…fuck. I'm surprised Hulk was even functioning.

With a soft sigh, Khan stood and stretched out, his thick muscles pressing tight against his t-shirt. "Too many memories here for him. Getting the fuck out of Denver and going somewhere to start over with a purpose and a new life to focus on is exactly what he needs."

I sometimes forget that one of the reasons Kahn was picked for the President position of the Denver Chapter was because he honestly gave a fuck about his men. "You think he'd be a good fit?"

"Yeah, I do. He's an honest man, smart as fuck with computers, and he's loyal. Plus, his brother is down there south of Austin, and Hulk could use some time with him."

"You will never, ever find a man more worthy of your trust," Breaker added in an unexpectedly serious tone, "When the man makes a vow, he keeps it."

"He got a woman to bring with him?"

"Nah. He's different from what you remember. Man got his priorities in order and realized that he wanted to hold out for a quality woman. The marryin' kind."

"Not many of those around here," Breaker said with a grin. "But if Beach and Smoke found those beautiful women of theirs down in Austin maybe there's hope for Hulk's old ass to grab some sweet young pussy as well."

"Fuck off," I muttered, glad for Breaker's humor to lighten the mood.

Kahn rubbed the back of his neck and stared at me for a bit, then something seemed to settle in his gaze and he nodded. "We're good for now. Go take care of things with your old lady, then find Hulk. He's doesn't know anything about this Enforcer shit, so I'd appreciate it if you keep it on the down-low. He's gonna be your right hand man here. Figured that would be a good way for you to see how he operates. He's great at tracking people down, so if you need someone, he can probably find 'em. Listen to me good—you can trust him."

I ran my hand through my hair, the weight of the day already pulling me down. "I want to get on the road tonight and scope some things out. What room is Swan in?"

Breaker motioned to me. "Come on, I'll take you to her."

Once we were outside the door and past the men standing guard, Breaker stopped me and looked around before saying in a low voice, "Hold up, brother. There's some stuff you need to know. I think one of the sweet butts might be a traitor."

"What? Kahn know this?"

"I tried to tell him," Breaker said with a sour twist to his lips. "But the fucker is old school and honestly doesn't think any of the sweet butts are smart enough to pull something on us. Me? I sit back. I watch things, and there's been shit goin' down that doesn't feel right. If one of those bitches is a rat working for Billie's crew, she'll probably try to get to Swan."

I snarled before I could stop it. "Over my dead fucking body."

"Chill out. We have all the hangers-on checked for weapons before they come in the clubhouse, a precaution we've put in place after the time one of the brothers' wives came after him with a gun when she caught him fucking around on her at the clubhouse. The chances of this bitch trying to kill Swan are slim to none."

I gripped my hands into fists, trying to calm down. "You motherfuckers are going to use her as bait?"

Breaker didn't look the least bit insulted. "Not really. Instead of bait, think of it as trying to attract sharks while she's safe and sound in a shark cage. Ain't no one touching her, I promise you that. While you're running around with Hulk, I'll be guarding your woman. She needs a chance to settle in tonight, but tomorrow you two are coming over to my place. Cathy, my wife, is gonna host a brunch with a couple of the other old ladies so Swan can meet 'em while we do some business."

I knew Swan needed to hang out with other old ladies to understand how her role in the world had changed, but I didn't like her leaving the security of the clubhouse. "Your place safe?"

"Absolutely. Gated community and all that shit. I stick out like a sore thumb among all the doctors and lawyers, but that works for us. Anyone who looks like they don't belong in my neighborhood is quickly spotted, and all the housewives get on the phone with security quicker than you can blink."

Taking a deep breath, I nodded, fighting my primal urges not to leave my woman with any man. No one could protect her like I could.

The racket of women shouting came down from upstairs, and all my senses went on high alert. Swan was yelling. "Touch me again, cunt. I fucking dare you," Her voice was ice cold, dangerous. Breaker and I exchanged a worried look, and I ran down the hall with Breaker, laughing, at my heels.

"Gonna be fun having your old lady round."

Knowing that the scene we were walking into wasn't gonna be pretty I muttered, "Tell me how fun it is ten minutes from now."

AUSTIN TX

Chapter Seven

Swan

Hulk lingered in the doorway of the small, but tidy guest room, his bulk filling up the whole frame. He watched me with unreadable soft green eyes that were such a startling contrast to his dark, cinnamon-tinted skin, and I tried not to fidget beneath his gaze. It was like he was waiting for me to say something, maybe complain about how plain the room was, but I was just happy it was clean like the rest of the upper floors. The quilt on the queen size bed was faded, but a faint scent of dryer sheets came up when I plopped the backpack on the mattress and it looked like the scuffed oak floors were recently cleaned. A hint of disinfectant scented the air, and someone had tried to warm the room up with a big painting of bright red flowers beneath a neon blue sky.

When Hulk still didn't say anything while he watched me futz around the room, and, my nerves tightened until I blurted out, "Why are you looking at me?"

That seemed to startle him and he blinked. "I was just curious."

"About what?"

Coming into the room then closing the door, he made sure to not get too close to me. He leaned against the dresser then crossed his arms over his chest. His whopping biceps were like cut slabs of muscle that flexed as he shifted, not as defined as Smoke, but solid. Big. Sheesh, this guy's mom must have had steroids in her breast milk. He reminded me of a professional linebacker. You know, a bulldozer with legs. Intimidated, I looked away and fiddled with my pack.

"Curious about how your mind works and how much of an asset you could be."

Scrunching my brow, I returned my gaze to his, surprised by his answer. "Pardon?"

"I do a lot of shit with computers—my mind is just wired like that—and I work with lots of brilliant, eccentric people whose brains operate just a little different from everyone else. I think you're one of those people."

"Those people?" I whispered, dreading his answer, waiting for him to call me a freak.

He studied me, then shook his head with a small smile curving his firm lips. "Yeah, *those* people. The brilliant ones, the people who see things just a little different than the rest of the world. If you're one of those people, and I think you are, you're gonna be a great help with finding your mom and ending this bullshit that's endangering all of us. I absolutely do not want Iron Horse to go to war with any gangs, the mafia, or other MCs. I want to keep my people alive in a situation that's pretty fucked because they're my family. I want to keep you alive not just because you seem like a decent lady, if a bit too hot-tempered for your own good, but because Smoke loves you, and I respect the hell out of that man. He's saved my sorry ass more than once and I owe him. In our world a man doesn't like owing a debt so he'll do whatever he can to make it even—in this case, keeping a beautiful young woman alive and happy."

His words came out a little too intense, his gaze a little too warm, and I looked away, "Uh...okay. You know I love Smoke, right? That I'm his old lady?"

"Yep, little girl, I do." He grinned at me. "Don't worry, I'm not hittin' on you. I'm not suicidal or a dick like that. I just...well, let's say I could really use the distraction of guarding you right now because it blocks out a bunch of personal bullshit. Besides, I've never seen Smoke as happy as he is with you. He deserves to be happy, have the love of a good woman and all that bullshit. I'm glad you brought my friend back, even if you do come with some baggage."

"I'm sorry about that. I wish I didn't present such a danger to you and your club." I sighed and rubbed my face. "Believe me, I wish we were meeting under better circumstances."

"Well, think about it this way. If you and Smoke can fall in love with all this shit going on around you, nothin' can tear you apart. I meant it when I said I've never seen him this happy. I guess what I'm tryin' to say is be patient with the man. This shit is as hard on him as it is on you because the crazy fucker loves you. Now, if he believes in you that much, you must have a good head on your shoulders, and we could use your help."

An unexpected flush of pleasure warmed my cheeks at the thought that Smoke's love for me was that apparent. Then I wondered if my devotion to him was as glaringly obvious. Damn, I needed to work on maintaining a blank face. People were more likely to try and take down someone they viewed as weak, and I didn't want to invite trouble, had plenty of my own, thank you very much.

I needed a moment to process what he said and opened the drawer of the small stand next to the bed, looking through the sample sizes of deodorant, wrapped toothbrushes, and the like. "Thank you, but I don't know how much help I'll be. I've been trained....well I've been trained to take care of myself, but I'm not a really good judge of people."

"I disagree, and more importantly Sarah disagrees."

"What?"

"Your sister passed through here with Beach a couple months ago, and I got to hang out with her at Khan's house. Nice kid, sweet and helpful, with the same ball-busting temper you got. We talked about the usual bullshit, weather, sports, and family. When she spoke about you her eyes lit up. She mentioned how special you were, and how smart you were and how much she admires you." I opened my mouth to protest, but he held his hand up. "We need your help, Swan, so this is what you're gonna do. At some point, maybe tomorrow night, you're gonna go scope out the sweet butts. We got a couple parties coming up—we're patching a new brother in—so it'll be a good time for you to get the feel of the crowd before the big celebration."

I could only imagine what the sweet butts would be doing tomorrow night when I 'scoped them out'. "Why the hell would I do that?"

"'Cause me and Breaker got a feeling that one of 'em is a rat and you're gonna help us find her. Don't worry, Breaker will be there watching you. He's been assigned as your babysitter since Smoke's gonna be gone most of the time."

My heart dropped and I clenched my hands together, trying to hide how much the thought of being here without Smoke bothered me in addition to all the other shit he'd just thrown at me. "Gone? Does he know about your plan for me to spy on the sweet butts?"

"Breaker's gonna talk to him about it, and if Smoke says no, then the plan is off, and you may not have to worry about this shit." His voice softened, "Honey, he's got shit to do that he can't focus on if you're with him. The distraction you cause him by just being in his presence could get him killed. And you have a big ass target on you that'll have fucktards trying to cash in on your bounty. But I swear, we'll keep you safe."

I sat down heavily on the edge of the bed. "Son of a bitch. So I'm stuck here? Locked away while Smoke is out and about?"

"Yeah, not the best of situations, but it also gives you the opportunity to wander the club. We'll have brothers watching you at all times, so don't worry 'bout anyone hurting you. You may not see us, but we'll be there."

"Shit. Any more happy news?"

He chuckled and moved off the dresser, his big muscles shifting as he headed for the door. "You get to meet the old ladies tomorrow at Breaker's house. Cathy, his wife, is throwing a welcome party for you. Don't worry, they're excited to meet you."

"Why?"

"'Cause you're Smoke's old lady and he's the founding chapter's Master at Arms. That means he's basically the Master at Arms for all of the Iron Horse chapters. The women want to be on your good side not only because they understand what it's like to love a biker, but for their old men's sakes. Also means sluts are gonna hit on Smoke, probably right in front of you…at least they will until Smoke makes it clear that he's off limits. No one wants to piss off your old man."

My mind spun with all the information he'd dumped on me, and I rubbed my temples. "Anything else? Am I going to have to go undercover as a club slut?"

He burst out laughing. "Fuck no, not unless we want Smoke to burn some unlucky mother fucker pig roast style over a bonfire."

"What?" The gruesome image tried to gain a hold in my mind and I shuddered.

After a moment of studying me, Hulk laughed. It was a nice laugh, deep and melodic, but it was also a fake laugh. "Just fuckin' with you, girl. Smoke'll be here soon and I'll give you a chance to get settled. Lock the door, but try to get some downtime, okay? Are you hungry?"

"We had dinner on the road so I'm good."

He gestured to the corner of the room by the dresser. "You've got a stocked mini-fridge up here so take whatever you want. Lemme give you my cell phone number. You need anything you call me."

I took his number then followed him to the door and clicked the deadbolt on the thick wood door with a sigh after he left. While I might be shit at understanding people, I had a feeling that Hulk was a good guy beneath all the biker menace. In fact, I had an odd feeling we could be friends if time allowed it, but that didn't mean I trusted him. I'd wait until I talked to Smoke before I did anything or believed anyone.

After turning off the bright overhead light and turning on the brass lamp next to my side of the bed, I collapsed back onto the firm mattress with a sigh. I stared at the ceiling with unseeing eyes for a bit, then pulled my backpack over and began to go through my knives. I looked them over to decide which ones I'd carry on me, and if I wanted to wear my bellyband to hold my weapons or if that might be overkill.

I tossed one of the suitcases, which had somehow made it to the room while I talked with Khan, onto the bed, eager to get out of the clothes I'd been traveling in all day. Thankfully, the weather up here was cool enough to warrant the tight, stretchy, brown pants and a cream, cashmere, long-sleeve sweater with what looked like angora around the wrists. I hadn't seen the pants or sweater before, but somehow seven outfits of the same sexy, but subdued style had been packed in a suitcase that belonged to Smoke. He said he had a bag packed for me, but I thought it meant I was going to be dressed by the hooker express again.

I was surprised there were no clothes that were blinged out, or over-the-top sexy, and I wondered who had bought them. My answer came in the form of a sealed envelope on top of the clothing and shoes. It was addressed to me, and I opened the pretty floral stationery envelope and pulled out elegant paper, surprised to find that it was from Smoke's sister, Julia. We'd met briefly back in Austin. I wasn't sure if she approved of me being in Smoke's life so I was hesitant to read the letter.

Hi Swan,

Miguel mentioned to me that he was having the party girls from his clubhouse buy you clothes. I can only shudder at the thought of what kind of stripper outfits you'd end up with, and I can imagine that you would be miffed that Miguel had those whores shopping for you. I got a little heated with him because I know our parents raised him better than to pull a stunt like that. In his defense, he is absolutely clueless about how a woman's mind works. He's never paid attention to any female long enough to care, so he didn't mean any harm. He's just dumb. It also doesn't help that the only two girlfriends who meant anything to him cheated on him. I know, his life sounds like a bad Spanish soap opera, but he's really trying his best to do right by you. He's just clueless, like most men, about the opposite sex.

Once I calmed down and explained to him how he'd fucked up by asking some woman he might have had random sex with in the distant past to buy anything for a woman he clearly loves, he saw the error of his ways.

126

Needless to say, he felt like an asshole, and it will never happen again.

I've been in the MC life for ten years now, and I know it's hard to adjust to at first. Getting used to a world where women are second-class citizens isn't easy, but your relationship can be anything you and your man want it to be. Just because some of his brothers may treat their women like shit and fuck anything that spreads its legs it doesn't mean Miguel will. For myself, I'd rather not be exposed to the skanks at the clubhouse, but that's not all the Iron Horse MC is. We're a family, and we love and take care of each other. The clubhouse isn't just used as a fuck pad. There are lots of parties there where the kids get to play together while the adults hang out. Those are the special times when everyone is together and you realize just how blessed you are to know these amazing people. I hope you realize that Smoke comes with a big group of people who love him and are delighted to see someone who makes him so obviously happy. You have no idea how long I've prayed for Smoke to find a woman who would love him for who he is. The way he talks about you, it's clear he is head over heels, and I hope you realize what a good man he is beneath all his bullshit.

I've rambled on enough, I'm doing an overnight shift at the clinic with some sick puppies, and I'm really wired on caffeine after shopping for you all day—which was totally fun, by the way. So, if you need a personal shopper in the future, let me know. My girls picked out some of your clothes, so I'm sorry about the bright red

127

and orange floral sweater. They insisted it was beautiful. Smoke bought clothes for my daughters in exchange for their help, so they took their job very seriously. ;)

You have no idea how grateful I am to you for bringing out the absolute best in Smoke. It's been years since he's expressed interest in a woman of any character or worth, let alone falling head over heels in love with her. I'm sorry I was so harsh with you when we met. I let my fear overrule my compassion. I hope that when we get to see each other again we'll go out for drinks. Stay safe and keep my idiot brother alive for me.

Welcome to the family.
Julia

I reread the note at least a dozen times, my eyes seeing the words while an unfamiliar feeling tightened deep in my chest when I finally accepted the fact that she had done something not only very nice for me, but true to my style. The clothes were comfortable for the most part—cute jeans paired with tops that showed a bit of skin, but managed to be conservative. There were also two of what I considered were 'club dresses', meaning they were short and ultra-sexy, but there was no risk of my tits popping out or my skirt riding up over my ass.

I placed the note on top of the clothing, determined to remember this moment of acceptance. A part of me had wondered if Smoke's sister would ever warm up to me. The thought of possible rejection hurt, but I'd tried to ignore it because I realized that just being around me was dangerous. Right now, I had a ton of baggage, and

I couldn't blame her for being worried about Smoke's safety, even if I wished she'd give me a chance. I know his sister was all that he had left and that he loved her very much. The last thing I wanted to do was harm their relationship, so her note lifted one of many burdens from my shoulders.

As I closed the suitcase, there was a brisk knock on my door. Conscious that someone would be watching my room and would have stopped anyone they deemed dangerous from getting near me, I only hid a couple knives on me, feeling Mimi's blessing as my fingers touched the cool surface of the blades. She'd had a perfectly balanced set made for me as a high school graduation present—along with a pearl bracelet. The brisk knock came again, as if the person outside was pissed at having to wait. I moved quickly to the door and took a breath to steady myself, praying it was Smoke.

I opened it and was greeted by the sight of three topless women who seemed surprised to see me. They were brunettes and each wore a Band-Aid-size skirt in different loud colors. I immediately dubbed them Slut #1, Slut #2, and Slut #3. In an odd way, they reminded me of the Three Musketeers. They all sneered at me, but I kept my face calm, laughing on the inside. If they thought the sight of some nipples was going to freak me out, they were way wrong. I leaned against the doorframe and raised a brow.

"Can I help you?"

The words were perfectly polite, but the tone was not, and the three topless women exchanged confused looks. The one in the lead, a brunette with layered bangs and a neon green skirt, narrowed her gaze. "We're here to see Smoke."

"And you are...?"

Her smirk turned mean. "They call me Cyclone. Smoke knows me real well...we're special friends. I always come visit with him when he's here. Every. Time. And he comes up here a lot. Who the fuck are you?"

"His girlfriend."

"Sure you are, honey. You're his little submissive bitch just like the rest of them. They all think they're special wearin' his collar, but they're nothing more than his fuck toys."

I would *not* kill her. I really wouldn't.

It was a struggle not to rise and take the bait, but my jealousy was burning, and I narrowed my eyes, still struggling to maintain my calm. "And what does that have to do with you stinking up the hallway with your dollar store perfume?"

Okay, sort of calm.

"Oh sweetheart"—she hissed the word—"you better get used to the smell of our perfume because Smoke's gonna be covered in it and in the smell of my pussy. When you kiss him you're gonna taste my come in his mouth."

I was so shocked, so angered at the mental image she shoved at me that I stood there, silent and assessing how quickly I could snap her neck even as I tried to ignore the pain radiating through my chest.

If I killed her, there would be a mess I didn't want to clean up.

Still, I was tempted.

This bitch knew she'd scored a direct hit because her smirk widened. "Better get used to it 'cause you'll never be able to satisfy him. I don't know if Smoke clued you in, but he's gonna fuck who he wants when he wants, and as his girl, you don't have shit to say about it. Now, we left work early to get here, and I'm done fuckin' waitin' so move your big ass. If you're nice I may allow you to suck the taste of my pussy off his cock when I'm done fuckin' him."

She tried to push her way past me, obviously thinking I would just step back and let her say that shit to my face.

How very wrong she was.

Territorial instinct overwhelmed me, and the thought of having her in my space, however temporary, was unacceptable. My training kicked in, and in one swift move, I had her slammed up against the wall, her tits cushioning her. I jerked on her arm, applying pressure in a most painful manner. She squealed and thrashed beneath me before I yanked up again not quite dislocating her shoulder. This time her cry of pain was real.

Her high voice drilled through my head. "What the fuck are you doing you stupid bitch? Let me go!"

The first thing that came to mind was one of Sarah's favorite sayings right before she got in a fight. "I'm gonna beat you like your daddy should've until you learn some fucking manners."

Slut #1 and Slut #2 looked at the chick I had pressed against the wall—it's all in the leverage—then back at me.

131

Slut #2 gasped. "Holy fuck, it's Sarah!"

It made me proud to hear the fear in her voice as she said that. "Try again, bitch. I'm Swan, her twin sister."

"Yeah," Slut #1 added in a high-pitched voice. "Sarah has bigger tits."

Beneath me, Slut #3, Cyclone, was making whining, whimpering noises while still calling me such filthy names that, on some level, I was impressed. Next time I saw Sarah I'd have some new phrases to insult her with. I pushed against Cyclone and whispered into her ear while gagging on her super sweet perfume, "Let *me* clue *you* in on something. You do *not* want to fuck with me. Ever. And fucking with me over my old man is sure suicide."

"He made you his old lady?" Slut #1 gasped with obvious hurt in her voice.

"Yes, but that doesn't matter. What you should be concerned about is how much I love him and how I will destroy anyone who tries to take what's mine." Unable to help it, I found myself growling out one of Smoke's favorite phrases. Damn, I was just borrowing badass sayings left and right tonight. Next thing you know, I'd be quoting Chuck Norris.

I could almost hear Smoke purring the words into my ear when I snarled, "Got me?"

"G-got you," Cyclone stuttered out.

I shoved her away and turned to head back into my room when Cyclone tried to hit me. Too bad for her I grew up with a sister who would try to sneak up and sucker-punch me on a regular basis. I have to admit that I had fun stalking Sarah in return then sweeping her feet out from under her before she even knew I was there.

132

We sparred, a lot, and all that practice taught me the signs the slut was about to throw a punch.

My reaction was pure muscle memory as I smacked her hand away with my forearm. She gave a sharp scream as I yelled at her to never try to touch me again, that I'd cunt punch her, rip her eyes out, shove them down her throat, and a bunch of other crazy shit stuff I'd heard my dad say when he was on a tear. Sluts #1 and #2 fled as heavy boots thundered down the hall, drawing closer. Cyclone tried to flee as well, but I booted her on her ass then smirked.

"Uh uh, you're staying here." If this woman was the one who was the rat, I wanted Hulk to get a good look at her.

Moments later, Smoke came around the corner and took in the woman cowering at my feet as she held her hand, then swore loud in his scary, deadly tone. Oh, shit, this was bad. When his gaze cut to me, anger snapped in his eyes, sending a shiver of apprehension down my spine. I knew he'd never hurt me, but fucking hell, he was pissed. It screamed from every line in his tense body and his powerful, irate gaze.

When he was sure he had my complete attention, he ground out in a low, scary voice, "What in the ever lovin' fuck is going on here?"

The first words that came out of my mouth did not help the situation.

At all.

"Did you fuck her?"

"Did I what?"

Without looking away I pointed at the skank on the ground. "Did. You. Fuck. Her?"

Hulk gaped at me while I squared off with Smoke, my fists clenched at my side.

"Jesus Christ, I do not have time for this shit." He grabbed me by the bicep and pulled me away from Hulk, who was now crouched over Cyclone and was checking her wrist that I may or may not have broken while she sobbed pitifully.

I jerked my arm away, unable to get the thought of Smoke having sex with her out of my mind. "Oh, I'm sorry to inconvenience you. See, your trash turned up at my door, and I had to deal with it while you and your boys were having your secret Pow Wow."

His jaw twitched and I thought he was going to explode, but he managed to control himself. "Get in the fucking room."

"What?"

"Get in our goddamn room, shut and lock the fucking door, and for the love of Christ, just do what I say for once. I don't have time to clean up your messes right now."

"My mess? *My* mess?" The last word came out in a screech.

"Enough!" I wasn't used to Smoke yelling at me and I froze. "Shit, just get in our damn room. And this time, don't be fuckin' stupid and open the door for strangers. Christ, woman, help me keep you alive."

At that moment I became aware that there were now around a dozen people in the hall watching us with interest, including a crying Cyclone. Stung at being chastised like a child in front of all these people, and hurt that he'd called me stupid, I flipped Smoke the bird while Hulk looked on with an unreadable expression in his frosty green eyes. My breathing abruptly hitched and with a burning nose I went into the room like I'd been told and slammed the door behind me, hopefully in time to cut off the scream of rage that escaped me.

What a complete and total fucking asshole.

A knock came from the door, interrupting my totally melodramatic self-pity fest. I shouted, "Fuck off!"

The knocking came again.

"Leave me the fuck alone. First person who comes in here is gonna lose a kneecap."

I knew it wasn't Smoke. He'd have barged right in, but I was not in the mood to listen to anyone's bullshit at the moment.

A moment later I heard a man's muffled voice. "Swan, it's Hulk. He didn't mean what he said, he was just pissed and worried."

"Hulk, I could really use some alone time. Please." I shouted and bit back my anger so I wouldn't yell hurtful shit at him.

"Swan, just give him a chance to explain. He may dig himself deeper into trouble with you, but you have to give the man a chance to learn from his mistakes."

At that point, I was totally over listening to anyone telling me what to do, especially when they were sounding rational. I was overwhelmed by everything, and a sick dread began to fill me. This was one of the things I hated about being me, my inability to handle too much at once. When I was a kid and things got too intense, I'd always flee to the wilderness, hiking and clearing my mind. That wasn't an option here, but

135

claustrophobia was sinking its claws into me. I had some issues with feeling trapped after my dad buried me in a coffin when I was fifteen. That'll give you issues, trust me. My therapist almost cried when I'd told her about it, and that memory wasn't helping me center myself, either.

I had to get out, but there was no way I would make it out that door. No doubt there was someone out there *now*, but I wondered where everyone had been when the three wicked bitches were banging on it. My palms ached as I dug my nails into my skin, needing the pain to help clear my head.

I stood quickly and scanned the room for the best escape route. There were bars on the windows, but they had a safety latch so the person inside could open them and escape in case of fire. I grabbed the notepad and pen out of the drawer and wrote down in big, bold letters for Smoke that I was fine and to leave me alone, then threw it on the bed. If Smoke thought he was going to come back in here and yell at me he had another think coming. My mind was fragile at the moment, easily wounded. I needed to shore up my emotional defenses and let myself zone out, or have a good crying fit.

Moving swiftly, not sure how much time I had, I went to the bathroom to get a towel and slung it around my neck, then went back and opened the window. The iron bars unlatched easily, and I took a quick look around outside. The side of the building we were on faced the dense forest, and I couldn't see much beyond the dim arc of a sodium light two stories below me. When I looked up, I could see a brick overhang that would make it easy to get up on the roof.

Thanking good genetics for my height and my love of rock climbing for my strength, I swiftly stood on the windowsill and hauled myself up, trying my best to not mess up my clothes. I took a glance around and saw the door for the roof access. I dangled over the edge and used my foot to close the iron bars. As soon as that was done I cursed the fact that I was wearing a white shirt that stood out like a beacon. My paranoia kicked in and I wrapped the deep burgundy towel around me, making me blend in a little more. I knew I'd be found eventually, but for right now, I just wanted to be alone and wallow in my misery.

Movement at the edge of the forest caught my eye and I scooted back, crouching down and watching the spot where I thought I saw something bigger than an animal moving. Staying as still as possible, I waited for any further movement, but whatever it was had either gone into the forest or was staying still and watching me. My spidey senses weren't tingling, so after a few minutes, I shifted back to my perch on the edge of the roof and wiped away a stray tear. Distant voices and the occasional growl of a bike engine came from the front side of the building.

Damn, this really sucked.

I sat up on the roof and watched the moon inch across the sky, my mind blessedly numb. The past few hours kept trying to intrude, but I refused to think about it. Even the briefest hint of how pissed off Smoke had been sent me into a downward spiral until I was sobbing into my towel. Sometimes a good pity party can get rid of a lot of stress, and if I didn't blow off some steam, I was gonna crack. The air had chilled, and I pulled the towel tightly around me. I was considering going back for the comforter, when a man's voice yelled, "Swan?"

A second later another male voice roared, "Where is she?"

Uh-oh, Smoke was back.

I had to fight the urge to yell that I was up here, but I didn't. Fuck him. He'd called me stupid, didn't even give me time to explain, just freaked out on me. I know I messed up but he had no right to hurt me like that. I wanted him to suffer a little bit for that epic bullshit. For fuck's sake, it was his past nasty ass booty call who started it. He had no room to try and take the high road.

In fact, he could kiss my round ass.

Below me Smoke was in a full on panic, shouting my name then yelling at whoever else was in there with him. They found my note on my bed and the rest of the men subdued a bit, but Smoke continued to rant and rave. I probably would have continued to hide up here if I hadn't heard the desperation behind his anger, the fear. The time I spent zoning out had relaxed me enough that I had let go of some of my anger. Enough that I felt a pang of guilt at how worried he sounded.

Stupid, fucking, soft-hearted me couldn't stand the sound of his distress so I yelled out, "I'm up here."

There was silence, then Smoke said in a rough, loud voice, "Swan?"

I sighed, wishing I'd never said anything. "I'm on the roof."

"What the fuck?" an unfamiliar man laughed out. "On the roof? I take it back. That beautiful pussy is way too high maintenance for me. You and Beach have my prayers."

The thud of something being hit reached me, even on the roof, as a man grunted. Then Smoke said in a low, really cold voice, "Do not disrespect my woman. Ever. That means you don't refer to her pussy, ever. That is my pussy. I own it, all of it, and you will respect my old lady if you want to continue to live without some not-so-pretty scars. Hear me?"

"Yeah…yeah I hear you. Shit, you hit like a fucking wrecking ball. Wife's gonna be pissed you gave me a bruise."

"Donkey, get the fuck out. Go tell Khan we found her."

I sat down on the edge near the window and dangled my feet. When I heard the bars open, I glanced down and into Smoke's worried face. Our eyes locked and he sagged against the frame and stared at me. "Swan? What the fuck are you doing up there? How did you even get up there?"

"I climbed." My voice hitched as I muttered, "Leave me alone. I'm fine, just go away."

He squeezed his eyes shut while a few more curious faces looked out the window before Smoke shoved them back. "Baby, please come down."

"No."

Yes, I realized it was a totally petulant answer, and maybe I was being dramatic, but I loved and hated him at this moment.

Closing his eyes, he spoke through clenched teeth. "Please."

"No."

A man said something I couldn't catch, and Smoke disappeared from the window, only to be replaced by Hulk. He looked up at me and grinned, then started laughing. I glared back at him, but that only set him off again. Still chuckling, he shook his head at me. "You are hot as fire, just like your sister. Way too much drama for me. Did you enjoy scaring the hell out of your man? I thought he was gonna stroke out."

I stiffened and glared at him some more. "Oh, I'm sorry. Was I supposed to wait around like a good girl for a man who yelled at me without giving me a chance to explain? Was I just supposed to hang out and wait for him to come back and shred me in front of everyone again? No fucking thank you."

Sobering, Hulk shifted to a more comfortable position to look up at me. "You know he didn't mean that shit."

"I don't care whether he meant it or not. He hurt me."

I'd almost whispered the last part but it must have been loud enough for Hulk to hear. "Guys say stupid things all the time when they're scared."

"He wasn't scared, he was pissed."

"You make a lot of assumptions, don't you?"

Startled out of my pity party for a moment, I frowned. "What?"

"Just sayin' that it seems like you assume the worst in people. How 'bout you give him the benefit of the doubt and let him explain why he reacted the way he did."

"Thank you very much, Dr. Phil, but I don't want to talk to him."

"Too bad," Smoke said in a silky smooth voice from right behind me, "because we aren't leaving this roof until we get some shit straight."

Chapter Eight

I froze and listened for the crunch of Smoke's boots walking across the gravel of the flat rooftop. His energy washed over me, and I bit my lower lip. A small part of me wondered if I could make the jump from the roof to the scraggly lawn three stories below. That might sound like a bit of an extreme reaction, but a lifetime spent with a not-so-stable father had left a scar on my psyche that I'd rather not examine too closely.

It was almost as if I could feel Smoke's heat as he stood behind me. He didn't say a word, and I itched to break the uncomfortable silence, to rail at him and curse him out for making me feel so bad. I wanted to sucker punch him for making me cry, but I remained frozen as my words stuck in my throat. When he took a seat next to me on the edge of the building, I stiffened and started to pull away, but he placed a large hand on my thigh, securing me in place like a butterfly with a pin through its poor heart.

"Babe, what are you doing up here?" he asked in that velvety, soothing tone that he only used with me.

The moonlight silvered the tips of the trees surrounding us and I pressed my lips together, refusing to answer him. If he'd yelled at me, I could have rallied my defenses, but when he was gentle with me like this I almost forgot what a prick he'd been. It took a great deal of effort, but I managed to keep my need to please him in check and pressed my lips together hard enough that it hurt.

"Swan," he tried again, "talk to me."

My muscles were tight enough to snap, and the effort to ignore him was getting harder and harder, but I bit my inner cheek sharp enough to taste blood and shifted farther away from him.

"Fuck this shit," he muttered a second before he snatched me up and pulled me onto his lap with my back facing the drop-off at the edge of the building.

I shoved at his arms, but he held me tight just like I knew he would. Pressed to his solid warmth with my legs wrapped around his waist, I refused to give him the satisfaction of looking at him. Rather than bitching at me, Smoke slowly stroked my back. I tried to resist his soothing touch, I really did, but my body relaxed against my will as he continued to stroke me.

He took a deep breath and let it out with a gusty sigh. "I should tan your ass for that stunt you pulled downstairs."

Oh, no, he fucking didn't.

Indignation filled me as I finally met his gaze and even in the silvery moonlight, I could read the stress and the fear on the harsh planes of his face. Before any misplaced empathy could rob me of my senses I snarled out, "I should cut your fucking throat for talking to me like that."

A hint of a smile ghosted across his lips before he sobered again. His eyes had turned to pure darkness in the moonlight, but they weren't empty. Even in those pools of black I could see a dizzying array of emotions swirling through him too fast to identify. His caressing touch stilled, then he slid his hand up so his fingers were stroking the back of my neck before he grabbed a fistful of my hair.

"Do you even have the slightest fucking clue why I'm mad?"

I tried to jerk out of his hold, to look away from his intense gaze, but he held me in place and I couldn't exactly fight free with my ass almost hanging off the edge of the building. "Because I'm stupid?"

"What?"

"You called me stupid."

He flinched as if I'd slapped him. "I'm sorry 'bout that. I lost my temper. Fear was runnin' my mouth."

Those words rang hollow to me, and I considered various painful ways to get off his lap. "Fuck off and let me go. I don't want to be around you. I mean it, Smoke. Red!"

The fact that I used my safeword seemed to upset him, and he leaned back enough for me to scoot off of him.

When I was a couple of feet away, I spun around to face him, my fists clenched so hard my nails were stabbing into my skin, probably leaving bruises...again. Yeah, I was fucked in the head, but pain gave me strength, a strength I desperately needed while squaring off with Smoke. I didn't want to argue with him—I loved him deeply—but we needed to get some shit straight.

Submissive in the bedroom?

Yes, it's the bee's knees.

Submissive out in the real world?

Um, no.

"You totally disrespected me in front of not just your buddies, but also the cunt who was insulting me and trying to get me out of the way so she could share your dick with those skanks. And then to call me stupid on top of that? Buddy you're lucky I'm still in the same country as you."

For a moment he looked genuinely puzzled. "What did I say?"

My skin tightened as I tried to spit out the words. "You don't even remember what you said?"

The lines around his mouth deepened. "Not really. I was pissed at you and worried."

Praying for patience wasn't working. "You know what? I'm done with this conversation."

"Wait!" I swear a look of panic came over him before he schooled his features into his usual cold mask. "I told you, now that I've had you I'm never lettin' you go, ever, and I mean it. You're stuck with me, Swan, and even though I'm a major fuckin' asshole, I didn't mean to hurt your feelings."

"You didn't hurt my feelings," I mumbled and hugged myself.

"Don't lie to me. I could see your pain the minute I lost my shit, and I am sorry about that."

"But it didn't stop you from running your mouth, did it?"

"Look, baby, I say shit I don't mean when I'm pissed."

"Don't you 'baby' me, Smoke. I'm a grown woman and I will not put up with you disrespecting me in front of people. You're supposed to build me up, not tear me down." I took a deep breath, trying to ignore the pained confusion twisting his handsome face. My impulse control had slipped its leash and a torrent of words spilled from me. "And don't tell me about being angry and saying shit you regret. That is a choice you make to lose control, 'cause let me tell you, if I wasn't keeping a tight grip on my temper you'd be dead right now. You think you have anger management problems? You have no idea what a terrible, horrifying thing true anger problems are. Before my dad got into therapy, he'd scare me so much I couldn't breathe. You think that being pissed gives you the right to be a dick? Well it doesn't, and I won't let you treat me like one of your whores."

"Swan," his voice broke and a look of understanding filled his eyes. "Fuck, I'm a dick. I get so wrapped up in my own bullshit I forget to think about what I'm saying. I'm sorry. Please forgive me. I swear you won't have to deal with that again."

"No, fuck that." I crossed my arms, more to hold myself together than to keep warm. "You are a dick, and just because you say you're sorry doesn't mean it's okay."

"I know, I know." He went to reach out for me, then let his hand fall between us. A surge of disappointment filled me when I realized he wasn't going to touch me.

The need for the calming effects his embrace was such a part of my world now that I craved it even though I was mad enough to bite him if he touched me. "Swan, I promise I'm gonna do better, and I'm a man of my word. Give me some time to adjust to having you in my life, yeah? Not makin' excuses, but I've been alone for a long time, and I'm used to having control over everything."

My lower lip trembled, and he sighed then closed his eyes. A moment later, he looked up and a bolt of warmth raced through me like the hot wind from a forest fire. In his shadowed gaze, I saw a deep, abiding love that was for me and only me. Crap, how was I supposed to resist him when he was being all nice and calm? This gentle side of his nature killed me, and I struggled to resist the lure of his embrace.

As if he sensed my weakening resolve, he smiled slowly and held out his hand. "Come here, baby girl. Let me take care of you. Give you what you need."

Double crap, I really liked it when he went all gentle, yet dominant on me.

My wet panties confirmed this fact.

I stared at him, taking in the entirety of his perfect masculine form, then stepped into his arms. He held me tight, pressing my face into the warmth and delectable smell of his strong chest. My lower belly fluttered even as I half-heartedly tried to push away.

"I'm still irritated with you."

"I know. I didn't handle shit right. Won't happen again."

"Fine." Okay, I sounded petulant even to myself, but I come from a family of grudge holders.

He ran his fingers through my hair and my muscles weakened. "Can you please tell me what the hell happened back there? I thought I was walking in on a scene where she'd tried to kill you. That was part of what made me overreact even though it was Cyclone."

"Did you fuck them? Those topless sluts showed up at the door to our room ready to shove their way past me to get into your bed. Impressive that you can handle three women at once, good for you."

His nostrils flared, but he didn't take the bait and nodded instead. "Yeah, I've probably fucked 'em. But I had nothing to do with them showing up. Cyclone said a brother she wasn't familiar with called her up at work to let her know I was coming into town and that I'd asked to see her and her...girls."

A shudder of revulsion went through me at the thought of what he'd probably done with those women, and I suddenly felt suffocated by his hold. "How many—"

Before I could finish my question he placed his hand over my mouth and shook his head. "I'm not gonna let you torture yourself with my past, it ain't gonna happen. We've had this discussion before, Swan. When are you going to believe that I'm not gonna fuck around on you?"

I hated the tears that burned my eyes, but he wouldn't let me go.

God help me, he was strong, and his determination radiated from him. "But that's not why I was mad at you. Do you know how easily Cyclone and her bitches could have been someone that wanted to hurt you? Do you have any idea how easy it would have been for one of them to be carrying a knife or a gun?"

I rolled my eyes and pried his hand off my mouth. "They were half-naked, Smoke. Unless they had a gun shoved up their skank hole I would have seen it."

"What if they were just there to lure you out of the room?" A hard tremble went through him. "You could have been taken from me. I could have lost you."

I softened slightly at the thinly veiled distress in his words and cupped his cheek, rubbing my thumb against the bristles along his jaw. "Smoke, you can't watch me 24/7. You have to trust that I can take care of myself and make my own judgment calls. I'm not stupid." The word sat on my tongue in a sour curl. "And I don't like it when you just flip out without listening to me."

He held my hand against his face and nuzzled his lips against my palm before speaking. "I know you're not stupid, and you will never be a burden. Trust me, Swan, I think you're one of the smartest people I've ever met. Your brilliance stuns me, but you don't have the experience with people that I do. Not just 'cause you were sheltered, but because you haven't been around people who want to use you, to do you harm. I have. I know how easily you could be snatched up and the terrible things they would do to you."

His voice dropped to a low growl at the end, and I wrapped myself around him, squeezing him with my arms and legs until there wasn't an inch of room between us. I was all too familiar with overprotective men, and as much as I loved Smoke, he had to know he couldn't obsess about my safety. It would drive us both crazy.

"I'm sorry I scared you," I whispered against his chest. "When they knocked on the door I thought it was you or Hulk."

"Where the fuck was Hulk?" Smoke growled. "He was supposed to be watching you."

"Maybe he thought one of those women was one of the sweet butts sabotaging the club."

Smoke stilled, the muscle of his jaw twitching against my palm. "He told you about that?"

"Yeah, and I'm glad he did. I want this to end. I want to find Sarah. I want to find my Mom. If finding out who the traitors are helps, then I'm all for doing what I can."

He rubbed his face against the side of my head, tension tightening his body beneath mine as he whispered, "I want to lock you away from the world so you'll never have you know a moment of sorrow. But I can't do that, and it fucking kills me. Protecting my people is what I do, what I've always done, but the one person who means more than anyone ever has is the one person I can't keep safe."

Now I was the one rubbing his back, soothing the unspoken fear that was at the heart of his words. "You're not God. You can't predict the future, and you can't be everywhere at once."

"We'll see about that," he muttered. "Just promise me, baby girl, that you'll take a moment to think before you act, that you won't put yourself in danger."

"I won't purposely put myself in danger, but I will deal with whatever comes my way. I love you, Miguel, with all of my heart, and I will fight to protect you, always."

He gently cupped my chin and lifted my face to his. The look in his eyes wasn't one of anger and fear anymore, but lust and determination. "Do you have any idea what you do to me? Any idea what you mean to me?"

"Of course I do." I placed a gentle kiss on his full lips. "Because you mean the same to me. But you're still an asshole, and if you keep this up, I'm going to punch you right in your baby maker."

His laughter ghosted over me and he shook his head, rubbing our noses together. "But then I wouldn't be able to fuck you."

I grunted. "Good point, you owe me an apology."

Light reflected in his eyes from the moon as he titled his head and gave me a slow smile. "I do, don't I."

His voice held a carnal edge that sent a shiver up my spine. "May I suggest something?"

I ran my hand over the firm expanse of his chest, trailing my fingers over the patches on his vest. "What would that be?"

He whispered the words against my sensitive lips, making me tingle from head to toe. "Sometime in the future I want you to torture me with orgasm denial."

"What…how?"

"You'll take me to the edge of coming, any way you want, then keep me from going over. By the time you do bring me to the edge for the third time I'll be out of my mind with the need to come. My cock will get harder than you've ever seen it, drip pre-cum for you while I strain to get you to make me shoot. But when you do give me permission to climax I'm gonna do it inside of you and wring a dozen rough orgasms out of that hot, pink cunt of yours. First time's gonna go fast, but I'll still be hard after I come. I won't pull out, I'll just continue to fuck you until you pass out. I've never given that kind of control up to a woman before, but I trust you."

Completely under his sexual spell at this point I faintly whispered. "Why don't we do that now?"

"Because right now I need to fuck you. I need to know that you're okay, that you're alive. I've never dealt with this kind of worry before, baby girl, so have some patience with me. Yeah? If I fuck up again, and I probably will, I promise I'll talk with you about it instead of shuttin' you out."

"Okay." I pressed my hips into his, grinding against his thick erection, but our lips still hadn't touched. "Smoke?"

"What is it baby?"

"Kiss me."

Our play quickly turned from a brush of lips to our tongues tangling together while we clung to each other. Smoke was holding me so tight I had trouble drawing a deep breath, but oxygen was overrated. Right now I felt like I could live off the divine sensations of his delicious lips, and survive on his breath and touch alone. Lovely, soothing pleasure unfurled in my body, and I embraced the distraction only Smoke could provide. My fears, the tension, everything was swept away in a tide of desire, and I was ravenous for him.

Smoke must have felt the same way because his cock was like a thick iron bar, and I rocked myself on him. We were separated by our pants, but not for long.

He cupped my breasts and squeezed them gently. "Gotta have you, baby. Take your pants off, but keep your shirt on."

"Can anyone see us?" I shot a quick glance over my shoulder at the area where I'd seen movement, but there was nothing there.

"No one's out here, but let's move back a bit in case anyone comes out back for a piss in the woods. No one gets to see your spectacular body but me."

He helped me stand then took me over to the portion of the roof with the door leading down to the clubhouse. Giving me a wicked smile that was a flash of white teeth, he spread out the towel then held his hand out to me. I slipped my fingers into his and he gently tugged me closer until our bodies were separated by less than an inch. His heat shimmered off my skin, and I leaned forward, taking a deep inhalation of his scent, richer now than it had been this morning.

He swept my hair over my shoulder with a gentle touch then ran his hands over my torso. "You are so damn beautiful, Swan, but as stunning as you are on the outside, your soul is even sweeter. I need to make up for being such a bastard and hurting you. I should kiss you until that pain goes away."

Before I could ask what he was talking about, he sank down onto his knees before me. The towel cushioned him as he settled back on his heels and tugged me forward. I was curious about what he was going to do while he studied me in the moonlight, his gaze tracing me like a caress. A pleased rumble escaped him, and he rubbed his face against my lower belly. I ran my fingers through his hair, toying with his loose curls, and absorbing his love.

Deft fingers unbuttoned my pants and slowly slid them down. A growl rumbled in his throat at the sight of my black lace panties. "Such a pretty baby."

The feeling of him licking the edge of that lace, his hot breath seeping through the delicate fabric, sent a bolt of hard lust through me. I buried my hands in his hair and tried to direct him to where I really wanted his lips. That aching little bundle of nerves between my legs pounded to the beat of my heart as blood rushed to my pelvis.

A ripple of shock moved through me when he grabbed the lace with his teeth then bit and tore at my panties until the crotch was shredded, my pussy exposed to him surrounded by the remains of my panties. My breath came out choppy as he continued to tease me, licking at my slit with feather-light touches as I tried to spread my legs wider and give him better access, but I was hindered by my pants, which were trapped around my ankles by my hiking boots.

The best I could do was hang onto his shoulders while I tilted my hips to his mouth. Adding to my frustration, he kept his touch light, teasing, and it drove me crazy with desire. I grasped his hair in my fists hard enough that it must have stung. My libido was firmly running the show right now, and it didn't give a shit what I did as long as an orgasm was the result. He groaned deep in his throat and spread my pussy lips wide open so my clit was fully exposed to him.

I sucked in a sharp breath when he placed a lingering kiss right on my clit. "Oh, God."

"Not God...Miguel" he murmured before he began to lick me in earnest.

While I knew he was exceptionally good at eating pussy, the way he was making out with my clit was a whole other deal. He kissed and sucked, and flicked that little bud with his tongue, driving me higher and higher until I was trying to hump his face, pressing my pussy into him like the shameless hussy I was. My lower stomach fluttered with small muscle spasms that were almost like mini-orgasms and I bit my lower lip, moaning with each flick of his tongue.

He lifted his face from my sex, his lips shiny with my arousal. "You gonna come for me, baby girl? Your little bud is all stiff and swollen, begging for me. Want me to make you climax against my face?"

The best I could do was whimper, and before I knew it, Smoke was on his feet and turning me to face the door. Shivers moved through me as he placed my hands on the cool surface of the door, his big hands enveloping mine while he ground his denim-covered cock against my bare ass. With my pants still around my ankles I was hobbled, which in an odd way, added to my arousal. Being at Smoke's mercy just flat out did it for me, and I loved it when he took charge of my willing body.

In response, I rocked my hips back against him in a tight circle and he groaned, then bit the side of my neck hard enough that I wondered if I'd have a hickey, not that I really gave a shit. I'd take bruises all over my body in exchange for the otherworldly pleasure of his touch. Trust kept me in place when he released my hands and bent me at the hips so my ass was sticking way out. Anticipation hummed through me like an electrical storm, and I found it hard to stay still. I needed to move to release this buildup of energy. I felt so alive, so present in this moment that the world took on a hyper-clarity. The cool night breeze danced over the exposed parts of my body, chilling me for a moment before Smoke resumed his dominant stance behind me.

When he rubbed the head of his cock through my arousal I let out a pained groan, my entire body throbbing with the need to have him inside of me.

He grasped my hair with one hand then jerked me back so my body was now bowed. Thank God I did a lot of yoga; otherwise, this position would have been painful. Instead, it only made me more desperate for him. I loved it when he took me over like this, when he forced my attention on him until the world faded away to nothing but this amazing, terrifying man behind me.

"Baby, while I've apologized for being an asshole, it's time for you to take your punishment for putting yourself in danger, for scaring the fuck out of me when you ran away, and for making me think that you'd been taken from me, that I couldn't protect you. You run, I'll always find you, always, because I can't live without you."

Despite his gentle tone, his grip was punishing. He continued to torment me, rubbing his cock over my clit, barely pushing the crest into me before pulling out. This cranked my arousal higher until I shook with need, but he still didn't give me any relief. He played my body until I was sobbing, begging him to end the teasing, begging him to fuck me and cool the burn inside me. I was so desperate to have him fill me, to feel that incredible connection between body and soul, but he continued to punish me until tears dripped from my eyes and onto the dark gravel under my feet.

"Please, please, Smoke, I'm sorry."

He teased my soaking wet entrance. "What are you sorry for, baby girl?"

"For scaring you, for doubting you, for doubting myself. Please!"

With a slight push he eased the first couple inches of his substantial erection into me and I screamed in pleasure. Fuck, his denial had worked me into a frenzied state. I don't know what it was about Smoke telling me 'no', but it got all my gears turning, and I was absolutely savage with lust. I needed him to want me, I needed him to love me and desire me, because when we were making love, I felt so connected to him that it was almost like our hearts beat as one and I knew I wasn't alone.

"You gonna do it again?" he taunted in a strained voice while holding my hips as still as he could with his superior strength.

"No!"

Another inch of his cock was pushed into my swollen sex. "Are you going to obey me?"

Even in my lust-induced fog those words made it to my brain, and I shuddered as I tried to think. "Probably not?"

He chuckled and stopped moving, leaving me bereft with my inner muscles squeezing hard on him. "Always a fighter. One of the things I love about you, but you need to let me protect you, and I can't protect you if you don't at least consider what I have to say."

I shot him an incredulous look. "You want to have this conversation now?"

His grin was pure wickedness as he flexed his hips into me. "Got your attention, don't I?"

All I could do was grunt as he buried himself to the hilt in a smooth glide. My breath came out in quick pants as I squeezed my eyes closed and began rubbing my clit hard and fast. Before I could reach my climax, my body hot and heavy with the building tension, Smoke snatched my hand away and pulled almost all they way out then pushed himself in balls-deep, making me keen and arch against him. He'd never released my hair and used it to control me even when I tried to buck against him, tried to ease the ache and the intensity of being so full of him.

And yet, I loved being controlled by him.

What did that say about me?

His breath was hot against my hair as he whispered, "Feel that? Feel the energy between us, the way your body fits mine perfectly? I've waited my whole life for you, Swan Anderson, and I won't let your pride get you killed."

Whatever reply I might have had came out in a strangled moan as he began to fuck me. My mind shut down and I sank deeper into Smoke's embrace, submitting to his masterful touch, giving myself over to him completely as he shoved himself all the way in me with a bone-melting grunt. The unforgiving impact of his body against mine sent a bright burst of pain through my pelvis as he hit my cervix. That little bit of discomfort quickly turned into harsh pleasure as he began to thrust into me, slow and hard. Despite wearing a bra, my breasts bounced and swayed with each thrust. I groaned low in my throat and ground my hips against him. He stilled then caught my rhythm, giving me exactly what I needed. The coiled tension inside of me released, my muscles trembling as I came hard enough that bright lights flashed behind my eyelids. Behind me, Smoke didn't miss a beat, pounding into me over and over again until I came three more times, changing the rhythm up with each climax to match what I wanted.

By this point, I was limp, held up only by my hands weakly braced against the wall and Smoke's grip on my hips. He'd released my hair after my second orgasm and was now running his hands over the exposed parts of my body while kissing along the side of my neck. I was damp with sweat and his scent overwhelmed me, his presence taking over every one of my senses. He completely covered me with his body, his hands pressing over mine on the wall, caging me with his strength. He managed to build me up again, my exhausted body trying to give him every drop of my pleasure.

His deep voice rumbled against the side of my neck while he did this twisting thing at the end of each thrust that made me see stars. I loved this man, this beast who rutted on me, but managed to hold his strength in check enough to keep from harming me. He fucked me like he owned me. Even though my inner feminist fought the notion, my inner slut loved it because it wasn't being owned in a negative sense. No, this was belonging to the most powerful beast in the jungle and considering him my equal.

"Gonna come," he growled. "Get on your knees."

My floating consciousness barely understood what he was saying, but when he slipped out, then spun me around and pushed me to my knees, I automatically opened my mouth for him. Looking up at Smoke, gilded by the moonlight and stroking his thick shaft glistening with my arousal, my anticipation of watching him orgasm was so intense that I began to plead with him to come, to give me everything. I wanted all of this man, including his pleasure. I wanted to taste him on my tongue, to give him as much satisfaction as he gave me. I leaned forward and began to lick his testicles while he stroked himself, the big muscles of his legs quivering as he made an erotic grunting noise.

He gripped my hair and jerked my head back, his breathing harsh and unsteady. "Open."

I complied, replacing my mouth on his balls with my fingertips, stroking the soft skin as it pulled up tight.

Smoke slipped the head of his dick into my mouth and I sucked eagerly, wiggling on my heels as my own passion ramped up. Knowing that he was going to reach his peak, knowing that I made him feel this good was an aphrodisiac on its own. When he cried out as I sucked him, my heart swelled with pride. Power— doing this for him was a rush of pure, sensual power. Fucked up or not, serving him fulfilled a need that, until Smoke, I never realized I had. I needed to surrender completely to him, to give him everything he wanted because he gave me everything I needed, and then some.

I pulled away long enough to say, "Give it to me, Miguel, I want your come in my mouth."

"Fuck!" He roared and bucked in my grip.

There was just enough time for me to seal my lips over him again. At the first hot burst of his seed on my tongue, I moaned low and deep, swallowing his slightly bitter liquid heat down as fast as I could. Even after I'd taken everything he had to offer, I kept sucking him, gentling my mouth until the stroke of my tongue against his length was a whisper of touch. He continued to groan and twitch, staring down at me while I worshiped him with my mouth. Doing this for him was also an attempt at an apology on my part, pleasure in exchange for putting up with me. I smiled up at him and peace filled me when he finally pulled me off my knees and helped me stand on my unsteady legs.

"Fuckin' shit," he whispered. "Holy fuckin' shit. Just when I think it can't get any better you do something like this."

I giggled then snuggled into Smoke, my emotions all over the place. He wrapped his arms around me and whispered something to me in Spanish about love, and beauty, and a bunch of other stuff I couldn't understand, but the fierce affection in his voice was easy to read. Hell, I felt his adoration in my bones. After an unknown amount of time spent petting each other, a cool wind blew across my bare ass and I realized I my pants were still around my legs.

With a smile at Smoke, I stepped out of his arms and pulled my pants back up and stretched out, arching my back with a contented sigh. As I did that, I noticed a faint, tiny red dot glowing beneath the overhang of the doorway, tucked back and impossible to see if I hadn't been exactly where I was. Curious, I tried to look closer, but it was too far up and hidden away.

"Smoke, can you give me a boost?"

"What?" He finished with his belt, walked over to me and followed my line of sight. "What is it?"

Realizing he couldn't see it because of our height difference, I pointed up. "Just lift me, please."

He boosted me up with ease so my head almost hit the top of the overhang and I frowned as I reached back into the little alcove, my fingers searching for the box and hoping I didn't encounter any spider webs. After a few seconds of groping in the dark, I managed to feel the box and a series of wires coming into and going out of it. I almost ripped it out of there, but left it alone because I had no idea what it was or what it did. For all I know there was a legitimate reason for this electronic device being there, but it didn't make sense that someone would go to such trouble to hide it.

"Okay, put me down."

"What's up?"

I chewed my lip, not wanting to make a big deal out of something that might be totally normal, but my instincts told me there was something wrong here. "There's some kind of electronic device hidden up there."

Smoke had his cell phone out before I finished my sentence. "Hulk? Yeah, I need you up on the roof...No, it's not for a fuckin' threesome. Mention that shit again and I'll personally stomp your face into the ground. Swan found something. Bring a ladder."

He hung up and turned to me, concern drawing the lines on his face tight. "How the hell did you see that?"

"I was stretching out and the flash of red caught my eye."

Shaking his head, he prowled around us, checking the overhang and following the wires to where they disappeared into the wall. I remained silent, not really having anything to offer until we knew if the device was suspicious or not. Knowing that people were on their way up to the roof, I worked on cleaning myself up as much as I could. As I finger-combed my hair Hulk burst through the door with another big man following right behind him. Even in the dim lighting I could see that the stranger's hair was probably a flaming red when the sun shown on it because it burned even in the moonlight and the dim illumination of the access passageway. He was closer to my age than Smoke's, but his serious expression made him seem older.

They all ignored me and turned right away to Smoke.

Hulk frowned at Smoke, his anger easy to read on his tense face. "What did you find?"

"Actually, Swan found it." He glanced at me before turning back to Hulk, and the redhead gave me a curious glance, like he was seeing me standing here for the first time. "Little box with a faint red light on the side. Any idea what it could be?"

"Nothing we put there." Hulk shook his head, then looked over at me with a grim expression. "Good find, little girl, but it's way past your bedtime. Smoke, why don't you go tuck her in then come back."

I wanted to protest that I should stay and see if I could help, but electronic surveillance wasn't my forte. I was fucking beat to the point that my thoughts were slow. My pussy ached from the hard fuck Smoke had given me, and the rest of my muscles were sore from all of our driving and lack of quality sleep. When Smoke gripped my hand in his I didn't protest, well aware of how closely we were being watched. While I didn't like what Hulk said, his voice wasn't sarcastic. I hoped that I'd read him right and he wasn't being a dick.

With my head stuffed full of the events of the evening, I didn't protest when Smoke tucked me into bed with a lingering kiss, or when he gave me my handgun. "Don't be afraid to use it."

I tucked the gun beneath the edge of the mattress within easy reach and was out in less than a minute.

AUSTIN TX

Chapter Nine

When I woke up the next morning it was after nine. I was stiff and felt like I could sleep another six hours, easy. While my mind slowly came online, I realized that the place next to me on the surprisingly comfortable mattress was empty. I vaguely remembered Smoke coming to bed and grabbing me to cuddle like a teddy bear, but other than that, I'd been dead to the world. With a sigh, I wiggled over to his side of the bed and took a deep breath of his scent, then another.

Before I could sit up, the door to the bathroom opened to reveal a damp and unbearably sexy Smoke. The moment he wandered into our small room, he sought me out. When our gazes met, I frowned at how tired he looked even as I basked in the warmth of his slight smirk. His eyes were red and the lines on his handsome face seemed to stand out more. Without thinking, I held my arms open to him, and he melted into me with his version of a happy sigh, which was more like a happy growl.

"Thought of waking up every morning to that smile...I'm a lucky man to have such a sweet baby."

My nether bits tingled and I shifted beneath the covers as his body curved into mine. He rolled off and tugged on his jeans while muttering about temptation and having shit to do. I ogled his tight ass without a drop of shame.

With just his jeans on, the top button unbuttoned, he came back over and picked me up from the bed and cradled me in his arms, holding me close while I peppered kisses on his damp skin. The scent of his soap was strong, and I rubbed my face against his chest, loving every second of being in his arms. He gave me a few tender, soft kisses on my forehead before gently tossing me back on the bed.

I gave a little girly shriek as my body bounced on the springy mattress, then I smiled up at Smoke. "Morning."

He yawned and stretched, making his well-defined muscles flex and dance as he cracked his neck. "Morning. You sleep well?"

"Yeah." I watched with interest as he went over to one of his suitcases on top of the dresser and began to dig through it. "So, you figure out what that thing was?"

"Hulk has his guys are going over it right now. The ginger who was with him last night, Joker, is really good with electronics. Had a bunch of training in the Air Force and shit. His cousin who's also a member of the Denver Iron Horse chapter, Donkey, did the same thing, and they both have their own separate security companies. Anyway, we know for sure that it tapped into the video feeds on the clubhouse along with some other crap."

"Shit," I whispered and looked around the room, wondering if someone had been spying on me the whole time I was in here.

He must have noticed my worried look because he shook his head while jerking on a pair of socks. "I already searched our room. Nothing in here or the bathroom, but they have cameras in some of the public parts of the clubhouse. Breaker's doing a sweep right now, then he's gonna come get you."

I glanced over at the door and rolled out of bed, heading for the bathroom. "Why is he coming to get me?"

While I took care of business, he spoke loud enough that I could hear him through the cheap door. "'Cause you're gonna meet with some of the old ladies today."

"Why do I have to do that? I thought we were looking for my mom and sister?"

When I went back out into our bedroom, Smoke was fully dressed in a pair of faded jeans and a crisp white t-shirt with his cut laying on the rumpled bed next to him. He was fiddling around with his phone, and I wandered over in his direction, stopping before him to run my fingers through his damp curls. My libido wanted me to run my hands over much more satisfying parts of his body, but my mind was occupied with the complex layers of the world I now found myself in.

"Go get dressed, babe." He grabbed my hand and placed a soft kiss on my palm before returning his attention to his phone. "I need you to meet the old ladies so you can get information on your sister and mom. Won't be all bad. They're good women, and I'll be there with Breaker."

"So I'm going to a biker tea party? What does one wear to such an event? I'm afraid Mimi didn't cover that social occasion in her efforts to make me a civilized woman."

He gave me a droll look and raised one eyebrow—I envied his ability to do that. It made him look aloof and…hot. A shiver raced through me, and my nipples hardened to sensitive points. Why the hell could I not be around this man without the sexual tension igniting between us? It was like I woke up hungry for him, as though sleep had deprived me of his touch. Evidently, the feeling was mutual because his gaze darkened, and he glanced at his cell phone, then back at me.

"Do you know what it does to me when you get all sassy like this?" He squeezed his hard cock through his jeans and I clenched the sheets like they were the only thing keeping me from throwing myself at him. "Makes me hard as fuck. Then again, everything you do makes me hard."

I smirked and tried to not act too pleased about his pornographic compliment.

His lips tightened as his teasing expression grew serious. "Now, while I understand you're uncomfortable, you gotta know you're stronger than your fear. You're the strongest woman I know, inside and out. Sometimes I'm a bit afraid of you, but then again, I think sometimes you're afraid of me so that balances us out. Don't be a chicken shit now. You've come too far."

Oh, I hated him at that moment, which perversely, made me want to fuck him all the more. No, not just fuck him, I wanted to seduce him until his control snapped, then ride him until we were both satisfied. And frankly, I didn't give a damn about anything else at the moment. With this lust thrumming through me and a desperate need to escape the pressures of the world, I tempted Smoke with something I knew he would love.

My sister had given me lessons on how to look cute and sexy. At the time, I thought it was part of the act she did for the teen pageants she was in. I didn't realize that she was working as a stripper, underage and behind our mom's back, at one of the better clubs in Vegas— and she was making a killing. Sarah used that money to run away from my mom and bought her freedom from the debts our mother owed. A year later, she surfaced again as one of the best pole dancers in Vegas, and not the stripper kind. Sarah was an athlete. She'd been a high ranking competitive skater before she broke her ankle when she was fifteen, and she used her strength and flexibility to pull off some crazy shit on those three-stories-tall poles she used for her burlesque show. She was incredible, and the raw sensuality Sarah could portray mesmerized crowds at the high-end casino show she starred in. So, I decided to see if I could use those same tricks to get Smoke to give me what I wanted.

It was a very empowering feeling to look up at Smoke from beneath my eyelashes and lightly lick my lower lip. The hitch in his breath hit me like a punch of adrenaline, and I knelt up so my breasts were visible.

Bright sunlight streamed down on me, and I was sure it made my hair glow around my freckled shoulders. Still giving him an almost mocking, shy look, I hesitantly brushed my fingertips over my nipple, squirming a bit at the pleasant sensation. With a soft sigh I pinched the tip and rolled it between my fingers, never looking away from Smoke. His lips curved in a small smile, all satisfied male arrogance.

"Look at my baby getting so bold, trying to take what she wants." His voice rumbled in a rough purr that sent my body into overdrive, and I boldly dipped my fingers beneath the edge of the blanket then stroked my slick, swollen pussy lips. Smoke had fucked me hard enough last night that my sex was a little sore today. After rubbing my clit a couple times I pressed harder, then winced slightly.

That was all it took. Next thing I knew I was on my back with a very concerned Smoke kneeling between my legs, his face close enough to my wet sex that his breath felt cool on my heated flesh. He made a soft groaning sound. "Baby, I forgot how tender you are."

I rolled my eyes and grabbed him by the hair, forcing him to look at me. "Smoke, you didn't hurt me. I'm okay. I'm still a little new to this."

"I'm sorry, sweetheart, I'll take it..."

If the next words coming out of his mouth were to tell me that he wouldn't fuck me hard like I craved I was going to punch him. He started this fire burning inside of me. He was the one who addicted me to his touch, and I was damn sure he was gonna give me his cock even if I had to tie him up, blindfold him, and then cover him in edible body oil and ride him until he was speaking in tongues.

Hmm, that might be fun. Lots of fun.

I didn't realize how deep I was into the fantasy of dominating Smoke until he nipped my clit and I screamed.

"What the hell!"

With a soft growl, he gently stroked my swollen labia. "Damn it. You're aroused and wet as hell, but I can tell that I fucked you too rough last night. I was too hard on you. Baby…you gotta tell me what you were thinking about when you went all quiet. Your pussy started to contract and your hips began to press just into the air like your body was about to take my cock. I watched you drip on the bed. I gotta know what the fuck you were thinking about so I can make whatever fantasy you found so hot come true. Nothing you can say is too dirty for me."

I couldn't help but laugh and blush, shocked by how honest he expected me to be. Still, he had a point. He'd been pretty open with me about what he wanted to do with me while I still avoided talking about it if I could. It was just so…intimate.

"I was thinking about forcing you to eat my pussy."

His grin was all delicious evil and full of soul-damning sin. "Do you want me to fight you?"

"No," I said quickly. "No, I just want to…to make you eat me. To know that you're being forced to do it, even if you really aren't. This is so hard to explain. Just forget it."

"Hey now. Don't get upset. If I know what you want, I'll give it to you. But first," he cuddled me close

171

and nuzzled my throat, "I need to reward you for being so honest with me."

I happily sighed and rolled my head to the side, exposing my heated pulse to his mouth. "Fuck yeah."

He laughed against my throat, and I would have hit him except he palmed my entire pussy and gripped me hard. The feeling was beyond superb, and I let out a soft whine. Still chuckling, he rubbed the heel of his hand over my clit while I gripped his hair. A low groan vibrated through his body over mine, and I reveled in giving myself over to his attentions and completely devoted myself to him. In the middle of all the intense lust mixed with love, I felt calm, safe, protected. The first inhalation against his warm skin filled me and I drew in a greedy lungful of his scent.

"You smell so sweet," he murmured against my throat, "but you taste all dark and tangy, like sex. I'm so fuckin' addicted to you."

I couldn't even tell him the feeling was mutual because his clever fingers where petting and caressing my sex, exploring how wet I was and teasing me until I wanted to snap.

My moans and efforts to get him to touch me harder were having no effect and I was beginning to get pissed off.

"Smoke,"—I was trying not to pant—"touch me."

He waited until I looked at him and when our gazes met he said in a deep, utterly seductive tone, "Make me."

The shudder that went through me almost pitched me straight into orgasm, but Smoke leaned back and wrenched my thighs open, preventing my climax and leaving me desperate to come.

He ran his tongue over his teeth while he stared down at me. "If you want me, you're gonna have to take me. That little pussy of yours needs a gentle touch so I'm gonna make love to you nice and easy, but first you're gonna ride my face until you come all over me."

Chapter Ten

I thought clapping my hands and yelling for joy might be poor bedroom manners, but that didn't mean I didn't give Smoke a huge smile. For a moment, he just stared at me, frozen, then he did a slow blink and smiled back at me. The dark lust was still there in his gaze, but it was banked for a moment by love. His affection poured into me, his amazingly strong will filling up the cracks in my soul the world had dealt me.

"On your back." I helped him along by giving him a push and my clit throbbed with anticipation.

While I didn't want to tie him up, I wanted those talented hands on me, and I couldn't wait to grind myself on his mouth.

Bad.

He tried to turn his face away when I attempted to straddle him, but I held his hair and got into a position that used leverage to my advantage. Not that he was putting up a real fight. It was token at best, but oh, God it made me hot. When I glanced behind me I found his erection dripping with pre-cum. Maybe after I came I'd lick it off his belly then lick him. The thought was somehow dirty to me, and I sucked on my lips while turning my attention back to the lovely view of Smoke's face between my legs.

His eyes were closed and I loved how long his eyelashes looked against his cheeks. I brushed my fingertips over his lashes. "Keep your eyes closed."

To my surprise he obeyed, and when I lowered my pussy over his mouth he twitched beneath me, but didn't make any move to pleasure me.

I hissed in frustration before rubbing my wet sex over his lips. "Eat my pussy."

His lips remained stubbornly closed.

Bracing my hands on the headboard, I tilted my hips and slowly circled my clit against his mouth. "If you make me orgasm hard enough, I'll make sure you come just as hard."

He laughed softly against my labia, and I shivered over him, no longer feeling the least bit in control as his big hands clamped down on my hips.

"Well then, I better make sure I please my little Mistress."

A strangled cry was my only reply as he zeroed in on my clit, quickly driving me almost to climax before he backed off.

Oh shit. He was going to make me pay for my momentary burst of dominance. My man loved control and knowing he was in charge of my pleasure. If I was being honest, giving myself over to him felt as natural as breathing. I loved submitting to him, and he always rewarded me with such wonderful devotion…after my punishment.

Damn.

Sure enough, he continued his oral assault on me, sucking on my clit until I was gripping his head with my thighs. My muscles were tight and his mouth on me was bliss, licking and sucking until I rocked myself against his tongue. Then he totally backed off and used his superior strength to hold me up and away from him just enough to tease me with little glancing licks.

I was about one more tease away from putting him into a submission hold so I could finally get off, but I didn't know if the pain would kill his erection. That would suck.

By now, the shameless harlot inside of me was in firm control, and I begged Smoke to fuck me, to lick me, just do something to make me climax.

His breath stroked over the skin of my wet sex as he whispered, "Time to go for a ride."

I let out a loud squeak as he plucked me off his face and positioned me to straddle his hips like I was a rag doll. When he threw me around like this it made me hotter. When I grasped his thick shaft and gave it a couple strokes before sliding him slowly inside of me, we both shivered. He watched me so intently, looking from where we were joined, up my body and to my face. The muscle in his jaw flexed while he reached up and palmed my breasts, letting their heavy weight rest in his hands before caressing them with a low sigh.

"Gently, baby, or you're gonna be walking around with an ice pack between those pretty legs."

I had to resist the urge to ride him like a bucking bronco, and instead, shifted ever so slightly, gripping him with my internal muscles. I was a little sore but not raw, and when I placed my hands on his chest and

176

slowly slid up, my body automatically clenched down on him, trying to keep him inside of me. Smoke was right. I was greedy for him, and I intended to gorge myself on his love and lust.

Our rhythm was easy, almost relaxing, but it only seemed to make every move all the more perfect. Every inch of my skin tingled and buzzed like I was standing in the middle of a fierce lighting storm. My body was too small to contain my emotions, and I found it was getting easier and easier to give myself over to Smoke all the way and trust him with everything I had. It was a wonderful, blissful feeling to surrender myself to him. As I looked down into his unguarded gaze I wondered if he felt the same.

Gripping my hips lightly, Smoke snarled at me and tilted my pelvis so I wasn't sitting straight upright, but rather curved over him so more of our torsos touched. A droplet of sweat gleamed as it ran down his cheek and I leaned forward, pressing our bodies flush while I licked the sweat from his warm skin. The taste of him exploded on my tongue and caused my body to tighten sending me rushing to my orgasm. Normally, Smoke seemed to like to control my climaxes, but today he let me rub myself against him with abandon as long as I kept the movements slow and gentle.

He wrapped his arms around me and held me close, our combined scent cocooning us while the sunlight further warmed my skin. The strong lines of his broad shoulders flexed and rippled, physical representations of the power and discipline of this man. His determination was reflected in everything he did and in all of his interactions with other people, including me. I loved the hell out of it when he controlled me in the bedroom, but there was something to be said for the slow slide of our skin together, for the way he kept whispering my name, calling me baby, each precise movement devastatingly gentle.

His thick cock stroked me over and over, driving me higher until he held me imprisoned in his arms while I strained to go faster and harder, to fuck my orgasm out.

"You wanna come for me," he growled out and I smiled against his skin, knowing that he wouldn't be able to resist the need to own my release.

"I want to squeeze down on your cock and take you with me."

He tensed beneath me and began to circle his hips while I continued to ride him just a little bit faster, enough that I entered that hyperaware state where everything became more—more intense, more beautiful, more everything. Time shifted and stretched like pulled taffy while we made love. Just when I thought I couldn't take this leisurely pace anymore, he gripped my hair and forced me to look at him.

"Who do you belong to?"

"You, Smoke."

"Who do you love?"

"You, Miguel."

The chords of his neck stood out when he lifted his head to mine and kissed me, as the perfect angle of his muscled groin rubbed against my hard clit just right. Fierce waves of pleasure overtook me. Each muscle twitch sent more gratification through my nerve endings, until I shouted his name and writhed on top of him while he held me as tight as he could and emptied himself in me.

The noises he made while he came were enough to arouse me all over again even as I drifted down from my own blissful orgasm. Resting my cheek on his chest I absently stroked the sparse hair on his arms, humming to myself while I enjoyed my post orgasmic bliss. I felt so connected to him, so loved, and I was trying with all my might to avoid thinking about the day to come. The small, scared, dependent part of me my father had tried so hard to destroy wanted to spend the rest of the day hiding here with my man, but I knew Smoke would never allow that.

Sure enough, his muscles flexed beneath my cheek as he sighed. "Time to get up, sweetheart. We have a brunch we need to get to and a traitor to catch."

His perfect, bronze skin gleamed in the sunlight, and I let out an appreciative sigh as he stood. He really was too fucking hot for his own good. "You think one of them is a spy?"

"The old ladies?"

"Yeah." I walked into the bathroom to quickly wash the remains of our activities away with a brief shower.

There was silence while I cleaned up, and by the time I came back, he was looking at his cell phone with a frown, busily typing something.

Whatever he was reading wasn't making him happy if the anger coming off of him was any indication, and I tensed as well, my body reacting to his non-verbal language. I watched him begin to pace, and my pulse picked up, throwing off the lingering afterglow from good sex. The only time my man paced was when he was struggling to hold back some strong emotion, usually rage.

Fear tried to worm its way further into my heart, but I concentrated instead on getting dressed in a pair of cute jeans, with elaborate stitching on the back pockets, and a lovely orange and pink bra that matched my panties. When he growled, I turned my back and tried to apply my lip gloss with a shaking hand, before giving up and watching in the mirror as Smoke paced behind me. When I'd first met him, I would have wanted to stop him from pacing, to try to calm him down, but now I knew him well enough to realize that this was his form of downloading. For Smoke, his ground-eating strides somehow soothed him, so I left him alone and slipped on my wrist cuffs, admiring the gleam of silver in the sunlight coming in through the partially opened shades and sheer, white curtains.

A harsh sigh escaped him when he finally stilled and met my eyes in the mirror. "It's not outside the realm of possibility that one of them may be a traitor."

As soon as the word traitor left Smoke's lips, memories of my father lecturing me on how traitors were the lowest of the low, the scum of the earth, raced through my mind. If there was a rat among the old ladies, I was gonna find her, fear of meeting new people or not. I would find a way to get through this and bring us a huge leap forward in my efforts to get this fucking hit off my head, and bring Sarah home. With this in mind, I turned back to look Smoke in the eye and he grinned. With his words, the training from my dad kicked in, and I gave him a slow nod as my mind

180

shifted from 'Swan, the woman' to 'Swan, the battle-trained survivor'.

"What do you want me to do?"

"Easy, mama bear. I don't need you clawin' anyone's face off."

That brought me out of my cold space a little bit and I shrugged. "I'm going to do what has to be done."

Still smiling at me, he nodded, and the light caught the hints of amber in his eyes, turning the irises to the color of melted chocolate. "I know you will. But for right now, just check them out. The traitor could be acting independently of her old man as well, so if a woman seems real unhappy with her man, she might be a suspect. Or if she seems really happy with everything, that might trip your female ESP as well."

"My female ESP?"

"Yeah, you know, that chick intuition shit. Look, we don't have time to sit around and bullshit right now. If we did I'd still be fuckin' you instead of talkin'. Damn woman, I can't seem to be around you without wanting you beneath me."

Heat rushed through me, and I squeezed my thighs together to try and stop the initial ache of arousal. "Okay."

My voice came out in a high-pitched squeak that made him chuckle. Not knowing what the day would bring, I chose a loose, long-sleeved, pink, silky shirt with a tight, white tank top beneath that, which was also a waist holster. As I got dressed, I waited for Smoke to come molest me, but he remained on the bed and focused on whatever he was texting. A renewed sense of purpose filled me, but there was also a growing sense of loss at being away from the safety Smoke provided me. He was the only person here I trusted, and I wasn't a big fan of being in unfamiliar environments, even if he would be there with me.

"Baby, what'cha thinkin' so hard about?"

Before I could stop the words, I said what I was really thinking. "I don't want to be away from you."

He sighed and looked up, watching me as I hid a variety of weapons. The weary look left his face and a slight smile curved his lips. "Make sure you don't go through any metal detectors."

Strapping a sheathed throwing knife to my forearm, I glanced up and raised my eyebrows. "Ha. Ha."

"I'll be there, but you'll be on your own with the women. If I hung out with you, it would be totally out of character."

I placed my handgun into its holster on my waist before securing it in place and tugging my shirt down.

As I moved this way and that in the mirror to make sure the gun couldn't be seen through the tank and shirt, Smoke laughed. "Does that thing have a laser sight on it?"

"Of course. Never hurts to have that little bit of extra help, but I don't use it much. If I relied on it, I'd be a shitty shot at night."

"Wouldn't you worry that the laser would show them where you are?"

"Not really. When I shoot, I shoot to kill."

"Baby, sometimes you scare me."

"Ditto."

Instead of being offended he smiled. "You'll be fine. I'm not sending you into the lion's den, just brunch with some chicks. What can I do to make this easier for you?"

"It…it would be easier for me if I had a mission goal." As soon as those words left my mouth I bit my lower lip.

Way to remind Smoke that I'm a freak.

For a long moment he studied me and I tried to keep my face blank, betraying neither my worry nor my embarrassment, but I was pretty sure I wasn't too successful if my burning cheeks were any indication. When he spoke, his voice was a soothing purr, and I knew he'd read me like a book. "You'll be fine. These women are connected to their community, they know lots and lots of people, a different group of citizens than their old men have access too. I need you to hang out with them. Tell them about your mother and sister, what they're like, and about places your mom and sister would be likely to go to. Those women have roots here, and that means they have lots of friends. They know people, and while the old ladies may not be able to go out looking for your family like my brothers can, they will have contacts that they'll use if they like you."

"But wouldn't that be giving the traitor, if there is one there, information they can use against us?"

"Not really. You're a very smart woman, Swan. You know what to say and when to shut up. I'm sure your dad trained you on hidden interrogation techniques."

Actually, he was right. If I fell back on my training, treated this like one of my dad's messed up tests, I could get through it. I wouldn't approach them like a woman meeting another group of women for the first time, like one of my teenage nightmares of rejection by the cool kids coming to life. I would treat this like I was interrogating suspects. Some steel returned to my spine and I was grateful that Smoke helped me find a way to deal with this.

Now I just hoped I didn't let him down.

I chewed on my lower lip while brushing my hair. "I don't know how helpful I'll be. I mean, I'm not the easiest person to get along with, and I'm not very good at schmoozing."

By not very good I meant horrible, but Smoke just shook his head. "Don't sell yourself short, baby girl. You're an amazing woman, smart, funny, and loyal to the bone. You'll be fine."

I watched in silence as he armed himself with a gun and a couple knives along with a pair of brass knuckles and a shiny silver Zippo lighter. "What are you going to be doing?"

"None of your business," He said it in a gentle voice, but I fucking hated those words.

"Why is it none of my business?" I gritted out through clenched teeth as I tried to keep my temper from flaring to life.

He obviously caught my tone because when he looked up while adjusting his shoulder harness his expression was guarded. "'Cause it isn't. You let me worry about handling my end and keep yourself alive. That is your number one mission goal. Live."

I took a deep breath and tried to calm myself down, but my anxiety level was getting higher by the moment. I could feel my inner bitch beginning to wake up as I began to go on the defensive.

"So I'm just supposed to trust that you're off taking care of business while I sit around and chat?"

I swore a chill raced through the room as displeasure tightened his features and goosebumps broke out over my skin. "You don't trust me?" Uh-oh. Obviously, I had inadvertently struck a nerve. "I do trust you."

"Then trust me when I say it's none of your business."

My emotions were flip-flopping between being pissed and wanting to soothe Smoke. "You do understand that's really screwed up, don't you? That it's crap of the highest order? If I said that to you, I have no doubt you'd throw a huge hissy."

"A hissy?"

The humor in his gaze made me want to smack him. "You know what I mean."

Smoke's phone beeped, and as he read the message, his face closed down into a cold, unreadable mask. While he typed he spoke in a tight voice, "Look, I don't have time for your chick bullshit right now, Swan. Can't you, just once, do what you're fuckin' told without riding my ass about it? Shit, I'm tryin' my best to keep you alive, but I can't do it if you're gonna fight me every step of the way. If you don't trust me, it could get us both killed. Like I don't have enough of a clusterfuck to deal with right now."

I stood there in hurt silence while he gathered up his shit. The part of me that needed to please the people I loved in my life wanted to apologize, but my inner bitch was having none of that. It was taking all my self-control not to pick a real fight with Smoke right now, but I had enough sense to know that this wasn't the time or the place. However, that didn't mean Smoke and I weren't gonna have a conversation in the near future about what kind of shit I would and would not deal with from him. Like dismissing me as though I was a moron who couldn't handle the truth.

I sucked in a deep breath and willed myself not to cry. Did I really want to be with a man who doubted me so much? Did I want to spend the rest of my life with someone who hid things from me? Memories of Smoke holding me like I was his lifeline, the way he looked at me, how sincere he sounded when he said he loved me battled with the fact that at times he could be a royal dick. I couldn't help but wonder if, in a screwed up way, I loved Smoke because he could be like my father, harsh yet caring. The ramifications of that thought scared me down to my bones, and I sucked in some deep breaths while staring at my reflection in the mirror and fighting off a panic attack. I didn't have time to freak out right now. It was an indulgence I had to ignore, because losing my shit right now could prove deadly. There was a knock on the door that startled me enough I dropped my brush on the dresser.

Before I could move, Smoke had his gun out and was standing to the side of the door. "Who is it?"

"It's Breaker."

Smoke holstered his gun before he opened the door and allowed the other man to stroll in. Breaker was wearing a faded Aerosmith t-shirt beneath his patched up vest and a pair of broken in jeans that flattered his lean waist. He gave me a quick once over, then turned his attention to Smoke. "You crazy kids ready to go?"

186

Smoke nodded, his attention back on his phone. "That tip we got earlier, any results?"

"Yeah," Breaker's gaze darted my way and then back to Smoke again. "We can talk about it at my house."

The men exchanged a look that was loaded with meaning only they understood before Breaker turned his charming smile on me. "You ready to go, doll?"

"Sure." I went to grab my helmet, but Smoke stopped me.

"You'll be riding with Breaker in his cage."

"My SUV," Breaker supplied helpfully at my puzzled look.

"What? Why can't I ride with you, Smoke?"

"Too dangerous, too exposed on my bike right now. I want you safe."

Obviously trying to lighten the situation, Breaker smiled at me. "Don't look so bummed out. I'll let you control the radio."

I shrugged, unable to form an answer for fear that I'd start crying over something as stupid as my feelings being hurt because I wouldn't be riding behind Smoke.

My man came over and gave me a soft kiss on the forehead. "Love you, be safe."

With that, I was left standing in the middle of the room trying to make sense of the events of the past few days, the here and now, and what was about to happen. With the way my mind worked sometimes, this was proving difficult if not impossible. I was good with straight logic, a whiz with numbers, great at calculating risks, but human beings utterly stumped me, and I hated how easily I was thrown off my stride.

Breaker ran his hand through his curly blond hair and sighed. "Girl, you gotta toughen up."

Those words cut through my scrambled thoughts, and I stood up straighter. No one accused Mike Anderson's daughter of not being tough. My breath hitched a bit, but I scrubbed at my face then busied myself with going through my pack. "Give me a second and I'll be ready."

When I grabbed my backpack with two of my dad's homemade grenades hidden in it, Breaker raised his eyebrows. "You don't got a purse?"

"My purse won't carry all of what I need."

The white lines around his eyes narrowed. "And what the fuck do you think you'll need at my home?"

"Never hurts to be prepared." Smoke's words about my lack of trust began to invade my thoughts, but I pushed them back into a corner of my mind to be dealt with later. If there was a later. "The people looking for me won't give a shit where I am. If they want me bad enough they'll come for me, and I have to make sure I'm ready for them at all times."

"Paranoid," he said with a small smile. "I like it. Makes it easier to keep you alive. Don't worry, my house is secure. You think I'd let anyone or anything near my old lady and kids?"

I tilted my head in acknowledgement. "Ready?"

We quickly made our way through the clubhouse, stopping a couple times so Breaker could introduce me to a couple different guys he called Enforcers. They treated me like I was a visiting dignitary, and soon, Breaker and I were going out the front door. I honestly had expected Smoke to be waiting for me on his bike, but only nature surrounded me as we got into Breaker's SUV. I buckled myself in and noticed a small, plush, pink panda on the floor of the vehicle. I retrieved it and held it up to Breaker with a small smile.

"This yours?"

He chuckled while we pulled out of the lot. "Toss it in back with the girls' other crap. I swear I clean their shit out of my cars constantly or it ends up looking like I have a fuckin' yard sale goin' on in my back seat."

The rough affection in his voice made me smile. "How old are they?"

"Eight, eleven, and fifteen." He gave a mock shudder. "All beautiful like their Mom."

I couldn't help but laugh, seeing shades of my father in Breaker in an odd way. "Oh, man, you're in trouble."

He sighed. "Don't I know it."

We were both quiet for the remainder of the ride, and I used that time to try to process everything that was going on or zoning out while I listened to the classic rock station Breaker had playing.

Around thirty minutes later, we pulled up to a really nice ranch house in a gated community with an amazing view of the mountains, and I blinked in surprise. This was a very pretty mega-home, perfectly landscaped, with a white Mercedes SUV in the drive along with a black Corvette, and a mini-van. Parked next to the Corvette was a motorcycle I was not familiar with, and I wondered if Smoke was already here and if that was his borrowed bike.

Breaker parked his SUV behind the white one and turned off the engine. He looked at me for a moment, studying my expression, before he said in a low voice, "Ain't none of my fuckin' business how my brother handles his woman, but I will say you gotta give Smoke a chance to figure things out. This shit with you is all very, very new to him and I know he's fuckin' crazy about you. Guy's crazy in general, but with you, he's a certified psycho."

I didn't disagree with this so I simply nodded, not sure what Breaker was getting at.

"Kid, one thing marriage has taught me is that communication is essential. You gotta listen to each other or you're never gonna work. You make him happy in a way I've never seen so I want you two to work. Even if you do turn him into a madman, you're good for Smoke, and it's obvious to everyone that he worships you. When a man is that wrapped up in a woman, he doesn't always think rationally, and sometimes he'll say stupid shit, but that doesn't mean he doesn't love you. Just means fear is running his mouth. Plus, you two are still learning each other. I've been married to my woman since we were seventeen, and I feel like I hardly know her even now. Show a little kindness to the man while he figures out how not to be an asshole."

My mind flashed to the clothing that his sister bought me and how much it meant to me when I realized that he understood he'd fucked up, and apologized in his own way by having her buy me some amazing outfits.

"Here we go. You ready to meet the old ladies?"

Before I could respond he was out of the car, and I had no choice but to follow him. The front door of the picture perfect home opened, and I half expected Donna Reed in all her pearl-clad glory to come stepping out. Instead, the auburn haired woman who greeted us was probably an inch or two taller than I was and blindingly attractive. She was dressed in a pair of black yoga pants and an oversized, stylish blue shirt along with Kermit the Frog socks, and she glowed with happiness. I swear she reminded me of Tawny Kitaen back when she was hot. As soon as her gaze landed on Breaker, a genuine warmth sparkled in her eyes that matched her bright smile. Her love for Breaker beamed from her like sunlight, and I wondered if that was what I looked like when I looked at Smoke.

Tears filled my eyes even as I scolded myself for acting like an emotional flake. We walked up the steps, and the woman gave me an odd look before she said to Breaker, "What did you do to make her cry?"

He actually looked panicked, and I took pity on him, not wanting to get his wife upset by a misunderstanding. "It's okay, he didn't do anything. Smoke was just acting like an asshole earlier."

I winced as the words poured out and waited for the stare that would silently ask if I was mental.

Clear, loud laughter poured out of the redhead, and there was nothing but understanding humor shining in her eyes. "Oh, honey, they're all assholes. No wonder he was so pissy when he pulled up a few minutes ago. Come on inside, everyone's on the back porch."

She ushered me in, and I noticed she didn't try to shake my hand or touch me in any other way. The home was as pretty on the inside as outside, decorated in bright, modern colors, and I could faintly hear women's voices coming from somewhere deeper in the house. The redhead turned to me with a smile. "My name's Cathy, and I'm a friend of your sister's."

"Hi, I'm Swan," my voice faltered, "I'm...I think I'm still Smoke's old lady."

She cut her gaze to Breaker and frowned. "What's going on?"

Breaker sighed and rubbed his face. "Young love between a stubborn woman and her pig-headed man. Not that we would know what that's like. They're good, trust me, Smoke is totally pussy-whipped."

With a giggle and a fond look at her husband, Cathy shook her head. "I've been waiting for years for Smoke to find the right woman. It'll be nice to see someone stand up to him, but I'll warn you now—that man is stubborn."

Breaker made a disgruntled noise. "I'm going down to the basement. Try not to fill her head with too much bullshit, and send Smoke down when you're done with him."

"Prick," Cathy said in a low whisper as she wrapped her arms around his neck.

They exchanged a long, lingering kiss that made me feel like I was intruding on their privacy. When their lips finally parted, Breaker whispered something in her ear that made her laugh, and she smacked his thick bicep before he let her go. She whispered something in his ear and giggled again when he growled a response. I wished Smoke was here. Pathetic but true. I felt so lost without him. I realized I was being very, very melodramatic and oversensitive, but I couldn't help it. Considering Smoke was my second boyfriend—maybe my first, because I couldn't count a guy who used me to cover up the fact that he was gay as a true relationship—I was way behind the curve ball on experience in a romance and dealing with new people in general.

Cathy smiled at me and said in a cheery voice, "Come on, honey. I've got us set up in the solarium and we have lots, and lots of booze to drown your sorrows."

"Thanks."

I trailed after her as she led me through the lavish home and into a solarium filled with plants in delicate, ornate pots. There was a comfortable seating area with a low glass table loaded with food and a rolling cart filled with alcohol and mixers. Overhead fans kept the room cool, and the vast windows were tinted enough that it cut down on the sun's glare.

Two other women sat around the table while the third was mixing a cocktail at the small bar on the other side of the room, while talking with Smoke. They were leaning close together, and Smoke had a smile on his face as he looked at the pretty blonde who grinned up at him. My jealousy began to roar to the surface. I managed to choke it back down after I noticed the large diamond ring on the other woman's finger as she poured some champagne into the crystal flute sitting in front of her, which contained what I assumed was orange juice. That didn't mean I was keen on the way she casually touched Smoke—not in the least—but I managed not to launch myself at her and rip her hand off his arm.

Jesus, I had to get a fucking grip before I started attacking any woman who even looked at Smoke.

Smoke seemed to sense my gaze on him. He quickly scanned the room until he saw me standing in the doorway, staring at him and the woman now sipping her drink and studying me with dark hazel eyes. She was a cute blonde, but not a threat. My gaze focused on her hand that appeared to brush against Smoke's firm ass and my fists clenched.

My attention was taken from her when Smoke crossed the room in three big strides, then lifted me by my waist to give me a devastating kiss that left me a little flushed by the time he released me. That delicious warmth curled through me, but I tried to not be distracted from my anger by his sudden demonstration of affection.

All too aware of the women watching us, and wanting to put on a united front, I reached up and buried my hands in his curls, tightening my grip enough that it must have stung as I whispered, "We're gonna have a talk, later."

His smile faded, but he nodded and leaned forward, forcing me to gentle my grip on his silky curls as he rubbed his nose over mine. "Later, when I can properly spank your round ass. Love it when your skin is all red and warm."

I snarled at him, but he laughed—the bastard—and gave me another gentle kiss before he turned me to face the room and wrapped me up in the warmth of his strong arms.

"I gotta go handle some business, but I wanted to introduce you to my old lady, Swan."

They all squealed and started talking at once, each expressing how happy she was to meet me. As I studied their faces, the pretty black woman in jeans and a red t-shirt, the blonde with dimples to match her cute smile who'd been talking with Smoke, and a dark-skinned brunette with full, red, painted lips, I tried to spot something that would tip me off as to their true intentions. I was pretty sure they were friendly. Still, my normal—or was it abnormal—reserve made me hang back.

In a stark contrast to their cheerful greetings, my hello was rather cold.

Smoke kissed my temple then released me. It took a great deal of effort not to cling to him, but when he whispered, "Remember your mission," I found the strength to let him go without too much pouting.

Cathy, who seemed to be a born hostess, gestured to a vacant chair, and I gratefully sank into its padded surface, nervous now that I was alone with these unfamiliar people. The other women arranged themselves around the table as the pretty black woman introduced herself as Sheena, the blonde as Alisha, and the woman with the full red lips as Bettie. Then Alisha poured shots for us and brought them to the table, handing me one then passing the rest out. As I studied the clear liquid that I was pretty sure was vodka, I slumped into the seat, worrying about Smoke while they introduced themselves. I was so nervous my answers were only one or two words.

The other women must have been talking to me for a bit before Cathy tried to get my attention. "Swan?"

I jerked, almost spilling my drink, and looked up to find them all watching me with confusion. "Sorry, my mind is elsewhere. Please forgive me for being rude. Thank you so much for going to all this effort on my behalf."

"What's bothering you?" Alisha asked in a soft voice. I couldn't tell if her concern was genuine or faked.

"I'd bet it's that six foot four package of trouble downstairs," Cathy said with a soft laugh. "Smoke said you were very new to the MC lifestyle, Swan."

"You could say that," I said with a sigh, trying to get my mind back on track. I should have been the one asking the questions here, but I was simply overwhelmed and tense. Something was tickling my senses, but I couldn't say exactly what it was. Maybe it was just my unease with being in a new place with new people.

"Now," Sheena said in a low, smooth voice while toying with one of her shoulder length dreadlocks, "why is your man being a fucktard? We've all been in the MC lifestyle for a long time now, and we might be able to give you some advice on living with a biker. They're pissy bastards, but they're also some of the best men you'll ever come across."

My mind wanted to lay out my problems for them and hope they had an answer, but I didn't trust them. I felt like I'd somehow be betraying Smoke if I talked about out private life, so I settled for the obvious. "Sweet butts."

A collective sigh came from the table and more than one woman lifted her glass and drank.

Cathy leaned over and squeezed my leg, "Don't let those bitches and their useless drama get to you."

"Fuck 'em," Bettie said with a great deal of heat in her voice. "When Frame and I first got together they tried to rip us apart, jealous that I'd managed to get a man they considered theirs."

"Frame? Is that his umm....road name?"

Alisha grinned, "Yep. Don't ask how he got it. You really don't want to know."

I almost asked anyway, then remembered the fucked up ways these bikers earned their names. "Understood."

With a sigh Sheena sat forward and refilled her shot glass from the bottle of clear liquor on the table. "I don't know how much experience you've had with MCs, but sweet butts will always, *always* be a part of your world. Like cockroaches, as soon as you get rid of one, another will take her place. We ignore them because they really aren't worth our time, and we know our men are faithful. Don't get me wrong, there are plenty of couples in our clubhouse where the man fucks anything that moves, but it's their business how they want to live their lives. Personally, Oak is my old man, my husband, and I let him know that if he screwed around on me I'd super glue his balls to his asshole. Some guys would have told me to fuck off and gone right on taking advantage of the free pussy, but Oak isn't like them, and I trust him."

There was something about Sheena's expression that caught my attention, and it snapped me out of my funk as I remembered the real reason I was here, and it wasn't to bitch about boys. Cupping my face in my hands, I took a deep breath to center myself. If someone here was a traitor it might help if they saw me as a weak woman, someone unsure about her relationship and vulnerable. It might make them slip up. Okay, so maybe I *was* unsure and vulnerable, but I could use that to my advantage. I looked up and found all the women watching me sympathetically.

"I want to trust Smoke, I do, but he…he yelled at me. Embarrassed me in front of other people. In front of the slut who was trying to shove her way into our room with her two skanky friends."

"Ohhhh," Bettie sighed as she refilled my glass. "That sucks."

Cathy frowned at me and sat back on the couch next to Alisha. "Which sluts?"

I rattled off the description of Slut #1 and Slut #2, then said the name Cyclone.

At the mention of her, all of the other women hissed with displeasure. The sound was so odd, like I was in the middle of a roomful of angry cats, that I couldn't help but laugh. It was funny, or at least what passed for funny to my alcohol-hazed brain. Realizing I was drinking on an empty stomach, I began to dig into the snack-type foods spread out before us. My hunger had returned with a drunken vengeance. The women all told me horror stories about Cyclone thinking she owned every man in the clubhouse. Alisha told me that on one of her infrequent visits to the clubhouse, she'd had the displeasure of glimpsing Cyclone in the middle of a group of bikers who were all jerking off on her face. When they came, she looked like a glazed donut.

I gagged and eyed the chocolate croissant in my hand, suddenly nauseous. I mean if that's your thing, awesome, but the germs…I'd bet she didn't screen those vile ass men for diseases before they shot one out in her face. "Fucking nasty."

"Totally," Sheena agreed. "I had to beat that bitch's ass until she got the message to stop messing with my man."

Looking back to Alisha, then Sheena, I took a bite of my cookie. "I thought the old ladies didn't come to the clubhouse? That you uh...didn't like to fight?"

"Girl," Bettie said with a husky laugh, "We don't go to the clubhouse because the sweet butts are the younger guys' problem. For the most part, they don't fuck with us and we don't fuck with them. For some, it's the thrill of bad boy cock. For others, it's what they like to do. For yet others, it's a way for them to try and get as much from a man as they can before he moves on. Or, as one bitch who tried to fuck my husband right in front of me said, 'guilt-free pussy'."

I made a little growling noise that was echoed around the room by the other women.

Huh, guess I wasn't the only woman who had a possessive streak that bordered on crazy.

Nodding at me and what I was sure was my disgusted expression, Bettie continued. "The fact that those transient women practically have the run of the place is the younger guys' fault. They need to learn to deal with their whores, not rely on other women to keep their sluts in place. I'm the fucking old lady of the Road Master. I'm not some fuckin' madam who'll keep their sluts in line, and they know better than to involve me in their shit. They do and my old man'll have a word about respect. They don't like it? That's their fuckin' problem."

"They also know better than to mess with Breaker," Cathy added in a slightly slurred voice. She'd had three drinks while I'd been here, and her lightly freckled cheeks were rosy. "And what Sheena said is true. Our guys, while scary as hell, are more than capable of taking care of themselves, don't care enough about the sluts to deal with them. They're hangers-on, bitches that just go in and out of the free-pussy-revolving-door of the clubhouse. Sad but true, these women really don't matter all that much to the men, so they don't see them as a real threat. And the older guys aren't going to waste their time babysitting skanks. So, until the younger guys man the fuck up and take care of their business, we're just staying away from the clubhouse other than for rides and family events."

"My advice to you," Alisha said while leaning forward enough to give a glimpse of her deep cleavage, "is to talk to your man about it when you're both calm."

My hands unclenched and ached as the blood rushed back into my fingers. Okay, I'd spilled my guts to them so hopefully that would get some of the other women to reveal things they shouldn't. I just had to listen carefully and try to find a pattern of behavior, or a break in one. That would be my first breadcrumb.

I hung out with the women, learning about the ins and outs of life as an old lady in the Iron Horse MC. They were surprisingly honest, telling me about the hard lessons they'd learned along the way. I found myself really liking these women and hoping none of them were betraying the club. As far as I could tell, they all seemed to be pretty legitimate, but the alcohol snuck up on me and I often forgot that I was supposed to be interrogating them.

Cathy rubbed her face after laughing until she cried as Bettie told outrageous stories about growing up in an MC out east, then set her glass down with a sigh. "Now, let's talk about the three hundred-pound gorilla in the room, your mom and sister."

All the women stared at me, and I struggled to decide how to handle this. Tension began to electrify the air, and all the good humor left their eyes. They were just as scary as their biker counterparts in an odd way. You could tell by looking at them, if you pissed them off, you would regret it. Then again, I didn't want them to see me as a threat. It really irked my pride to appear weak, but the sympathy card had worked for me so far so I let the tears come to my eyes as I whispered, "I'm so worried about them."

Just like that the uncomfortable energy dissipated. I tried not to flinch as Alisha patted my hand, her touch sending an electrical storm of misfiring nerve impulses through my muscles and skin. It took an enormous amount of effort, but I managed to keep my stomach under control while I moved my hand away from Alisha's touch.

They all made soothing murmurs and comments, each one saying nice things about Sarah. To me they all seemed sincere, but I thought Stewart had been honestly in love with me as well, so what the hell did I know? They finally settled down, and I tried to keep breathing normally while I waited to find out if they could help me or not.

Cathy spoke up first. "I met Sarah when she was here with Beach, and I've gotta say, I'd be more scared about her coming after me than some of the men."

With a laugh Bettie sat back and shook her head. "That bitch can throw a punch."

I looked around the circle of women. "What happened?"

"What happened," Alisha said with a small smirk, "Is that Tila got into it with Sarah but Tila was fuckin' Sm...ummm..."

I stiffened and tried to keep the smile on my face. "It's okay, I'm aware that Smoke had a rather...sordid sexual history before we got together."

"Right," Cathy said as she briskly rubbed her hands together. "So anyway..."

With perfectly horrible timing Smoke's voice rang through the room, "Babe?"

It took a great deal of effort to turn my head and smile at him, but I think I managed okay. "Yes?"

Tension filled his expression and he crooked his finger at me. "Come here."

I wanted to snarl at him that I wasn't his puppy to come and fetch when he called, but I once again played the role of dutiful old lady and went to his side. There had better be a big plate of brownies in my future for putting up with this shit. When he went to reach for me I stepped back, but he only took a big step forward and crowded me against the frame of the doorway. I stared up at him, loving and hating him for having shared such an intimate act with other women, while he examined my face.

"I don't know what they said to you, but I need you to focus past it for a second. Please baby girl. There is some important shit I gotta share with you."

Compared to the effort it took to let go of my anger, doing a hundred mile hike with no shoes seemed like a breeze. I'd never realized just how hard it was to control my temper, and I wondered if this was how my father felt before he flipped out. It was the memory of being on the receiving end of his anger that gave me the strength to swallow those destructive emotions down like jagged shards of glass tearing up my throat.

He cupped my face and stroked my cheeks as he whispered, "I got a text from Mimi. Now, I've gotta go, but Breaker will take you back to the clubhouse."

"Mimi?"

My heart lurched and I grasped his forearms as his hands slid to my shoulders. The child inside of me who worshiped my stepmother hoped that she'd found a way out of this mess for me even as my adult mind scolded me for thinking everything would end so easily. Smoke nodded and something dark and scary passed through his gaze.

"Yeah. Evidently Mimi has contacted your grandfather and he was not pleased with the situation. Mimi said there are a couple of your Stefano cousins either in town or on their way. She wouldn't tell me which, only that they'd remain out of sight and not contact you directly for fear of tipping the Russians off and starting a war between the two families."

I sucked in a quick breath. "Holy fucking shit."

"Yeah, just when I thought this clusterfuck couldn't get more complicated here comes the Stefano mafia." A small smirk twitched his lips. "Should I expect some of your daddy's special ops friends to be stopping by?"

"Probably, but if they do, we won't see them," I muttered. Crap, I should have known my parents weren't going to let us drive away without interfering. I prayed that my dad wouldn't show up here. With his temper, he'd be beating up bikers left and right for looking at me. "Did she say which cousins?"

"No, only that they're not 'officially' here, although they are here because your grandfather loves you and is worried. They won't be contacting us unless absolutely necessary in an effort to stay under the radar."

"So, I guess she decided there was something going on that she needs to share with you." I tried not to be upset that Mimi didn't want me to help, I mean, yes, I was a big, blonde, walking target, but it still stung like I'd been rejected somehow.

With a tender touch Smoke rubbed his thumb over my lips. "You miss her, yeah?"

"Yeah." I sighed. "Give her my love, please."

"If I see her, I will. For all I know I'll be meeting with one of your cousins."

The muscles in my jaw tightened as I considered my macho, protective, overbearing, prone-to-thuggish-behavior cousins. "Tell them if they breathe on you wrong, I'll be coming for them."

He laughed. "Damn, you're cute. Not because I don't think you couldn't kick their ass, but because you would."

The thump of boots hitting wood floors came from our right, and Breaker appeared at the end of the hallway, his curly blond hair in disarray, as he stepped over a pink toy convertible with a doll shoved haphazardly inside. "We've got confirmation of the drop-off."

All the warmth abruptly went out of Smoke, and he released me. "Gotta go. Breaker, anything happens to her and I'm coming for you."

"You go take care of your shit. I'll guard your old lady like she's my own. There's some stuff I need to square away first, then we'll head out."

Smoke went to step away, but I caught the front of his shirt and hauled him down to me for a quick, hard kiss before whispering against his lips, "You annoy the fuck out of me, but I love you, so please come back to me in one piece."

He pulled me into a tight hug then abruptly released me. "Ditto."

I took in a deep, shuddering breath as I watched Smoke walk away before I turned back to Breaker. "How long until you're ready?"

"Not too long—hour or two maybe. Go hang out with the old ladies, and I'll come get you in a few."

"Okay."

None of the women asked me what was going on, and I found it odd until I realized that this secrecy was normal for them. They were used to the cloak and dagger bullshit that came with club life and their nonchalance put me at ease. We talked about places my mom and sister could probably be, and by the time I had to leave, I felt like I wasn't any closer to finding my family than before, but I might have made some new friends who seemed to genuinely like me. We exchanged numbers, and I promised them that once things calmed down we would hang out.

Once Breaker and I were on the road he glanced over at me. "Feel better? Old ladies help you figure some shit out?"

I nodded and shifted to adjust the gun in my waistband. With my ebbing adrenaline, lack of quality sleep, and the drinks, I was pooped. Hell, it was only the middle of the afternoon, and I was ready for a nap. "Yeah. They're really nice."

"Cathy is a good judge of character, and she likes you. I'd hazard a guess she's circling the wagons around you right now, and Sheena is calling her girls to see if there's any gossip going around about Billie. Looks like you got their seal of approval. They'll move heaven and earth to help ya now."

"What do you mean?"

"Old ladies look out for each other. Alisha's husband, Donkey, had some medical problems last year, and the old ladies took care of them both, cleaned their house, made 'em food, all that shit." He sighed. "Don't get me wrong, some of the old ladies are cunts, but those women back at my house are some of the good ones."

That caught my attention, and I watched Breaker while we pulled out of his neighborhood and onto the main road leading out of his subdivision. While we'd been inside, the sky to the west had clouded up, and I was pretty sure it was going to start pouring soon. The air smelled like rain, and I could see some dark clouds piling up over the mountains.

"And who would the cunts be?"

"Just a few of the old ladies who have chips on their shoulders, nothing to worry about."

"Still, I'd feel better if I knew who they were so I can watch out for them."

He glanced at me and his brows lowered. "Don't worry about it. They wouldn't fuck with you, and if they did, they know they'd have to deal with Smoke. A few of them are going to be at our party tonight. Word is already spreading to steer clear of you, that Smoke's a little possessive."

"Party?"

Images of the drunken orgy that I'd seen yesterday when we arrived flashed through my mind and I grimaced.

"Yeah, a new brother is getting patched in and there's a big party after." He flexed is hands on the wheel and his forearms tensed. "I doubt Smoke'll allow you to go."

"What do you mean 'allow' me to go?" I actually had no desire to go, but I didn't like this whole 'allowing' me thing. "Will Smoke be there?"

"Little girl, you don't wanna be there. Trust me on that."

"Why?"

Fat raindrops began to hit the windshield as we pulled off the busy highway. "Because there's gonna be a lot of stuff going on that you don't need to see, and no fucking way Smoke's gonna expose you to that."

A hint of jealousy curled in my stomach, and I tried to ignore it, but my tipsy mouth ran away from me. "Why? So he can get a little time with Cyclone?"

Breaker whipped his head around to look at me and his glare made me shrink back in my seat. Man, he could be scary when he wanted. "You couldn't be more fuckin' wrong. Smoke doesn't want anything to do with any of the sweet butts, a fact he made abundantly clear when he had me spread the word that any club whore who touched him would deeply regret it. He's keepin' you away from the party, because with the couple hundred people jammed into the clubhouse, it'll be practically impossible to protect you."

That made me simmer down a bit, and I leaned my head against the cool window, watching the beads of water race down the glass. The truck had decent size side mirrors, and I frowned as I noticed a silver sedan about three cars back that would switch lanes every time we did in the busy suburban Denver traffic. When the sedan blew a red light to keep up with us, I knew we had problems.

He pulled off at an exit, which led to what looked like an older part of the city, leaving the silver car on the freeway behind us. "Gonna grab some lunch. You hungry?"

I nodded and fifteen minutes later in the pouring rain I was chowing down on a really good hot dog with mustard, chili, and relish almost dripping off of it. My buzz had completely faded by this point, but the post drinking hunger had kicked in, and I devoured my meal. I shoved the last few bites in my mouth then grabbed my soda and took a big drink. My gaze drifted to the passenger side rear view mirror and something caught my attention. I realized that a car had been following us since we left the drive through hot-dog place, but it wasn't the silver one anymore. This time, a

208

burnished copper sedan kept a couple cars back, but they were for sure keeping up with us. A burst of adrenaline hit my blood stream, and I sucked in a slow breath.

"Breaker, we're being—"

"Followed? Yeah, I know."

He abruptly changed lanes again. "Don't worry, I got a couple ways to get us to the clubhouse. Unless they have wings, they ain't gonna be able to follow us."

I drained the rest of my drink for the sugar and caffeine boost, then grabbed my pack to double check my weapons and get my extra ammo ready. As my fingers brushed two very illegal guns and a couple other deadly toys, I prayed we wouldn't have to use them.

The truck abruptly shifted and I yelped, clutching my pack to my chest and bracing my arm on the dash. We'd left the road and were now driving over some rough terrain to reach the next major street ahead. "What the hell?"

"They try to climb that curb in that sedan and they'll rip their undercarriage out."

Impressed, I smiled. "Nice thinking."

He gave me a wink. "I might've had to do this a time or two. You manage to get the license plate?"

"Yep, but it was hard to see inside the car, like the windshield was extra tinted. If it was a custom tint job that might help."

"It would, but they have shit you can put on and peel off your windshield now that's like a giant sticker you can get on the Internet."

"That sucks."

Breaker called Khan to let him know that we were safe but that we had been followed, and he was gonna drive around a bit just to be sure we'd lost our tail. I turned over the puzzle of the sedan following us in my mind, grateful for the distraction from my gut wrenching worry. We didn't say anything else, and I lost track of the world around me as my brain sifted through the last few hours. We were driving down a one lane gravel road on the west side of Golden, Colorado, according to the welcome sign we'd passed a ways back, when the two front tires on Breaker's SUV suddenly went flat, sending the vehicle skidding over the wet gravel and into a tree with a bone-jarring thud.

AUSTIN TX

Chapter Eleven

Miguel 'Smoke' Santos

Me, Hulk, and Frame, one of Hulk's Enforcers, pulled up to the warehouse on the south side of Denver and parked out front along with a white mini-van with a cleaning service logo on the side. The van belonged to Sheena, Frame's old lady, and it had been used to bring something other than cleaning supplies to this massive auto and motorcycle parts warehouse. In this case, it was a present from Mimi.

I'd hoped she or Mike would contact me with some information, but I didn't expect it this soon. In all the shit that was going on, I'd lost sight of just how deadly Swan's loved ones were, and I couldn't help but feel a little bit of hope that I could get my baby girl though this bullshit relatively unscathed—a miracle that had been appearing less and less probable as time went on. Now we had something…or someone to work with.

The clouds were gathering overhead and a brisk breeze had stirred up the dusty land in the industrial complex, throwing stinging grit into the air that pebbled my skin and skipped off my leather. Thunder rumbled across the distant mountains, and it looked like we were going to get one hell of a storm. I hoped that Breaker would get Swan back before the skies opened up.

We were all wearing protective facemasks. Mine made the lower half of my face, from just below my eyes down, look like a skull. My brothers were all wearing equally intimidating masks. Hulk's made him look like Frankenstein, and Frame's was a snarling demon face. Normally, I'd just wear my plain black face protector, but today, we were here to get some answers from a very unwilling piece of shit, so it helped to have the psychological advantage of intimidation. And it would help mask the smell if our target happened to shit, piss, and/or puke himself. That's one side effect of torture that they don't tell you about on the news, that the area will stink to high heaven until you bleach the hell out of it or burn it down.

And burning hair leaves a funk that'll never come out.

As I dismounted the Harley Davidson Road King I borrowed from Breaker, I pulled my black gloves out of my back pocket. These gloves were specially designed to keep any and all body fluids from reaching my skin and I carried them everywhere with me. As I stretched them over my fingers I had to turn my face away from the growing wind. Gonna be a hell of a storm.

"Let's get the fuck inside." Hulk yelled over the increasingly loud gusts that whipped between the buildings, throwing more grit into the air by the second.

I nodded and follow him with Frame close behind me, squinting my eyes against the fine grit being picked up by the approaching storm front. The door opened and my brother Icarus' old lady, Wild, ushered us in. Her dark hair was streaked with silver, and she had more lines around her eyes and mouth than when I last saw her, but she was still hot and knew it. Wearing jeans that looked like they'd been painted on and a black tank top with a plaid shirt over it, she appeared right at home surrounded by spare parts despite looking like an aging super model. After we were all inside, she slammed the door and bolted it to keep the rising storm outside. The squall against the steel framed building created an eerie howl, and I brushed the sand off and gave Wild an apologetic look.

"Smoke." Her cigarette-roughened voice hadn't changed, and she gave me a hug that smelled of tobacco, motor oil, and a faint hint of perfume. "So good to see you again, honey."

I returned her hug before releasing her. "You too."

"Talked to Breaker a little bit ago. He wanted me to let you know that he and Swan had left his place and he'd call you as soon as he met with Khan."

The urge to ask Wild if she knew how Swan was doing and was my girl was okay burned in my gut, but I didn't want to look like a pussy-whipped schmuck in front of my brothers. Fuck, I hated to admit it, but I was worried. My gut was going crazy right then, and the

213

feeling that someone was sneaking up behind me was making my back twitch. I had this bone-deep feeling that something wicked was headed this way, and I didn't like it one fuckin' bit. Liked it even less that my baby girl was out there somewhere right now without me to guard her back.

I regretted that I'd been a prick with Swan earlier this morning, but there was a lot of shit coming down on me right now, and I was afraid I'd slip up and she'd get hurt. The last thing Swan needed to deal with right now was knowing that back home in Austin my sister-in-law Veronica had lost it, big time. My sister, Julia, had texted me earlier to let me know that Veronica had been taken to the ER last night after another suicide attempt, which meant I might have to go down to Texas at some point and deal with all the legal red tape that came with being her guardian. To complicate matters, Veronica was off her meds again and out of her damn mind. She needed to be committed, but no one wanted to bother my brother-in-law right now to let him know his sister was goin' to the insane asylum. He'd been under deep cover for about a month overseas with no contact with home, and we were all starting to get worried. I didn't know what my sister would do without him, and I didn't want to find out.

That thought made my fear for Swan roar to life. I was in the fucked up situation of having to decide between my family and my woman. It was possible Veronica could be released after a three day psych hold. If she was off her meds, for her bipolar disorder, my sister was pretty sure Veronica would try to off herself again, and she might succeed. This was the fourth attempt to kill herself that I knew of, and it seemed like the older Veronica got the crazier she became.

The last attempt that I knew of had been when she called me the day I took Swan to meet Mr. Sokolov, known to his friends as Tom. I had told Swan the reason I had to leave was because Veronica was too drunk to drive, but the real reason was that she had called me absolutely off her rocker and was threatening to slit her wrists. I swore to my brother-in-law that I'd look after her, gave him my oath that I'd protect her from herself. I knew my sister was freaking out and couldn't physically handle Veronica when she was on the downslide of her bi-polar swings. Julia was the one who'd found Veronica in her car with the engine running and the garage door sealed shut during a previous suicide attempt. That scared me more than Veronica's previous threats, because I knew the irrational bitch didn't have the guts to end her life in a violent way…but slipping into death by carbon monoxide poisoning would be something she would do.

My family needed me right now, but if I left, Swan could end up dead. My soul ached and caused a physical hurt in my body that clenched my gut. This shit had to end.

I had to get the motherfucker downstairs to give us some information if I had any hope of keeping Swan alive.

Frame moved to my left, the glint of his copper orange hair catching my eye. "What's down there?"

At his words, my focus shifted from my own personal bullshit to our captive in a cold heartbeat.

One thing I love about Wild is that she's a no-bullshit kind of woman who would do anything to protect those she loves, but she also doesn't pull any verbal punches. "You mean Smoke's engagement present from some psycho-scary bitch?"

I swallowed. "What did she look like?"

When Wild described her I knew right away who she was. "That was my future mother-in-law."

Wild stared at me for a moment, then burst out laughing, tears in her eyes and trailing down her high cheekbones as she clutched her sides. "That was your soon-to-be mother-in-law? Oh boy, I thought my mom was bad, but you? You are fucked."

Everyone started to chuckle again and I cut them off. "Laugh later. We got business to attend to."

That sobered everyone quickly, and I exchanged a look with my men, letting 'em know playtime was over.

We wound our way through the various aisles, passing a few brothers who worked for Icarus, before Wild led us to a secret door in the floor beneath the computer desk in her office. We moved her desk, and when the trapdoor swung open, we could hear a man shouting obscenities. There was good soundproofing, which would be handy. None of us flinched at the ragged cries. Wild, her lips curled in disgust, glared at the floor like she could see through it.

Hulk went down first, and I followed soon after, our heavy boots thumping on the stairs. A musty tang flavored the air as we went down the long run of steps, and I wondered how the ventilation was down here. If it wasn't that good, I couldn't burn much of anything. Nothing like getting smoke damage to my lungs from a burning corpse. Plus, I didn't like fire in small places.

Shit could go bad quick. I, more than anyone, had respect for the damage fire could do, and I gave it the respect it deserved.

The harsh glow of fluorescent lights illuminated a medium-sized, concrete room with two drains in the floor and a man securely taped to a chair in the middle of the room. He was blindfolded, but that didn't stop him from cursing us. You know, the usual bullshit— he'd never talk, yada, yada, yada. A growl rumbled through my chest at the sight of his Los Diablos cut. My fingers itched to start to work on him, but first, we had to talk to Icarus who waited on the far side of the room. He stood against the wall, his arms crossed over his big chest, next to a folding table covered with instruments of torture...including a blowtorch.

He grinned at us, his gold tooth flashing in the light before he pushed himself off the wall and gave me a quick hug. "Good to see you again, man. Though I must say, I wish your friends would've called before they delivered this present to us. I almost shot their asses."

I sighed and shook my head. "Feel free to tell Lady Death to call first when she feels like she's doing you a favor. Be sure to let me know how it goes."

"That was her? Jesus Christ." Icarus actually paled beneath his tan and rubbed his mustache. "Fucking hell. How the fuck do you know Mimi Stefano?"

"She's Mimi Anderson now and my future mother-in-law."

Icarus smirked and Frame laughed. "Good luck, my friend. You're gonna need it."

"Thanks."

"Well your mother-in-law left a message for you. She said that her boys spotted this fucker following a car with a woman that looked an awful lot like Billie in it."

"What the fuck? Why didn't they skip this douche and get Billie?"

"'Cause they found it on surveillance tape at a grocery store from three days ago. Billie headed west out of the city and out of the range of traffic cameras while homeslice here stayed in the city. Lady Death said he was a clean take-down, and no one knows we have him. She also mentioned that he pimps underage girls for Los Diablos. She hopes he will suffer."

I made a mental note that the next time I saw Mimi I was going to give her a pair of nice diamond earrings for this gift.

Frame stared at the man in the chair with hatred in his eyes. Three years ago, Frame's sister was killed by her old man, a Los Diablos member who beat her to death. As a result, Frame had absolutely no mercy for any member of the rival MC. This was one of the reasons we brought him with us. Another one was that Frame was an ER Physician's Assistant and could keep the asshole tied to the chair alive for a very, very long time while we took care of business.

I noticed little white buds in the man's ears. "Can he hear us at all?"

"Nope, he ain't hearing shit but the music right now."

Nodding, I stretched out, my mind going to that empty, dark place inside of me that allowed me to do what needed to be done without compassion or guilt.

"You tell anyone about this yet 'sides me and Breaker?"

"Nope." Icarus grimaced. "I don't trust phones, computers, or any of that electronic shit right now. Especially after you found all that same crap had been used to spy on us."

After we cleared out the clubhouse last night we discovered more surveillance equipment that Khan swore hadn't been there a week ago when they last swept the place. Whoever had done it knew what they were doing, and they'd done it quick. A professional for sure. On the suspicion that there was more equipment we hadn't found yet, I didn't blame Icarus for being vague. I never realized how much I used technology until it was taken away, leaving us scrambling to seal up all the leaks. Fuckin' A, it was safer to use carrier pigeons at this point.

Hulk cracked his neck and began to stretch out his fingers. "So who is this child molester?"

"His name is Steve Miley, just got patched into Los Diablos last year. Got caught sleepin' on top of a seventeen-year-old girl he pimps."

"Nasty bastard," Hulk muttered.

Frame snorted. "Stupid too, thank fuck."

"Yeah, good for us."

Frame started to put on what looked like protective gear that one would wear in a hospital and Icarus tossed a pair of thick nitrile gloves to me and Hulk before putting his own on. I held the gloves and gave Icarus a questioning look. I mean, yeah, I used my gloves to protect my hands, but hazmat gear seemed a little much.

Frame caught my expression and gave me a serious look. "Last year we had an incident with a guy we were questioning. Turns out he had HIV. None of us got infected, but it was a scary couple months there."

"Terrible shit to have hauntin' the back of your mind, wondering if a scrape on your arm got infected." Icarus muttered and grabbed one of the gowns after he'd put his gloves on. "Frame tested all of us for six months, and I'll tell you what, every time I was waiting for that test to come back I was shittin' bricks. The thought of having possibly brought that home to my wife, maybe my kids? That's the kind of worry that'll have you suiting up in hazmat gear."

I was glad I had obsessively used condoms for sex and blowjobs with everyone, well everyone but Swan. My baby girl had come to me a virgin. Since she was the only woman I planned on doing anything with for the rest of my life, I was glad I wasn't playing sexual roulette with my cock anymore for brief moments of pleasure. Even last night when a drunk Cyclone had tried to hit on me, I felt nothing but disgust even though I knew how well that bitch could deep throat a cock. After I pissed Swan off, we questioned Cyclone after she'd had a couple shots to calm her down, and I believed her when she said she'd been told that I wanted to see her. I could have had her banned from the club, but I'm pretty sure she was just a pawn in someone else's game, so I just told her to stay the fuck away from my old lady. Besides, Swan had almost snapped Cyclone's arm, and I think she was afraid that I'd let my woman settle the score.

I couldn't forget the blank, hard look on Swan's face when she'd first glanced up at me while standing over Cyclone like a fucking Valkyrie bent on destruction. When our eyes met, even in my own fury at the danger she'd put herself in, the killer inside of me recognized one of its own. Sometimes it was hard to remember that she was so much more than my beautiful baby girl, but I needed to keep in mind that she could take care of herself. Hell, she could probably take care of herself and me if it came down to it. I needed to get my mind wrapped around that fact so we could work together as a team, not just me doin' the work while she sat back and stayed safe, hatin' my guts for keeping her out of the action.

With a sigh, I pulled on the rest of my gear and looked at the men around me. Suited up in our hazmat clothes we all looked like a bunch of extras out of a medical thriller. Hulk stared back at me through his medical face shield. "Good cop, bad cop?"

"Yeah. I need you to keep a clear head and do most of the talking while the rest of us take care of business."

Normally, I questioned people, but I wanted to see Hulk in action. I was pretty sure he'd make a good fit down in Austin, but I had to see if he had not only the brawn, but also the brains to do a proper interrogation. It would also free me up to devote myself to this pedophile's pain. I wanted to have a turn with this piece of shit before us not only for my own personal satisfaction, but because I also wanted to make him suffer for helping to run one of the biggest sex slave rings in the world. Fucker deserved every single bit of agony coming his way, and I burned with the need for vengeance for all of this fucker's victims. We selected our preferred tools without saying a word. In my case, I pulled out my brass knuckles while Frame took a wickedly big, razor-sharp scalpel, and Icarus grabbed the hammer before turning to look at the man duct taped to a sturdy wood chair in the center of the room.

All emotion, and all thoughts about anything other than getting what I needed from this fucker faded away, leaving me in my killing space.

"Let's do this."

Less than an hour later, the barely breathing piece of meat coughed out blood as he moaned. So far, we'd learned that he was hired by an unknown male to make the electronic box that hacked our security system along with a couple of other pieces of technology to invade our clubhouse four months ago, but that he had no idea who the customer was or what the device was for. If he'd known it was going to be used on the Iron Horse clubhouse he would have charged a lot more. Los Diablos were known for doing anything for money—anything—and by this point in our...conversation, he was begging for death.

Hulk squatted down and looked into the man's face. I doubt the piece of shit in the chair could see him after my brass knuckles had crushed the bones of his eye sockets. "Steve, I can make this end right now. Just give us something worth putting a bullet in your brain and I'll make it happen."

"Don't...know...anything else."

With a sigh Hulk rocked back on his heels. "You know something? You're just not givin' it up. Why? Do you need some more encouragement?"

I stepped forward and calmly whipped my knife out and cut off a portion of his right ear before Frame stepped in and harshly bandaged the wound over the man's ragged screams. "Talk, motherfucker, or I'll keep you alive for weeks and every moment of the rest of your short life will be agony."

"I can't." He coughed again, more blood spraying from his lips as the empty spaces in his gums where his teeth had been pulled out continued to bleed, making his words hard to understand. "Kill...my mother."

For a second, I almost felt some empathy for the fucker, but it quickly vanished as I remembered all the sins he'd confessed to, shit dark enough to make even my gut clench with nausea.

"What if we keep her alive, get her out of here and find someplace for her to be safe?"

Steve cried, but the tears were lost in the blood and sweat coating his face in a grizzly mask. "Swear."

"I swear it, and you know I always keep my word."

He sucked in a couple rattling breaths. "Billie is here. Knows Swan and Sarah here. A Russian team...going to retrieve Swan. Can't get to Sarah."

Without thought I lunged at the fucker, but Frame held me back by whispering into my ear, "Let him finish. We need this information."

"Are they already here?"

"Yeah. Arrived last night."

"How did you know Swan was here?"

"Spy…in your clubhouse."

"Who," Hulk almost whispered.

"Don't know…swear. Some bitch. Down with Los Diablos. Owes…lots of money."

At the confirmation that a sweet butt was giving out info on us, I exchanged a look with Icarus that promised a swift death to whoever it was. I didn't give a fuck if the traitor was a female. She betrayed us, and that shit did not fly regardless of gender. Especially when she'd helped lead the Russians right to Swan.

Panic sped up my heart rate, and I struggled to not whip out my phone and call Breaker. His phone was at the clubhouse with everyone else's being checked for any kind of bugs. He had a burner, but I hadn't programed the number into my phone yet. Sweat dripped down my back beneath the blood-stained gown and I began to pace. Hulk watched me with a grim look.

"Anything else? The more honest you are the harder we'll work to keep your mom safe. Think hard, Steve, 'cause that sweet woman's life is in your hands. I'd hate for Los Diablos to track her down. You know what they'd do to her, you sick fuck, the same things you've done to dozens of women."

The guy wheezed. "Trap set for Swan."

"What kind of trap," Hulk said in a soothing voice.

"Cameras you don't know on…on all roads leading to clubhouse." He sagged in his chair, a low moan tearing from deep in his chest. "Ambush. Anderson twins bounty alive three million. Private…collector wants 'em."

Icarus jerked his head at me. "Call the clubhouse. I don't care if it is bugged to shit."

224

After stripping off the blood soaked gloves and gown I jerked my cell out and called Breaker. The phone rang and sent me straight to his voice mail. A sick feeling hit me right in the chest and I called the clubhouse next. Thank fuck this time I got an answer.

"Hello."

"Listen, this is Smoke, I need to talk to Khan right the fuck now." He was the only one I knew I could trust there right now. Terrible visions of someone hurting Swan bombarded my mind, making me close to insane with worry.

"Got it."

Less than a minute went by but it felt like hours before Khan answered. "Smoke?"

"Are Breaker and Swan back yet?"

"No. Talked to Breaker a while ago. Said he had a tail but lost it and was gonna drive around a bit to make sure. What's going on?"

"Listen to me. Someone is getting ready to ambush Swan and Breaker at the entrance to one of the roads to the clubhouse. I need you to get a bunch of your men out there and find them. The Russians have cameras on the road, and they've been tracking everyone's comings and goings. Los Diablos tipped them off. They have an ambush set up to get Swan and are probably armed to the teeth."

Khan didn't even bother to ask how I knew this. Instead, he started shouting out orders. "We won't let anyone get your old lady."

With my heart in my throat I hung up and turned around just in time to see Hulk end Steve's evil life with a bullet to the head. Thankfully, Hulk had used a silencer or we'd have all been deaf from the gunshot echoing in the cement room.

"Icarus, you got any automatic weapons on hand?"

"Absolutely. I'll have my boys take care of this garbage. Let's go find your woman and our brother."

Chapter Twelve

Swan

Breaker swore as he fought the wheel, trying to get his SUV under control while we slid on the gravel. My seatbelt locked, pinning me against my seat as I struggled to brace myself. There was another loud series of bangs that I now recognized as gunshots, then the windshield took a hit, the glass cracking into a haze. The front airbags deployed and my entire body shook as we hit something hard enough that Breaker's head busted the window on his side of the cab. I got a pretty good thump on my own skull from the impact. When we finally came to rest it took me a minute to get my bearings as the airbags slowly deflated. I took my seatbelt off as soon as possible, my heart pounding as I jerked my handgun from my waist holster before looking over at Breaker.

He was shaking his bleeding head, the limp white bag in front of him smeared with his blood, and when I grabbed his chin to look at him I saw that his pupils were huge and he was looking at me without comprehension.

Shit, no help there.

Outside, the rain was really pouring down now, creating a curtain between the SUV and whoever was shooting at us. Despite the fact it was late afternoon, the storm clouds had dimmed the area. The instincts that my father had honed within me to a razor sharp edge kicked into gear, and I knew that time was running out. I stripped off the pink shirt I was wearing and laid an unresisting Breaker down as gently as I could onto the floor boards then pressed my shirt up against the wound on the side of his head where he'd slammed into his window. I tied the arms of the shirt together around his head to make sure it would stay on.

"Breaker, can you hear me? You have to keep pressure on your wound."

He groaned and tried to talk, but his words came out all scrambled and I worried that he had a major concussion.

"Just hold your hand here and stay down."

He slowly did as I asked, but his hand had no strength in it as I placed it on the wound.

Fuck it, we didn't have many options at this point. So far, none of the bullets had struck me, probably because I was worth more alive than dead—can't prostitute a corpse—but they were for sure trying to flush me out. I dug around in my bag for my phone and spent a few precious moments trying to get a signal, but all I came up with was the no-service icon on the screen.

Okay, I just needed to hold on long enough for someone to come to or from the clubhouse. I mean the wreck was halfway in the road, glaringly obvious. Someone had to come by soon. Please God, let someone come by soon.

I quickly scanned the area where we'd come to rest as a huge clap of thunder rattled hard enough overhead that my teeth felt like they were vibrating. I took a deep breath and kicked out the rest of the shattered glass in the window on Breaker's side, using the rumble of thunder to try and mask the sound. Movement outside my window caught my attention, but I managed to slip out Breaker's door with my pack before I crouched down and scanned my surroundings.

The SUV had come to rest against a large tree and provided a small space where I could hunker down that kept the big tree at my back and the hood of the vehicle at my front to provide some shelter. With all the tires shot out, I couldn't crawl under it for cover, so I made do with what I had. For as far as I could see, there were just trees and more trees interspersed with large exposed boulders. Unfortunately, the nearest rock that might provide some shelter was far enough away that dragging an injured Breaker there wasn't going to happen.

We were well and truly fucked.

It was time for plan B.

Take them out first.

That beautiful, deadly emptiness filled me completely, blotting out thoughts of having to tell Cathy how her husband died, of dying myself, or even worse—being captured.

It wasn't going to end that way.

I wouldn't let it.

Adrenaline and a host of other chemicals flooded my body, making my heart race as I became hyperaware of my surroundings. Rain still darkened the area and it made catching anyone moving around even harder as the vegetation moved in the wind. Human instinct in situations like this was to run away, escape. In my case, my training demanded that I stand my ground, protect myself, and eliminate the threat.

Knowing that Breaker was depending on me helped me focus even further until I was reduced to what I had been trained from childhood to become in these circumstances.

A killing machine.

I squeezed farther into the gap between the deflated front tire and the tree where the SUV rested, trying to see and hear through the rain. In the distance, thunder rumbled repeatedly and the storm seemed to be gaining strength. In front of me, there was nothing but more trees and brush, making it hard to see through the sheet of rain. The storm continued to rage around me but I no longer paid attention to my own physical discomforts. While whoever had shot out our tires remained hidden, I pulled out a few toys from my pack and set them to the side.

Silent, watching, I almost laughed at the sight of a bright red laser sweeping through the dim, humid air, pointing straight to at least one of the shooters. I'd been taught to never assume I was facing one enemy when there could be an entire army surrounding me, but if they were all dumb enough to use a laser sight in the rain then this might be a short fight. A bullet passed through the window where I'd been sitting and I hoped that Breaker was still lying down.

I followed the line of the laser to a thick bush and sent six bullets into the dense leaves, my lips curving in a savage smile as a man began to scream. A voice came from my left while another yelled out somewhere else to my right, hidden by the thick trunk of the tree. Panic started to stir in my gut and I began to shake in fear as I listened and realized they were probably speaking Russian. If that was the case, we were in deep shit. I'd rather face dozens of bikers than one group of Russian assassins. Mimi had studied for a while in Moscow with the Novikov *Bratva,* and she said they gave her the shivers.

Bullets peppered the side of the truck, and I had to grit my teeth and resist the urge to drag Breaker through the window. They appeared to be trying to flush us out, and I hoped they thought I was still inside. More gunfire mixed with the thunder, and I tried to calculate where they were coming from. They could be using the shots as a distraction for a member of their group to sneak up on me.

Stealing quick glances over the hood of the truck, I caught movement right before a bullet whizzed past my ear close enough that I could hear the scream as it parted the air.

I sucked in a deep breath, trying to calm my racing heart while I jerked my pack open and pulled out a flash-bang and two regular grenades.

My dad had packed them for me reminding me that it was always better to be on the offense than the defense.

At the moment, I was the most concerned about the man shooting from somewhere to my left, but I needed to know his general location. Lightning struck close enough nearby that I could smell the ozone, and the fine hair on my arms and the back of my neck stood on end. Hoping that the men hunting me were distracted by the display of nature's fury, I stood and threw the flash grenade in middle of the road. I managed to duck and cover my head and ears before it went off a few seconds later.

Even crouched down into a ball on the opposite side of the truck, the flash was bright enough to be seen through my eyelids and the bang rivaled that of the thunder overhead. The screaming man had gone silent but a barrage of bullets slammed into the truck and three into the tree well above me. All it took was a quick glance at the shredded bark behind me to figure out the general area of the gunshots, and I pulled the pin on the grenade and stood long enough to launch it, catching the bright flare of muzzle flash and adjusting my aim at the last second to launch the grenade in that general direction. Something hot grazed my bicep and I dropped back down with a barely muffled scream right before that grenade went off.

I heard what I thought was another round of yelling in Russian, but my ears were ringing and it was hard to place where it was coming from. I lifted my arm and quickly inspected the wound, the rain washing my blood away and turning it a watery red as it dripped down my fingers. I choked on a yelp as I gently probed the wound, relieved that it appeared to be only a graze. Thank fuck I didn't have to dig a bullet out. Moving quickly, I jerked my waistband off and wrapped it around my bleeding left bicep, cursing beneath my breath at the fiery pain radiating from my arm.

Breaker moaned inside the truck and my heart lurched as I wondered if he'd been shot. I wanted to check on him, but I didn't dare. It wasn't like I could do much for him medically anyway. I had one grenade left and two spare clips, all I could do was hope it was enough.

Sadness pierced my heart at the thought of what my death would do to Smoke, then I gave myself a mental slap for acting like a weak ass bitch. I hadn't lost yet, but if I psyched myself out to the point where all I could focus on was my death then I might as well put a bullet in my head now. My father's voice rang in my head telling me to suck it up, to keep fighting, to never ever give up. Thousands and thousands of hours spent enduring the pain of my training allowed me to think past it, to get back into my cold headspace. On some level, I knew my body's uncontrollable reaction to being shot would kick in and hinder my ability to fight, so I couldn't try to hold out anymore in the hope of someone coming. For all I fucking knew, the Russians would shoot some innocent bystanders, and I'd have their deaths on my soul.

I heard something and I froze, not even daring to breathe as I tried to listen over the rain, which was finally slowing down as the thunder rumbled on its journey to the east.

A branch snapped and I couldn't help but smile. Whoever was sneaking up on me from behind wasn't very quiet, but I didn't dare use another grenade this close to me and Breaker. Instead, I calmed my breathing and tried to ignore the bullets flying through the air in an attempt to flush me out. It was a much smaller barrage than before, and I was pretty sure it was only coming from one gun. Moving slowly, I crouched down as low as I could and trained my gun in the direction of the person trying to sneak up on me. At the first glimpse of grey hair from behind a tree to the right, I aimed, and as soon as I saw his eyes I gave three direct shots at his head.

One of my dad's number one rules is that if you have the ammo, take three shots at your enemy because one of them is bound to hit some part of your target.

I'm an expert marksman and they all hit.

Time slowed, and it seemed like there was an eternity between each shot when I knew that it was only a second, if that.

For as long as I live, I'll never forget the destruction those three shots wrought on the grey haired man in dark clothes. First shot took out the top portion of his skull in a bright burst of red exploding into the air. Second shot caught him in the neck as his head whipped back from the recoil, and the third in his chest right above his heart.

My father would be proud.

Nausea gripped me at the horrifying sight, and I choked back the urge to throw up. I didn't want to die on my hands and knees in a puddle of my own vomit.

A roar filled my ears and I sucked in a deep breath, shaking my head to try and clear it. If I passed out I was done. Even though the rain was cold, a hot sweat coated my skin as my mouth filled with saliva. In an effort to clear my mind, I pressed down on my bicep where I'd been grazed. The pain shot through me, bringing with it a burning wave of clarity, as my brain switched from trying to cope with the trauma of killing to survival.

There was one shooter left. I popped up, trying to draw his gunfire so I could find him. After returning quickly to my crouched position I listened, but the roaring in my ears was only getting louder. Worried I was going to pass out I tried to slow down my pulse, to do some deep breathing, but the bloody corpse of the man I'd killed seemed to keep moving on the edge of my vision and I found myself constantly stealing looks at the nearly headless body to make sure it wasn't somehow crawling toward me, that he wasn't still alive.

When I realized that roar wasn't in my head, but rather the rumble of what I hoped were bikes coming closer, I shuddered. I had one grenade and two clips left, not very good odds if they had fresh reinforcements. My body was beginning to stiffen up, so I shifted slightly and tried to get to a good spot where I could see who was coming. It was for sure someone on motorcycles, but it could be either Los Diablos or Iron Horse. At the first glimpse of a group of at least two dozen bikers roaring up in the slacking rain,

I let out a shuddering breath when I recognized Khan in the lead. Then the horrible thought that the last shooter was still here raced through me and I darted around the tree, staying crouched but shooting my gun into the air four times.

One of the bikers I didn't know on a hunter green bike spotted me first and pointed me out to Khan. He drove right up to me and pulled a big handgun out from his shoulder holster, his gaze darting from my bleeding arm, to my face and back again while the rest of his men spread out around us. When no shots rang out— not that I could hear them much over the roar of the bikes—I swayed. A hard shudder tore through me, and my thoughts started to get muzzy as the shock of my wound and the events of the last few minutes raced through my nervous system. I could hold myself together mentally, but I had no control over my body's reaction to what had to be a huge amount of adrenaline leaving my system.

My dad's voice echoed in my thoughts, lecturing me about what to expect if I was wounded, and I slowly stood, determined to make sure Breaker was okay before I crashed.

Mind over matter.

Willpower over pain.

Life over death.

Khan parked his bike in front of the wrecked truck while I shuffled over to him, my gun pointed at the ground but ready to take out anyone or anything that tried to hurt me or the men Smoke considered brothers.

"Breaker's in the truck," I said in a shaky voice as I fought off the urge to puke. "As far as I can tell there were four shooters. I got two for sure. Another may be in that bush. I have no idea where the fourth is."

Moving slowly, Khan gestured to my arm, the rain dripping off the ends of his silver hair and rolling down the hard lines of his face. "You get hurt?"

"Gr-grazed," I stuttered as a chill raced through my soaking wet, stressed out body. "Smoke?"

"On his way, sugar. Just hang in there."

Khan began shouting out orders while I took some unsteady steps back to the truck to check on Breaker. Instead of going through his window again I made my way to the passenger door, my stomach curling as I saw how many bullets peppered the truck. Everything in my body started to ache at once as the last of the adrenaline faded. I was pretty sure I was going into shock, but I had to see if Breaker was all right.

One of the bikers crowded in close behind me, and without thinking, I whipped around and pressed my gun to his forehead. "Back the fuck off."

He did with his hands held high and his eyes wide. "Easy, honey. I'm not the enemy. Just trying to check on Breaker. My name is Darren, and I have battlefield experience treating the wounded. Fought in the Marines with your old man."

My gun wavered the slightest bit as my hand began to shake. "I don't know you."

It was a testament to my distracted state that Khan was standing between me and Darren without my even realizing he'd moved. "Swan, take it easy. Let us help Breaker."

It took a moment for his words to penetrate the post-battle haze filling me, but I didn't lower my weapon until he gently wrapped his hand around it, a look of quiet understanding filling his eyes. I didn't protest when he lowered the barrel to the ground, but when he tried to take it from me I snarled at him. Truth was, I was feeling as weak as a baby kitten and couldn't have stopped him from taking my weapon from me if I tried. But at this point, I didn't trust anyone but Khan.

"Sweetheart, Breaker needs us. Let me help him. Smoke's almost here."

Tears filled my eyes, and I nodded. Before I moved aside I glanced at Breaker, the side of his face resting in a pool of blood. The only thing that stopped me from losing it completely was the shallow rise and fall of his chest. When I stepped back, Darren quickly went to work on Breaker while I told Khan what had happened. By the time I reached the point in the story where they'd arrived, my teeth were chattering hard enough that my words came out in a terrible stutter. While I talked, the other men gathered around. I heard one of them whisper to Khan that they'd found the man in the bushes. He'd bled out from shots to his torso. I also heard that the guy I'd shot in the face was going to be hard to identify.

The memory of his face distorting as the bullet hit ran through my mind in a terrible, slow motion reel.

When the nausea filled me this time, I couldn't stop it. I stumbled a few feet away and hung onto the side of the truck as I dropped to my knees and threw up until I had nothing left but the dry heaves. My stomach cramped and ached, bringing new tears to my eyes as I gagged uncontrollably.

I barely noticed Khan holding my hair back while I tossed my cookies. When I was done and just shivering, he moved me away from the contents of my stomach and had me sit down with my head between my legs before he handed me a bottle of pop. I rinsed and spit a couple times before taking a long pull of the sugary drink. My thoughts were a weird, jumbled mess, and I couldn't really feel my body anymore, just a spreading numbness. While I knew about the physical reactions to being shot and trauma, it still freaked me out when I realized I was about to pass out.

"Swan!"

I tried to lift my head to see if that voice really belonged to Smoke or was the sound just my wishful imagination, but it was just too heavy. My ears rang, and tiny black spots began to dart across my vision as I stared at the muddy ground between my legs. Tears and rainwater dripped off my nose, and I struggled to breathe, totally overwhelmed to the point where I almost felt catatonic, but even that didn't stop me from forcing my lips to form one word. "Miguel."

The heat of his body washed over me, and in the next instant, I found myself in his arms, staring up at his pale face, worry and fear etched into every inch of his expression. I tried to raise my wounded arm to touch him, to reassure him that I was okay, but the pain stopped me before I got very far. It was at that moment that I truly realized how much I meant to him, how if anything happened to me, I would be taking the piece of his heart—and his soul—with me. Even as I welcomed the oblivion and the quiet it would bring to my mind, I struggled to stay conscious so that I could tell Smoke I loved him. The soft, velvety darkness closed in anyway, and I finally gave up and let it take me secure in the knowledge that I was safe in Smoke's arms.

When I came around again, I was being carried somewhere that smelled of cleaning products and Smoke. I managed to open my eyes and found that I was cradled in his arms as he practically ran with me. My tongue felt numb so I didn't even try to form words. The only sound I made was a soft moan that sounded weird to me even in my messed up state. He looked down at me, and the intense relief on his face swamped me, and I began to cry again.

"Shhh, baby girl," he said in a low, tortured voice. "You're safe."

Since I couldn't get my stupid tongue to move, I tried to look around as best I could while Smoke carried me into what appeared to be a roughly put together exam room that didn't look like any medical office I'd been in despite the tools of the trade neatly placed around the big space. Paper crinkled as Smoke laid me down, and I noticed we weren't alone. There was a slender guy with wet, dark red hair reaching past his collar washing up at the sink. Next to him an older woman in blue scrubs with kittens all over them was setting up a tray with stuff I couldn't see.

Someone propped me up and someone else behind Smoke handed him a plastic cup with orange liquid inside.

Wiping my hair back from my face Smoke murmured, "Can you drink this?"

I was still physically weak as hell, but my brain was coming back online, and with Smoke's help, I managed to drink what turned out to be orange juice, washing the bitter aftertaste of vomit and fear from my mouth. My teeth began to chatter as I shivered and the nurse appeared at Smoke's side, her kind gaze meeting mine.

"Here you go."

When she went to put the warm blanket that smelled like fabric softener around me, Smoke blocked her and grabbed it, then wrapped me up in the delicious heat, leaving my hastily bandaged arm exposed. The blanket must have been in the dryer because it felt like heaven and my tense muscles began to spasm, then relax. Smoke stroked my cheek, and I returned my attention to him. The need to comfort him, to take away that terrible fear in his gaze, gave me the strength to talk.

"I l-love you."

"I love you." He closed his eyes and took a deep breath, his nostrils flaring. "Thought I was gonna be too late."

A man cleared his throat. "Smoke, I need to look at her arm."

I could tell Smoke didn't want anyone near me, but he moved just enough to allow the guy I assumed was a doctor and his nurse to start working on my arm. The man gave me a small smile, the fine lines around his pale green eyes deepening. "Swan, my name is Frame. Can I take a look at your arm?"

"Ye-yes."

He nodded and set to work gently cutting through my makeshift bandage while Smoke began to breathe heavily next to me. I reached out and grasped his hand, giving it a good squeeze when the soggy cloth was peeled off my wound. Glancing down at the injury, I was glad to see that while it would probably leave an ugly scar, it wasn't that bad. At the sight of the blood, my scattered thoughts shifted to Breaker.

"Is he okay? Breaker, is he all right?"

"He's fine. Take more than a bump on the head to put him out of commission," Frame said in a soothing voice. "I'm going to give you a shot so we can numb the area and stitch up the wound."

"Okay." By this point, I was still a little woozy and my whole body ached, but I was alive and so fucking thankful. "Where am I?"

Smoke stroked my hair back from my face again, his hand faintly trembling. I grabbed it and placed a kiss on his palm as he said, "At the clubhouse. We've got a small clinic set up here for emergencies that we'd rather not have to deal with hospital bullshit over. Don't have the equipment to do brain surgery, but we can fix someone up after a gunshot or two."

Men's voices came from outside the door, and a moment later, Khan walked in along with Hulk and three other men I didn't recognize. Smoke stepped closer to me, hovering to the point that Frame nudged him with his shoulder. "Gimme some room."

Instead of moving away, Smoke sat on the exam table and moved me back into the cradle of his thighs. His wet warmth surrounded me and his heart beat against my back as I shifted my blanket around as best I could with one arm to cover him as well. Wrapping himself around me he remained silent, but I could almost sense the aggressive looks he was giving the other men. I shifted enough so Frame could give me a shot. Thankfully, the area of burning pain began to numb quickly, and I slumped against Smoke with a relieved sigh.

Khan closed the door after himself and leaned against it, watching me closely. "Swan, can you tell us what happened?"

He wanted a debrief. Now, when my mind felt like day old pudding. Okay, I could do that. I went through what had happened, reliving the memory. My voice broke a couple times. When I got to the part about my phone not working, Khan told me one of the men found a jammer on one of the guys I'd killed. My mind tried to deal with the fact that I'd taken lives today, but I forced that knowledge down deep and continued. When I got to the actual gunfight, Smoke began to breathe heavily. By the time I finished the report, my wound had been stitched up and bandaged. The mood had shifted to one of suppressed, tightly controlled rage. Smoke growled out, "When I find the motherfuckers responsible for this…"

I'd had my fill of violence by this point and really, really needed some time to process—and sleep. "Can I please go to my room?"

Smoke swept me into his arms. "Hey, I can walk."

He spared me a glance, his dark eyes glittering with a mixture of intense emotions that I couldn't even begin to identify. "No."

Well aware that arguing with him was a lost cause, I sighed and rested my head against his damp shirt, exhaustion now hitting me full force.

"I'm taking her to bed," Smoke said in a no bullshit tone. "Let me know if you learn anything.

"Will do, brother."

We were now in what looked like a hallway, and there were several other men standing around. Khan cleared his throat. "Swan, you did well today, I'm proud of you. Not many men that I know, let alone a little girl like you, would have made it out in one piece. That's a good woman you've got there, Smoke. Hold onto her."

The other men murmured similar things, but I ignored them as Smoke carried me through the hallway. We didn't say anything, and even though I wanted to just go to sleep with every beat of my heart, I managed to stay awake until we made it to our room. Once we were inside, Smoke set me gently on our bed, and I sighed in relief. Instead of joining me, he searched our room, then pulled an Uzi out of his bag and set it on the table next to the bed. Outside the grey twilight had given away almost completely to a dark, night sky, and I curled in on myself, my mind totally unable to cope with anything at the moment.

I have no idea how long I laid there in a dazed state, but soon I found myself being picked up. It was a testament to the depth of the numbness surrounding me that I didn't take a moment to grope and admire him, instead, letting him prop me up against the wall in the bathroom while he efficiently stripped me out of my cold, wet clothing. Steam filled the air, and he guided me into the bathtub with him. Part of me was aware of the sensation of the warm water on my body, but I almost felt like an observer from the outside looking in.

Smoke hummed a song I wasn't familiar with, while he carefully washed me, his touch so gentle, so welcome, that I began to rise from the fog protecting me from the events of the last few hours. By the time he was working conditioner through my long hair, untangling any knots he found with care, I had my arms wrapped around him, clinging to him like someone would try to take him away from me. Resting my cheek against the broad expanse of his chest I could feel the rumble of his humming against my cheek mixed with the steady beat of his heart.

It was beautiful.

"What song is that?"

"An old Spanish lullaby my mother used to sing to me when I was a kid and couldn't fall asleep."

"It's lovely."

When I didn't say anything more he went back to caring for me, the melody of the song seducing me into relaxing. As I became aware of my body, I also became aware of his heavy erection pressed against my stomach. Despite the growing ache from my arm, I began to crave a different kind of touch from Smoke, and I pressed my hips into his, loving the way he groaned while he stroked my back with a light touch that sent little electric shivers through me. My love for this man roared through me like a flash fire, fed by the fear I'd endured. I tipped my head back and my heart ached as our gazes met, and I saw everything I felt for him reflected back to me in his eyes.

Sliding up his torso, I placed a kiss on his sinfully full lips, a kiss that soon turned hot and dirty. We devoured each other, our teeth clashing as our tongues stroked together, imitating the way we were rubbing our bodies in a sinful rhythm. I was overwhelmed by an intense arousal, mixed with some frantic emotion I couldn't name, as I reached between us and stroked his hard length. My pussy throbbed with my need for him to be inside me, my flesh swollen and wet. As our desire built, so did my aggression until I had Smoke pressed against me tight enough that it was a little hard to breathe. He kissed his way from my jaw to my neck, murmuring to me how much he loved me, how much I meant to him, and how proud he was of me.

And thankful, so very thankful.

Warmth blossomed in my chest like a flower opening, and I told him how much I loved him, how much he meant to me, and how scared I'd been. But mostly, I tried to make him understand what he did to me, how I couldn't imagine how I survived before him, and I begged him to never leave me.

His lips returned to mine and he fisted my wet hair, pulling me back enough that he could look into my eyes. "I've been through some terrible shit in my life, done some horrible things, but I'd do it all over again because at the end is you, my reward, my blessing. Baby girl, you own me—wretched heart and wicked soul."

I placed my fingertips against his lips. "You do not have a wicked soul. I wouldn't be able to love an evil man."

He gripped my wrist and held my hand to his chest over his heart. "This beats for you. When…when I thought I wouldn't make it in time, I swear I felt like I died. You're my life now, and I promise I'll do a better job protecting you. I'm so fuckin' sorry I failed you."

The way his voice broke on those last words, the guilt saturating his voice, made me angry. "You. Were. Not. Responsible. Do you hear me?"

"I should—"

Slapping my hand none too gently against his mouth I growled out. "Stop. Just stop that fucking bullshit right now. I'm not some delicate princess waiting for Prince Charming to come rescue her. Just because I have a pussy doesn't mean I'm weak. It doesn't mean I can't take care of myself. I did what I've been trained to do. It fucking sucked, and I was scared out of my mind, but I don't regret what I did. I don't regret those men's deaths, nor do I blame you."

He closed his eyes and lifted me up until my arms were wrapped around his neck and my legs were around his waist. I was slick and slippery from the water, but he managed to keep his grip on me, his fingers digging into my ass, while I licked the drops of water from his neck and he carried me out of the bathroom then into the bedroom. I bit him gently over his throbbing pulse and tasted his skin. That elicited a delicious growl from Smoke, and I sank my nails into his shoulders, holding on while he laid me on the bed, following me onto the thick comforter and surrounding me with his presence.

A feeling of being safe and protected enveloped me, and as we kissed, tears burned my eyes. The reality of how close I'd come to dying made me frantic for more, for him to be a part of me in an undeniable way that proved we were alive. My arm ached as the anesthetic Frame had used began to wear off, but the pleasure of Smoke's touch was overwhelming. He shifted his attention to my breasts and gathered one in his large hand, squeezing gently while his thumb played with my nipple.

"So pretty. Love the way your nipples get so hard for me, how they press against your shirt when you look at me with those big, blue, fuck-me eyes."

The more he touched me, the more I needed him, until I was writhing beneath him, the urge to fuck became overwhelming. His musk, mixed with mine scented the air with a unique combination that was us, and filled me with a sense of satisfaction that this magnificent man belonged to me and only me. I believed him when he said he loved me, when he said we were going to be together for the rest of our lives, and I believed him when he said he was made for me, because it was the absolute truth.

If I was his blessing, he was my gift.

One of his hands slipped between us and stroked the slippery entrance of my sex, a low growl vibrating against my nipple that seemed to be connected to my clit. Each draw felt like a pull on that little bundle of nerves, and I ground myself against his fingers, shameless in my need for the life-affirming pleasure that only he could give me. His thumb began to rub little circles on my nub, and I panted out his name, straining for my orgasm.

Beyond shame at this point, I pleaded with him in a strained voice, "Miguel, please, let me come."

He shivered and I groaned, arching into him, loving how deeply it affected him when I said his name. "Baby girl, who do you belong to?"

"You, always you."

"Come for me."

He slipped a deliciously thick finger into my empty sex and my inner muscles clamped down him. I swear my heart skipped a beat, and I exploded in ecstasy as an intense climax raced through me. I became aware of the blood rushing through my veins, the joy of being alive and how precious every second was. Smoke continued to gently rub my clit until I was trying to push him away, overwhelmed by his touch on my sensitive flesh. Little aftershocks of gratification stole my remaining senses, and I made small mews of pleasure as I twitched beneath his heavy bulk.

His warmth left me, and I reached out for him, begging him to come back to me but unable to say the words. Delicious, gentle waves of desire still moved through me, and when he ran his hands down my waist and groaned, all I could do was smile. His love for me was evident in his touch, and I drank down every drop of his affection as it chased back the lingering shadows of fear and panic trying to invade my mind.

"So fuckin' beautiful," he whispered. My hips jerked when he ran the thick head of his cock against my sensitive clit, teasing me.

I struggled to open my eyes, and when I did, I was greeted with the pussy clenching sight of a naked Smoke next to me staring down at where he was rubbing the crest of his dick against my stiff clit. His muscles stood out in stark relief, and I wished for an ounce of artistic talent to preserve that image because he was so damn beautiful. From the dark disks of his nipples to the sharp V leading to his groin, he was perfection, and I wondered if the sight of him would ever grow old. Using my good arm, I caught one of his hands in my own and lifted it to my lips, placing gentle kisses on his bruised knuckles. He looked up at me, and the warmth in his gaze made my whole body buzz as hormones flooded my system.

The mood between us changed when he moved over me, and my back arched to meet him as he slowly entered and filled me. The slight pressure of my body accommodating his thick girth made my toes curl, and I couldn't help the moan that escaped me. He felt so damn good, and my pussy contracted then released with each gentle push of his hips. I swear his steel-hard cock throbbed deep inside of me, and my skin tingled everywhere he touched me.

"Swan, look at me."

I hadn't even realized I'd closed my eyes, but when I opened them I found myself drowning in the warm, brown velvet of his eyes. He cupped my face and watched my expression as he pulled out, my pussy gripping him in an effort to keep him inside of me. He pushed back in with a fluid roll of his hips. Holy shit, my man could move his body in ways that destroyed me. Our eyes held while he made love to me, building my orgasm while I watched so many emotions race through his gaze. At this moment, I felt as if we were one person and submitted to him fully, allowing him into my soul, like he was in my body. Our breathing sped up, and soon, I was lifting my hips to his. A high-pitched sound of pleasure escaped me when he ground his pelvis against mine, his thick cock splitting me wide with each thrust.

He sat back on his heels, still not looking away from my eyes, and lifted one of my legs so that it laid across his chest with my toes pointing up at the ceiling. This allowed him to move deeper in me until each building thrust made him bottom out inside of me. I felt owned in every sense of the word and reveled in his adoration. I treasured it, valued how he took complete control of our lovemaking in order to bring both of us the most pleasure possible. As if his physical prowess wasn't enough, the way his gaze captured mine sent me racing to the edge of my release.

"Damn, you feel so good. Hot little cunt wrapped around me. Hold on, baby, don't come yet."

I gritted my teeth, trying to hold back as he did this thing with his hips and hit a spot inside of me that made me grip the sheets as hard as I could.

"Can't...please...too much."

"Do *not* fucking come," he snarled in a way that only turned me on even more.

He seemed to be impossibly hard inside of me, as if his cock were made of granite, and I rhythmically squeezed my inner muscles around him, determined to make him climax.

"Fuck, fuck, that tight pussy is gonna suck the come out of me."

"Give it to me." I whispered in a voice so sultry I surprised myself.

My focus turned from my own climax to his, and I pulled him down to me and kissed him with all the passion he built inside of me.

His tongue rubbed against mine as we became lost in each other, our sweat-slick bodies moving together. This position rubbed my clit, and I whimpered into his mouth. The effort of holding back made me shake. He began to slam into me, and I tore my mouth from his, my body strung tight and lights flashing behind my eyelids.

"Gonna fill you up," he growled.

"Miguel!"

"Shit," he hissed. "Now."

Burying himself as deep as he could our lips met again, and I exploded around him.

I swear our bodies were so synched together that my sex pulsed in time with his release. There was no beginning or end to us. We were one in every way possible. Tears raced down my cheeks as I climaxed hard enough that I simply lost myself in him. He groaned and cried out with his face pressed against my neck, his hips jerking against me, pressing deeper into me as I wrapped myself around him. I buried my hands in his hair, while clinging to him like he was the only thing keeping me on this earth.

For some unexplainable reason, I couldn't stop the tears, and he hushed me gently, stroking me and cuddling me while he was still inside of me. Smoke said all the nonsense words that people say to each other at times like these, but when he said it was going to be all right, I believed him. When my sobs finally subsided, he pulled out of me and rose from the bed. I shivered at the absence of his warmth and realized for the first time that the sheets beneath us were damp from our shower and my hair was probably a tangled mess.

Smoke came out of the bathroom, gloriously naked and confident. I must have looked a sight because he gave me a small smile and shook his head. He went to the closet and pulled out some clean linens from the top shelf. When I rolled off the bed and stood on unsteady legs he watched me carefully.

"You okay?"

My lower lip trembled, but I managed a small, brittle smile. "I am. I just need to clean up."

He nodded, his gaze never leaving me as I shuffled into the bathroom. At the sight of myself in the mirror, I let out a low groan. I was officially a hot mess. The first thing I did was clean myself up and then tried to brush my hair out as best I could using only one arm. I winced when I pulled at the tender roots where I'd bumped my head. After a careful exploration of the goose egg on my head, I splashed cold water on my face and brushed my teeth.

During all of this I avoided looking into my own eyes. When I finally did, I wasn't surprised by the haunted look there. I didn't feel guilt over ending those men's lives—it was a kill or be killed situation—but I couldn't help thinking of the families they'd left behind and the people who would suffer because of their loss. I began to imagine these faceless people grieving, and I had to give myself a mental shake to snap out of it. If this misplaced guilt was something my father felt after he killed someone, I could understand why he was a little bit crazy.

There was a soft knock on the door. "You okay?"

"Yeah. Be out in a sec."

I took some deep breaths to calm myself and gathered my thoughts.

When I came out of the bathroom Smoke was waiting, dressed in a pair of black boxer briefs. He held a green and blue, super soft robe that must have been in with the clothing his sister bought for me. He helped me into the robe, leaving my injured arm uncovered with the sleeve draped on my shoulder.

"Come on, baby, let's change your bandage."

I sat down on the edge of the bed, my whole body hurting now that my post orgasm bliss had faded. We didn't say anything while he changed my bandages, but he kissed all around my stitches, as though his lips could heal me. I ran my fingers through his damp curls, taking comfort in his soothing touch. After tending to me, Smoke helped me take the robe off and put on a pair of comfortable, silky green pajama pants and a thick black tank top. A knock at the door startled me while he was sliding thick socks on my feet, and I was hovering on the edge of grabbing the Uzi stashed beneath the bed.

"Yo, Smoke. Got your grub."

My man must have noticed that I was starting to freak out, because he kissed my cheek and ran a comforting hand down my neck.

"Easy. It's just Hulk with some food."

The big black man came in carrying a tray with sandwiches and a big bowl of soup. A delicious smell wafted up from the food and my stomach growled. I was too tired to do much more than nod at Hulk, and the sympathy in his gaze made my throat tighten.

254

"Hi, sugar." Hulk spoke in a gentle voice as his pale green eyes studied me carefully.

As fragile as I felt at the moment, I didn't say anything as I nodded then turned my attention to the soup.

While Hulk and Smoke talked in lowered voices, I listlessly picked up the bowl of what smelled like chicken soup and began to eat it. The warmth of the broth slid down my throat, and I relaxed marginally. I didn't really taste the food, but I did begin to feel better. By the time I finished half of the peanut butter and jelly sandwich, Hulk had left and Smoke knelt before me. He stroked my cheek, then handed me two pills.

"Take these."

I didn't argue—I didn't have the strength to fight with him—and dutifully took the pills, washing them down with a gulp of milk.

"Want any more?"

I shook my head, laid down on my good side, and watched Smoke devour the rest of my meal. He turned the lights down until the room was only illuminated by a soft, dim light on the dresser. He joined me on the bed, tucked us in, and turned on his side so he could face me. He was close enough that I could feel his breath. We stared at each other—no words were needed—while he gently stroked me beneath the blanket.

"I feel bad for killing those men," I whispered, hoping he didn't think me weak, hoping he wouldn't yell at me like my father would for being a coward.

"Why? Those fuckers were trying to kill you and Breaker. You did the world a favor by taking out that garbage."

"I don't feel bad for killing them, but I feel bad for their families."

"Swan, they were responsible for their actions. It was their choices that led to their deaths, not yours. I promise you, those men were all criminals, demons in human form."

Intellectually I knew this, but it still bothered me. "Okay."

"Get those fuckin' thoughts out of your head." His grip on my hip tightened. "I haven't been in your same exact situation, but I have been where you are mentally right now, and you can't let it fuck with you."

My lower lip trembled, but I swallowed hard, determined not to cry. "How do you deal with it?"

"By living my life. I'm not saying I don't think about some of the shit I've done, or that it doesn't bug me, but life goes on. Here in the States we aren't used to violence. We're spoiled by our safety, but I've been in parts of the world where it's kill or be killed, and my enemy wouldn't give my death a second thought. I can tell you it helps to talk about it, and over time, it will fade. I will always, *always* be here for you for anything, including dealing with this. And I know your dad and Mimi are the same way."

"But the families..."

"Stop. If you think like that, it'll drive you insane."

I opened my mouth to argue with him, but he silenced me with a kiss that was as delicate as butterfly wings. I gave myself over to him, letting him pet and cuddle me until the last of my negative thoughts drained away, and I drifted in his arms, absorbing his love, and letting it heal my heart.

AUSTIN TX

Chapter Thirteen

The sunlight streaming through the barred window warmed my skin as I sat across from Khan at his massive desk and fought the urge to gut-punch Smoke.

With fire in his gaze and his lip curling back in a silent snarl, Smoke glared at Khan. "No fucking way."

Equally pissed, Khan snapped back. "We don't have a choice."

"No. I forbid it."

I cleared my throat, trying to get Smoke's attention while being mindful of playing the part of his dutiful old lady. "Smoke, I can do this."

It was like I wasn't even there. Neither man stopped trying to stare down the other. Hulk stood against the wall in the corner, and I looked to him for help, but his attention was entirely focused on his President. His freshly shaved head gleamed in the late afternoon sunlight, and he was armed to the teeth. There was a savage, angry look on his face I'd never seen before, and I hated the heavy the atmosphere in this room. I felt as if I was choking on testosterone.

I hadn't woken up to do anything other than pee, drink water, and stumble back to bed until sometime after noon. The pain pills I'd been given kept me in a deep, healing sleep. My arm was looking a lot better, and while it still ached, I was able to take a lower dose of pain meds this morning in an effort to keep my wits about me. The food and lots of milk had helped, and I actually felt almost human...ish. The pills had mellowed me out enough that I'd been able to bite my tongue—so far—as they'd discussed what had happened while I slept, but now, I was just about done playing the meek, obedient old lady.

Especially when I learned that Sarah had been spotted in town again, but managed to ditch the club member who tried to follow her...after he saw her coming out of a local free clinic looking, in his words, 'worn down and sick'. My worry for her had reached epic proportions, and I was frantic to find her. Just the thought of her suffering and alone hurt deep inside my heart.

The big muscles of Smoke's biceps clenched as he crossed his arms. "She is not coming to the party tonight!"

Khan's expression closed down, but the muscles of his neck tensed. Shit, the men were about to get pigheaded with each other. "Swan is our best bet to get the traitor or traitors to show themselves. With everyone who'll be here for Brown's patching-in, it'll be the perfect opportunity for someone to try to snatch her. We need to tempt them into doing it. She'll never be in any real danger. You're in charge of her safety at all times. She'll never leave your side."

A shiver raced through me as Smoke slowly stood up and put his fists on the table. He reminded me of a silverback gorilla as he gave Khan a deadly look. "No."

Hulk shifted behind me, a concerned look tightening his full lips. "Smoke..."

"I said *no*." He didn't yell. He didn't even raise his voice, but the level of determination in his tone was clear to everyone in the room.

When Khan stood and placed his fists on the desk, his position mirroring Smoke's, I sensed shit was about to go downhill fast.

Kicking my man's leg I muttered, "Smoke—"

"Shut it, Swan, now is not the fuckin' time."

I knew he was scared, maybe even terrified, for me, that he wasn't thinking clearly, but I agreed with Khan. I needed to be there tonight. I needed to end this, and we weren't any closer to finding my mom or sister than when I'd first arrived. If he thought I was the kind of woman content to sit home and knit hats while he was out having fun, he was out of his mind. We were partners, equals, and equals didn't tell each other to 'shut it' about major, life-changing decisions.

Besides, Smoke was being a dick.

I pulled out one of my knives and slammed it into the table between the two of them hard enough to embed the first few inches into the wood. That made them shut up and look at me. I glared at both of them. I would be calm. I would be rational. I would let them know how things were going to go in a non-antagonistic way. At least that was my intention.

"Smoke, I love you to death, but this isn't your decision to make. I'm going tonight, and you can either help me or you can get the fuck out of my way. This shit needs to end, and I'll make it happen with or without your help."

"You are not! Sit your ass down!" He actually yelled at me.

The only thing that kept me from gutting him was the fact that his concern for me was pouring off of him in waves. I had to remember Mimi's advice about dealing with him when he felt like I was keeping him from being able to protect me to his high standards. That didn't, however, mean I was putting up with his temper, so I raised my middle finger and flipped him off.

Smoke's nostrils flared, and the air around him seemed to grow heavy.

There are women who would have been pissing themselves by this point, but I'd faced down a dangerous man who tried to control every aspect of my life for far too long to put up with Smoke's crap.

"Yes, I am going to work with your brothers to help end the threat," I yelled back. "I can take care of my own fucking self! Shit, I think I proved that yesterday. Give me some damn credit and stop trying to stash me away like I'm a liability."

His face turned red and he loomed over me, his irritation burning my skin even as fear chilled his gaze. "You got lucky."

Oh, that pissed me right the hell off and adrenaline surged through me, fueled by my frustration and pent up anger.

"That wasn't luck, asshole, that was skill—and you know it. I've been training my entire life for this shit. When you were a kid, you were out fucking around with your buddies. I, on the other hand, was learning the best way to break a man's neck. I know what I'm doing, and I *will* do whatever it takes to end this."

"I know you can take care of yourself. But it kills me that you have to." He surprised me when he sank back into his chair, holding his head in his hands. "I can't lose you, Swan, I can't."

I went to him and knelt before his chair, aware of Khan watching us, and rested my hands on his knees. "Please, I have to do this. I'll be safe, I swear."

Lifting his gaze to mine, my heart pounded when I saw the absolute agony in his dark eyes. "Please, don't do this."

I wanted to give in to him, to soothe him, but I just couldn't. "I have to."

Khan cleared his throat, but Smoke and I didn't look away from each other. "We'll constantly have our eyes on her, brother. She'll never be without one of us looking out for her. Swan's your old lady. You know we'll protect her 'cause she's one of our own."

Smoke closed his eyes and desperation etched his features. "Doesn't fuckin' matter what I say, does it? You're gonna do whatever you want."

Trying for patience, I gave his knee a squeeze. "I'm not going to get hurt."

His phone rang, and he grabbed it out of his pocket and looked at the screen. I knew Smoke well enough at this point to easily read his sudden tension. He abruptly stood, and walked away from me. Before he left the room, he looked over his shoulder and said, "Do whatever the fuck you want, Swan. I've got shit to take care of."

With that, he went out the door and slammed it behind him while talking on his phone, leaving me still on my knees and slightly stunned. I knew what was going on between us wasn't normal, and I couldn't help but wonder if my life with Smoke would always be like this. Would he always try to make the decisions for me? Could I spend the rest of my life living with a man who could be so tender one moment and such a colossal asshole the next?

Khan cleared his throat. "You okay, girl?"

I stood and turned my back for a moment, hoping they didn't see me rub away a tear. "Yeah, I'm good. So what's the game plan?"

Six hours later, I sat on the edge of the bed in our small bedroom, and watched Smoke pace in front of me. He was looking hot as sin tonight in his dark jeans, his vest, and a very tight t-shirt that hugged all his yummy muscles. And I wasn't looking so bad myself. Alisha had come over and helped me slut-up biker style. Turns out Alisha had spent some time as a sweet butt before she settled down with her old man, Donkey. The way she described it, you could tell it hadn't been easy for her to make the transition to old lady, but now that she'd been with her old man for seven years, she was starting to feel at home.

Alisha had dressed me in a pair of butter-soft leather pants that laced up the sides with black lace through bright steel rings and rivets. They were sexy, kick ass, and I loved them. They were also super easy to move in, and the leather was high quality which meant it would protect my skin. The shirt I wore was an empire waist black top that dipped low enough to give me some major cleavage, but was loose enough at my middle so I could wear a holster. The long-sleeved shirt looked sedate from the front, but the top half of the back was almost totally exposed beneath a thin layer of black lace. That see-through back wouldn't look good with a bra, which meant my breasts trembled with each breath and my major cleavage became positively obscene despite the decent amount of chest support the top provided.

While Alisha was wearing a pair of comfy slippers, I was forced into some far from comfortable boots that would be a pain in the ass to stand in for any period of time. My arm still ached, but Smoke had given me some more pills and the pain was already fading. Hopefully, it would also help me endure my footwear.

I was being careful not to cry as Smoke continued to ignore me because Alisha had laid the makeup on thick. When I looked in the mirror, I swore my sister was looking back at me with her pouty pink lips and expertly done smoky eye shadow. Sarah would rock this outfit with her strong self-confidence without a second thought and look like a model strutting on a runway. I was just hoping that no one was around when I had to take the stairs—slowly—while holding my tits.

With a rough sigh, Smoke stopped pacing, but he didn't look at me. "You ready?"

He'd spent the last fifteen minutes pleading with me not to go tonight, and I was rather surprised by his abrupt change of attitude.

"Yeah," I said in a low voice, waiting for the argument to begin anew.

His gaze raked over me and his nostrils flared as he lingered over my exposed cleavage with a look that was positively possessive. "Who put the sparkles on your tits?"

"Alisha, but she never touched me. It was just with the brush which was okay."

Actually, she had touched me a couple times and my stomach had clenched harder each time. It wasn't her fault, makeup involved touching people, but it still made me ill. I'm not one for self-pity, but sometimes I really hated being me. Right now, I especially hated my body for becoming aroused any time Smoke was around. This was ridiculous, I couldn't continue to function like this or I'd lose my edge. But oh…how I wanted him and the blissful oblivion his affection offered even as I tried to focus on the upcoming mission.

He knelt before me, setting his hands on either side of my waist, pulling me into his seductive warmth. "When we get through this, you and I are gonna have a long, long talk which is going to end with your ass spanked so red you won't sit down comfortably for a week."

My libido quickly responded, "Will you fuck me as hard? Make my pussy as sore?"

Smoke blinked at me, then grinned. "I'll do my best."

I smacked his chest, not wanting him to think he was off the hook for being a dick. "Smoke, focus."

"I'm not the one talkin' dirty," he muttered before standing. "You are not to leave my side, ever."

"Isn't that going to make it a bit hard for me to act as bait? I mean how can anyone approach me with you being my human shield? Come on, I have Hulk, Khan, Frame, and Alisha with her old man Donkey watching over me. Not to mention all the prospects that trail after me like hulking puppy dogs. I'm not sure how whoever is after me can even think they'll be able to get to me in this fortress. Just trust me to be okay. I…I love you so much, but I can't take it if you keep trying to swaddle me in cotton and lock me away like I'm made of crystal. Please have faith in me."

He clenched his hands, and as I saw his anger ramp up, I gathered the courage to try and calm him down. I placed my hand gently over his then uncurled his fingers one by one. Once his hand was loose in mine, I placed it on my cleavage, over my heart. Where speech would fail me my body wouldn't. It was so much easier for me to express my love physically than with words. I looked up at him, sensing his internal battle and hating that I was at the root of it.

"First, you are brilliant. I would never, ever say otherwise. Second, I have faith in you, it's the rest of the fuckin' world I don't trust."

"Miguel, I need you right now. Please. I need you to keep me safe *and* let me do what I can to take care of this situation. I'm sick of it, sick of the constant fear, the tension, the never ending emotional roller coaster.

While you may know me well, thanks to your disturbing level of stalker behavior, I don't have the same advantage. You're still very new to me, and even though I've felt like I've known you forever, it's only been a few weeks. I want time to just be with you. To enjoy falling in love without constantly watching our backs, and that won't happen unless we end this."

He closed his eyes and swallowed hard, then his features began to slowly go blank. The lines of worry smoothed out, and his lips firmed. Before my very eyes he was making the transformation from Miguel to Smoke, and I found it fascinating. I had studied this man so much, obsessed over his every delicious feature, that I knew his expressions better than my own. When he opened his eyes I found the killer I needed looking back at me. His expression had gone blank, scary, and his entire body seemed to grow and somehow become bigger, more intimidating. He took a half step closer to me, and I once again felt the size difference between us on every level.

Unable to help myself, I sucked in a little gasp as lust and fear combined inside of me. His gaze darkened even more as he placed his hand on my chest and slowly flexed his fingers over my heart. "You keep this alive and well for me, got me? Don't do anything stupid or dangerous because wherever you go, I'm coming with you. They will have to kill me to get to you, and I would gladly give my life for yours, but I'd rather spend the rest of my hopefully long, long life loving you. I'll do anything, sacrifice everything, to make that happen."

My heart slammed against my ribs hard enough that he had to feel it against his palm, and it began to race as panic roared through me at the thought of anything happening to him.

"No, please...please Smoke. Don't do anything to endanger yourself. I'm begging you."

He gave me a laugh that wasn't nice and stroked my cheek. "I'll tell you the same thing you tell me, Swan. I have to do this."

I gaped at him, unable to come up with a smart retort, while I wondered if this irrational panic I was experiencing was the same thing he felt. This was an epiphany, an understanding that gave me a small peek into the way he thought. Okay, now I understood a bit what it was like to go insane with fear. It wasn't a nice feeling.

"I'm sorry."

He blinked at me, but the predatory look stayed on his face. "For?"

"I think I understand. Your worry, I mean. When I think about anything happening to you it makes me wild to stop it." I sighed and stood, smoothing down my top and going over my weapons before checking my hair where I had a couple surprises hidden. "I'm sorry you feel that way 'cause it sucks. How about we promise to keep each other alive, okay? Let's not fret about who's going to die for whom. I don't know about you, but that sounds like melancholy Romeo and Juliet emo drivel to me."

He gathered me up into his arms so quickly that I didn't have time to even yelp. One instant I was fixing my upswept hair, held in place by two black lacquer chopsticks, the next my body was pressed tight enough to his that I could feel his heart thundering against my cheek. He buried his nose against my hair and took a deep breath while I hugged him back. We remained like that for a long time, just holding each other while loud voices began to echo up and down the hall.

Finally he pulled back and kissed me softly on the lips. "Ready, baby girl?"

"As I'm ever gonna be."

AUSTIN TX

Chapter Fourteen

I was pretty sure I was gonna puke, and it wasn't because I'd been drinking.

We'd been wandering around the party for about four hours, and I'd seen just about every sexual act human beings could do to one another. At first it had shocked me, maybe even titillated me a little, but now I was over it. Smoke, bless his heart, was trying to shield me the best he could from the depravity, but about half an hour ago he'd given up, and I'd spent most of my time focusing my gaze on the wall above the action happening down lower. No wonder the old ladies never came to parties like this, it was just so unhygienic. There were people having sex all over the place and none of them were putting down a towel first. For someone with minor germ issues like myself, it was enough to make me cringe.

Guys dropped their condoms on the floor. Right on the fucking floor! No wonder Scarlett, the Iron Horse Secretary's old lady back in Austin, yelled at Smoke about it. I had no idea whose job it was to clean this place up, but they should be doing it in hazmat gear. And Khan needed to cover all his furniture in thick plastic.

I wished I could go outside where the picnic benches and stuff were, to get away from the crowd, but there was no way Smoke and my self-appointed guards were going to let me out of their sight.

People from all over the state had come to celebrate with Brown as he got patched in, which as far as I could tell, involved a new vest and a lot of drinking, smoking pot, and manly hugs as well as willing women as far as the eye could see. News about the little ambush I faced had been kept on the down-low, and no one asked me about it. I think I was the only old lady still there, other than Alisha who stuck around to help guard me. She was around here somewhere in her blue micro-mini dress hanging out with her husband, Donkey. The rest of the old ladies and serious girlfriends had taken off after the ceremony hours ago, after telling me how glad they were I survived, and thanking me over and over for saving Breaker. The one good spot in this night was when I learned that Breaker would make a full recovery, and that even though he had a mild concussion and blood loss, it could have been much worse.

Cathy called me from the hospital earlier, sobbing, and we had a very uncomfortable conversation where she basically blubbered incoherent shit, and I said a couple 'you're welcomes' before I basically hung up on her. It felt weird to realize that in addition to taking someone's life, I'd saved someone else's. I mean, I knew I'd saved his life, but I really hadn't processed the ramifications yet. The knowledge that I'd saved some little kids' Dad made my heart ache like someone was squeezing it in a fist.

Shit, I did not have time to get all melodramatic. I was on a mission, which meant I needed to focus. But damn, I was tired of standing around. The noise was overwhelming, and I was starting to feel a little claustrophobic. Smoke had slipped me another pill earlier, and it was making me tired. The room was so packed with people now that my personal space was almost nil.

It had to be nearing midnight, and I was wondering if anyone was even going to make a move. In all my planning for tonight, the one thing I hadn't counted on was how fucking bored and fatigued I'd be. The fornicating going on around me held absolutely no interest for me, because there was no emotion involved. Just a lot of groping and grunting, then they would get off, and the guy would discard the woman with about as much regard for her as for the used condom. Not arousing for me in the least.

Because of the sexist pig nature of most of these bikers, I was pretty much ignored whenever a new bunch of guys approached Smoke. It was the same every time. Smoke would introduce me as his old lady, the biker would make some kind of comment about how hot I was, and Smoke would growl or tell him to fuck off. The guy would then act surprised, then apologize for real to me, all of them grinning or laughing while congratulating Smoke for landing such a hot old lady. It was macho male bonding at its finest.

Then that stupid male 'I need to talk to you, bro' look would happen and from that point on they would ignore me and just bullshit with each other about biker stuff. I swear to God it was like dating an accountant and listening to him talk numbers with his colleagues. Instead of figures, they were talking about a buddy of theirs who was currently in jail, or using that stupid biker slang, that I didn't totally get, and losing me altogether.

I never doubted that Smoke was on high alert. Despite his relaxed demeanor, he was never more than a couple inches away, but I was still getting restless. Thankfully, the long-sleeved shirt and pants kept me from feeling most touches, but every once in a while someone would brush my hand, and I'd have to swallow hard. Smoke must have noticed, because he soon gave me a bottle of water, rubbing my hands when he did, and the yucky sensations vanished.

Alisha's voice came from next to me, and I twitched, startled by her sudden appearance. Dressed in a low-cut, pale blue, sparkly dress with almost as much makeup as I was wearing, she blended in with the sweet butts in spite of her bubbly, innocent looks. "You need a bathroom break?"

"No, I'm good. Smoke took me a couple minutes ago."

A frown flitted across her face as someone bumped into her. It happened so quickly, I wasn't sure I'd even seen it before her dimpled smile returned. "Okay, how about a beer?"

Exquisite Danger(Iron Horse MC, #2)

"No beer," Smoke growled, turning his attention momentarily back to me.

I pointedly looked at the beer in his hand and gave him my best 'Really?' look. "Why not? You have one?"

"You're on heavy pain meds. One beer and you'll be fucked up, and not in a good way."

I had no good comeback for this, so I just glared at him.

He stared at me, but before we could start arguing, Donkey motioned for Smoke, and he took a couple steps away, leaving me with Alisha. I leaned down and spoke close to her ear. "Fuck him, get me a beer."

With a giggle, she moved off through the crowd, leaving me with the small victory in my minor rebellion and easing the knot in my belly.

Returning to scanning the vast open space, I thought I heard a familiar laugh to the right of the room where the bar stretched out along the far wall and tended by women in cut offs and bikini tops. I could have sworn it sounded like Sarah, but from my vantage point, all I could see were brunettes, blondes and a couple of auburn-haired women among the mass of bodies. Cyclone was now over there as well, huddled up on the couch with a stacked redhead. I quickly moved my gaze from them, not wanting to even think about that skank. I'd hoped that she was the spy, and we could take out at least one threat, but Smoke swore Cyclone was loyal to the club and wouldn't betray it. He told me that she would be at the party, and since she'd been set up, he asked me not to pick a fight. Of course, if she said anything to me, I was welcome to beat her ass, but Cyclone had been told to keep away from me. She was currently on the other side of the big room, as far away from me as she could get, talking to the redheaded chick with large breasts. She hadn't so much as looked my way, so I tried to dismiss her from my mind.

Alisha returned a few minutes later and handed me a water glass with an inch of amber brown liquid in it and held an open beer bottle in her other hand. "Here, shot of Southern Comfort."

Grinning at her, I took the glass and quickly downed it before taking the beer with a gasp. "Thanks."

"Welcome."

She vanished off into the crowd with a guilty look thrown at Smoke's back. He was now talking to Hulk with another two guys I didn't know, the men forming a cluster of black leather while they leaned in to mutter with each other. I turned my back to Smoke and took a long drink of the beer, grateful for the bracing chill racing down my throat as the bitter taste filled my mouth and replaced the sweet, syrupy burn of the Southern Comfort. The heeled boots I wore weren't super tall, but they were high enough that my feet were starting to hurt after standing around for hours despite my fading pain meds. I could have taken a seat, but every surface of this place had been or was about to be defiled, so I put up with my sore feet and wondered when I would be able to go to bed.

I was fucking beat and the beer and SC shot were mellowing me out since I drank on an almost empty stomach.

Last time I'd had a beer, I was standing in my parents' backyard watching the wind move the trees in the valley below our hillside spread. It felt like a million years ago instead of just a few days. A time when I was just a woman trying to survive, not a killer in my own right. The image of shooting that man began to play out in my mind, but I ruthlessly locked it away, and wondered how my father was ever able to ignore the memories of the people he'd killed. A man getting a blow job in a corner roared out his orgasm and snapped me out of my dark thoughts. I took another drink of my beer, trying to focus on the here and now. Like the fact that Breaker was alive and I'd landed in the uncomfortable role of hero. I didn't need or want the recognition. My dad taught me to blend in, and I was doing a craptastic job of it so far. Time to focus.

I was positioned in the room so I had a good view of the staircase leading upstairs. From my vantage point I could see a pair of sparkly blue hooker heels, with dolphins on them, that I instantly coveted and a couple pairs of men's motorcycle boots. I was so busy admiring the woman's shoes that I didn't register something small and dark had been dropped from the stairs while she quickly walked away. As it rolled down the last few steps, I realized what it was and screamed.

"Grenade, everyone down!"

Smoke crushed me to the floor an instant before a big bang hurt my eardrums and the lights went out. I couldn't hear any screams over the ringing in my ears, just muted shouts of panic as the room filled with dense smoke and chaos. The lights flashed on and off, in an almost strobe-like effect that made me dizzy. Smoke grunted as someone stepped on his back hard enough to push him into me. Fear clawed at me as I considered that we could get trampled to death as the crowd started to panic. I was completely blinded by the time we got to our feet, and Smoke clung to me, telling me to stay close.

He got us up against a wall, and it afforded us a bit of safety from the crowd.

"We should head for the stairs," he yelled then coughed. "Front and back doors are too dangerous."

Instead of answering, I nodded right before loud bangs and screams came from the front of the room. Smoke and I immediately drew our guns and began to edge along the wall. I almost shot Hulk when he appeared out of the dense smoke, but I recognized his shape enough that I pointed my gun at the ground instead of him.

Smoke jerked him down to a crouch, and I followed suit. The air was better down here and I scanned the area while Hulk told Smoke that there were snipers, one out front and one out back, firing warning shots at people. He eyed me and lowered his voice, then Smoke nodded.

"Let's go."

I found myself being pulled between them and was almost to the stairs when a second smoke grenade when off somewhere to my left. A moment later, I was completely blind as someone grabbed me out of the oppressive gloom. Then another hand from a different direction grabbed my shirt. The hand on my forearm was a woman's hand, and I went to break her wrist when she twisted me in a move my dad would have envied, jerking me away from whoever had a hold on my shirt and said in my ear, "Swan, it's me, Sarah. We need to get you out of here. Up to your room, now."

My heart stopped as I recognized her voice, but I couldn't see shit. "Prove it."

"Your first crush was Slater on *Saved by the Bell*. You had a pillow with his face on it that you kissed because you're a pillow-molesting pervert."

"Sarah!" I coughed out a sob, reaching out for her and finding her other hand.

Smoke roared out somewhere to my left, and I tried to tug Sarah toward Smoke's bellowing voice but she dragged me in the general direction of the stairs. "He'll find us. We need to go, now, up to your room. All the guest rooms have security doors, and it'll be easier to make a stand there than down here. Los Diablos and a couple bounty hunters with tranqs are in here looking for you and trying to flush you out. If they find out we're both here, we're fucked, so I need you to *move*."

Without another word, I followed her as best I could, sliding around people, taking the stairs in a stealthy manner that would have made my father proud. Windows must have been opened because the smoke was beginning to clear, but people were still yelling, and I saw more than one gun out in the open. I'd somehow lost mine during the tug of war downstairs. As the air cleared, I caught glimpses of Sarah's green dress and the crazy auburn wig she was wearing along with what had to be a big prosthetic nose through the fog still clouding the stairway. I grew dizzy and disoriented for a moment, but managed to gather my thoughts and push through.

At the top of the stairs were two prospects in gas masks who ushered us up to the third floor while they continued to scan the stairs with their guns trained on the crowd below. Thank fuck they were on my side. I could hear Khan roaring from somewhere behind me in the area of his office, but all I could really focus on was the fact that Sarah was here, alive, and dressed like a high-class hooker. We were almost to my room when I felt a sudden weakness rush over me, and my fear went into overdrive.

Shit, I knew this fuzzy feeling all too well.

Fuck.

"I don't feel good," I managed to mumble out from my numb lips.

"What? How?"

"Don't...know. Feel weird. Stoned."

"Did someone drug you?"

"Pain meds...did a big shot of Southern Comfort. And beer."

She snarled at me. "You dumbass! I can't believe you did that!"

I tried to walk with her but it was getting harder, and she was soon supporting me. "Don't you fucking puss out on me, bitch. Get your ass in gear. *Fight.* Never give up."

That managed to get me three more steps, and I slumped against the wall as warmth flowed through me.

This was nice. I really didn't care about anything at the moment. I could probably withstand torture if I felt like this. Mellow.

Shit.

My life was so utterly fucked up.

Sarah flung my door open, dragging me behind her, and when I went to look behind me I saw an unfamiliar guy dressed like a biker with a couple days' worth of

beard. The rage distorting his face, as Sarah slammed
the door shut behind me, I threw back the lock. Sarah
went to shove the dresser in front of the door and I
helped her as best I could in my current state, my breath
coming out in ragged coughs as I struggled to free my
airway from the smoke I'd inhaled downstairs.

A sickening lethargy spread through me, and I
limply grabbed onto Sarah's arm as she dragged me
into the bathroom. She hauled me over to the toilet and
stuck her finger down my throat. Despite the increasing
lassitude, my body knew what to do when my gag
reflex was triggered. I threw up until my stomach was
cramping. Sarah eased me back, then cleaned me up
and massaged my stomach, easing the pain until I was
lying there panting, sweaty, and exhausted. My last
thought before unconsciousness claimed me was that I
was really fuckin' tired of passing out.

I woke up sometime later to the harsh noise of Sarah
in über bitch mode going off on someone. My thoughts
were slow and muzzy. We must have been drinking
pretty hard last night, because my head ached and my
mouth tasted like someone had taken a dump in it while
I was sleeping. Moving took too much effort, so I just
pulled in a deep breath and shouted, "For fuck's sake,
Sarah, can you stop yelling at Dad for ten damn
minutes. Shit. And go get me some orange juice and
some aspirin."

I managed to pull the pillow over my face, already
half asleep, when it was rudely jerked away from me. I
had to close my eyes against the light searing my
pupils. Rough fingers touched my face, and I squinted

and focused on what turned out to be the somehow familiar face of a super hot guy. Blinking at him, I reached out and traced his lips, and the sight of his red eyes disturbed me enough that I blinked against the stinging light to try and see him better.

I cleared my throat and croaked out, "Do I know you?"

An expression of fear crossed his face, and my sister spoke from the side of the room, "She'll be fine. Give her stupid brain a chance to surface past her attempts to kill it with alcohol and drugs."

"Bitch." I lifted my head to look at her, then clasped my hands over my throbbing skull as I tried to hold it together. "Owwww."

Slender fingers pried my hands off my eyes and Sarah looked down on me. The wig was gone as well as the fake nose, and her pale blonde hair brushed her shoulders while the remains of heavy makeup streaked her face. Her blotchy, swollen face told me she'd been crying. Neither of us shed pretty tears. She'd lost weight and appeared really, really run down.

I reached up and touched her sharp cheekbone. "Sarah, are you sick?"

Pressing her lips together, she glanced around the room then back to me. "I'll talk to you about it later."

"Khan is on his way," a man said from the other side of the room and Sarah swallowed.

I licked my dry lips as memories began to surface. "Khan…like the wrath of…he's scary."

My sister gave a brittle laugh. "He can be, but he's also a pussy cat. What else can you remember?"

The breath left my lungs in a low rush as my mind began to fill with my life. "Smoke."

I immediately reached for him, and he picked me all the way up, cradling me in his arms. His body shook, and I clumsily tried to pet and soothe him. If he started to cry I was fucking done for.

"Hey, hey, I'm okay."

When he looked up I realized he wasn't shaking with sorrow, but rather anger. "You're okay," he repeated in a low voice.

"I'm okay, I'm here, I'm alive," then I kissed him to prove it.

"Alive," he whispered against my mouth with apparent profound relief.

Before our kiss could get dirty Sarah said, "Ha! I knew you had a thing for her."

I turned my head so I could see Sarah, but didn't let go of Smoke. "What?"

She ignored my question, and gave Smoke a smug smile. "How the mighty have fallen. I bet every sweet butt from here to New Mexico is crying herself to sleep."

It looked like Sarah felt comfortable with Smoke and had a good relationship with him in her own messed up way. She gave him shit like he was family. From the spark in Smoke's dark eyes he was about to give as good as he got.

"Speaking of fallen," Smoke said in a silky voice, "Beach is waiting for you to call him back, Sarah. He wanted me to remind you of your agreement with him, one phone call a day, every day. And my Prez also wants you to know that Papi is on his way, and that you're his now, princess. Get ready for a life of spoiled leisure after he punishes you for scaring ten years off his life."

Watching the blood rush out of her face might have been comical if she hadn't looked like she was about to faint. Before she could stumble, Hulk was there, gently supporting her. She smiled gratefully up at him and patted his arm. "Always there to catch me. You need to get a new hobby."

"You need to stop falling down around me."

She took a deep breath and looked Smoke in the eye, a light flush heating her cheeks. "Well, I guess I'll be taking the next seven years off from working full-time to sit on my ass and eat bon bons."

Confused by their inside conversation and the state of the world in general, I thumped Smoke on the shoulder, "Can you let me down? I need to talk to my sister."

"We all need to talk to your sister," Hulk muttered while Sarah had the good grace to blush as her defiant expression fell a notch.

Without another word, I grabbed her hand and tugged her into the bathroom, ignoring the protests of the men. As soon as we were inside I turned on the shower and locked the door, then spun to face her. We stared at each other for a moment before Sarah cracked a smile and said, "You look like you're doing okay for yourself."

"Yeah, other than people trying to kill me every time I turn around I'm having a great time."

She winced, then looked down at her hands. "I'm sorry I haven't caught her yet."

I grabbed her in a fierce hug. "I don't give a fuck about that, you stupid bitch! You're alive, that's the only thing I care about. I love you so much, I was so worried about you, and I'm sorry I've been such a crotch nugget to you. Where the fuck have you been?"

"It's…complicated." She hugged me back hesitantly at first then harder until she started to sob. "I'm so sorry I got you dragged into this. I didn't know Los Diablos would be at the bar. You got there before I did, I got caught up in traffic, and by the time I arrived they had you. I followed them as far as I could, then called the clubhouse and left an anonymous tip."

For a moment I had no idea what she was talking about, then I thought back to when this roller coaster ride from hell began in Dallas when I'd been kidnaped for the first time.

"Hey, it's not your fault. I wasn't paying any attention. I should have seen them. I guess my paranoia was out of practice. Besides, Smoke saved me, and I started to fall in love with him that night."

She blinked quickly, something I did as well when I was trying to fight off tears. In many ways watching Sarah was like watching myself, and she was easier than anyone for me to read. I mean yeah, she was my twin, but it went deeper than that. I was filled with a sense of shame for having given up this special bond with my sister for someone as stupid as Stewart.

Sarah sighed and tucked a wayward strand of my hair behind my ear. "I'm so proud of you, and so sorry I still haven't managed to nail our mother down. That bitch is slippery, and I can't get too close to her without tipping off her watchdogs. Please forgive me for dragging you into this, but I couldn't do it on my own."

"You didn't drag me into anything, it was our waste-of-space mother. I'm so proud of you for going after her even if I want to strangle you for putting yourself in danger like that! Where have you been? What have you been doing? And why the hell wouldn't you contact me?"

"I couldn't. Nothing I sent to you could be trusted not to end up in the wrong hands. They have hackers that make Stewart look like a rank amateur. This is the big league, Swan, and they don't play around. I got the jewels that will make Hustler happy, I got the codes that will make the Russians happy, and I know for a fact that we can trade them for our safety. The Russians will not only forgive our mother's debt, they will add their protection to us. That leaves the Israelis, and I'm hoping that'll work itself out." She took a deep breath and let it out slowly. "So we'll have a strong enough shield of people guarding us, the kind of people who will seek bloody retribution on our behalf, and we should, in theory, be able to live the rest of our lives in relative peace."

I stared at her, completely stunned. "Are you for fucking real?"

"Absolutely." Something…mesmerizing flashed in her blue eyes for a moment then she sat taller. "The Iron Horse MC is my family. Nobody fucks with my family and most especially, nobody fucks with my blood. I love you honey, so much, and I'm so, so happy to see you. I missed you."

She told me that Beach had taught her about unconditional love and how she felt so at peace now. It had taken her awhile to get used to the idea that someone could love her for who she is, that she was worthy of that love, but Beach was nothing if not determined. I just held her and listened, letting her pour out her feelings and emotions. That's how Sarah coped with things. She needed someone she could trust enough to confide in, someone to talk it out with. It had been a long time since she'd done this with me, and I couldn't help but wonder if Beach filled that role in her life now. Smoke certainly filled my need to be held and cuddled, but it still felt good to hold my sister in my arms.

I eventually pried her off of me and handed her a wad of toilet paper so she could blow her nose. I wiped my own eyes and studied her, noticing that she'd lost at least ten pounds, and underneath the cheap bracelets she wore stacked on her left arm she had 'Beach' tattooed on her inner-wrist. My mind tried to switch to her fiancé and thoughts of how relieved he was going to be, but right now my focus needed to be on Sarah. My heart ached with love for her, and it took everything I had not to grab her and hug the shit out of her again. We didn't have much more time before the guys intruded, and I needed to talk to her, but only after she pulled herself together.

Everything was going so fast that my filter couldn't catch up. "I'm going to sing *Wind Beneath my Wings* for you at your wedding."

"You better be ready to sing it in Vegas," Sarah said with a grin as she wiped at her face with a washcloth. "Because I've been thinking about marrying Beach there since the day I met him, and it's going to be a hell of a party."

A giggle bubbled up out of me before I could stop it, and I was transported back in time to my sister watching one of those bridal dress shows with me and telling me how she was going to get married in some tropical paradise.

"What happened to the palm tree-themed wedding?"

"I decided to save that for the month-long honeymoon Beach and I will go on. You have no idea how much I want that man to myself. I don't want to share him with anyone, just soak up the sun and love him."

Empathy surged through me as I imagined doing that with Smoke, and how good it would be. "I hear ya. Once this shit is settled, you tell me when and where, and I will be at your wedding...as long as you do one thing for me."

"And that would be?"

"Could you have a reception party at Dad's after? It would mean a lot to him and Mimi."

"I'm not getting married without Dad and Mimi being there. Nice side perk of being Beach's old lady is people try to kiss our asses—a lot. So we get things like free use of private jets and all that thrown at us all the time. Although Beach is more likely to just go out and buy one if it comes to that. Boys and their toys." Her lower lip trembled, then she began to cry again.

Flustered, I patted her back. "Girl, get a grip. You can't cry like this in front of those guys, they'll be terrified of Beach thinking they made you unhappy. Time to woman up."

After dragging in a few watery breaths she sighed and whispered, "Sorry, hormones are making me a fucking mess. If Beach thought I was crazy before wait until he has to live with me for the next nine months."

"Hormones?"

The look in her gaze was tortured as she said, "I'm pregnant."

I took one deep breath, and another, then squealed and clapped my hands as her words fully set in. "Congratulations! A baby! Oh, my gosh, that is amazing."

A new tear raced down her blotchy cheek. "Swan, I'm not happy about it."

"Why the hell not? Beach is going to be overjoyed. He loves you so much Sarah. He'll be happy that you're going to have a baby. You have nothing to worry about. That man would move heaven and earth for you."

"You don't understand. I know he'll be a wonderful father, and he wants to have a baby with me so bad...but I'll be a terrible mother."

"What?" The conviction and self-hatred in her voice struck me like a blow. "No, you will be a wonderful mother. You're such a good person, and while I may have been too dumb to see it, you take care of those you love."

"But what if I end up like...her? I couldn't do that to my baby. I've been trying to be better, but every once in a while my temper slips and I hurt people's feelings. What if I did that to my child?"

"When's the last time you lost it?"

"On Beach. We had a big fight, and I flipped out and said some pretty bad stuff."

I blinked. "Okay, well, what about before then?"

"Um, when Beach and I started dating, I shaved a sweet butt bald for fucking with me."

Before I could help it I giggled. "Right. Well those were adult fucked up situations. You won't be like that around your child because you're their blood. Think about the way the baby cousins flock to you for cuddles. They love you and you're so good with them."

"Mom was good with us when we were young, loved and protected us…then look what happened. That could be me if I'm not careful."

I wanted to go and hunt down my mother right now for screwing my sister up so much that she was afraid to love her child.

"You won't. You aren't, and you never will be like that bitch." I held her head between my hands and made Sara look at me, noting how dark the circles under her eyes were. "You would never do this to anyone, let alone your child."

She blinked back some tears and her lower lip trembled, but she nodded. "You're right."

A knock came from the door and Smoke said, "We need you out here."

"Be right there," I yelled back.

"Beach is going to hate me," she suddenly whispered, her face ashen. "Even though he says he loves me, he's going to hate me for endangering his child."

I shook my head at her. "God you're an idiot sometimes."

That brought some color back to her cheeks. "What?"

"Look at you! Fuck, woman, you faced down bikers and the mafia, then managed to save the goddamn world by yourself. You're a fucking superhero. Any child would be blessed to have you as a mom. Your past is just that, your past. And when did Sarah Anderson, *Playboy* Centerfold, Pole Dancing Champion, and Ice Dancing Junior Queen of Nevada give a fuck what anyone thinks of her?"

"When those two pink lines came up on the pregnancy test."

There was another knock on the door and we opened it to a scowling Hulk. "Hate to interrupt your tea party, but you have some people waiting on you."

After turning off the shower, Sarah slipped her hand into mine and we walked out of the bathroom together to face the waiting crowd of men. There was a collective gasp from the group staring at us as we stood before them. I had to resist the urge to roll my eyes as everyone did the back-and-forth thing, comparing me to Sarah and vice versa, as they tried to wrap their minds around the idea that we really were identical twins. Khan broke the silence first with a growl as he took a step forward and picked Sarah up, twirling her around before setting her on her feet again with a loud, smacking kiss on her cheek.

"You scared ten fuckin' years off my life! Where the fuck have you been? Why didn't you come to me?"

She darted a glance around the room, but bitch Sarah was rising to the surface and I watched as my sister swiftly rebuilt the walls between her heart and the rest of the world. "That would require trust, and you know I don't trust anyone except Beach and my family."

I expected Khan to be angry, but he just shook his head. "Should've come to me, trust or not."

Smoke moved behind me, and I gratefully relaxed into his arms. He touched me softly to reassure himself that I was okay while I did the same, stroking the fine hair on his arms. His scent enveloped me, and my body relaxed into his safety.

The wild look in Sarah's eyes eased as she took in the sight of Smoke wrapped around me. "My goal, Khan, is to stay alive. I will do whatever it takes to make that happen. As will my sister. It's how we were raised."

My dad had done his best to catch my sister up on my training, but she preferred to fight with him rather than do some of the more crazy stuff. I was a huge fan of Sarah telling my dad off and getting her way, because that meant I didn't have to do some of the bullshit I hated. Like mountain climbers. If I never did another fucking mountain climber in my life it would be too soon. Sarah was super strong when we were teenagers—she did competitive ice skating—and she could march my dad into the ground, but if she didn't want to do it, so she wouldn't. Drove my dad bug fuck, but I think Mimi was proud that Sarah stood up for herself—and me. It was after her first confrontation with our dad where she came out the winner—we didn't have to spend the night in the snow with no tent—that I began to open up to her and our friendship began.

I wanted those days when we were tight back, and I could feel like she was one of my best friends again.

Smoke, ever aware of my mood, leaned down and whispered, "She's not leaving our side tonight until Beach gets here. I'll sleep in the chair, but I want you two in bed and tucked in."

Was I a horrible person because for one brief instant I was sad Smoke and I wouldn't be able to physically reconnect? Then I looked at my sister, and I couldn't imagine letting her leave my sight. It was going to be hard to let her go, but I'm sure Beach was just about insane with worry at this point, and I wasn't getting in his way once he arrived. Even if she'd been calling him once a day, I'm sure Beach had been ready to tear his hair out with worry. For all I knew, the psycho could be on his way via private helicopter.

Smoke's phone beeped, and as he read the text, the corner of his lip curved up in a grin. "Beach will be here in two hours. He says he wants to talk to you in person."

I could hear Sarah's sharp inhalation, then she let out a shaky sigh. "How can I love and hate him at the same time?"

"Because you're a crazy bitch," I muttered.

Smoke just gave her a solemn look. "Which one are you gonna embrace, love or hate?"

Sarah's brow crinkled. "What?"

I rolled my eyes at Smoke's fortune cookie answer. "Just let go of your bullshit already and marry the guy. You're obviously stupid for each other, so just make it official and live your happily ever after."

Hope brightened her eyes to an intense sky blue and she wiggled her toes. "Just like that?"

"Why not?"

"But there's so much between us…"

Smoke chuckled. "Women...always over-complicating shit. Here's what you're gonna do: when Beach comes in you are going to tell him you're sorry, then kiss him until he stops trying to talk. I'll clear the room across the hall out, and you can take him in there and remind him how much you love him. Then, you're gonna take your punishment from your Papi like a good little girl."

I blinked rapidly, waiting for Sarah to knock his ass to the ground for calling her a little girl but she just grinned. "Sometimes being a bad little girl is fun."

"Tell me that tomorrow after you've had a night with Beach, knowing you scared the fuck out of him."

"He'll be fine," she said with a breezy wave of her hand. I wasn't fooled by her nonchalance, she was shaking in her boots, quite literally. A fine tremor ran through her, and I thought she might cry, but instead she burst out laughing. "Okay, he might be a little tiny bit irritated with me, but he acted like a dick."

"True. In fact, I think he might still owe you," Sarah beamed at Smoke and he shook his head, grinning back. "Remember to make him beg for it if you really want an apology. Make him hard until his dick hurts and he'll forgive you for anything once you give him that pussy he's been starvin' for."

Sarah and I blushed as Smoke went out into the hall to let the guards know what was going on. She ran her fingers through her hair. "I look like shit."

"Well, let's kick Smoke out so we can get you ready for Beach and get something to eat."

When Beach finally arrived, I swear I knew it before the man was even in the building because suddenly Sarah sat up straighter and nervously smoothed her hand over her slightly rounded stomach. She wore a pretty white dress that had a loose, almost poncho style top that hid her bump, but when she flattened the fabric it was easy to see that she was a little over four months along. Evidently, Sarah had found a way to get pre-natal care while on the road without alerting anyone, and her baby was as healthy as could be, unhurt by Sarah's intense morning sickness. She even knew the sex, but she wouldn't tell me until she told Beach first. My respect for her grew by leaps and bounds as I imagined how much courage it took to head out, alone, pregnant, and sick to try and hunt down our mother. The marvel of a little baby being inside my sister still hadn't faded, and I had a hard time keeping my hands off her belly. Thankfully, Sarah didn't mind, she'd just place her hand over mine and smile at me.

Smoke and I stood as well, and when the door slammed open a tension-filled minute later, I didn't even bother to go for my gun, because Beach's aura filled the room like ocean waves in a storm. I knew that sounded goofy as shit, but I could have sworn I felt his energy rush over my skin the moment he saw Sarah. In less than a heartbeat, he had Sarah in his arms, and she was clinging to his neck with her legs wrapped around his waist. I could hear her whisper, "I'm sorry," before they cinched into a lip lock while desperately grabbing at each other that made me blush.

"Sarah," Beach groaned against her mouth and my heart hurt to hear the anguish, the pure relief and overwhelming love he put into that one word.

My blush heated further when Sarah and Beach began to tear at each other's clothes to the point where I was shoving them out the door and into their own room. As soon as they were inside Smoke slammed the door shut and laughed, his mood visibly better than it had been twelve hours ago.

"Hulk, I need a man on both doors, one on each end of the hallway, and teams on the roof and the grounds. I'm sure they'll surface at some point, but right now Beach will shoot any motherfucker dumb enough to interrupt them—even me. So leave 'em the fuck alone."

I glanced around and saw a bunch of rough-as-fuck smiling bikers. Their genuine happiness for Beach and Sarah touched me, and I smiled back. These strangers had helped bring my sister back to me in their own way and kept me alive to see her again.

I didn't have words for how awesome this moment was, but I had to try.

In an uncharacteristically bold move that drew everyone's attention to me, I raised my voice a bit and said, "Thank you, so very much, from the bottom of my heart. You have no idea how much everything you've done for us means to me. I'll be forever in your debt. Just…thank you."

Hulk slung his arm around me and gave me a tight hug that made my nose burn. "You don't need to thank us, sweetheart. You're family."

Before I could start bawling, Smoke led me into our room and I rushed into his arms.

Ahhh, instant, narcotic, loving comfort.

We fell into bed together after we quickly kicked off our shoes and shed our clothes. Soon we were nude and my nipples peaked as I took in Smoke's smooth, tanned skin stretched tight over muscle. When Smoke shut the light off and set our guns and knives out, I couldn't help but laugh.

"Always prepared."

He let out a deep breath. "Ain't nothin' that could have prepared me for tonight. Shit."

I traced my fingertips over his face, utterly mesmerized by the texture of his scruff against my fingertips. I was beyond exhausted, and the moment my head hit the pillow my eyelids dropped as well. A soft sigh escaped me, and I was almost asleep before I remembered that I forgot to tell Smoke what Sarah said.

"It's over!"

He looked up at me in the dim light like I'd lost my mind. Maybe I had. "What's over?"

I quickly told him what Sarah had said about the jewels and the weapons, everything but the Israelis, and that Sarah would take care of that as well. My sister was a fucking superwoman, and I was so damn proud of her I was sure Smoke could hear it in my voice. By the end of my explanation, he laid on his back and stared up at the ceiling. When he didn't move for a few seconds, I worried that maybe he'd had a heart attack, but before I could touch him, he let out a whoop so loud it had Hulk pounding on the door.

"You okay in there?"

"Perfect," Smoke bellowed back.

"If your sister wasn't doing things to Beach right now that are probably illegal in most states, I'd go give her a big fuckin' kiss. I *knew* that ballsy bitch was smart

296

as shit, but to have pulled this off...fuck. She's right, Beach doesn't give her enough credit."

I smiled and hugged him back, lazing in the warmth of his joy as he rocked me gently.

"Gonna be different now baby, you'll see. Just you and me."

Placing a gentle kiss on his lips I yawned as I said, "I can't wait."

He kissed my forehead and held me close. "Go to sleep."

Grumbling, I did as he demanded and drifted off with relief.

AUSTIN TX

Chapter Fifteen

Miguel 'Smoke' Santos

I've been through a lot of shit in my life, and I'm not saying that to brag.

I'm saying that because even though I've been through all that inanity, this was by far the most surreal, unbelievable scene I'd ever witnessed. We were at the epicenter of a gathering of the heads of criminal organizations unlike anything I'd ever encountered, and my baby girl was handling them like a champion. Earlier this morning Sarah had set everything up for the exchange with Mimi's help. At 7 a.m., Mimi showed up at the clubhouse with a ton of breakfast takeout and two of Swan's male cousins. She wouldn't answer any questions as to where she'd been or what she'd been doing, but she did say that she could now openly help the girls without starting a mafia war.

But it was Sarah, with Beach on one side of her and Swan on the other, who was clearly in charge of the negotiations. Mimi just looked on with cold, dead eyes across the wide conference table at the men on the other side. Bet that badass bitch had enough knives on her beneath that fitted burgundy business suit to kill everyone in the room in less than a minute. I was glad she was on our side because that woman was on the warpath. These were Mimi's daughters, and the mafia Mimi's father headed had leant their full support. The essence of danger clung to her just like her classy perfume.

While Mimi, Beach, Sarah, and Swan sat at the table, I stood behind them along with a wall of muscle. There were bikers, members of the Stefano mafia, and a whole bunch of retired Special Forces motherfuckers, some of whom were now hitmen of the highest caliber, who were all here to represent Mike. Swan's dad was God-knew-where doing God-knew-what, but I think we all agreed it was a good thing he wasn't here. We didn't need him flipping out and gunning everyone down.

And Swan was hovering just above her killing space, waiting for one hard shove to send her into violence.

Our group would be enough to intimidate even the most hardened criminals, but the stone-faced guys sitting on the other side of the table didn't give anything away, and neither did their partners, the Israeli mafia.

Now most people in the States would laugh at the thought of an Israeli Mafia, but they are real. They're the most secretive of the world's various criminal organizations and deadlier than most—except possibly the Russians. But they're also practical men known for not letting their emotions get involved in business, which could work in our favor. They're lethal if double-crossed, but they're also fair-handed and open to negotiation. Growing up in a world of violence and in a country that was constantly on the edge of war tended to make a man less likely to take a life if he didn't have to.

Sarah laid out the terms of the deal with them. The missiles had been found right where she had said they would be and were recovered, but they'd been abandoned before they were found, so we didn't get a chance to capture and interrogate anyone. That really chapped my fuckin' ass, because we still didn't know who our rats were. At this point, the only men I trusted were Beach, Hulk, and maybe Breaker. Khan's security was sloppy enough that my girl almost got really fuckin' hurt, and I would be addressing that with him in the near future. I also needed to ream out Alisha's ass for giving Swan alcohol after I'd told her not to. But I returned my attention to my future sister-in-law and her razor-sharp tongue and watched her lecture one of the high-ranking members of the Boldin *Bratva*, Mr. Loktev.

Her tone was smooth and uncompromising. "You and I both know that your reputation hasn't been harmed, because not only did you find the items she stole from you, I know there were some very expensive, very interesting toys there as well that will make you a ton of money. And don't try to bullshit me. I saw them with my own eyes, and I know what they are worth."

Mr. Loktev tilted his head to the side, then narrowed his gaze at her. "You do not know this for sure. Since you were not there, you can only assume that the extra weaponry was where you said we'd find it."

Sarah calmly smoothed her shoulder-length hair
back, and I noticed the tips of her ears were red,
something that also happened to Swan when she was
pissed. No matter how relaxed Sarah appeared, she was
getting really, really angry. I hoped she could hold her
temper long enough to deal with this asshole. Beach
was also close to losing it, and I couldn't blame him.
Sarah offered the fucking Boldin *Bratva* everything
they'd lost and more on a silver platter in exchange for
Swan's safety as well as hers, but the old bastard was
hedging.

Sarah leaned forward slightly and glared at him.
"We had an agreement."

"If," Mr. Loktev said with a grim smile, "you paid
the interest, dear Sarah."

I tensed, ready for Sarah to flip out, but before she
could, there was a loud knock on the door. Everyone
turned as one of the bodyguards opened it and Tom
fucking Sokolov, one of my oldest friends, breezed in
with a smug look on his slightly nerdy face. He was
wearing a dark blue suit and looked like he was late for
a board meeting as he adjusted his thick, black-framed
glasses. I blinked—twice—sure I was imagining things.
Last time I'd talked to Tom he was speaking with his
relatives on Swan's behalf, but he hadn't sounded too
optimistic—said something about having to talk
directly to his uncle and ask for help.

I guess his talk with his uncle had gone well because
there was more than a bit of cockiness in his smile as he
surveyed the room until he found me.

Moving quickly through the crowd, he leaned in and whispered, "After this, we're even."

For a moment I frowned, then understanding filled me. Five years ago, I'd saved Tom's niece from being molested by a serial child rapist. She was just four at the time, and her mother had been beaten into a coma before the molester took Tom's niece. I found him with the little girl before things got too far. Once I had him alone I'd done things to that piece of filth who got off on destroying children, which still gave me nightmares to this day. If there was such a thing as Hell, that man was there, but I made sure his last hours on this earth were a taste of what was to come. Tom had tried to pay me, to give me anything and anyone I ever wanted in return for saving his niece and extracting revenge, but I turned him down. I didn't want or need any of that stuff, so instead, we worked out a deal. If the world went to shit around me he'd be there to bail my ass out of the fire.

If Tom truly thought that whatever he had to say was going to cancel his mark, I allowed myself trace of hope that brought my mind back from the killing edge.

Trying to cover my stunned reaction, I nodded, and Tom's grin grew into a wide smile as he said in a low voice, "Good choice. Sit back and enjoy the show, my friend. I'm about to pull a feat of magic like you've never seen. Just like you did when you found Amy. Watch and be amazed at the awesomeness that is me."

Without even pausing, he went straight to the table and brazenly took a seat next to Mimi, who appeared to be considering the idea of stabbing his smug ass as he flashed her a charming smile.

Before I could get over my shock of him appearing out of thin fucking air, Tom placed a manila envelope on the table with a serious, no-bullshit expression. In an instant the room chilled, and Swan briefly met my gaze, her confusion evident, before she returned her attention to Tom. I met Beach's eyes next, and whatever he saw on my face made him visibly relax. He leaned over and whispered something to Sarah, who quickly grabbed Swan's hand beneath the table.

As everyone stared at him, Tom inclined his head in greeting to the men seated across from him. "Marat Loktev, how good to see you again. My uncle, Petrov Dubinski, sends his regards. He says he looks forward to meeting with you when you return to Moscow."

I knew in theory that Tom had overseas relatives who were big in the Russian crime world. I'd even partied with a bunch of 'em at a luxurious BDSM dungeon in Moscow when I went over to help Tom with some issues a few years ago, but I had no idea how big until Loktev paled and looked like he might throw up. "Mr. Sokolov. It is good to see you again."

I had to fight a grin at the way the man seemed to choke on calling Tom Mister instead of by his first name. No wonder Tom insisted on Mr. Sokolov if this was the kind of reaction he got. Leaning back in the chair like he didn't have a fuckin' care in the world, or a bunch of people one heartbeat from pulling their guns on him, he tapped his fingers on the envelope as if bored. "We would like to propose a trade."

"I don't..."

"This is not a trade for you, but for your boss, Mr. Boldin." He switched to Russian and continued on.

If I thought the guy paled before, he was positively ghostly now. I really hoped he didn't have a heart attack. Stealing a glance at Swan, I saw her looking carefully between Tom and Loktev, her brilliant blue eyes focused and intent. I wished that I could have read her mind to become privy to the astonishing speed of her thought process. Because I was watching her so intently, I noticed instantly when she began to relax. Her shoulders slumped and the tension in her face eased. While I was sure she didn't speak Russian, she was very good, in her own way, at reading body language, and whatever she saw reassured her.

"You would make this trade?" Loktev switched back to English, his voice strained. "What do you want?"

"It's not what I want, it's what Ms. Anderson wants. Agree to all of her terms and drop all penalties. I'm aware of exactly what you received in addition to the missiles." He chuckled and it wasn't a nice sound. "We're taking care of your import, and you will split the profit 50/50 with the Anderson sisters. None of these terms are negotiable. Do we have a deal?"

I was waiting for Mr. Loktev to waste time calling his boss or some other stall tactic, but to my surprise he nodded. "Then it is done. Ms. Anderson, the Boldin *Bratva* agrees to your terms. We will discuss payment arrangements with Mr. Sokolov."

He leaned across the table to shake hands and Sarah stood, but instead of shaking his hand she took a piece of paper out from her bra and handed it to Loktev who seemed nonplussed for a moment.

"The codes," she said in a cool voice and Loktev nodded.

A small smirk twisted Beach's lips, while Swan looked from Sarah to me, the joy brightening her eyes to sky blue while her beauty knocked me on my ass.

Now, usually I'm fuckin' solid in a situation like this. I've done plenty of hostage negotiations and dealt with some truly psychotic motherfuckers, but this time, it was my heart, my life on the line. I'd been fighting to protect her from the day I laid eyes on her, and since then, I'd not had a moment where my worry for her wasn't a background hum in my mind. I found it hard to let that worry ease as I stared into her eyes and found everything I felt for her reflected right back at me.

Jesus Christ, she was finally safe. Somehow this managed to happen with only a little bit of bloodshed and few dead bodies. Including the men my girl had to kill. It still roasted me with anger and guilt when I thought of how I hadn't been there for her, that I wasn't able to protect her, but I was getting better at focusing on the future than the past.

"That is all lovely," the Israeli representative, Mr. Dahan, said in a thickly accented voice, his dark eyes cold and empty, "but there is still the little matter of what your mother owes us, Ms. Anderson, that priceless item she stole so easily. Unless you have it. Do you have it, Sarah?"

"I...no," she whispered, and I carefully eased my hand to where my gun was strapped to my thigh.

The relief dropped from everyone's face, but then Tom's quiet laughter filled the silence. "I was wondering when you were going to speak up, Mr. Dahan."

Mr. Dahan gave Tom an almost a sorry look before his expression went bland. In his early thirties, the guy had almost as much arrogance as Tom, but there was something about him that made me edgy. For some reason, my instincts said this fucker was more dangerous than Mr. Loktev and his guards. He'd been nothing but polite so far, and yet, now that the attention was on him, it was easy to see the anger simmering below the surface.

"I am sorry, but even for you, Mr. Sokolov, this is out of my hands."

With a casual flick of his wrist Tom flicked envelope over to Mr. Dahan. "Inside you will find something better than the product.

"And what would that be?" Dahan asked with no hint of real interest.

"The person who made it."

A hint of surprise flashed through his dark eyes and his eyebrows rose a bit, but he didn't reach for the envelope in front of him. "A very generous offer, but it will take at least a year to make. Even this will not save them from paying the price for their mother's sins."

Shit, this asshole wasn't going to let it go. I might need to eliminate him. Not an easy job with so much collateral in the room. I stole a quick glance at our side of the table, taking in Beach furiously whispering to Sarah while Mimi slowly lowered her hands to her lap. My heart beat faster, then I looked and found Swan, hoping she'd calm me down, but she was staring across the table with murder in her eyes.

Fuck.

Leather creaked around me and movement seemed to flow through the group like water rushing over river smooth stones. Adrenaline flooded my bloodstream and everything around me sharpened. The tension between our two groups caused the hair on the back of my neck to stand up. Across the room from me, one of the Israeli bodyguards caught my gaze and held it. We stared at each other, both promising a swift death to the other once the violence started, before I turned my attention to Swan, waiting for her to make the first move.

Tom sighed then rubbed his square jaw. "My cousin, Dimitri Novikov, is calling in his marker."

What the fuck? Even I knew Dimitri Novikov was a bad ass. The man would swiftly eliminate anyone who threatened him and his new wife, Rya. Oddly enough I knew her dad, a biker that I done some rides with in the distant past. Good guy, down to earth. I'd had dinner with them at their palatial penthouse the last time I was in Moscow, and they were gracious hosts, but Dimitri radiated a silent menace whenever I looked at Rya for what he deemed too long. Tom had attended their wedding, and when he described the lavish event, I joked with him that it sounded fancier than a royal wedding. He told me then that it was a royal wedding in the world of the *Bratva*, and that Dimitri was kind of like a crown prince.

Evidently, he wasn't bullshitting because Dimitri Novikov's name clearly shocked most of those in the room. Sarah and Swan were confused as shit, but Mimi gave Beach a smug smile for some reason. He was too busy staring down each of the bodyguards on the other side of the room to notice.

Mr. Dahan gave Tom an openly surprised look, then sat back heavily in his chair before nodding. "I will have to verify this."

He held out his hand and one of his bodyguards placed a phone in it, whatever number he needed already dialed. I moved through the crowd, aware of everyone's gazes on me, but I needed to be next to Swan to calm her down. I'd originally stationed myself by the door because I wanted to be the first line of defense between my girl and anyone who might try to get in here and harm her, but now I needed to stop her from doing anything stupid. I watched her gaze dart across the room, no doubt cataloging risks and assets in case things went to shit. I managed to reach her before she started inching for her gun.

I knelt next to her and grabbed both of her hands in mine. "Easy, baby girl. Let Tom take care of this."

She sucked in a quick breath, and I rubbed my thumbs over her wrists. For whatever reason my touch seemed to ease her anxiety, and sure enough, her blue eyes softened as she stared down at me, distracted from her volatile feelings. In Sarah's case, the situation appeared to be reversed with Sarah trying to calm Beach down. Yeah, good fuckin' luck with that. Now that Beach knew he was gonna be a daddy, he was gonna be damn near impossible to live with. Sarah would be lucky if he didn't put her in a suit of armor before she left the house.

I stood and placed my hands on Swan's shoulders as Mr. Dahan had a conversation with someone in Russian. We all watched him and when he chuckled, I allowed myself a bit of hope that we would once again beat the odds and get out of this unscathed—something that seemed a lot more likely when Mr. Dahan actually smiled at Sarah and Swan.

"Ladies, it is a good day when two beautiful women such as yourselves are given a second chance. Your debt to us is forgiven and you are now under our protection. Congratulations Sarah and Swan Anderson. You have become untouchable."

Tom looked over at me and cocked his head, giving me a mocking look that made me want to punch him right in his smug face as he silently asked if we were good.

I nodded once, amazed that he'd managed to pull this off but tried to keep those feelings off my face. Our marker was clear, and after I spent two days alone with my girl, just loving on her, I was gonna have to find out exactly how Tom pulled this magical rabbit out of his ass. Someone must have been talking with him. I watched Sarah as she stood, went over to Tom and gave him a huge hug. I was pretty sure at that point who'd called him in. He laughed about not wanting to crush the baby, then Sarah leaned in, cupped her hand around his ear, and whispered something far too low for anyone to hear.

After about a minute of this Beach started to grow agitated. As if sensing this, Sarah glanced back at him, then gave Tom a kiss on the cheek before returning to her crazy possessive fiancé. Not that I had room to talk, I wanted to kick the ass of every guy in here who was checking Swan out. The need to stake my claim filled me, and I stalked back over to Swan's side, picking her up out of her chair and holding her against me with one hand in her hair and one hand on her fine, fine ass. She gave a little squeal as I nipped her lower lip, but as soon as I sucked gently on it to soothe her, she melted against me and our bodies curved together perfectly.

Mine. All fuckin' mine, every sweet damn inch.

AUSTIN TX

Chapter Sixteen

Sitting back in the white leather lounge chair on the enormous balcony of the presidential suite of the Four Seasons in downtown Denver, I took a full breath for the first time in months as the poisonous cloud of worry eased deep within me. Shit, felt like fuckin' years. I'd experienced this same lightness in my chest after surviving battles when I was in the Marines. It was the deep breath of someone realizing they were still alive and well enough to take one.

Only this time, I was better than alive. I was reborn. The promise of a future with Swan was now a fact. Someday there would be a wedding, then a honeymoon someplace where I could put her round ass in a really small bikini and take her to a public beach. The mental image of her coming out of the ocean in a tiny bikini, all wet and tan, made my cock twitch. Yeah, yeah, I'm a pig, but I love showing my girl off knowing other men are envious of me. It's not a nice or pretty thing to admit, but it's how my fucked up mind works. Now, if any of those men look at her for more than six seconds, we got problems.

Life was pretty good when my biggest concern was a man boldly eye fucking the perfection that is my woman.

It was hard to believe Swan was now untouchable, that she had an invisible shield around her that was bomb proof. The sun was setting over the Rocky Mountains in the distance while Beach and I ate our dinner. The balcony was enclosed with clear glass so that it looked like we were perched on the edge of the roof. Our girls were together in the palatial bathroom with its own sitting area while Sarah took a soak and talked 'girl shit' with Swan. They'd scarcely left each other's sides since the meeting this morning, and it made my throat thicken to see how absolutely overjoyed they were to be together again. I had a feeling they had a lot of catching up to do, and even though I'm greedy as shit about spending time with Swan, I knew she needed to reconnect with her sister.

Plus, Sarah had threatened to feed me my balls if I ate the surf and turf I'd ordered for dinner in the suite. Evidently the smell of beef made her sick. So Beach and I ate our meat after the girls disappeared to hang out. With pregnancy hormones in full effect, neither of us wanted to piss Sarah off. I gotta say, after seeing Sarah in action today, my respect for her had grown by leaps and bounds. Yeah, I knew she was a force to be reckoned with, but knowing and seeing are two different things. Bitch is tough, yet still a lady, and Beach couldn't be any prouder of her.

Speaking of proud, I found my friend sipping the 40-year-old Scotch he'd ordered while he looked out at the glittering lights of Denver coming to life for the night.

"Congratulations, by the way, on the baby."

We clinked our thick crystal glasses and smiled. While Swan was sipping champagne in the bathroom, Beach and I were savoring the good hard liquor. We'd talked about a little bit of club business—I updated him on my ideas for security upgrades—but neither of us wanted to poison the atmosphere right now. The girls were feeling playful, jacked up on their victory, and I couldn't wait to celebrate the spoils of war with Swan. Shit, just the thought of her sighing as I slowly pushed into her tight fuckin' pussy caused my dick to harden at an uncomfortable angle.

I had a feeling we'd be indulging in some kinky play tonight. My girl just had that look in her eyes that told me she needed my dick, always touching and rubbing up against me, and I was so fucking looking forward to being alone with her it wasn't even funny. I wanted to love her, to celebrate a victory over what had felt like insurmountable odds. And Beach couldn't keep his hands to himself when Sarah was within four feet of him. He was my buddy, but I really didn't want to watch him make out. It wasn't all Beach's fault. Sarah's hormones were apparently running the show, and she seemed to be insatiable for him. After we left the meeting, the first thing Sarah and Beach did was go into a bathroom and put a couple of prospects on guard duty at the door to ensure their privacy. Just the thought of

Beach's smug look and Sarah's hot blush when they came out again made me chuckle.

Beach glanced over at me, the harsh lines that had carved his features since this shit started had eased, making him appear younger than his true age of thirty-eight. "What are you laughing about?"

"Just thinkin' of how red Sarah's cheeks were when she came out of the bathroom at the office building."

"The cheeks on her face weren't near as red as her ass. But it wasn't me that dragged us in there. My woman's hungry for me." He gave me a wink and sat back in his chair, satisfaction oozing from him. "Think I'm gonna like her being pregnant."

"Congratulations, again."

"Thanks," Beach replied in a voice that was even raspier than usual. He held his glass up to the dying light, inspecting the liquid within, his gaze distant and focused entirely on the glittering amber liquid. "Never, ever would have imagined I'd be this in love with a woman, that I'd willingly destroy the world to protect her. Sarah's not like anyone. She's extraordinary. And she's having my baby. Our baby. They're mine."

I had a hard time suppressing my laughter at my Prez, a man hard as fuckin' nails, looking like he was gonna tear up, but I knew how the poor bastard felt, so I took mercy on him.

"You need some tissue there, Sally? Is your period coming?"

Beach burst out laughing then slammed his drink back with a satisfied sigh. "Fuck you very much. Don't act all high and mighty. You're so far up Swan's ass it's sad."

"I'd like to be up her ass," I muttered.

314

With a dirty chuckle, Beach leaned forward. "It's nice, real nice."

"What's nice?"

We turned to the doorway where we found Sarah and Swan standing in the silky, kimono style robes they'd bought down at one of the high end boutique shops off the hotel lobby.

A blush warmed my baby girl's cheeks, almost matching the pink shade of her robe. She wore more makeup than usual with a thick black liner around her eyes that made them glow like aquamarine jewels. All I could think about was what that makeup would look like after I fucked most of it off or she'd cried it away while she came hard enough to shake the bed. I looked closer and noticed that she was swaying the slightest bit. Evidently, that champagne was getting to her. She met my gaze, and I sucked in a breath between my teeth, turned on hard and fast by the mixture of lust and nervousness on her innocent face. That look made me pretty sure she and Sarah had been talking sex, and my pulse raced. Sarah liked to think of herself as an unofficial sex therapist, and if they did talk about it, that meant my baby might be wantin' to try out some new, kinky things with me tonight.

Fuck yeah.

Beach's chair scraped the floor as he pushed back then held out his hand. Sarah came over to him right away and let him pull her into his lap with a low growl. He cupped her cheek, then looked up at me and smiled. "Time to go."

I laughed and finished my drink before ambling over to Swan, who had her hands clenched at her sides. While I liked her a little nervous, I didn't want her scared. With a soft touch I held her hand in my own, forcing her fingers open, then placed my hand in hers. That connection, that trust, turned me on as much as watching three women fight over sucking my dick. I led her into the modern, well-decorated living room of the suite, the low golden lighting gilding Swan and making her glow. God, she was so fuckin' beautiful. I could stare at her for the rest of my life and never tire of the view. Just looking at her was pleasure.

Moving slowly, I gently stroked her face, her gaze going soft as she melted into me. It always made my heart, and other parts of my body, swell with pride when she gave in to me like this. Having her against me, feeling the heat of her skin, drove me fuckin' wild. The world around us faded away as I continued to calm her, massaging her back while she cuddled.

"How you feelin' baby?"

"Mmmmm, good."

"How much champagne have you had?"

"Enough that I'm ready to call in your marker."

Startled, I leaned back and looked down at her. "What?

"Your marker." She flushed and looked down at my chest. "You know…the…umm…the orgasm denial."

Those last words came out in an embarrassed whisper and I grinned. "Sounds like my girl is feeling naughty."

"Very."

My cock instantly pushed against my pants at the heat in her burning blue eyes as she looked up at me, the golden mass of her hair framing her face. "Anything you want, I want to give you. If you want to experiment with my dick, who am I to stop you?"

Her self-satisfied little grin sent a tingle of warning through me. "Good, because Sarah gave me some tips."

A hard burn went down my spine and my balls tightened.

Fuck. Yeah.

Without another word we went back to our suite down the hall. I practically dragged her behind me in my haste to get to our room.

As soon as the door opened, she pushed me in, her aggression surprising me.

It also surprised me even more when she shoved me up against the wall and kissed me until I was pushing my hips into her, incredibly turned on by her hunger and by how rough she was being.

She broke our kiss and buried her hands in my hair, stroking it and making my dick ache to be buried in her. I never knew someone playing with it could turn me on until I met Swan. Looking up at me, she tugged hard on my hair, then smiled.

"You know one of the things that makes me crazy about you?"

Evidently, a tipsy Swan was a talkative Swan. The champagne flavored her mouth and breath. I wanted to kiss her again, but there was no way I was gonna turn down the opportunity to learn about what pleased her. I needed to give her everything she wanted, to let her know that I loved her in a way that couldn't be denied, that no one could satisfy her like I could.

"What's that?"

"How you take charge in the bedroom. You make me feel free, and pleasing you is like pleasing me. I didn't think I'd get off on being aggressive, but being dominant is kinda fun."

While she was nowhere near dominant, I liked how she seemed happy with herself, and I wanted to fully encourage her to explore her sexuality. What a lot of people don't realize is that it is possible to be dominant by submitting. It sounds like bullshit, but it's true. I'm giving her what she needs, allowing her to play. Hell, I'm all for letting Swan's kinky side loose.

"It is," I agreed. "What are you going to do to me?"

She grinned and my heart squeezed tight. Fuck, I loved this woman. "Go get me a pillow from the couch."

I did as she asked, my mind going through a million and one kinky things that she could want me to do with this pillow. Instead she dropped it to the floor, then knelt before me. Giving me a quick, almost shy look that made me want to fuck her in the worst way, she began to unbuckle my belt. Once she had my fly down, she pulled the pants down my legs, but left them on. Then she sat back on her heels, the kimono parting enough that I could see the swell of her right breast almost to her pink areola.

Reaching out with one hand, she gently stroked my cock imprisoned beneath the thin cotton of my boxer briefs. Her lips parted on a sigh, and she unerringly trailed her finger down the thick ridge on the underside to the piercing on my balls. She paused to rub the bit of metal, giving my nuts a good massage at the same time. My need began to grow, and instead of fighting it, I gave her what she wanted. With a groan, I leaned back against the wall, my hands falling to the sides instead of buried in her hair. I was afraid if I touched her right now I'd hurt her.

Swan leaned forward and placed her mouth on the head of my cock as she blew a hot, moist breath on me. I groaned and my hands twitched with the need to hold her still so I could sink my shaft between her pretty pink lips. The sting of her teeth as she nibbled on my shaft made me groan, and she hummed in return.

She pulled back and looked up at me, holding my gaze while she freed my cock from my underwear, licking along the head with her clever little tongue. At the first push of her soft tongue against my tip, I fisted my hands behind my back. She took just the head of my cock into the wet heat of her mouth and groaned, her tongue lashing the slit of my dick. It felt so damn good, the toe-curling sensation of her coaxing out a small amount of pre-cum, which caused me to thrust forward.

Instead of taking me deeper, she pulled away altogether and grasped my dick firmly. My breathing began to speed up as she spit in her hand and started to jerk me off. The smile she gave me was positively wicked while she tugged at the belt holding her kimono closed with her free hand. Instead of pulling the silken fabric off she let it drape open to frame her killer body. The pink of her robe was much paler than the bright pink of her nipples. I loved playin' with her pretty tits, and I promised myself that once her teasing was over I'd make her come just by suckin' on 'em.

Swan began to pinch and pull her nipple, sending hard arousal bursting through me, making my dick ache as her smooth fingers stroked me. It wasn't long until I was getting close to my orgasm, and not touching her was a constant struggle. I could smell her wet pussy now, the rich scent an aphrodisiac like I'd never known. I loved that she got off on servicing me, how sucking my cock made her horny.

Then her grip loosened, and she was barely touching me as she slowly slid her hand up and down, denying me what I needed to come.

She stared up at me, passion heavy in her gaze. "That was one, right?"

"Yeah."

"Good, I want to take you to the peak two more times." She licked her lips, then my cock. "You are so hot when you're about to come. Your dick gets really, really hard and I can trace the veins with my mouth like this."

The silken tip of her tongue began to draw torturous paths up and down my shaft, teasing me to the edge of another orgasm. By this point my self-control was severely strained, and I wondered if I'd made a mistake. I hadn't expected Swan to be so good at this, but I should have known better. She may have lacked physical experience, but my girl loved her porn, and she always got an A for effort.

"Fuck." I groaned and started to thrust my hips. "Come on, baby, stop playing."

She gave my cock a wet, erotic slurp before returning to jerking me off. My whole body twitched like I was being electrocuted. My nuts throbbed with the need to release, and I growled at her. Instead of giving me what I needed, she continued to tease me until I was a sweaty, shaky mess, a constant stream of groans ripped from me by the hot, soft suction of her mouth on me.

"Need to come, Miguel?"

My control snapped and I lunged at her. The way she squeaked out a scream then giggled only made me want to fuck her harder and establish my dominance. After kicking off my jeans, I carried her over to the couch and set her down. The silk of the kimono framed her body against the dark beige sofa, highlighting the perfection of her curves. The savage need to take her filled me and I gritted my teeth. Eager to feel as much of her as possible, I ripped my clothes off. I loved the way her eyes widened as she began to squirm on the couch.

See, orgasm denial is a double-edged sword for a woman like Swan. In denying me, she was also denying herself, and she had to be almost as worked up as I was. When I slid my fingers between the folds of her swollen labia, I groaned at how slippery wet she was. Curling my fingers, I fucked her with first one, then two, then three. By the time the third finger was in, she was screaming my name, thrusting herself against my hand. I felt every twitch of her stretched out pussy. The delicate, but strong flutters were getting closer together, and just when she was about to come, I shoved her legs up onto my shoulders so her body was almost bent in half, then braced my arms on the couch so I could shove ram into her.

She arched as much as she could, pinned by my bulk, then wailed out my name, turning it into a sound of pure pleasure. Satisfaction mixed with my lust, and I fucked her, hard, the smooth grip of her little cunt a paradise on earth. My whole body buzzed with need for this woman, this young, complicated female who owned me heart and soul. She sank her nails into my biceps and grunted while I slammed into her, never letting up, while trying to thrust harder, deeper. Her next climax took me by surprise as she writhed beneath me, then bit my forearm while her body squeezed and released me with a ball-draining clench.

There ain't a man on earth who could resist a pussy sucking on him like that. After the orgasm denial, I didn't even want to try. I followed her over the edge, every inch of my dick squeezed tight by her cunt. The first jet of release sent me out of my head, the world going white around me as I gasped in a deep breath. Fire burned through my body while I filled up my woman with jerking pumps of my hips that I couldn't control.

When I came back to myself my hips were still moving me in and out of her. Swan was whimpering and moaning with each thrust, her breath coming in harsh pants. Knowing I'd used her roughly, I pulled out gently then knelt between her trembling thighs.

At the first stroke of my tongue on her puffy pink sex, she tried to sit up. "What are you doing?"

"Licking you to orgasm."

She laid back with a shocked look that only made me want her more. "But you just came in me."

"And? It's not like you haven't tasted yourself on my dick."

Before she could argue, I swiped her clit with my tongue, rubbing and gently sucking on that little bundle of nerves until the tender tip emerged from its hood. With a pleased murmur, I looked at her while cleaning her with long, slow swipes of my tongue. Then I probed the entrance to her sex and licked my come off her, holding her hips still as she tried to push harder against my mouth.

"You're so dirty," she murmured in a sexy purr that, combined with her cunt in my mouth, made my dick get hard again.

"Yep."

I returned to the task at hand, building her up again so I could fuck her nice and slow while I pressed her against the floor-to-ceiling windows that looked out over the lights of Denver at night, showing the whole world what belonged to me and only me.

Late afternoon the next day, my arm was curled around a warm armful of sleeping woman as Swan snuggled up to me in the front cab of my truck. I'd fucked my sweet baby twice after taking her on the couch, once in front of the window and again on the kitchen counter. I loved how insatiable my girl was, and I gave her all she wanted and a little bit more. Just the thought had my cock rock hard, and I shifted uncomfortably, trying to position it better as I drove.

Mimi and Swan's cousins had flown back today with a promise that Swan would come for a visit as soon as possible. Her male cousins had tried to question me about my intentions with Swan once they got me alone, but Mimi scolded them and told them that they didn't need to worry about my intentions, because I knew that if I hurt Swan, Mimi would be coming for me. That shut them all up. And I'll admit it, I can think of about a million people I'd rather have after me than Mimi. Not that it was a worry. My future with Swan was lookin' so good I had a hard time believing it wasn't a dream. Swan's parents would see that I have nothing but love for their girl.

Back in Denver, Hulk was packing up his life to move down to Austin as one of my Enforcers. Vance had been none too happy that I was bringin' along a new addition to my security company, but I didn't give a fuck that he didn't have the time to train anybody. It wasn't like Hulk had no idea what the fuck he was doing. That man had proven himself to me over and over again, and I trusted him completely with Swan, which meant I trusted the big bastard with just about anything. Once Breaker was fully recovered, he'd be the Denver chapter's Master at Arms, and I was pretty sure he'd do a good job. Khan was cleaning house with both the sweet butts and the brothers, letting 'em know that party time was over. From now on the clubhouse was gonna be a little more picky about the pussy it let waltz through the doors.

Swan had told me about the shoes she'd seen a woman wearing before the shit hit the fan at the party, but so far, no one else could remember seeing them. Blue sparkly heels with dolphins on them were pretty distinct, and I was hoping someone would remember something. In the meantime, back home, I had my guys going through every fucking bit of electronics we had, making sure that whoever the fuck the rat was in the clubhouse, we weren't going to make it easy for 'em.

I took an exit off the freeway that I'd scoped out earlier in the day, one that led to a really nice and isolated cabin where Swan and I were going to spend the next two days alone. No one except Beach, Sarah, and Mimi knew where we were going, and I planned on keeping it that way. Yeah, it was fuckin' selfish of me to want to keep Swan to myself, and we both had a ton of shit to do back home, but I didn't give a fuck. We were gonna spend the next two days in bed and I was gonna spoil the fuck out of my girl and ask—beg if necessary—her to marry me.

Chapter Seventeen

Swan

For some bizarre reason, I was nervous as Smoke took our luggage upstairs to the bedroom in our private cabin. You'd think that after all the stuff we'd been through together, all the kinky things we'd done, I would be more at ease, but I wasn't. There was a tension in Smoke that was different from anything I'd experienced with him before, and I didn't know how to process it. The tightness around his eyes wasn't from fear or worry—I had those expressions on his face down pat—and it wasn't from being tired. It was…something else. More nervous than tense, but his emotions put me on edge as I looked around the spacious, cozy great room and open kitchen of the cabin. The place wasn't huge, but the vaulted ceiling and exposed beams made it feel larger. It was beautifully decorated, and it was so quiet. After spending the past few weeks with bikers, constant noise had become a part of my life.

This silence, something I was once so used to, now became unnerving.

Smoke had told me he was going to take a quick shower and that I should relax while he cleaned up. My libido had been hoping that he'd ask me to shower with him, but instead, he'd left me in the living room with its many windows. I fiddled with the draped neckline of the grey silk tank top I was wearing and glanced around the room, cataloging weak spots in what could become a defense perimeter. As I made mental note of possible escape routes, I also identified things that could be used as weapons, like the fire poker on the hearth, or a horse bridle that decorated the far wall. Hell, I could grab the stool near me and take pretty much anyone down.

I should've been breathing free right now, having been declared untouchable by some of the most powerful groups of men in the world, but my mother was still out there somewhere, and I'd never fully relax until she was found and locked away so she couldn't cause any more trouble. The fact that we still didn't know who the traitors were in the Iron Horse MC made the hair on the back of my neck stand up and did nothing to calm me. Whoever had set up that heist was gonna be pissed, and they weren't gonna go away. Until they were caught, I wasn't ever going to be really safe. None of us were.

With that sobering thought weighing me down, I wandered onto the very private deck, no other buildings for as far as I could see from our position on the edge of a large hill, just forest, and plains, and beautiful rock formations.

At least there was noise out here, the sigh of the breeze, the scurrying of animals, and I marginally relaxed enough to do some deep breathing, the kind I used during yoga. I tried to center myself in the moment and stop worrying.

Didn't work.

As beautiful as the view was with the late afternoon sun still bright in the blue sky, my gaze began to scan for animal runs and natural hiding places in the splendor of the Colorado Rockies.

When I was finally satisfied with knowing at least six ways to flee the cabin, I turned my attention back to the house and found Smoke, clad in a pair of very worn jeans, watching me with his arms folded across his bare chest, his blue and green dragon tattoo drawing my gaze to his pierced nipple. Water still dripped from the ends of his curly hair, and I had a hard time reading his expression at first. I thought he looked worried, then angry, but he didn't hold an emotion long enough for me to identify it.

A hollow feeling ached in my chest, and before I could stop myself I whispered, "I need a hug."

It was easy for me to recognize the profound relief lightening his gaze to brown velvet and I met him halfway across the deck, eagerly burrowing into his chest. When he enveloped me in his chiseled arms and cushioned me to his warm chest, I let out a watery sigh as my morbid thoughts of death and avoiding it grew fainter with every beat of Smoke's strong heart. God, he was so...alive. And warm. And he smelled good, so damn good.

Awareness of my body began to return, drawing me out of the mental loop of worry I'd been stuck in. Sometimes I hated my brain, hated that it made me weak, that it didn't work like other people's did, that it made me weird. I know that I'm a unique and beautiful snowflake—la, la, la—but I worried sometimes that it made me hard to like.

In Smoke's embrace, I knew that he loved me, and that he cherished, worshiped, and all those other inadequate words used to describe this feeling, this moment of bliss that reverberated through me on a soul-deep level.

"You okay?" he whispered against the top of my head.

The scent of his soap was strong on his skin, and I rubbed my face against his damp chest, the soft mat of hair a delicious tactile sensation against my cheek. "Yeah. It's just…a lot to deal with."

He stiffened against me, then let out a long sigh. "You're overwhelmed, right?"

The thought of lying and saying I was fine flitted through my mind, but there really wasn't a point in fibbing to Smoke, not when he held me this close and could read my body better than I could. "Yeah."

"Mmm-hmm," he nuzzled his lips against the crook in my neck before placing a series of feather-light kisses over my skin. "What you need right now is some tender care, baby girl."

I frowned, unsure if he was teasing or being serious. My attempt to push away from him was met with resistance as he pinned me against his chest. He looked down at me, his eyes dark. As playful and indulgent as Smoke was with me most of the time, there were occasions where I'd push him too far and a different side of him would come out. Still kind, still protective of me and loving, but darker. This was a man used to getting his way, and he radiated a silent command that sank into my bones, warming me, and making me pliant against him.

Shit, if he could make me melt with just a look, I was well and truly fucked in every sense of the word.

He stroked my hair back from my face with a gentle touch, his rough fingertips dragging lightly over my sensitive skin. "We're gonna take things slow—"

I smacked my hand over his mouth and shook my head. "No. No, we are not taking things slow. You are going to fuck me until the world disappears and it's only us. I want you in me, now."

His teeth sank into my palm hard enough to sting and I yelped, jerking my hand away. With a soft growl, he fisted his hand in my hair and tilted my head back, the tingle of pain from my scalp turning into hot desire. Oh my, the look on Smoke's face was positively feral. Hopefully, I'd pushed him enough that he would make rough love to me, but not far enough to really make him angry.

"We're thinkin' different thoughts, sweetheart. By slow, I mean I'm gonna build you up to your orgasm, take you to the top again and again, until you're beggin' me to fuck you hard and make you all relaxed and whimpering on my cock."

My nipples tightened to painful tips, and I ran my fingers through his hair, the sun warm on my skin, and a bit of the fear surrounding my heart faded. I was alive, and my odds of staying that way were much, much better. For the first time since I sat on the other side of the table from men intent on selling me into a fate worse than death, I allowed myself to take a deep breath. I wasn't sleepy, but I was mentally exhausted. The day that Smoke had in mind for me sounded perfect, and I surrendered myself to him, cuddling up to him and rubbing my cheek against his chest.

"Oh…well, in that case I think I can endure it."

"That's gracious of you." A soft, rumbling laugh echoed against my cheek and I smiled. "Love how you feel in my arms, baby. Love everything about you and I'm so fuckin' thankful that you…if something had happened I would…fuck…so, yeah…I'm thankful."

The hitch in his voice killed me, and I fought the sting of tears. It was my turn to comfort him, and the love that we gave each other grew into something bigger, something better. I'm not sure who started touching who first, but Smoke had me naked before I was even aware of it, his deep kiss taking me over. Our tongues slid against each other, the lush softness of his lips pillowing mine as he lifted me and urged me to wrap my legs around his waist. With a low groan, I did as he asked, all too aware of the thick bulge behind his boxer briefs. His kiss was delicate, gentle, a tease that made me even greedier for him.

I let him know this by sucking, hard, on his tongue.

He stumbled as we entered the cabin, and I laughed while he swung me around to carry me in a cradle hold, his lips curving into a smile when he made his way across the room again, this time keeping his eyes on our surroundings. I tried to protest when he started to carry me up the stairs, but he paused long enough to throw me over his shoulder with my ass in the air, and spanked my pussy. I let out a sharp hiss of air, his questing fingers combining with the blood rushing to my head, which made me dizzy. Up and down his fingers slid, playing with the wetness coating my sex, driving me crazy. I wiggled against him, urging more, but he removed his hand and slapped my ass.

"Behave or I will punish you."

I was curious as to what kind of punishment it would be, but the sight of his ass flexing as he carried me up the stairs was fantastic enough to distract me.

I soon found myself being lowered into a huge bathtub full of bubbles. Smoke was being careful not to get my hair wet and draped it over the side. After he placed me in the warm water and I became engulfed by the foam, he turned the faucet off. The trill of birdsong filled the air, and I let out a relaxed sigh when I'd realized he'd opened the windows, letting fresh air into the humid room. Wiggling my legs beneath the water, I enjoyed the feel of it sliding over my skin. I smiled at Smoke, trying to put into my gaze how happy I was, how happy he made me. He grinned back, and with efficient moves, swept my hair up into a messy bun, and secured it on top of my head.

We didn't exchange any words, but then again, we didn't really need to. The time for talking was past, and right now, we were just living in the moment. It amused me how much Smoke seemed to enjoy taking care of me, and I couldn't help but giggle when he made a satisfied, humming noise deep in his throat as he began to wash me. Soon, my eyelids were at less than half-mast, my gaze unfocused and blurry while his clever fingers glided up and down my arm, stroking from the sensitive skin of my inner wrist to my shoulder. Then his touch became firmer and turned from a caress into a muscle-melting massage. He was careful to avoid any lingering bruises, but each time he discovered one he would gently lift that part of my body to the surface and kiss it with what felt like reverence.

When he reached the healing bullet wound, his hands trembled enough that the water moved in little shivering waves. A desperate look flashed through his eyes as he glanced up at me, then at my healing arm. With my free hand I lightly touched his jaw, loving how smooth it was after his shower. He didn't look up from my arm, so I leaned forward and shifted to my knees so my bubble-covered breasts were in his face instead.

The switch from pain to pleasure in his expression was so swift that they merged for a moment, making him look so beautifully tortured.

Feeling bold, I squeezed my breasts then pulled at my nipples. "Smoke, please."

"Don't move." Startled, I let my hands drop and he made a tsking noise. "I said don't move."

He grasped my hands and returned them to my breasts, coaxing me into pinching my nipples again. Once my fingers were positioned the way he liked them, he squeezed his grip over mine, making me pinch harder. A startled squeak escaped me, but he just chuckled. I was pretty sure that he was more than a little sadistic in bed at this point, a theory that was quickly proven true when he left me kneeling there in the tub, pinching my breasts so hard an ache radiated from the tip and soaked into my body.

The fading sunlight hit him as he came walking back in, and I couldn't help my dreamy sigh despite the sharp ache filling my body. "You're so hot."

He gave me that grin that was only mine, a happy and relaxed expression that I never saw on his face when he wasn't alone with me. Other women may have had his body, but I bet his eyes never glowed with deep brown fire for them the way they did for me. With every step he took closer to me, my body heated and burned, my craving for his touch making me squeeze and release my nipples with a sharp gasp.

"Naughty baby. You just can't help yourself can you? Always gotta push me to see if I'll follow through with a punishment."

The grin on his kissable lips turned downright evil, and I froze. Dominant Smoke was coming out to play, and a delicious thrill of apprehension and pleasure skittered through me. I studied his face, and when he gave me a hard look, my nipples tingled beneath my unmoving fingers. Fuck, I loved it when he took control like this.

"I'm sorry…um...Sir."

"I know you're new to this baby girl, and you'll make mistakes, but it makes me so proud of you when you do as I ask. Shows me that you trust me to give you all the pleasure you can take, to surrender yourself to me and let me show you what I can really do."

I blinked. "You've been holding back? Is that even possible?"

"Had to let you get used to me first, to show you some things and gauge your interest." He leaned forward and licked my lower lip before retreating again. "And now I know you are very, very interested."

He sank to his knees again, the edge of the bathtub hitting his lower stomach. Pure happiness tinged with raw lust flooded me, mixing with the throbbing needs of my body and somehow making it all the more intense. I had to tilt my head to meet his gaze and the pleased look in his eyes relaxed me. He was satisfied with me, and I loved making him happy and hearing the praise he gave out so easily, which meant so much to me. Getting a kind look or a compliment out of my father was next to impossible. I guess after a childhood spent trying to please a man who was even worse with emotions than I was, it had programmed me on some level to crave the praise of a strong man.

Thank goodness I'd picked someone worthy of my devotion.

With a gentle touch he eased my fingers off my swollen, bright pink nipples and let out a little groan while I whimpered and tried to absorb the pain.

Never taking his eyes from my chest he made a shushing sound. "Easy, baby girl. I'll take care of you. Hands behind your back, fingers laced."

I did as he asked, my breasts thrust out and trembling with my rapid panting. Instead of taking my nipples into his mouth and soothing the burn with his magic tongue, he flicked first the left nipple, then the right, making me yelp and glare at him. Darkness stared back at me from his gaze and my clit throbbed even as I snarled at him.

"Ohhh, look at the fire in those pretty blue eyes. Makes me hard, but your temper has no place here. This is about lovin' you." He flicked my left nipple again, harder this time. "I'm just gonna love you rough."

Despite his aggressive words and tone, he simply took a handful of water from the space near my sex, his fingertips brushing my floating pubic curls, before dripping that water over my nipples setting my entire body aflame. The tips of my breasts were so sensitive now that even the water felt like someone touching me, and I gasped. He repeated the motion again, tickling and tantalizing me with the liquid warmth before he captured my right nipple in his mouth and sucked hard while rubbing that bud against the roof of his mouth with his firm tongue.

Lighting zipped along my nerves, and I almost lost my hold on my hands behind my back. I wanted to run my fingers through Smoke's hair, but I'd been too well trained to break form that easily. I clutched my hands together, somehow trying to ground myself against his sensual assault. He was stealing my thoughts, rendering me into nothing but a hungry animal intent on mating.

I let out a little growl when he finally released my breast, then flicked it again. A shriek escaped me, and he plunged his hand beneath the water and ran one thick finger between the lips of my sex. My arousal was even slipperier than the water. My pussy clenched, hard, when he teased the entrance to my sheath. Smoke, the bastard, just chuckled.

"Such a hungry cunt, always tryin' to suck my cock, my tongue, or my fingers inside of you." To my embarrassment, those words made me clench up again as his fingertip probed my entrance, pushing in a couple inches, then slowly dragging back out. I shuddered with each penetration and keened softly when he began to suck and bite my nipple, the other one throbbing as the cool air dried the wet heat on my skin that had been left behind from his mouth. Soon he had his finger all the way in and was increasing his pace as he switched from breast to breast, continuing to give me more pain and make me burn hotter.

I almost slipped when he pushed a second finger into me, and I tried to shove myself down onto it.

"Hold the edge of the tub," he rumbled without lifting his mouth from my aching tip.

With a shuddering moan, I complied and held on for dear life while he drove me higher and higher, but wouldn't let me go over.

I began to beg, the need hurting at this point, my pussy swollen and craving a rougher touch, a harder rhythm. That's what Smoke always gave me, a good hard fuck that soothed every hunger I had. Knowing he could relieve me, I whispered all the dirty things I wanted to do with him, rocking myself against him and shuddering when he began to work a third finger in. The feeling of being stuffed so full was intense, and I soon found myself leaning against him for support while he drove me crazy.

"Smoke," I whimpered when he removed his fingers from my grasping sex.

"Love you all wet like this, but I want to make you wetter. Trust me, baby girl?"

I gripped the edge of the tub hard enough to make my hands ache, which was still less painful than the throb of my overstimulated sex. "Yes, please, anything you want, just make me come."

He let out an unsteady breath that almost sounded like a soft moan. "Get out of the tub, and lay down on the bath mat."

Giving him a dubious look, I did as he asked, giggling when my unsteady legs almost collapsed as I tried to stand. There was no humor in Smoke's eyes as he lifted me out of the tub and gently laid me down on the oversized, lush blue bathmat. It was long enough that my head and torso were cushioned with my legs resting on the floor. I wiggled slightly, enjoying the tickle of the softness beneath me.

Smoke grabbed a towel and folded it before kneeling next to me. His gaze moved ever so slowly over me, lingering on my nipples then on my hip. His fingertips scraped along my skin and he said in a whisper, "Still want my dragon on you?"

I blinked at him in surprise. "Of course I do."

The edge of his mouth quirked into a half-smile and he continued to stroke my hips, running his fingers just above my pubic hair. "So soft."

Tingles raced through me at his touch and I felt sparks gather between my legs, quickly ramping my arousal back up as he traced his hands down my inner thighs, spreading me wide and murmuring to himself in Spanish.

"Gonna make you come so hard you're gonna pass out, then I'm gonna fuck ya back to life."

"Umm...yeah...awesome."

Normally, I would have been embarrassed at my babbling, but he chose that moment to hold my sex wide open with his thumbs, just staring at me with a ravenous expression. With a small grunt, he began to stroke my pussy, pulling at my clit and handling me in a much rougher manner than in the tub. I loved it, loved his commanding touch, his complete confidence in both himself and me. I groaned and clutched at the rug beneath me, winding my fingers through the long fibers while Smoke began to finger-fuck me again. He made a low, hungry noise while he did it and by the time he was back up to three fingers I couldn't control myself.

I had so much delicious tension running through me, all I could do was revel in his caress and groan out my pleasure.

He twisted his hand and began to rub his fingers along the top of my pussy from the inside, zeroing in on a magical spot that felt insanely good when he pushed on it. My eyes flashed open as he pressed, hard, inside of me and I stared up at him, mesmerized by the raw lust curling his upper lip into a silent snarl. He was totally focused on my sex, and he kept licking his lips like he couldn't wait to feast on me.

"Oh yeah, it's gonna be easy to make you squirt."

That penetrated the fog of my blissed out mind for a moment. "What?"

"Gonna make you come, hard, so hard that you're gonna soak my hand." He began to rub the magic spot and my toes curled before my thighs trembled. "When you feel like you're gonna come, I want you to push out with your pussy"

"What?"

His gaze snapped to mine and he growled, "Don't question me, just do it. I want this from you, Swan, I need you to give this to me."

I slowly nodded, but it was hard to get back in the mood as I fretted over his words. He must have sensed it because he gave my clit a sharp smack with his other hand and I hunched forward, a harder, deeper need filling me as that pain radiated out. He began to move his hand again, stretching me, making me burn, and I rocked my hips into his thrust. I didn't even need to tell him that I was getting close to coming, he could read me like a book. The delicious tension built and when he pressed his free hand down firmly on my lower belly just above my pubic bone I screamed out my pleasure. That was good, so fucking good. I wasn't even coming yet, and he had me sobbing as my over-stimulated body tried to adjust to his harsh touch.

"That's it baby, feel me. Feel my fingers shoved into your tight cunt, stroking you deep, rubbing and flexing inside of you. Come for me and I'll fuck you good. Now."

It felt as if he was tapping the magic spot inside of me and my breath froze in my lungs, my body tensing, then shattering.

"Push!"

Already caught up in the first contraction of my orgasm I did, and as he slid his fingers out I came so goddamn hard I thought I might be dying.

Something about his hand pressing down on me extended the orgasm and I felt hot, liquid warmth spilling over my bottom. I'd read enough erotica and watched enough pornos to know that I was experiencing female ejaculation, but I had no idea it would be this *intense*. Before I'd even coasted down he slid his fingers back inside my quivering sex and started rubbing and tapping again, making me writhe for him, his hand on my belly the only thing holding me still for him. This time, when I came, he let go of my belly and quickly rubbed my clit, making me double over as the pleasure became too intense. Another cascade of warmth, another body shattering orgasm in what had to be record time for me.

My mind drifted away at that point, and I floated in happy warmth. I was completely aware of Smoke gently rubbing me, giving me a massage that turned me into a puddle of mush. When he picked me up I just kind of flopped in his arms and he laughed while kissing the top of my head. Soon I was lowered to a soft mattress on my belly, and I sighed with happiness. Oh man, he was good. Utterly devastating. When I shifted my hips, my pussy was still sore, this time from hard use.

Smoke's warm, naked body blanketed mine and he placed his thighs on the outside of mine, pressing my legs together while he rubbed his cock against the crack of my ass.

I was so out of it that when he spread my butt cheeks wide enough that the cool air brushed over my anus I didn't even protest. Anything and everything he wanted to do with me at this point was totally okay with me. The brush of his swollen cock over my bottom was nice, but when he slid lower and the fat crest of his dick pushed into me I sank deeper into the mattress, rough and incoherent noises falling from my lips.

"Fuck, sweetheart, your pussy is so swollen, makes it incredibly good to sink my dick in you."

His position made it impossible for me to move, and I allowed myself the bliss of giving my will over to him as he fucked me. His scent enveloped me, and I rocked back into him as best as I could, absorbing every bit of pleasure he had to offer me and savored every minute of his enjoyment as well. Smoke grunted as he thrust, not holding back and giving me everything he had. I was surrounded by him, and I felt so loved. My next orgasm was just an extension of that bliss, a slow, deep release, and I cried out softly beneath him.

"So fuckin' pretty when you come," he said in a gravely voice. "So fuckin' beautiful."

I felt so amazing that I wanted to share it with him, to bring him the same level of satisfaction he had brought me. Bracing my arms a bit, I wiggled with his thrusts, grinding little circles on his pelvis with my ass and gasping at the new range of sensations. Smoke moved my hair over to the side and sank his teeth into my shoulder hard enough that I bucked up against him. That was all he needed to slip a hand beneath my belly and pet my clit.

"Oh, oh shit," I whispered and squeezed my eyes tight.

"Gonna fill you up, sweetheart," he whispered into my ear and nipped the tender lobe.

"Please, please come inside me."

Using three fingers he rubbed my clit just the way I liked, and I bit the blanket beneath me, crying out into it while his thrusts became unsteady. He buried himself inside me, his cock throbbing with his release, while he whispered about how much he loved me.

By this point, I was a panting, dehydrated mess but even in my blissed out state I made sure that he knew how special he was to me, how he made my body sing, and much I loved him.

Eventually, he rolled off of me, and I just laid there like a cat in a patch of sunlight, content to drift in my post-coital haze. Damn, my man could fuck. I had no idea how long I lounged there in dreamy bliss, but soon Smoke was back with what looked and smelled like enchiladas on a serving tray along with two beers and a side plate of brownies. My stomach roared to life, and I rolled over and held out my hands.

"Gimme."

Still naked as the day he was born and semi-hard, Smoke set the tray on the table next to the bed and slid into bed with me. Cuddled up together we quickly ate, and when we were done, I was wiped out. By this point, I was spread out over Smoke's chest while he ran his finger along my spine.

"What'cha thinkin' about, baby girl?"

"Absolutely nothing, what about you?"

He tensed slightly, then sighed. "Bunch of things, but mainly about you."

"What about me? How totally awesome I am?"

He gave my butt a light slap. "About all the places I want to take you, the things I want to do with you. We have more than enough money that you could stay home if you wanted to, you wouldn't have to work."

I poked at his chest. "I *want* to work."

"Then how about you work for me?"

"What?"

I lifted my head and found him smiling at me. "Yeah, that would be perfect. You would be a great fuckin' asset to the company, and anytime you need an orgasm you can just *come* in my office."

I laughed, unable to help it when he gave me a look filled with such mischief and happiness. "You're a dork."

He yawned, then nodded. "Only around you. Woman, you have no idea how much you've changed me, how big an impact you've had on my life. Never knew I could be this happy with someone, never knew what I was missing."

I rested my head on his chest and resumed running my fingers over the defined ridges of his muscles. The thought of working at his security company appealed to me, and not just because Smoke was there. Smoke loved the Iron Horse MC and considered them his family. As such, I wanted to protect them, to help them figure out who the traitors were and to make everyone as safe as I could, because if they got hurt, Smoke would hurt. Maybe this was how he felt about Lyric, or how Beach felt about me. Huh.

With those thoughts rolling through my mind, I drifted off to sleep in Smoke's arms, images of us working together at his security company like a couple of badass ninjas sending me off into dreamland.

AUSTIN TX

Chapter Eighteen

Miguel 'Smoke' Santos

The fine golden hair on Swan's arms gleamed in the shaft of sunlight coming through edge of the curtain. It was close to noon, and she showed no signs of waking up anytime soon, much to my disappointment. The desire to give her the engagement ring I held tightly in my fist was now almost a compulsion. A small, sane part of my mind urged me to wait and go with my original plan, to ask her at sunset after a hike up the side of the mountain near our cabin. I'd scoped out the perfect place earlier when I'd left Swan alone for a little quiet time this morning. The fact that she was still sleeping by the time I got back and showered made me realize just how tired she was. The dark circles beneath her eyes had finally lightened and she looked relaxed, content.

Instead of being a selfish fuck, I knew I should let
her rest more, but she'd slept for ten hours so I figured
she would be fine for at least the next few. I would put
her back to bed after I'd fucked then fed her. Or maybe
both at the same time. Sliding into her body was all
slick heat and tight muscles. When her pussy clamped
down on me as she climaxed it was always a battle to
hold back, but I was greedy for her orgasms. I loved the
fact that she's mine, and only mine, that I would be the
only one who would ever give her pleasure. Every
word, every sigh belonged to me, and I was so ravenous
for her that I slipped the ring onto my pinky finger and
slid beneath the sheets.

Moving slowly, I lowered myself between her legs.
At some point, she must have gotten up because she
wore a pair of soft, pink cotton panties with little
sparkling gems along the dangerously low waist band. I
wondered where the hell Swan had gotten such a sexy
piece of lingerie, then my mind flashed to my sister
who'd bought clothes for Swan, and I immediately
banished any further thoughts from my head.

I refocused on my task and slowly parted Swan's
legs, then found out the panties were crotchless. Swan's
pretty pussy lips with their golden fuzz were
surrounded by smooth pink cotton and begged for my
lips. It was so unbearably sexy, I knew right away
who'd gotten them for her. Hustler. Don't know how
he'd managed it, but that bastard did it to fuck with me,
I'm sure. When I got back, I was going to beat his ass
for giving my girl panties.

The light down of her golden curls felt soft as rabbit
fur beneath my fingertips as I slowly, ever so lightly,
stroked her cunt awake. I didn't want her mind to

realize she wasn't dreaming quite yet, but I wanted her pussy soaked so that when she did wake up, it would be to instant arousal. She really got off on her clit being sucked, and I wished I had thought to grab my toy bag, but there was no way I was leaving the warmth between her legs. Not when her labia were slowly beginning to flush, swell, and grow wet.

Trapped beneath the sheets I was surrounded by her scent and when I saw a drop of liquid arousal seeping out I couldn't hold back any longer. My cock fuckin' hurt with my need to be inside of her, to soothe me in the way only she could. She shifted slightly and sighed as the movement rubbed the hood of her engorged clit against the slit of her panties. Moving carefully, I lifted the side of her panties just enough to use the material to rub against her. That made her moan, and she said something that was a garbled mumble. I grinned and did it again, watching with fascination as her clit swelled, emerging fully out of the hood.

Yeah, now she was ready.

I repositioned the sinful bit of cloth over her slit so I had the maximum usage of that small space. She wore these panties for a reason and I wanted to show her what fun they could be. I admit it, I got off on teaching her new things, and I had enough dirty ideas of what I wanted to do with her for three lifetimes. The first lick on her clit caused her stiffen, then shift restlessly with a gentle arch of her spine.

The way she lazily ground her mound against my face let me know that she was awake.

"Mmm, Miguel…what are you doing?"

I growled when she used my real name, and a bolt of lust drew my balls up tight. Fuck, every time I was with her I felt like an adolescent who had to fight busting his nut constantly. She's just so fuckin' sexy, and she didn't even know it. Even better, once I got her going she was shameless in her need for pleasure and that made me even hotter. Having her wet pussy in my mouth, gave me plenty of cream to lick up, and I hovered on the edge. The only thing that held me back was the ring on my pinkie. I wanted to give it to her now, but I was going to do it in a way that insured she'd say yes.

She lifted the sheet, and I was greeted by the sight of a relaxed, happy Swan. Her smile shot straight through me, and I sucked her clit hard before I released it. Her big blue eyes were glazed with lust and she gave me a pleading look. "Don't stop, please!"

I slid a finger into her and was rewarded when her cunt gripped down on me. "Who gave you these panties?"

"Hustler." She bit her lower lip, then gave me that cute, sexy look of hers that shredded me. "Does it matter?"

I shoved a second finger roughly into her, which earned me a groan. My dominant side rose a bit as I stared at her, knowing the effect it would have. Even with my face buried between her thighs I was the one in control here, the one who gave her pleasure and took it. A hard shudder vibrated my bones when she dropped her gaze, a softness crossing her features that entranced me. She slipped into submissive mode so quickly that I sometimes worried about it. I wondered if she needed a harsher hand, but I always dismissed the notion because of one simple truth. No matter how submissive she appeared, Swan was a wildcat and would rip into me if I really pissed her off. I loved the fact that she was dangerous. It made me want to screw her brains out in the worst way.

"Yeah it fuckin' matters that Hustler gave you panties. What the fuck?"

She gave me an impish look. "He also loaned me a book all about sexual positions. I want to try every single one with you. Can we do that, Miguel?"

This sweet, not-so-innocent girl knew just how to play me, and even though I knew I was being manipulated, I didn't care. Swan was just coming into her own as sexually active woman, and I wanted to encourage her to express her passion, to always get what she needed, and be brave enough to ask for it. It would make my job of satisfying her easier if I knew what she wanted.

I rested my chin on her pubic bone, looking up the long line of her lean, muscled body to her soft face. Perfection. The first time I ever saw her in the sunlight I just about had a heart attack. Swan went jogging that day while I watched her from the parking lot in my surveillance vehicle and my dick had fallen in instant lust with the hot young blonde in the tight, white yoga shorts and amazing ass. High, round, fuckable.

And those tits. Bouncing with her every step.

Mine.

My attention was drawn back to the present as she ran her fingers through my hair. "I love it when you look at me like that, Smoke. I have no words for it, but you make me feel...so much."

Suddenly any nervousness I had was gone and it was the most natural thing in the world to slip the ring off my pinky. I moved up a bit so my elbows were on either side of her ribs and settled some of my weight onto her, knowing she liked it. Sure enough, a small smile curved her lips as I pressed her into the mattress, and she continued to entwine her fingers in my hair. Each little tug made my dick jerk in response and I gritted my teeth, fighting the urge to fuck her.

"Swan, I need to ask you something."

As she studied my face, her brows drew down and her jaw tightened. "What's wrong?"

"Nothing's wrong."

"Yes, yes, there is. I can see it in your eyes. They're not brown velvet like they should be right now. What is it? Please, tell me. I can take it."

Shit, this was not going as I expected. "Just calm down. I'm nervous, but not because something is wrong, but because everything is right. How it should be."

With a sigh she removed her fingers from my hair. "Fortune cookie."

"Then let me be as plain as I can then." I looked her right in the eye and said the words that would change the rest of my life. It would never be just 'me' again, always 'us'. "Miss Swan Anderson, will you marry me?"

Her eyes grew bigger, and bigger, and bigger until I had to bite back laughter. She just looked so astonished as she gazed at my mother's ring, the three one-carat diamonds sparkling in the warm light. The expression on her pretty face was so blank that I had no idea what she was thinking, no way to know if I needed to back off or keep pushing. This was the most important moment of my life, and I was at a loss for what to do to make her see, to understand, that we were meant to be.

"Like for-real marriage? Not some stupid biker shit?"

I burst out laughing. I couldn't help it. She was scowling, so suspicious, so damn adorable as she glared up at me, but her lips were twitching in a smile. My hard dick ached enough that I had to press my pelvis into the mattress.

"No, no stupid biker shit. I want to own you in every way I can, baby girl, to provide you with anything you could ever want or need. I don't care what you do, as long as you do it with me at your side. I want to be your husband, 'til death do us part."

She beamed at me, then held out her left hand, her ring finger slightly extended and shaking. "Ye-yes. I'll marry you, Miguel."

I kissed the tip of her finger before I slowly slid the ring on. It was a little bit loose, but the fit was close enough. As I held her hand up to the light to admire the brilliance of the ring sparkling on her hand, I had a vivid memory of doing the same with my mother, sitting next to her as a kid and gazing at the big stones as they threw rainbows onto our bodies. Now the rainbows were shimmering on my fiancée's face, and it felt right all the way down to my soul. I liked to think my mom and dad were with me right now, giving us their blessing, but they needed to beat feet back to heaven soon because things were about to get real dirty down here on earth.

We kissed and as our tongues stroked across each other I think we both groaned at the same time. Her wet, soft pussy pressed up against my erection, coating it with slick moisture as she wiggled against me. My whole body was on fire, my dick throbbing with the need to be inside her, surrounded by the wet velvet of her pussy. With one shift of my hips, I was in her, and I couldn't get close enough. I wrapped my arms around her and buried my face in her neck. She clung to me, only letting me pull out a few inches before pressing me back in with her legs wrapped around me.

I licked and bit at her neck while she did the same to me, our control gone and lust building like a thunderstorm. Our movements were so flowing, so in sync that I felt like I was just following what her body wanted, what she needed. I loved givin' it to her.

"That's it, baby girl, just like that. Squeeze me with that tight pussy of yours."

She groaned against my neck and bit me hard enough to make me wince. "You feel so good. So hard and deep. Love you."

My orgasm started to race up my back, spurred on by her words. Thankfully, Swan seemed to be approaching her own peak. After a little more dirty talk, she shattered around me, her pussy tightening and releasing in a way that swiftly pushed me over, and I groaned my way through the intense pleasure of emptying myself into my woman, every sensation dragging a shudder from me. As the last wave of pleasure flooded my system I collapsed next to Swan, rolling her over so she could cuddle into me. I loved holding her like this, draped on my body, boneless and purring. My feelings for this girl had grown beyond words, and I was so fuckin' happy she'd taken my ring without hesitation.

We were having lunch in bed when my phone beeped to alert me that someone had sent me an emergency text. I stiffened as a wave of foreboding moved through me. Somehow I knew the peaceful moments we'd stolen for ourselves wouldn't last long.

Swan must have noticed because she rolled off of me. "What's wrong?"

"I told Beach I only wanted to be contacted if the shit had hit the fan."

She stared in the direction of my phone and her anxiety was contagious as I dug for it through my pockets. It only took me seconds to open the text from Beach:

Call me ASAP. It's about your family.

Icy dread curled around my spine, and I was barely aware of Swan on the bed behind me. I think she said my name, but I was so intent on finding out what was going on that I didn't respond. Shit, my brother-in-law, had he lost his life overseas like too many of my buddies? Or was it my sister, or—please God, no—my nieces.

I began to pace, and when Beach picked up on the second ring I barked out, "What the fuck is going on?"

"Brother, I need you to remain calm, okay? I need you to listen and remain calm. You might want to consider leaving the room if Swan is there."

I swear my breath stuck in my lungs as I waited for him to tell me my brother-in-law was dead. My heart slammed in my chest as my breathing picked up, bone-deep fear racing through me. I fuckin' hated being afraid. It sucked, but I'd be damned if I could control it. Glancing behind me, I found Swan watching me with open concern as I battled with leaving the room or staying. As I watched her, I calmed enough to keep from having a meltdown, and I knew my decision. My girl was a part of my life in every way now, and I wasn't gonna hide shit from her.

"It's all good. Now what the fuck is going on?"

"I'm so sorry to tell you this, but Veronica either committed suicide or was murdered on Hustler's back porch last night. I need you home to help your sister with funeral arrangements. We're takin' care of her, but she needs you right now and so does Hustler. I'm so sorry, man. I promise you, I swear to you, that if someone did murder her we *will* find them and take care of them."

A dull roar echoed in my head as I tried to figure out what he was saying. Veronica couldn't be dead. It was my job to protect her, to keep her safe and I'd failed. Failed my family. My throat tightened up, and I managed to grit out, "We're on our way home."

"Got tickets waiting for you at the airport in Denver, you and Swan."

"Leave your truck there. Khan'll have one of his boys bring it down. You okay? I can get one of the brothers to drive you if you need it. We're here to do anything we can for you. Understood?"

"Yeah, I understand."

There was a long, awkward pause where I swear I could feel Beach's sorrow through the phone then I hung up without saying goodbye.

I have no idea how long I stood there, staring at the wall, before Swan's voice tugged me out of my shame, guilt, and deep sorrow. "Smoke? What's wrong?"

What was wrong was that Veronica was dead because I wasn't there to take care of her. I didn't even come back to help her when she slit her wrists. While I didn't regret my decision to save Swan's life, I couldn't help but think about how my selfish actions had helped lead to the death of a woman who had so much potential when she stayed on her meds. And Hustler…shit, he must be losing his mind. I wondered if he was in jail right now as I dialed my sister's number, dreading the call.

After four rings she picked up, her voice thick and exhausted. "Hi, honey."

I swallowed hard and turned to face the wall, not wanting Swan to see me with my soul wounded like this. "How are you?"

"Not so good." She gave a watery sigh. "I haven't had the heart to tell the girls yet, and the military is still trying to hunt my husband down."

"I'm on my way. Just hang in there."

"I heard about the miracle Sarah managed to pull off. Congratulations."

While there was absolutely no accusation in her voice, I flinched anyway. "Thanks."

"A bunch of Tricks' relatives are on their way to help, and you know the club has been bending over backwards to take care of us. Right now, Scarlett is cooking up a storm while Birdie and Gina are with the girls, giving me some time to get my shit together. I'm hanging in there with lots of support."

"How's Hustler?"

For the first time her voice broke. "Not so good. He's a suspect, of course. Iron Horse's lawyers are talking with him right now."

"Wait, so it wasn't suicide?"

"No. Jinks and Track checked the scene out before the cops got there. Veronica was shot in the back of the head at an angle impossible for her to reach. She was for sure left there for Hustler to find. We just don't know why."

I was a total shit of a human being because that news made me feel a little better and eased my guilt. Anger built in me and filled my mind with thoughts of bloody, terrible revenge. I couldn't help but picture Veronica being shot. Someone was going to pay, big time.

"I gotta go, Julia. Love you and the girls. I'll be home soon."

"Is Swan coming with you?"

For the first time, I hesitated about that question. Of course, I wanted her with me, but I really didn't feel comfortable with her meeting my extended family at a funeral. Not that anyone would give a fuck. They'd probably be too shocked by the fact that I was getting married to care. Man, that sucked even more. I couldn't even celebrate my engagement with my family right now. Swan deserved the best I could give her and that wasn't showing off her engagement ring at a wake.

"I think I need to focus on you and the girls right now."

"Miguel Santos!" My sister shouted into the phone. "You better not fuck things up with her. You bring her with you and I don't want to hear another word about it."

"What?"

"She is so good for you, such a strong woman, and I've talked with Cathy up in Denver a lot this week, checking up on you."

"You have?"

"Of course, you're my brother. Do you really think I wouldn't worry my ass off about you? But I knew that you didn't need the distraction of my fretting. I don't think you really understand how much you're loved and by how many people. I met Swan's Dad earlier this week. Intense guy, but he said I was the closest thing you had to a mother and he wanted to make sure you and Swan were a good match." Her laugh was harsh, but when she spoke again her voice was a little lighter. "I found myself pointing out your very dubious virtues to him, and I felt like I was trying to pimp you out to a reluctant buyer."

"Mike Anderson came to visit you?"

On the bed, Swan gave a loud, dramatic moan of despair.

"He was a perfect gentleman, Smoke. Never once made me or the girls feel uncomfortable. In fact, they swarmed all over him. He said if yours and Swan's babies are half as pretty as mine he might forgive you for stealing his daughter from him."

My gaze darted to Swan almost against my will, afraid of what she'd read on my face. I was a fuckin'

mess, my mind not really engaging, and I hurt inside.
No matter how much I wanted to avoid thinking about
it, Veronica was dead. Funny how when someone
passes we forget about the bad shit and remember the
good.

"I gotta go, Julia. According to the info Beach sent
me I should be landing around 6 p.m."

"I'm coming to pick you both up," she said in a firm,
no bullshit voice. "Swan's dad mentioned the ring so I
know she's going to be part of our family soon. Right?"

"I just gave it to her," I murmured while finally
daring to look at Swan again.

She knelt among the messed up sheets and blankets,
now dressed in a pair of jeans and a sedate emerald
green top. Her big blue eyes were filled with worry, and
she had her hands fisted in the sheets tight enough to
turn her knuckles white. With a start, it dawned on me
that she was so freaked out because she thought the call
was about a threat to her. And maybe it was. I doubted
Veronica's death was a random act of violence. It might
be a form of revenge. Whoever had stolen those
missiles had to be fuckin' pissed about losing them.

Julia yelled to someone in the background, "Hey,
I'm going to pick Smoke up from the airport at six. You
mind watching the kids?"

Holding Swan's gaze, I tried to let her know that it
was gonna be all right, that she didn't need to worry,
but she only looked even more alarmed. Her attention
kept darting to where her guns were stashed and I knew
I had to get off the phone and calm her down. Taking
care of her helped center me—simple as that.

"Gotta go. Love you."

She sounded distracted as she replied, "Love you too. I'll see you *and* Swan at six."

"Roger that."

I hung up and turned back to find Swan standing about two paces from me now. Damn she was sneaky, and quick. When her steel-blue gaze locked on mine, I sighed internally as I realized just how quickly she'd slipped into survival mode. While she was still stressed, she was done with me not telling her anything.

Sure enough, "Smoke, if you want me to be your wife you have to be on the level with me. What is going on? Tell me. I can take it."

My voice sounded tight and choked as I forced out, "Veronica was murdered last night on Hustler's back porch."

Her eyes grew impossibly wide and she pressed a hand to her chest like her heart hurt. "Oh my God, you're serious. How?"

"I don't know the details, but she was shot in the back of the head."

Tears glimmered in her eyes and she continued to press her hand to her chest. "That's awful. I'm so sorry."

Yeah, the whole fuckin' thing was heartrending on so many levels it made a Greek tragedy look like a romantic comedy. I was gonna break down soon, I could feel it nipping at my heels and even though I wanted to go mourn by myself, I also wanted to hold Swan while I let my grief go. I just worried that it would be too much for her to process, that she wouldn't understand that while Veronica was far from my favorite person, she was still my family and didn't deserve to be shot and dumped on Hustler's porch like a piece of garbage.

Swan took the decision out of my hands by pulling me gently back into bed with her. She sat with her back against some pillows and the headboard, then drew me down until my head was in her lap. I wrapped my arms around her legs and held her tight, closing my eyes at the simple pleasure of her playing with my hair. Flashes of my life with Veronica kept spilling into my head as I tried to deal with the fact that she'd never have the chance to enjoy the sensation of someone playing with her hair again. It was such a weird thing to focus on, but my brain seemed to be stuck on it, stuck on all the things Veronica would never experience. Shit had gotten bad with her over the last couple years, but at one time, before her bi-polar disorder took over her life, she was a nice woman with a bright future.

The tears started of their own accord, and I turned my head to Swan's thigh, pressing my face against the warm cotton of her jeans and gripping her hips harder. She began to whisper sweet words of love and healing, trying her best to ease my pain. I can't tell you how good it felt to have someone who loved me hold me while I cried. Now I know some guys think it's a pussy thing to cry in front of their woman, but that's bullshit. Crying over the loss of a loved one isn't a sign of weakness, it's part of what makes us human.

Eventually, I wound up wrapped around Swan, tired and feeling empty. She watched me closely, petting me and loving me, easing my grief. With a soft groan I rolled over to my back, hauling her on top of me. She traced the bow of my lips then said in a quiet voice, "My heart aches for you and your family."

That squeezed another tear from me, and I held her tight. Loving the gentle give of her body and her warmth as she wrapped herself around me. I slowly relaxed, and my mind cleared. I held on to one absolute truth. As long as I had my woman, everything would be all right.

The flight back was uneventful. Beach had booked us first class seats and Swan slept most of the way, her head on my shoulder, while I stared out the window as the world sped by. We had to leave our weapons with Khan because taking that shit through airport security was impossible. I know Swan had been irked to leave her knives behind, but she didn't complain.

As we stood around waiting for our luggage, I kept a constant eye on my girl, making sure no one got too close to her or looked too hard. I swear guys were eye fuckin' her left and right. Not that I could blame them one bit. She was probably the hottest woman these gaping motherfuckers would ever see, but I made more than one man take a step back when I caught him staring at her a little too long. Swan was oblivious, busy texting her sister. She kept running her tongue over her lower lip, and I wanted to kiss her hard enough to make her melt. But I knew she probably wouldn't appreciate me mauling her in a busy airport, so I kept my hands and my lips to myself.

I tried calling my sister, but there was no answer, not that I really expected one. Julia never answered her cell phone while driving, so I sent her a text letting her know we were here and asking where we should meet her. By the time I was done, I noticed a guy approaching us out of the corner of my eye. I turned quickly, ready to knock someone right the fuck out if they messed with Swan, but I quickly recognized the man grinning at us. It was Cruz, a member of the Iron Horse MC and an old friend. With his full grey beard and large size he was a physically intimidating man, and Swan hung back, slightly behind me, as I introduced her to him.

Cruz shook my hand. "Smoke, sorry to hear about what happened to Veronica, man."

I stiffened, then nodded, not wanting to talk about it here in the baggage area. "Thanks."

He shifted uncomfortably, shoving his hands into the pockets of his worn jeans then sighed. "Damn shame. Anyway, Julia sent me to pick you up."

"Is everything okay?"

"Yeah, yeah everything is good. They managed to hunt down Tricks, and she was talking to him on Skype when I left."

My stomach clenched as I imagined the conversation my sister was having right now and the need to be with her and take care of her, dug into my gut.

While Cruz and I talked about what had been happening at the clubhouse Swan stayed slightly behind me, her gaze darting around as her body language broadcasted her increasing unease.

I leaned down, brushing her soft hair away from her ear to whisper, "You okay?"

"I'm okay," she whispered back. "Just…there's a lot going on."

While I wasn't sure if she meant what was going on around her or all the bullshit that we'd been through, I knew the limit of her tolerance for the crowd was reaching its peak. She'd worn a peach long-sleeve turtle neck along with a pair of dark jeans to cover as much of her skin as possible in order to avoid freaking out over the accidental brush of a stranger. Right now she'd pulled the cuffs down over her hands and had fisted the fabric, shielding her exposed skin as much as possible.

Cruz continued to go on about Los Diablos being a dangerous pain in the ass—something about them beating the hell out of one of our prospects—but I was more distracted by my worry for my baby girl than the threat of an all-out war between the two clubs.

I gave Cruz a hard look. "Why the fuck do they want to go to battle with us? They know they'll lose."

It was true. Not only was Iron Horse bigger than Los Diablos—our men were hand selected for not only their physical strength, but their quick minds as well—we could outmaneuver, outshoot, and basically crush Los Diablos if it came down to it. If drawn into a fight, losses would be great on both sides, to us and our allies, as well as to Los Diablos and their allies. The thought of my brothers and their families facing that kind of danger made my protective instincts go full out. As soon as I got shit settled with my family, I'd have to deal with this new hot fuckin' mess.

Swan moved away from me and I realized that while I was thinking our luggage had popped out onto the conveyer belt. As we gathered our bags, she was quiet, tense, and constantly scanning the crowd. Her big blue eyes met mine and the unease I saw there made the hair on my arms stand up. Before I could ask her what was wrong Cruz took her suitcase with a smile.

"Let me take care of that, darlin'."

Swan handed her suitcase over without protest, and I gave Cruz a hard look that let him know flirting with my old lady was off limits. My closest friends got away with it because they were cocky fuckers I knew would never make a real move on my woman. Cruz hadn't earned the right to smile at Swan like that. His gaze lingered on her breasts pressing against her peach shirt but before I could say anything, he looked away.

"Come on, let's get out of here."

I followed Cruz, the wheels of my suitcase bumping over the ground as we left the terminal and made our way to the parking lot. It was around ten o'clock at night, and the vast parking area was pretty much deserted except for the occasional random traveler off in the distance. The scent of Austin mixed with the smell of jet fuel filled me, and I was glad to be home. A few days ago, I'd been pretty sure that I would die trying to save Swan's life from some pretty fuckin' overwhelming odds. If we could beat those and come out the other side with our love stronger than ever, there was nothin' we couldn't do.

We stopped at a light blue mini-van with a 'My Child is an Honor Roll Student at Lake Travis High' bumper sticker on the back. I recognized it as Julia's mini-van and an ache of homesickness went through me. Knowing my sister was probably a wreck by now tugged at my gut, and I was eager to get to her. We stopped near the back while Cruz fumbled with the keys.

"Isn't this Julia's ride? Where's your Mercedes?"

Cruz owned his own lawn company that was doing pretty well if his lavish lifestyle was any indication. "Julia wasn't sure how much luggage you were bringing with you. My convertible isn't really built for hauling shit around."

Swan stayed by my side, scanning the parking lot. As I watched her I wondered how long it would take her to decompress and what I could do to help her deal with all this bullshit. Thankfully, I wouldn't have to figure it out on my own. Mike and Mimi were coming down to stay with us for a few days, and I wanted to take some time to sit down with them and talk. Sarah was also within driving distance, but I knew she has enough of her own shit to deal with at the moment, not to mention Beach. I'd be surprised if he let Sarah out of his sight ever again.

"Fuckin' trunk is stuck," Cruz muttered. "Swan, go ahead and have a seat inside while Smoke and I screw around with this."

After a moment's hesitation she nodded, and when Cruz opened the sliding passenger door for her, three things happened at once that turned my world into an absolute nightmare.

An unfamiliar man jerked Swan into the van and held a gun to her head. Two more guys spilled out of the trunk, with their guns trained on me, while a third quickly put a cloth over Swan's face. The two guys from the back of the van I recognized as Los Diablos members, kept their guns pointed at me.

"Don't you fuckin' move," the older guy with his salt and pepper hair and bad teeth snarled. "You so much as flinch in our direction and your bitch pays for it."

I desperately wanted to go to Swan as she struggled against her captors, impotent rage churning in my gut. She had gotten a couple of good punches in, but whatever they drugged her with soon slowed her movements. Her eyes locked with mine right before they rolled back into her head and went limp.

Cruz took a step forward, refusing to meet my gaze as he looked into the van. "My part's done. Where's the money?"

While that betraying bastard talked with whoever held Swan, the other two guys approached me with duct tape and evil intent in their gaze. I tensed to fight when the old man shook his head. "Don't be stupid. There is no way you could take on all of us. And even if you tried, we've got a couple of brothers in the lot waiting to shoot your ass. If you want to keep us from ass-fucking your girl until she bleeds while we ride to our destination, stow it and cooperate. Otherwise... "

Wrath filled me, making me vibrate with the need for violence, but we were well and truly fucked. The thought of Swan being raped pushed me dangerously close to the edge, but I knew I couldn't let go. I looked in the van and saw Swan was being held in the lap of some buck-toothed fucker who was currently grabbing a handful of her tit.

"Get your fuckin' hands off of her," I snarled.

The men laughed, but the older guy who was talking to me shook his head. "Sorry, you don't get to call the shots here. Demon'll keep his dick to himself, but I won't begrudge him a li'l feel of those big titties."

They shoved me into the back of the van, and I kept my gaze on the man holding Swan, who was now mauling her unconscious form. Disgust, rage, guilt, and the need to kill boiled inside of me. They secured my hands with a zip tie and put some tape over my mouth. My nostrils flared as I took a deep breath, already regretting that I went with them without a fight. There had to be something I could have done other than just giving up, but I couldn't let Swan pay the price for my rebellion. If I died she'd be all alone, so even though it went against every instinct I had, I didn't protest when they pulled a black hood over my head.

The last thing I saw was Cruz's guilty look before nothingness overtook me.

AUSTIN TX

Chapter Nineteen

Swan

My mouth tasted terrible and I couldn't move.

Those were the first thoughts I had as I came back to the real world from the drug-induced slumber.

This being knocked out thing was really getting old.

As I struggled to open my eyes, bits and pieces of the last day came to mind in a confusing whirl of colors and emotions. I shifted and my extremities filled with pins and needles that cut through my disoriented thoughts. As I slowly surfaced, panic sped up my pulse rate, and the adrenaline in my system began to force everything awake.

Before I dared to open my eyes I listened hard, to see if I could hear anyone. Somewhere off in the distance there were faint voices, but nothing in here. The air had a musty smell to it, but no dampness, so I probably wasn't in a basement again. I gradually, carefully opened one eye and found myself staring at a pale green wall with a peeling wallpaper border that had old lady style roses embossed on it. A quick glance showed a battery operated lantern not too far away from me on an old blue milk crate. I slowly lifted my head, waiting for someone behind me to say or do something, but I appeared to be alone. My neck strained as I tried to see where I was and despair filled me. A small part of my heart had hoped that Smoke would be here with me, but I was alone.

It was quiet enough for me to be sure I wasn't in the city, but I thought I heard other faint sounds coming from somewhere in the house. For a moment, I imagined I heard a yell that sounded like Smoke, then nothing. Fear sat heavy in my chest and I strained to hear if it really was him but there was only silence.

Dreadful images of what they could be doing to Smoke right now, if he was still alive, tore at my mind and willpower. Without realizing it, I'd begun to struggle against my bonds, only to end up hurting myself as the zip ties chaffed my wrists. I was well secured to a folding steel chair and soon I slumped against it, my breath heaving out of my lungs as sweat trickled down my face. A boarded over window to my right let in a small amount of what I assumed was moonlight from outside, and from what I could see, it was still dark.

Something I was pretty sure was a generator of some kind roared outside, and I hoped that maybe I could use the noise to try and cover our escape—once I found Smoke.

I wanted to cry, to sob out my pain and hurt over the thought of anything happening to Smoke, but I managed to choke it back.

No, I had to hold on, had to save him.

With a renewed sense of determination, I began to shift my chair around, trying to minimize the scrape of the legs across the old wooden floor.

My senses were on high alert so when the squeak of the door opening filled the small space I froze, waiting to see what monster I had to kill in order to get out of here.

The person who came into the room was indeed a monster, but not the kind that I could ever kill.

No, this monster had my blue eyes, my blonde hair, and at one point, claimed to love me.

The monster was my mother, and she looked terrible.

Her once beautiful face had aged, making her appear haggard, like the wicked witch in a fairytale. She had scabs and open sores on her arms. When she smiled, I noticed that her once gleaming white teeth were yellow, and her gums had receded. Her appearance made her big smile all the more terrible, like some kind of insane clown from a child's nightmare.

She had tried to put makeup on, but her hand must have been unsteady because the black eyeliner that she normally wore was smeared over her eyelids and her lipstick was a bright pink slash on her surgically plumped up lips. She wore a short-sleeved shirt, with a plunging neckline, which showed off her abundant cleavage, but even the skin of her chest was damaged. As I watched she absently scratched at her forearm hard enough to peel one of the scabs off, but she didn't appear to notice.

I was so stunned by this zombie image of my birth mother that all I could do was stare at her. She came in and shut the door behind her while nervously licking her lips. When she leaned back against the dull wood and watched me, I became aware of a black cloth bundle clutched in her right hand and the fact that her pupils were pinpoint. I'd been around her enough while she was high to know that she was wasted right now. Far in the back of my mind, past the shock of my mother's appearance and betrayal, a cold, practical part of me was happy that she was here because she was way easier to overpower than any of the Los Diablos members who had abducted me earlier.

"Swan," my mother said in her husky voice. "I'm…"

When she just continued to stare at me with watery eyes I snapped. "You're what? Sorry that you had me kidnapped? Sorry that my fiancé is probably dead right now? Sorry that you almost got Sarah and me sold into sexual slavery? Or is it because you used to beat Sarah for years? Maybe you feel bad for pimping Sarah out to a casino owner when she was sixteen. What part are you sorry for, *mother!*"

I was close to screaming and Billie crossed the small room, a panicked look on her face. "No, no. Shhhh. You have to be quiet. They don't know you're awake yet, and I want to help you. I'm going to make sure they don't hurt you."

Sudden hope bloomed within me. "Are you letting me go?"

She looked down at her hands and I noticed for the first time the track marks going up and down her arms among the scabs and scars. Oddly enough, she had massive bejeweled rings on every finger, the real kind, a fortune in jewelry on dried skin that looked like it belonged to a mummy. My stomach sank as she slowly shook her head, and I had to fight back tears when she looked back up, her apathy filling the air. She was utterly weak...defeated. Always so damn fragile. Even though I hated her for what she'd done, I also despaired at what she had become— a drug-addicted whore who would help in the kidnapping of her own child.

"No, Swan, I can't let you go. If I do they'll just find you again and take away my medicine." She ignored my bitter laugh at calling whatever she'd been taking 'medicine'. "This is for the best, really. The Chief wants you, and he's promised me that he'll keep you safe and take care of you as long as you behave. I think he has a crush on you."

She gave a girlish giggle, like we were just gossiping about cute boys, and the sound made my skin crawl.

"Who the hell is the Chief, and what the hell are you talking about? Are you trying to tell me some psycho wants to be my boyfriend? Is that somehow supposed to make me feel better? To know when he's raping me that my mom considers him relationship material?"

The familiar shutter came down behind her eyes, the almost visible wall that she put up around herself, when I was saying something she didn't like, so she could pretend she never even heard me speak. "He'll be here soon so you need to be good, please. Smoke is going to pay for messing everything up—the bastard. The others wanted to sell you, but Chief wants you for himself.

372

Please don't make him mad. If you do, he might let them have you, and you do not want that. I've seen what they do to women."

She gave a hard shudder, her gaze haunted as I scrambled to understand what was going on. "So I'm supposed to play nice with Chief? Who is he?"

Billie seemed to drift away for a moment, her jaw slack and her hands motionless. I realized that she must have shot up right before she came into the room and hate filled me. Here I was, a prisoner and about to be given to some sadistic man as his toy, and if I displeased him I'd be handed off to a group of men to be raped to death. Perfect timing for my loving mother to escape reality and get fucked up.

A pang went through me at the knowledge that I might never see Mimi and my dad again, my real parents who loved me unconditionally. I had to shove away the deluge of emotions that accompanied that thought and refocus myself on my mother who was now brushing my hair off my face with a dreamy look. I tried to not show it, but my skin crawled at her touch.

"Swan, I can't say who he is, if I say who he is he'll lock me in a closet without my medicine and make me pay. He has a plan for you, and I can't tell you about it. But he won't hurt you. He promised, but you must cooperate with him. Do what he says and try to hold your tongue. His temper is…just don't get him mad, okay? He can give you a real nice life as long as you mind him."

"Have you lost your damn mind?" Desperate to reach her, to try and get past her drug-induced fog, I begged in a desperate voice, "Mom, please, help me get out of here. We'll run together, you don't have to stay here. You could be free."

The desolation in her red rimmed blue eyes, so like my own, killed what little hope I had. "You can't escape them. Ever. You'll just run from one devil to another. All you can do is survive and find beauty where you can. Like wild flowers in a garbage dump."

"But I have found happiness. Smoke loves me and I love him. We're going to build a life together."

The harsh grate of her laughter scratched along my skin. "Love? You think he loves you? I know Smoke and that psychopath doesn't love anything or anyone."

"No, you're wrong. He does love me and we're getting married." I sucked in a quick breath and tried to get through to her. "He's fought for me, killed for me, and he even stood up to Dad for me. He loves me."

From the bundle in her arms she brought out a bottle of water, opening it then putting a straw in before holding it to my lips. "Drink."

Arguing with her might have been an option if I wasn't suddenly so thirsty I'd drink a puddle of dirty rain water. After guzzling more than half of the big bottle, she pulled it away and offered me a few peanut butter crackers in silence, then some raisins. I ate them without comment as she hand fed them to me, arguing with myself that I needed the strength, that I couldn't allow myself to spit the meager food back at her.

Once it was gone, I stared at her, trying to find a drop of humanity to appeal to.

She licked her dry, cracked lips with a quick flick of her tongue like a lizard, then her gaze darted to the closed door. "Chief will be here soon and he'll want to touch you. I know it's going to hurt you since he's a stranger, so I brought you some medicine so you won't feel anything bad, only good. You're going to love it."

I swallowed hard, a horrible suspicion filling me that had me suddenly panting with fear. "What are you going to do to me?"

Instead of answering, she crouched next to my chair and unrolled the black cloth she held and laid it and the contents on the ground by the lantern. There was a small syringe filled with a brown liquid as well as what looked like a piece of rubber tubing that had been carefully wrapped up inside. My heart lurched, and I had to fight the urge to struggle uselessly as I realized my mom was going to shoot me up with something. I had no idea what was in there. I whimpered as I imagined myself becoming an addict like my mother and turning into a walking, rotting corpse.

If she touched me again I might go mad.

No, I had to find my calm, I had to think.

But oh, God, please have mercy on me, and don't let her inject me with that. Don't let her put that poison in my body.

She calmly opened a small package and pulled out an alcohol wipe, swabbing down my arm and then her hands, grinning like she was about to do something really fun. After that, she pushed my shirt sleeve up to expose my inner elbow and touched me there, probing my arm. My heart raced so hard I thought I might pass out as she cleaned the skin on my inner elbow with another alcohol wipe.

"Mom, no, please," I whispered, utterly horrified as she picked up the syringe and turned it this way and that, admiring it in the light coming from the two portable lanterns. She cleaned that as well with an alcohol wipe and I knew then that she meant to put that shit in my veins.

"Whatever it is, I don't want it."

"Yes, yes you do want this." I swear her smile was positively loving as she looked up at me, "Chief is generous, and he has the best stuff. This is the finest heroin money can buy, sweetheart, clean and pure. Trust me, it takes everything away. It's hope for the hopeless."

She didn't look away from the syringe and its contents as she turned it in the light and stared at it like it was a beautifully faceted diamond. At that thought, I squeezed my fingers together, reassuring myself that I still wore Smoke's ring. Pain lanced through me as I wondered if I would ever see him again, and I begged my mother to help me, but I might as well have been talking to the wall. There was a rapture in her expression that chilled me to the bone, and I knew if I didn't reach her somehow, she'd continue putting God knows what kind of shit into my body until I was as addicted as she was.

When she began to move the sleeve of my shirt up even higher I let out an involuntary sob. Fuck, she was going to turn me into a slave to heroin before handing me off to 'Chief,' whoever the fuck he was. I'd seen first hand what people would do for drugs, and I had a vision of me begging someone for a fix before doing a bunch of horrifying shit in order to get it. I tried again, desperation like I've never known filling me as a stinging sweat broke out over my skin.

"No, no, no, mother, please no, *please* don't. I don't want this. Please don't do this. Let me go, please, please, *please* let me go. I don't want that needle in my arm. Mom, no, just stop." Tears streamed down my face and slid over my lips and into my mouth the salty taste blending with the taste of my terror.

"Shhh, don't worry, this is a brand new, clean kit," my mother whispered, totally entranced now as she felt around on my arm on the inside of my elbow, no doubt looking for a vein before tying the rubber tube around my bicep. "Stop moving or the needle may break off in your arm. They won't take you to a hospital, so please stay still for me, or I'll have to dig the broken tip out. I promise this will make all the pain disappear. You won't have to hurt ever again as long as you have your medicine."

My broken sobbing didn't move her, and I had to fight against myself to keep from jerking away. She was going to inject me, there was nothing I could do about it, so I needed to not complicate things further by risking breaking a needle off in my arm. With her this close, the scent of her unwashed hair and cloying perfume suffocated me, making each bit of air I struggled to inhale tainted by her. She was going to do this, there was no stopping her, and I could only hope I survived it. All thoughts of anything but the needle pressing into my vein fled my mind, and I held my breath as the plunger was slowly pressed down. I felt the burn as the drug entered the vein while I prayed that she really was using a clean needle.

It took fifteen of my heartbeats for her to empty the syringe. As she slowly released the tourniquet the burn crept up my arm then straight into my heart. My lungs burned like they were on fire, and I struggled to take a deep breath of air while my stomach churned with intense nausea.

It was torture. I couldn't understand why people would do heroin because this shit hurt like fuck going in. My chest felt heavy, then it felt like someone was pressing on my brain, and my mouth flooded with saliva as I fought the urge to puke. My mother caught my frantic gaze and a small smile curved her chapped lips.

"Feeling it, yet? That warmth that's better than anything you've ever experienced filling you, melting the ice inside?" She shivered before rubbing her arms. "I remember my first hit. It was after I left your father….so long ago. How did time pass by so fast? How did things go so wrong so quickly?"

The burn inched up my neck, and my skin began to tingle. I sucked in a breath of air and my mother smiled wider. Something was happening inside of me, and no matter how hard I fought it, my thoughts were beginning to slow and grow disjointed.

"There you go...now you're getting to the good stuff. Don't fight it. Just let it happen." Her face fell for a moment and tears swam in her eyes. "That's the best thing to do when you're with men that you don't want to touch, but they make you. Don't fight them, just let them have you, and it'll be over before you know it….it'll be over before you know it."

By this point, I had no idea what she was saying. The drug had flooded my brain, and I was trying to deal with this new version of reality that I'd been shoved into. The part of my mind that was freaking out got quieter by the second until I was humming with pleasure, writhing in my chair as the most wonderful feelings of joy filled me. Everything was perfect, beautiful, and when I looked over at my mother tears filled my eyes. I was blind to her faults now, only seeing the woman I wanted to love me as much as I loved her. Once, a long time ago, she'd been a good Mom. If I hadn't been so fucked up, I would have been sobbing over how stupid my heart was.

"Don't cry," she said in a cracked voice before digging into the pocket of her loose jeans. She took out a little folded up piece of paper and opened it, my uncaring gaze observing her snorting whatever was inside. A muscle in her cheek twitched, and she let out a soft sigh and leaned back against the wall near my chair. "No more tears. No more feeling."

I have no idea how much time passed as I lazed in my drug-induced vacation from reality. The cracks in the walls were endlessly fascinating, and my vision seemed to narrow into an odd tunnel. Every once in a while my mom would make me drink water or eat something. Once she helped me lean up enough to pull my pants down without untying me so I could pee on a couple of towels. Other than that, I really didn't pay her any attention. While it was amusing to look around and become obsessed with things like a spider web moving slowly in the little bit of breeze coming in through the window, moving seemed like way too much effort. I was too high to freak out, even when my mother stood and approached me with the black hood, sniffing and rubbing her nose.

"I have to put this on so you don't see the Chief. He always wears a mask. Hell even I don't know what he looks like and neither does Cruz." She gave me a conspiratorial wink and lowered her voice, "Cruz is going to leave his wife and marry me, you know. Take me away from all of this, and we're going to live on a beautiful beach and never have to worry about money again. He's such a great guy, and he provides for me. That's the kind of life you could have with Chief if you make him happy. He has *obscene* amounts of money."

Forming words was beyond me. When she placed the hood on my head, I was lost once again in the magic that was flowing through my veins, my vision cloaked in darkness, and time ceased to exist.

I think I fell asleep at some point because when I woke up the world was muzzy, and I had no idea about the passage of time since I still wore the black hood. My mother was no longer in the room, or if she was, she didn't respond to my rough words. The dryness in my mouth was terrible, and I longed for just one sip of water. Hunger also panged in my gut while my mind caught up to reality and one thought consumed me.

Smoke.

Oh God, Smoke!

Tears rolled down my face, wetting the fabric of my hood as I let out a sob that tore at my throat like I'd swallowed glass.

As I cried, I swear I felt my dad's presence in my mind, in my heart, giving me the strength to uncurl myself and focus on getting out.

I did some breathing exercises to try and rid my mind of the sticky ghost of the heroin, and I pushed back against the depression that threatened to stun me into inactivity. Everything felt so futile, so doomed that I had a really hard time rallying the willpower to keep fighting. It would be so damn easy to give up, to let Chief do what he wanted, to try and end my life rather than be some man's slave.

But I couldn't. I needed to find Smoke, to see if he was still…he was still alive.

And if he wasn't, I would avenge him.

Voices came from behind me, and I tensed at the squeak of the door opening followed by a draft of air through the room.

"At last," an oddly distorted man's voice said from behind me. "The beautiful Swan."

"Remember," my mother whimpered. "You said you wouldn't hurt her."

"Of course. If she cooperates." Someone touched my face through the hood, and I hated how helpless I was. "You want to be a good girl, Swan, because if you're a bad girl, I'll cut off a little piece of Smoke and make you eat it."

I gagged, the image so repulsive that my mouth was flooded with the bitter taste of bile. There was no way I was going to throw up in this hood, but I was coming close. I took in deep breaths, forcing my body to relax even as I shuddered.

A light, hesitant touch brushed my shoulder then slid down to the exposed curve of my cleavage. I braced myself for the crawling sensation to come, but to my surprise, whoever was touching me wore some type of gloves, leather I think. That could mean one of two things, either he didn't want to leave prints, or he knew enough about me to realize what the touch of his bare hands would do. A thick sob escaped me before I could stop it.

"Where's Smoke? Is he alive?" I said in a voice with a small tremble in it.

I hoped Chief thought it was fear instead of rage.

"For now."

The floor creaked as he moved around me, his hand running over my upper chest. Then he paused and swept my hair over my shoulder, continuing to touch every inch of me he could. When he moved from my shoulder down my arm to where my sleeve was still pulled up to expose my vein, I swore I could feel a sudden tension fill the air. He took in a sharp breath, then his fingers were grasping my elbow. When he touched the sore injection site his breath hissed out in a rush.

"What the fuck is this? You doin' drugs now, Swan? Smoke got you hooked on that shit?"

Before I could censor myself I blurted out, "What? No, it was my mother, asshole."

As soon as those words left my lips I knew I'd made a mistake. His growl reinforced that notion, and I quickly said, "I mean, it's from donating blood a couple days ago."

"Billie," he said in a low voice, "get the fuck out of here. I'll deal with you later."

My mother let out a whimper, "But I—"

Then the sharp crack of leather contacting skin rang in my ears and my mother let out a shrill scream.

Oh no, oh fuck. "No, no wait, she didn't—"

"Get out!" Chief roared.

The door slammed and I knew my mother had left me alone with a monster.

"Please don't hurt her—"

Pain lanced through my chest as he cruelly pinched my nipple, stopping me in mid-sentence as I struggled to get out of the hold he had on me. "Shut your fuckin' mouth and listen. Just 'cause I don't want Billie turning you into a junkie doesn't mean you're gonna get away with any shit with me. Either you reel that attitude of yours in and be nice or I'll cut Billie's drugs off and let her die of withdrawal, locked in this room with you. Understood?"

"Yes."

"And you will respect me or Smoke will pay for it. I would love to spend the next five years torturing him until he begs for death, but if you're very, very nice to me I'll keep him alive and relatively comfortable. He might be missing his legs so he can't run, and his arms so he can't hit, but we'll take care of his torso. All you need to do is be as sweet as sugar and never tell me no, understood?"

Hate wasn't a big enough word for what I felt for this man.

But my fear for Smoke was so great that it wiped away any idea of resistance. "Understood."

His touch gentled and I hissed as my nipple stung. "I don't want to hurt you, Swan, really I don't. Of all the things that Smoke has that I want, you're at the top of the list because he loves you more than anything. Seeing you in my arms is going to hurt, real, real bad, in a way that physical pain can't. And that cunt sister of yours will be in misery for the rest of her life at the knowledge that she failed you. Fuckin' uppity bitch. She's throwin' a fit about you back in Austin right now, keepin' Beach occupied tryin' to calm her ass down. Stupid bitch thinks Los Diablos has you and she's about ready to storm their compound."

I didn't say anything, not trusting myself to let one word pass from my lips. This son of a bitch was going to destroy everyone and everything I cared about, and I was too shackled by my love for Smoke from trying to stop him. My feelings were so explosive, I knew I'd fuck up and say something that could get Smoke—and my mother—hurt. I cursed myself for caring about her after everything she'd done and wondered where she was right now, if maybe she was going to try to call for help. Surely she could see how wrong this was.

Okay, I needed to regroup. Obviously, help wasn't coming from my mother, so I was on my own. I should have been gathering intelligence, asking the guy leading questions, dissecting his answers for some clue as to who he was, gathering information for when I escaped, not if. The weird electronic hum to his voice revealed he was using a voice modulator, so that might mean he was afraid I would recognize him. Or that he was hiding who he was from whoever else was here. Why would he do that?

The chime of a cell phone sounded and the man left the room for a few minutes, leaving me wondering how long I could sit here before real pain set in from being in one position for so long.

To my relief, and dismay, the mystery man's voice came from behind me. "I need to go, but first you need a little object lesson, and I need something to make me smile. You and your sister really fucked things up for us, so knowing that when Smoke sees you he's gonna hate you for being sweet to me, I'll eat that shit up. Fuck around and screw up, and I guarantee I'll make you both hurt."

"Wait," my mind scrambled for some way out of this. "You said you wouldn't hurt me."

"And I won't, at least not physically, but I do plan on breaking you." He gave another cruel pinch to my nipple that made me hiss in discomfort before I could bite the sound back.

The squeak of the door opening interrupted whatever else the monster casually touching my breasts was about to say.

"You called, Chief?" A man's unfamiliar voice came from behind me.

"Yes. Take Ms. Swan to use the bathroom and freshen up, but do not remove her hood. I want her out at the shed in five minutes."

"Understood."

The man with the odd voice leaned down and whispered, "You're going to want to hurry, because if you make me wait, I'll take out my boredom on your man."

There wasn't a doubt in my mind that he would, so instead of trying to escape, I allowed the new man to lead me across the room, and he was a real dick about it too. He let me bump into the doorframe, trip over a loose board, and all kinds of bullshit so he could have an excuse to grope me. Thank God he was touching over clothes, but even that was bad enough that I was shaking with the need to rip his balls off. Whoever he was, he had that familiar smell of motor oil to him that most bikers did, and when he crowded me from behind, his beard brushed against my ear.

I counted steps, fighting to remember how many paces it was from one spot to another when I was thrust into a small room.

"Don't move," he said in a cold voice. "I'm gonna cut your zip ties loose, then I'm gonna handcuff one of your hands to mine. Hope you ain't shy 'cause I'll be right inside the doorway while you take care of business. Give me any trouble and I'll personally fuck Smoke up. I would love to have an excuse to get my hands on that arrogant, hypocritical bastard."

"Understood."

I took care of business one-handed as quickly as I could, ignoring his lewd comments about golden showers and other sick shit. After I stood and buttoned up, I decided that now was probably my best chance for dealing with this situation. "May I wash my hands please?"

"Sure, take all the time in the world, princess. It's Smoke whose gonna have to entertain Chief. And let me tell ya, that is one sick, creepy bastard with a real hard-on for your man."

I wanted to scream in fury at the knowledge that my rapidly forming escape plan would mean Smoke was going to suffer more pain. My escort pushed me forward a couple steps with a firm shove to the back and my fingertips came up against cool porcelain that was probably none too clean. I pretended to feel for the taps and braced my free hand on the wall in front of me. When the smooth, silken texture of a glass met my fingertips I smiled, unconcerned about my triumphant expression hidden by the hood. There hadn't been any sounds from anyone else in the house and I hoped they were all either sleeping, or outside, anywhere but here. I was pretty sure my mother was still here, hopefully out of her mind, and I could only pray she wouldn't raise an alarm at the noise I was about to make.

After I rinsed my one hand off I pulled the other, which was handcuffed to my captor. I was just about to yank forward and use one of the nastier moves my dad taught me to send this asshole's head right into the glass and hopefully snap his neck, when I heard footsteps approaching us. The man behind me shifted, not so gently dragging me out into the hall with him. I cursed that I hadn't been just a little bit quicker, then dismissed that thought. As long as I was alive there was always another chance.

"Cruz and I have some business to attend to," Chief said from maybe a foot or two in front of me. "Buck, Weed, Custer and Flea are comin' up and should be here in about twenty minutes to relieve you. But don't worry, sweet Swan, I've left you with some incentive out in the shed. After she's been properly motivated, bring her back here and lock her up in the closet."

"Will do."

Hands grabbed at my breasts again, and I had no idea if it was just Chief or Chief with one hand and the guy behind me with the other. I held my breath, and fought the screams that were so close. The sense of violation and helplessness made me mad. No, I couldn't give into my instincts. I had to hold on…had to fight to remain calm.

With one final, hard squeeze the hands were gone. "Have fun, sweetheart. I hope you like my present."

The sharp tang of blood filled my mouth as I bit my lip and strained not to fall into mindless panic. I still had one hand free, and if I could somehow get this stupid hood off my head, I'd have a much better chance at survival. While I could fight relatively well without sight—my Dad is a big *Star Wars* fan and had me train blindfolded more than once—I couldn't do it well enough to ensure a victory, especially when I had no idea how many people were here with me or my surroundings. A misplaced kick could send my leg into trouble instead of a soft stomach.

My arm was rudely jerked, and the man leading me dragged me after him until I was able to catch my balance and walk properly. We went down a set of stairs and I was trying to figure out if we were still above ground when a guy's thick voice from somewhere to my left shouted out, "Motherfucker!"

The guy leading me stopped and I bounced off his back falling until he wrenched me back to my feet. "Baldy? What's up, man?"

Baldy—no one I knew—yelled back, "I think Billie's OD'd. What the fuck do I do?"

"Son of a bitch," the man that I was cuffed to yelled. "Go get the adrenaline kit out in the shed. I'll be right there after I secure this cunt."

"I don't think the kit's gonna help her."

"Just get the fuckin' kit!" the man next to me roared.

I was stunned in that moment, frozen in time at the idea of my mother dying just a few feet away. That shock lasted right up to the point where my brain realized on some level that the cuff next to mine had just been removed. In an odd way, my mind felt split into two parts. One part was methodically going through scenario after scenario of ways to escape while the other, childlike part of me was wailing in grief.

"Shut the fuck up," The man who spoke was jerking at my cuff.

It took me a moment to realize that the part of me screaming in denial and pain wasn't inside my head, but what was happening to my body. A primal need to protect my blood overcame me. I had to help my mom, I had to save her. My scream abruptly cut off as I felt him trying to fit the cuff on something.

My body and thoughts caught up to each other in the calm dreamscape of my killing space.

I braced myself on his shoulder like I was feeling faint and quickly calculated where his throat was. In one smooth move I lifted the hood enough to free my mouth, then sank my teeth into his flesh as hard as I could. I tried not to let the sensation of his beard against my face and in my mouth bother me, or the metallic tang of his blood. My teeth sank deep into the meat of his throat and I bit down hard enough to crush most of his trachea and esophagus. He tried to scream and shove me away, which only made it easier to tear out a nice size chunk of his throat.

The moment I was free of him, I jerked my hood all the way off while spitting out his blood. I turned in the direction of the horrid, wet sucking sounds the guy made as he tried to breathe. In a surreal moment, our eyes met, and I watched in morbid fascination as he tried to stop the bleeding with his hands. He stumbled away from me while the hard pump of his heart sent surge after surge of blood pouring past his fingers. One thing my father never told me was how fucking messy death could be.

When one of his blood-covered hands fumbled at his lower back, I realized he was probably drawing a gun, and that snapped me out of my daze. I crossed the room in three steps then reared back and kicked him right between the legs like a soccer pro going for a goal. If he'd been able to make any sound he probably would have been shrieking loud enough to break the windows, but the only sounds he made were those disgusting sucking, gurgling noises. He was nearly unconscious from blood loss as I pushed him with my foot onto his stomach then grabbed the gun from his lower back, a loaded Smith and Wesson .38 Special.

With one threat essentially eliminated, I focused on where the guy looking for the adrenaline kit had gone. Once I got rid of him I could get to my mom. My shoes squished through the growing puddle of blood flooding the small, empty foyer. I glanced around and found nothing to indicate that anyone actually lived here. This place must be outside of town because my screams would have been enough to alert any neighbors or people walking by. The house vibrated slightly as a door was thrown open. I hid behind the edge of the wall, and stole a quick peek at the man who must be Baldy running down the hall with a look of panic on his craggy face.

Taking advantage of the element of surprise, I stepped around the corner and placed a bullet right between Baldy's eyebrows, the gore of the shot blending into the darkness whirling around my mind. He hit the ground with a thump. I crouched down and waited fifteen precious seconds for someone to come investigate the sound of a shot being fired.

My ears were still ringing from the gun blast, but I decided that it was safe enough to scoot forward and grab the backpack from the still warm grip of the body that was now a corpse. The harsh rasp of my breath halted when I saw my hands were coated in blood. For a hysterical moment, I freaked out about having the bearded man's blood all over me, but I managed to fight past my disgust and fear to focus on the pack.

My mother needed me. Smoke needed me, and I didn't have time for the luxury of a freak-out.

I opened the first door to my right off the hall and found an abandoned washroom with a pair of rusted out avocado green appliances and a funky, moldy smell thick in the air.

The next room I glanced into was empty except for some crap in one corner, and I saw that one of the boards over the window had slipped enough to let sunlight in.

There was one door left and I took a deep breath, my exhale turning into a keening wail as I opened it and found my mother lying on an inflatable mattress that had been shoved into one corner.

Her sightless eyes were turned to the ceiling, and dried puke ran down the side of her face from where it was pooled in her mouth. It was obvious she was dead. I staggered into the room, still crying, and went to touch her to see if I could find a heartbeat, but I couldn't bring myself to place my fingers on her unmoving body. She had rubber tubing wrapped around her upper arm and the syringe was still in her vein. The wounds and scars of her years of abuse to her body showed dark against the gray-green parlor of her skin.

I wanted to sit there and cry, and wait for someone to come rescue me, for some miracle to bring my mother back to life, but I couldn't. The practicality that my father had drilled into my head forced me to stand and go back out into the hall, and strip the man there of all his weapons. In addition to the gun I'd taken off the first thug, along with two guns and a couple of knives from the other, I retrieved a cell phone that actually had service.

For a moment, my mind went blank as I stared at the phone, then I swiped at the screen with a shaking finger and dialed Sarah's number.

After three rings she picked up. "Hello?"

"Sarah," I sobbed.

"Swan? Oh, my God, Swan! Where are you?"

"I don't know. I need help. Mom's dead, I don't know where Smoke is, and there are bad guys on their way."

There was shouting and yelling in the background, but Sarah's voice was almost too quiet to hear. "Mom's dead?"

"Yeah. She OD'd."

A second later, Beach's familiar, raspy voice came over the line. "Swan, where are you?"

"I don't know. Look, this phone has a good charge left. I'm going to try to hide it in this house, then go get Smoke. I don't know where he is, if he's alive, or who may be with him. Five guys are on their way up here, and I don't think this abandoned house is good for making a stand. I'm going to find Smoke, then we're going to run."

"Help's on its way," Beach said in a tight voice. "You just keep alive and we'll find you. Do you know who took you?"

"No idea, these guys aren't wearing cuts, but I think the mastermind of this whole thing is a guy they call Chief. Oh, and Cruz is involved."

Beach started to rant, but I cut him off. "I have to go find Smoke. We'll be waiting for you somewhere nearby."

After placing the phone on the top shelf of an empty cupboard in the dilapidated laundry room, I stepped out onto the back porch, all too aware of the hard snap of the weathered-out boards beneath my feet. The feeling of time running out spun through me, and I hurried across the dried out yard. There were no signs of any other homes or the rumble of traffic, so I was pretty sure wherever we were was in the middle of nowhere.

I didn't have a problem finding the rusted shed at the back of what passed for the yard next to the huge, rotting barn that was slowly falling in on itself. There was a generator set up not too far away, and I followed the bright orange chord to the shed door. I did a quick recon of the building, but there were no windows to see if anyone was inside. With my heart in my throat, I banged on the side of the shed, then waited for some kind of reaction. When nothing happened, I did it again, and this time there was a low moan that made the hair on my arms stand up.

Smoke.

Without another thought, I raced to the door and tugged at it, sending a prayer of thanks as it rolled easily upwards.

That prayer died the moment I took in the man tied to a metal bedframe in the center of the room.

His shirt hung in tatters and blood marred every surface of the beautiful body I knew as well as my own. Bruises covered his face and if I didn't recognize his tattoos covered in dried blood, I wouldn't have recognized this man as Smoke. He appeared to be passed out and my stomach threatened to empty itself when I caught sight of a table filled with what had to be torture tools, some of them covered in dried blood.

"Please, please be okay." I staggered to him and dropped to my knees on the side of the bed, the various guns and knives sticking out of my waistband digging into my ribs. "Smoke?"

No response, just a low groan that made it hard for me to breathe.

I was afraid to touch him, or even breathe on him, but if I left him here we were both as good as dead. A quick scan around the room revealed a pallet of bottled water, like the kind that you'd get at one of those super stores, up against the far wall next to a beat up, old, white fridge. The refrigerator was humming steadily, and I ran over to it and jerked it open. There were chilled bottles of water inside, an answer to a prayer, and I grabbed two before running back to Smoke.

Turning his head to the side so I wouldn't drown him, I poured the cold water onto his face and got an immediate reaction. He sucked in a huge breath, and his blackened, swollen eyes opened, the barest of slits. With a pained moan he tried to sit up, but the rope around his wrists kept him pinned to the bedframe. I placed my hand on his right shoulder, the only place I could find that didn't seem to be injured, and pushed him back down.

"Smoke, it's me, Swan."

He blinked up at me, "Swan? Alive?"

"Yeah, I'm alive and so are you. We're getting us out of here, now."

"Where...rest?"

"I killed the two men in the house, but five more are on their way up."

"Chief?"

"Gone."

"Billie?"

"Dea...dead. Overdose."

"Baby...so...sorry."

That, in a nutshell, showed just how much I mattered to Smoke. Here he was, looking like he'd been dragged behind a truck then set on fire, and he was trying to comfort me over the loss of my mother, one of the people responsible for doing this to him...to us. I dared to place one feather-light kiss on his bruised and cut lips, trying to convey in that gentle touch how much I loved him, and how thankful I was that he was alive.

"Hang in there, my love, I'm going to get us out of here."

Chapter Twenty

My hands trembled as I carefully cut the rope away from the skin of his sore, abraded wrists. When I went to cut his legs free, I was happy to see he still wore his boots. His shirt was a total loss, but I thought his jeans, other than being crusty with blood from cuts on his stomach, were serviceable. Every wound, every slice, felt like my own, and by the time I was done, I was in agony over his pain.

I helped him sit up and poured more water over him, washing away the blood on my hands and on his injuries. There were lots of small knife cuts, but only a couple deep ones, at least from what I could see. There were also patches of his skin that were burned and blistered, making my heart and body ache as if his wounds were my own.

"Anything hurt inside?"

He slowly shook his head. "Hurts, but I don't think broken."

My hands fluttered over him as I tried to figure out where to start. I had to bandage the worst wounds and pray the others didn't get too infected. Then again, if I wasted any more time we were dead anyway. Time to get moving.

"Smoke, I have to go see what supplies I can grab from the house. Can you walk?"

He took a deep breath and slowly rolled his neck, his battered face pulling up tight. "Yeah, they didn't break bones. Eyes swollen shut, but okay. They were savin' takin' 'em out for later."

I wanted to slice Chief up into little bits and feed him to himself, but that wasn't an option right now. Instead, I gave Smoke one of the guns I pilfered, wrapping his least damaged hand around it the best I could. "Hang in there. I'll be right back."

His reply was lost in a pained moan as he stretched his arms out, and I had to bite back a sob when I saw that someone had burned away part of his dragon tattoo, and that his nipple ring had been ripped out.

A blinding rage tried to descend, making me want stay here, to seek revenge and make everyone responsible for this pay, but Smoke was in no shape for a fight. I wanted to be out in the forest, where I had the tactical advantage, than in a house I knew nothing about where we could get trapped inside. I had no idea how long it would take Beach to find us, but when I spied our luggage opened with our stuff strewn about in the back corner of the kitchen I grabbed my empty oversized duffle and shoved a change of clothes for Smoke and myself inside. I had no idea how long we had left, and we both needed to get out of our blood-soaked garments.

A quick search of the kitchen didn't reveal much other than a half empty box of cereal in the cupboard along with some protein bars and an unopened bag of chips. All of those went into the duffle along with as much water as I could comfortably carry. Before I went any further, I took a few precious seconds to wash myself off in the cold, mineral-smelling tap water from the sink, getting as much of the blood off of me as I could using the anti-bacterial hand soap. A disturbing thought about all the nasty diseases that could be in the blood that had gotten in my mouth, spun through my mind, and I fought not to think about it.

Even in the warm air, I shivered from the chill of the water, but it helped clear my head the faintest bit. I needed to see if there were any more weapons stashed around the house…and I needed to get what I assumed was the medical pack from the room where my mother was.

My scavenging yielded a really nice rifle, a Knights SR-25 carbine, along with about one-quarter of a box of ammo. Unfortunately, the carbine didn't have a sight, but if it came down to it, I was a good enough of a shot to compensate. In the living room area, I found a six pack of soda along with some folding chairs, a half empty bag of chips, a full ashtray, and an old tarp. The soda was heavy so I opened one can and chugged it as fast as I could to get the sugar and caffeine running through my system. I also ran upstairs and grabbed the lantern, taking a peek out through a broken window to try and figure out the best way to go. The old house faced a large open forest on one side. Across the road was a big hill with some boulders and exposed rock ledges. If we could get to one of those rock overhangs I figured there would be one deep enough for us to hunker down in.

Much easier to defend a cave than sit in the middle of a forest.

I just hoped Smoke would make it.

With my heart slamming in my throat, I went back to the room that held my mother and looked down at her. I hated to leave her in such an undignified state for the others to find, but I knew I didn't have the time or the emotional strength to clean her up. Instead I laid the tarp over her and left the room at a sprint with the backpack securely on my back, the duffle over my arm, and the loaded rifle in my free hand.

I found Smoke leaning against the entrance to the shed, squinting into the sunlight. He tensed when the door slammed behind me, and I called out, "Can you walk? The only things here are bikes. I don't know how to drive one, and I'm pretty sure you're in no shape to drive anything right now."

"Yeah, hand is fucked up…no shifting." He heaved in a breath. "Fuckin' hurts but I can walk."

"Here, I brought you a clean shirt." I reached his side and helped him remove the shredded remains his old one. At the sight of his back I retched and had to step back and bend over with my head down. Someone had either cut out or burned off the Iron Horse MC Symbol in the middle of the church on Smoke's back. It was now a raw, nasty wound that must have hurt like a bitch.

"Smoke…"

"Later, baby."

"Right. Come on."

Before we'd even taken two steps I knew Smoke was in no condition for any kind of hike. He staggered, then used me as a crutch. His weight along with the packs made it almost impossible for any kind of speed. We were three steps out of the shed when I heard the rumble of motorcycles in the distance. I couldn't tell how far away they were because of the odd way sound moved through the hills and the forest.

My heartbeat accelerated, and I looked between the house, the shed, and an old barn that was leaning like it was about to fall in on itself. I quickly decided the barn was the best place because it looked like one of the least likely places to hide. Even as we shuffled to it, I was afraid to open the side door. It took a couple tries but I finally managed to yank it open and step inside.

It was a fucking mess, and perfect for hiding. There were old boxes, furniture, farm equipment, and just about everything known to God and man crammed into the barn. It was all moldering junk now, but whoever owned that house must have been a hoarder at some point. Next to me, Smoke panted, the heat of the barn oppressive, and I propped him against the wall for a moment before scouting out a path.

"Lean on me, I know this hurts, Miguel, but you need to go just a little farther."

He gave a rusty, pained laugh. "Hearin' you call me Miguel made me get a semi. Guess I ain't gonna die after all."

I shot him a brief, disbelieving look before pushing and pulling him through the mess. I made sure to block our path again and tried to erase any interruptions in the dust.

The bikes were a roar now, and I struggled to help Smoke climb the rickety ladder to the rafters that were also stuffed with crap, praying neither collapsed beneath our weight. By the time he was half way up with me helping him as best I could, the bikes had been turned off and I waited with sweat pouring down my back to hear the first sound of alarm.

Thank fuck we were in the loft by the time a panicked cry came from somewhere outside. Soon more shouts joined it as I set our packs down and began to pull out weapons. When I glanced up at Smoke, he was the color of cheese and I knew I had pushed him too hard. Fresh blood seeped from his wounds, and I wanted to rant and scream about how unfair it all was, how this was such bullshit. My mother was dead, my fiancé might be dying, and we were outnumbered and stuck in the middle of fucking nowhere with a limited number of weapons and very little ammo.

Basically, we were fucked.

For a moment, I gave into the hopelessness and stared at the dust motes dancing in the sunlight pouring through the cracks in the boards.

The cracks in the boards... What could I see through those cracks?

Grabbing the rifle and ammo I tried to pick my way past a pile of rusty bikes that could trap my feet and spill me to the floor. Then, I tried to avoid a large blotched mirror that showed a monstrous reflection of me. I was coated in dried blood and looked like I was a stunt extra during the bucket of blood scene in the movie *Carrie*. When I gazed at myself, my eyes were empty and cold, and I saw someone savage, someone absolutely capable of killing to defend herself staring back at me, and that made me smile.

I looked through one of the larger cracks, stealing a glimpse of the back yard where the motorcycles were. One of the three men stood there yelling on a cell phone. I bit my lip, racing through all the implications of trying for a shot now. The rifle wasn't mine, I didn't even know if it worked, and it would be a huge risk for just one man.

Then another joined him and I decided on my course of action and stuck to it.

My breath came out in a smooth, cool rush as I shut down. Nothing mattered, not my body, not my bruised heart, not my grief over my mother or my anger at the people who had done this to us. It was all inconsequential now.

Nothing mattered but the shot.

Line up the sight.

Wait for an opening.

Take the shot.

In two successive, loud bangs I ended the lives of two more men, and a distant part of my mind that I tried to ignore, reminded me of my growing kill tally. Of all the families that now hated me, the children who would grow up without fathers. The mothers missing their sons.

I watched carefully, waiting for more men to run out.

Sure enough, a guy appeared on the porch, a big black man with long grey dreads. Just as I took the shot he moved, resulting me in missing the first one. The second and third caught him in the stomach before he disappeared around the side of the house so I was pretty sure he was out of commission by his pained screams.

From the other side of the barn came more men's voices, and I tried to hear what they were saying, but I couldn't make anything out from where I crouched.

After the initial round of voices, things went quiet and I began to worry.

I liked them shouting, running around panicked, but I didn't like not knowing where they were and what they were doing.

I didn't have to worry for long because it soon became apparent what their plan was and it really sucked.

The first thing to catch fire was the house.

At first, I thought I was imagining the smell of a burning building, but the flames soon flickered into my line of sight and my heart dropped.

They were trying to flush us out.

My mouth went dry as I wondered if they'd do the shed next, and then the barn.

What if they were lighting the barn on fire right now?

I grabbed my rifle and tried to get back to Smoke as quick as I could but I got tangled up a couple of times in my haste, making a racket I would have worried about if the fire burning the house hadn't started to roar and snap like an angry dragon. Large fires get loud, extremely loud. With that horrible noise playing as the soundtrack to my own personal hell, I came back to my man, only to find him passed out with a thready pulse. "No, no, no," I whispered and tried to find a place on him I could touch, frantic to keep his heart beating. "Please, Miguel, please don't leave me alone. Please stay with me. I promise I'll save you, I swear it. Don't go. Hold on."

His pulse fluttered against my fingers but kept beating. I have no idea how long I sat there in a daze, watching him and willing him to live, before smoke began to burn my eyes. Snapped out of my desperate trance, I wasn't sure if the smoke was coming from the outside or inside, but I'd run out of time. I'd rather die from a gunshot than burn alive.

With no regard to making a racket now, I shoved aside piles of garbage with a strength I didn't know I had, moving heavy furniture to the side so I could make it to the part of the loft that sagged closest to the ground. It was still at least a one-story drop, but that was better than two.

Grabbing a rusting metal chair with a faded 1970s floral print cushion, I swung it at the already mostly broken window, smashing out the rotted frame and making as big a hole as I could. Next, I grabbed a moldering mattress, hoping that we didn't get impaled on a rusty spring as I tossed it out to the window and to the ground. Even when I stuck my head out no one took a shot at me. The air was thick with smoke, and I slipped my shirt up over my nose and mouth to filter out as much of it as possible.

By the time I made it back to my man, I was having a hard time seeing and had to rely on touch to get through the nightmare maze of crap to the busted out window.

My lungs felt like I had inhaled shards of glass, but I ignored the pain and pushed past it like I'd been trained. In that instant, I was thankful for every bit of my father's harsh discipline, thankful for every ounce of determination he'd given me to do what needed to be done without regard to my own suffering. If I'd had one drop less of willpower, I never would have been able to get Smoke's heavy body over the ledge.

He landed mostly on the mattress and didn't give any indication of having felt the drop.

I know he was still breathing because he coughed weakly a couple times, but a numbness was growing inside of me, a whisper of unbelievable loss. Not wanting to jump onto Smoke I tried to aim to his left. One moment I was crouched, the next airborne as I fell. The gunshot that hit me mid-fall took me by surprise, sending fire spreading through my leg. I landed with a harsh scream, the pain excruciating as I grabbed my thigh, knowing that the bullet had hit bone.

A man approached me out of the haze of smoke whirling around in a harsh wind that revealed hints of the landscape around me, like bits of a grey cotton wall torn open. He raised his gun, and I prayed that God would take care of my loved ones as I waited for my death and got ready to meet Smoke in Heaven, promising myself that if he was in Hell I'd find a way to join him.

There were five loud shots, but I didn't feel anything, then something thumped down near my feet.

It was the shooter, and I struggled to understand what had happened.

My first thought was Smoke, but a quick glance in his direction showed him still passed out. I looked in the other direction and found a man in a skull facemask with dark riding glasses on approaching us. Something about him was familiar, but I couldn't quite place where I'd seen him before.

He raised his gun in Smoke's direction, and I thought he was going to shoot him, but another voice yelled from nearby, "Vance! Any sign of 'em?"

Slowly, ever so slowly, he lowered the gun then yelled back while he lowered his facemask, "Hulk, I've got 'em! Tell Beach we're gonna need medical help, lots of it."

Okay, that was it, my brain officially gave up.

We were safe.

Against all fucking odds, we were safe.

My vision was fading fast, but I strained to reach up and touch Vance's cheek as he knelt next to me then pulled him down to give him a kiss on the lips. Surprise showed in his dark eyes, but I cupped his cheek and forced myself to say, "Thank you, thank you for finding us. You saved my life. Please, don't let Smoke die."

For a moment I swear he looked conflicted, but I could hear people approaching and he nodded. "Take it easy, sweetheart, we'll do what we can to help him."

After that, everything became a whirl of people talking too loud, mixing with pain in my leg and anguish over Smoke's condition, and I fell straight over the edge into darkness.

I sat uncomfortably beside Smoke's hospital bed waiting for him to decide to rejoin the land of the living, but he continued to sleep on.

Almost every inch of his strong body was bandaged, and where it wasn't covered in white cloth, scabs and scars were forming. I was currently in a wheelchair, as comfortable as I could be with a fractured thigh bone, a couple dozen stitches, and a bunch of other bullshit including the fact that I fucked up my lower back up when I jumped and fell wrong.

When I woke up, I was still mostly out of it, but the first thing I wanted to know was how Smoke was doing. No one would tell me anything for fear of upsetting me. Just as I was gearing up to rip out my IVs and go to look for him, Julia showed up. At the sight of her, I burst into tears, and she gathered me into her arms, both of us ignoring the nurses telling us to calm down, that it wasn't good for me to have so much excitement. I learned that Smoke suffered a pretty severe concussion, multiple burns, broken bones in his hand, and various other injuries that she didn't go into other than to say that he was expected to make a full recovery, but they had no idea when he'd come out of his coma.

When I next surfaced from my deep sleep, I found out they had me hooked up to a morphine pump, and I freaked out then babbled about my mom shooting me up and begging them to take it out of my arm. Everyone in the room stopped moving at once and stared at me. The nurses, doctors, interns, fuckin' everyone including Beach and Hustler gaped at me with a range of expressions I couldn't even begin to process. Even though my mom was the one that put that shit in me, I felt ashamed. Like my blood was dirty. After about two seconds of silence Beach had flipped out and started ranting and raving.

Hulk had come over and leaned down real close, eye to eye. The medical staff didn't stop him because they were busy dealing with Beach, and I stared up into his frosty pale green eyes set off by his smooth, dark skin. "Listen up, Swan. If you ever feel the need to do that shit again, don't. It will take your soul, change who you are, and destroy the world around you for the feeling of false love. And I will personally hunt you down and put you in *my* version of rehab. Trust me, you don't want that."

My mouth, loosened by painkillers, decided to let Hulk know that wouldn't be necessary, but thanks for the offer. "You are out of your fucking mind. Do I really look like someone who had the desire to do drugs? My mom tried to shove them on me all the time, and I turned her down because I will not ever touch any shit like that. I watched my mother turn into a monster, Hulk, a cruel, screwed up, narcissistic woman who shot her daughter up with heroin in a misguided attempt to save me from the discomfort of being raped. So trust me when I say you can kiss my lily white ass, the only man I answer to is my fiancé, and you aren't him, so fuck off."

The last words came out in a shout, and I soon passed out after hitting my pain pump, not giving a shit if it was morphine at that point because I was incoherent with agony.

After that, I had a brief reunion with my parents and sister before the doctors came in and ushered everyone out while they examined me. When I was shot, the bullet grazed my thigh bone and I fractured it when I landed after I jumped out the window, leaving the leg fucked up. Basically, I'd be doing rehab for a while and there was a possibility that I would walk with a limp. I hated to admit that my vanity was pricked by that, but I'd gladly hobble for the rest of my life as long as I could spend it with Smoke. They weren't ready to let me see him yet, but I made it clear nothing would stop me from getting to his side. The docs gave in, but only as long as they were satisfied with my progress and if I behaved, then adequate arrangements would be made.

The next time I woke, my parents and Beach along with Sarah were there, and everyone was very, very careful to keep calm around me. I would have found Beach's attempt to be mellow funny if his worry hadn't been so evident. I'd told them what I remembered and learned that two days prior Cruz had been found dead in a garage with a bullet through the back of the head. With my new information, they figured that whoever Chief was, he probably worried about Cruz talking so he eliminated the threat. The other men I killed had either been Los Diablos members or guys that they hadn't been able to figure out a connection to yet.

When tears came to Beach's midnight blue eyes as he thanked me for helping to save Sarah and their unborn child as well as Smoke, I lost it and ended up crying while I hugged Beach, and my parents hugged me, and Sarah just sat there bawling.

Things hadn't been easy these past few weeks, that was for sure, and I spent a lot of time when I was alone trying to cry away the stress. Sarah and I also spent a lot of time talking about our mother and trying to come to terms with her death. The club had taken over planning her funeral since she really didn't have any friends or family who would come to a wake if we had one. With that in mind, we decided on a quiet ceremony and burial at a local cemetery since Austin was our new home.

Sarah was blissfully happy with Beach, and her bump was getting bigger by the day, making me think about her future with Beach and my future with Smoke.

Now, a week later as I sat beside Smoke's bed, I gently stroked the hand that hadn't been crushed and hummed softly. I was doped up on some pretty good non-addictive painkillers and was content to sit here for the rest of my life until he woke up. The part of my mind that hadn't dealt with everything I had been through insisted that if I left his side he wouldn't wake up. Even though I knew it was irrational superstition, I planned on being here as much as possible.

Across the room, Hulk and Hustler sat in all their dark and broody, good-looking glory and pretended to watch TV while I tried to pour my love into Smoke. Things were kind of weird between the club members and me because sometime in the past few days I'd somehow achieved mythical status among the members of Iron Horse. Sarah said they were telling tales about me that made me sound like a cross between a Valkyrie and Rambo. She also said she was pretty sure there were some members who would rather face Smoke than me in a fight.

I was totally flattered and couldn't help smiling every time I thought about it.

Hell, being a bad ass was better than being a dead ass, that was for sure.

Because I was watching Smoke so intently, I noticed that the fine lines around his still swollen eyes were twitching. Holding my breath, I leaned closer, ignoring the twinge of pain from my battered body and held my breath. Sure enough he began to move a little more, soft groans rising from his lips. Hulk and Hustler both stood up, but I waved them back.

"Smoke?" I spoke in as strong of a voice as I could manage when all I wanted to do was burst into relieved tears.

"Hmm?" He grunted, then frowned. "Hurts."

My fingers trembled as I stroked the thick stubble covering his cheeks. "Easy, you've been through a lot. Take a second to catch up. You're in a hospital and you're pretty beat up, but we're safe."

"Safe…safe…" He seemed to be testing the word out, and he tried to open his eyes, then closed them again. "Bright."

Without having to ask Hustler hit the lights and Hulk closed the shades. I gave them a quick nod in thanks before returning my attention to Smoke. "Better?"

He tried again and his muzzy gaze quickly searched me out. "Baby girl."

"Hi," I said in a broken chirp.

"What happened?"

"What's the last thing you remember?"

"I think it was when they tied me to that bed. There are bits and pieces after that, but nothing useful." Grave shadows of what had to be remembered pain tightened the fine lines around his eyes. "What happened?"

Before I could say anything, Hustler spoke up in a rough voice, "I'll tell you what the fuck happened. Swan went all Berserker Barbie on us and killed every mother fucker there, except one that Vance got."

I swear there was anger in Smoke's gaze and he opened his mouth to say something, but Hulk cut him off, "You're real lucky to have such a good woman, Smoke. Without her you'd be playin' pool with the devil right now. I expect you to use the rest of your sorry life to let her know how much you love her and how much she means to you. A woman like her is a gift from God. You better respect that gift, or he'll take it away."

To my shock, the anger dissipated, and Smoke sighed while I blushed at Hulk's profuse praise. Smoke slowly lifted his good hand and placed it over mine before looking at Hustler. "Tell me everything."

Hustler glanced my way. "Maybe we should wait until later."

Smoke gave my hand the gentlest squeeze. "No, she stays. Swan's a part of me, and anything you can say to me you can say to her."

With a shrug Hustler nodded. A week ago he might have fought Smoke on revealing club business to me, but Veronica's murder had changed him. He didn't joke like he used to, and he was disturbingly quiet. It didn't help that there was a rumor going around that Hustler was the traitor, and Veronica had known it, so he killed her. The very idea was outlandish, but the whole club was in an uproar knowing that someone among them was pretending to be their brother, a man they trusted, a man who still had a grudge against Smoke. I couldn't help but wonder if the rumors behind Hustler being the traitor were started by Chief, but I brushed that thought to the side.

All I wanted to do right now was spend every moment I could with Smoke, to try and satisfy my never ending need for my man. As the guys discussed the political situation within the Iron Horse MC, I didn't really pay attention, focused only on how vitally alive Smoke was in spite of the beatings he'd taken. Color had returned to his face, and he somehow appeared bigger, more alive than he had while he slept.

The moment Hulk left to go get Beach and Hustler left to go get a nurse, to let them know Smoke was awake, I leaned down and whispered in his ear, "We should have babies, soon."

He blinked a couple times. "What?"

I flushed and gently stroked his curls. "Babies. I've been thinking about it, and I want to have them with you. Without a doubt you will be a wonderful father."

He tried to smile, then grimaced. "Can we wait until I'm a little more healed up? I'm all for starting right now, but I'm afraid that while the mind is willing the flesh is weak."

"I didn't mean right this instant, dork. Just that I want to have children with you in the near future. I have it all planned out."

The edges of his bruised lips twitched. "Do you now?"

414

"Yeah. We're going to get married, then have a big reception at my parents' place for all of our friends and family, including the club. We'll live in your house, maybe add on some rooms for the kids and an office, then I'll do freelance accounting work. I can either get online gigs or come work for you, like you suggested, as an independent contractor. We can do that for however long we want, and when we're ready, I want to have at least four kids with you."

"Four? Why four?"

"It's a good, even number." I shrugged, trying not to wince as the action pulled on my sore muscles. "I don't know, it just sounds right for us."

He gave a soft, strained chuckle. "It does."

"You on board with this plan?"

"I am, but I want to make a couple requests."

"Like what?"

"One, I want permission to pamper and spoil you whenever I want."

"I can deal with that."

"Two, I want you to promise me you'll always come to me if you have a problem. No running off and playing hero. We're a team, and we have to trust each other."

"Agreed."

"Three, I want to get married as soon as possible. We can have a ceremony later but I want you to be Mrs. Swan Santos by tomorrow."

"What?"

Hulk chose that moment to come back in the room with a pretty middle-aged Asian nurse at his heels. She didn't look happy to see me, and I couldn't blame her. I wasn't very nice to the staff whenever they tried to keep me away from Smoke, but when she caught sight of my man her smile was genuine. "Mr. Santos, it's so good to see you awake. The doctor is on his way."

Smoke sat up a little bit and gave her his no bullshit stare. Even with his swollen eyes and battered face, it was pretty effective. "I want a marriage license and a justice of the peace as soon as possible."

He glanced at me as if asking if it was all right and I glared at him, then turned back to the nurse. "No, we don't."

Smoke made a pained noise and I turned back to him. "You don't want to get married?"

"What? No, of course I do. But I want a real wedding, Smoke. Not here in the hospital on painkillers. Our wedding album would not be pretty. I want to do it right and we are spending the rest of our lives together, regardless of any stupid paper." I touched his hair as gently as I could. "You own my heart, Miguel. I'm your old lady. Papers don't mean shit."

That familiar soft, warm, velvet brown that I adored filled his gaze as he roughly purred, "Baby."

The nurse cleared her throat, and I glanced over at her then followed her wide eyed gaze, finding that yes indeed, a certain part of Smoke's anatomy had made a full, vigorous recovery.

I didn't care for the way the nurse was staring at his crotch so I covered him with my hands and said, "Mine."

Smoke started to laugh, then groaned, and I quickly removed my hands, watching the blood drain from his face and other parts of his body. "Fuck, laughing hurts."

The nurse recovered from the magic that is Smoke's sexual voodoo and shook her head before saying, "Yes, well Mr. Santos you are a very lucky man. Ms. Anderson, if you could leave us for a few minutes there are some tests that the doctor will need to perform on Mr. Santos. I can call your nurse and she can help you freshen up."

As soon as she said that, I became aware of the overall grungy level of my appearance and wanted to scrub the hell out of my hair ASAP.

"Yeah, that would be nice. Promise me I can come back?"

With a sigh, the nurse started fiddling with the machine next to Smoke. "I don't think we could keep you away."

I met Smoke's gaze and fell into the warmth there, wrapping myself up in his all-encompassing, unconditional love for me.

"No, you couldn't."

Epilogue

Miguel 'Smoke' Santos

I stood beneath an archway of twining branches woven together and decorated with teal and silver ribbons along with, I shit you not, eight thousand dollars worth of flowers and other girly bullshit surrounding me on the soft green grass of the Anderson family's compound. It was a beautiful early summer sunset, and the Christmas lights woven through the trees surrounding us, burned like fireflies. The perfect amount of warmth still filled the air, and the scent of everything growing mixed with the perfume of the roses, white lilacs, and orchids that decorated the end seat on each row of white-cloth-covered chairs.

It had been a long, hard winter and spring full of grief and healing, but right now, I felt like I was starting over again, like I'd been given a chance at a newer, better life.

The audience of over four hundred people all stared at me and my groomsmen, making me unusually nervous in my black tuxedo, while off to the side, a six-piece band played classical music. Even in the outdoor setting, the ceremony itself was elegant and high class, the result of Sarah's obsessive wedding planning. Give that woman something to decorate and you better just hand over your credit card and get the fuck out of her way.

Especially when her pregnancy hormones were in full swing.

My good mood dimmed for a moment as I surveyed the audience, wondering if that mother fucker 'Chief' was out there somewhere, smiling and pretending to be happy for us while he plotted against me. That bastard had a shit ton to answer for. When I found him—and I would find him—he would pay. Motherfucker was slick and well connected. Right around the time we were being rescued, Cruz and his nephew Dipper, from the Iron Horse MC Austin Chapter, had been murdered, along with Donkey and Alisha up in Denver, probably to cover Chief's tracks. Dead men tell no tales and all that shit.

Breaker and his men found all kinds of evidence in their home, including taped conversations that Donkey had made during his dealings with Chief, which had been hidden in a place where Khan could find them. Those tapes didn't get us any closer to finding out who Chief was, but we did find out that Donkey and Alisha had turned because of some massive gambling debts they both owed. They'd also found a pair of sparkly blue shoes with dolphins on them in Alisha's closet.

It had been a real blow to the fuckin' chest for the club. Everyone was still wary about it, all of us wondering who else might be selling us out. Beach and I were hoping that this wedding would help bring people back together, to remind them that we're family, and that we're worth fighting for through the bad times to get to the good. My heart swelled with pride as I looked out over the crowd and briefly met the gazes of so many decent men and women who would always have my back, always be there for me, and for them, I would do the same.

Beach and Sarah's four-month-old, blonde daughter, Kylie, sat on Beach's Mom's lap, who was crammed into the crowded front pew of the bride's side with Mimi. Next to Mimi sat her sisters and father, the Don of the Stefano mafia family, which pretty much controlled southern Texas. Mimi dabbed at her eyes as the music for the wedding march started up. I'd met Swan's grandfather yesterday at the rehearsal dinner that had turned into a big party. He had to be in his eighties and stood at about five-foot-two, but I believed him when he said he could make me disappear if I hurt Swan. My girl had actually gotten teary eyed at that statement and ambushed her grandfather with a hug. Yeah, that was the kind of family I was marrying into, and I couldn't be happier.

The band struck up the opening music for the wedding march, and I took a deep breath, happy that the long wait to make Swan my wife was almost over.

There was movement at the flower-draped entrance to the giant, white-cloth-covered pavilion, easily as big as a circus tent, where dinner would be served. Three little brunette flower girls appeared, my nieces, dressed in their fancy gowns, chucking the pink and peach flower petals from their white satin baskets like baseballs. From the moment they met Swan at a family dinner my sister had hosted for us after I'd healed up a bit, they'd fallen in love with her, constantly wanting to brush her hair and do her makeup. They kind of treated Swan like a big doll, but she didn't seem to mind. When I had my nieces over to spend the night, Swan spent the entire evening with them painting their nails, watching cartoons, and eating their body weight in brownies. Seeing her so at ease with them had been a punch to the gut in the best way, knowing that someday she'd have the same patience and love with our kids.

Next came the ring bearer, one of Swan's young cousins from Mimi's side of the family, a dark-haired kid who stared at my nieces. I narrowed my eyes at the way he gawked at them, not sure if he was scared or fascinated. Either way, I needed to keep an eye on him.

Julia followed them in a slinky pink silk gown that showed more of her curves than I was comfortable seeing. My brother-in-law, Tricks, was home and it looked like he was on his way to a medical discharge. His back was screwed up, and after the loss of Veronica, he didn't have the heart to leave my sister and nieces. At the thought of Veronica, I closed my eyes for a moment and said a silent prayer that wherever she was, she was happy and I asked my parents to take care of her.

Once the girls were done flinging flower petals and settled into their seats, Lyric came out of the pavilion tent, her head held high and her long, wavy, brown hair flowing down her back. She looked cool and composed, but her flowers trembled visibly, and she kept nervously licking her lips. I fiddled with the edge of my jacket and watched as Lyric, Swan's best friend, walked down the aisle in a silver sparkly gown that hugged her voluptuous hourglass figure usually hidden by dowdy clothing.

She'd shown up without an escort from the cult, but appeared worn down and exhausted at the party. Right now she seemed fine with a bright blush staining her cheeks and her light brown eyes sparkled. I made a mental note to get my guys to keep an eye on her tonight. With her innocence, she was like a sheep among wolves, and I wasn't going to deal with Swan being pissed because Lyric got her heart broken by one of my friends. She glanced at my groomsmen and blushed harder, but I had no idea if she was looking at Hustler or Tom.

The last bridesmaid was Indigo, Swan's hippy friend who could easily pass for an Asian Bettie Page with an elaborate floral tattoo sleeve taking up her entire left arm from wrist to shoulder. She sashayed down the aisle, leaving a trail of gaping mouths in the wake of her well rounded, rolling hips working her tight dress. The look she gave one of my groomsman wasn't timid in the least, rather a bold sexual challenge along with a heavy dose of disdain. When I glanced over to see who it was, both Tom and Hustler were looking straight ahead with identical frowns while Beach was grinning.

Sarah came in last and strutted her way down the carpet looking good in her form fitting silver dress. Her body had bounced back nicely from her pregnancy due to her hard work, and she knew it. Her smile was radiant, lighting her up from within, but it wasn't for me. Nope, she was beaming at my best man, her husband, Beach. They'd gotten married in Vegas a month after I got out of the hospital, and we were sharing our reception together. The girls were really keen on the idea, and whatever Sarah and Swan wanted, we gave them.

All thoughts about anything or anyone other than Swan fled my mind as she appeared on her father's arm, wearing a long, draped white gown that clung to her figure and made my pants tighten uncomfortably. Her dress had to be silk because nothing else shimmered and flowed like that as she slowly walked toward me. What I liked best of all was that beneath that clinging silk, on her right hip, a tattoo of my dragon curved over her pubic bone, guarding my treasure.

Her beautiful, blonde hair hung long, but she'd put waves in it that reached her waist, and her elaborate veil shimmered with crystals. At the time, I couldn't figure out how the fuck a veil could cost a couple grand, but now that I saw it on Swan, I would've paid five times what I spent on it. The top of the dress was nice and tight, giving her some rockin' cleavage, and when I finally looked up to her face I felt like I'd been punched in the gut.

Beautiful. Amazing. Mine.

This woman had killed for me, fought for me, and saved my life in more ways than one.

The audience laughed as I broke tradition to walk toward her, and she giggled, the flash of her smile doing heady things to me. They took it slow, because technically, Swan should have been using a cane to help her walk. She had threatened to shoot me if I mentioned it one more time, so Mike and I had agreed to support her up and down the aisle. Mike handed her off with a grumble and some warnings about death and dismemberment, but I ignored him, too caught up in my woman's beauty. We just stood there and stared at each other for a long moment, her eyes shining for me like I was the most amazing thing she'd ever seen.

The new scar on my jaw from my time spent in Chief's gentle care, pulled a little when I smiled, but I didn't give a shit. Every ache, every pain was proof that I was alive and whole. And goddamn was I thankful for that right about now. My baby girl's smile was so bright it was like looking into the sun, and I grinned as I caught sight of the gleaming, turquoise wrist cuffs I'd given her the night she met my sister. I fuckin' loved that. She wore my cuffs, she was marked by my bite on the side of her neck, she wore my patch, and soon she'd have my name and my ring. I was so goddamned blessed. Gratitude overwhelmed me that at the end of all the bullshit in my life I had this beautiful young woman waiting for me with open arms.

She placed her hand over mine and leaned into me as I led her to the flower-covered archway, trusting me to take care of her, because she knew she was the most important thing in the world to me.

Now and forever.

The End

Up next, 'Exquisite Redemption(Iron Horse MC, #3)', Beach and Sarah's book. In their story we get to see into the past including how they met, fell in love and what happened from Sarah's point of view when she was chasing after her mom and how she pulled a miracle out of her ass in order to save the lives of everyone she loves.

ABOUT THE AUTHOR

With over forty published books, Ann is Queen of the Castle to her husband and three sons in the mountains of West Virginia. In her past lives she's been an Import Broker, a Communications Specialist, a US Navy Civilian Contractor, a Bartender/Waitress, and an actor at the Michigan Renaissance Festival. She also spent a summer touring with the Grateful Dead-though she will deny to her children that it ever happened.

From a young Ann has had a love affair with books would read everything she could get her hands on. As Ann grew older, and her hormones kicked in, she discovered bodice ripping Fabio-esque romance novels. They were great at first, but she soon grew tired of the endless stories with a big wonderful emotional buildup to really short and crappy sex. Never a big fan of purple prose, throbbing spears of fleshy pleasure and wet honey pots make her giggle, she sought out books that gave the sex scenes in the story just as much detail and plot as everything else-without using cringe worthy euphemisms. This led her to the wonderful world of Erotic Romance, and she's never looked back.

Now Ann spends her days trying to tune out cartoons playing in the background to get into her 'sexy space' and has accepted that her Muse has a severe case of ADD.

Ann loves to talk with her fans, as long as they realize she's weird and that sarcasm doesn't translate well via text. You can find her at:

Website
http://www.annmayburn.com/

Facebook
https://www.facebook.com/ann.mayburn.5

Pintrest
http://pinterest.com/annmayburn/

Twitter
https://twitter.com/AnnMayburn

CPSIA information can be obtained
at www.ICGtesting.com
Printed in the USA
LVHW080313110519
617522LV00031B/522/P